Merde Happens

Stephen Clarke

BLACK SWAN

TRANSWORLD PUBLISHERS
61-63 Uxbridge Road, London W5 5SA
A Random House Group Company
www.rbooks.co.uk

**MERDE HAPPENS
A BLACK SWAN BOOK: 9780552773515**

First published in Great Britain
in 2007 by Bantam Press
a division of Transworld Publishers
Black Swan edition published 2008

Addresses for Random House Group Ltd companies outside the UK
can be found at: www.randomhouse.co.uk
The Random House Group Ltd Reg. No. 954009

The Random House Group Limited supports The Forest Stewardship
Council (FSC), the leading international forest certification organisation. All
our titles that are printed on Greenpeace approved FSC certified paper carry
the FSC logo. Our paper procurement policy can be found at
www.rbooks.co.uk/environment

Typeset in Janson

Printed in the UK by CPI Cox & Wyman, Reading, RG1 8EX.

2 4 6 8 10 9 7 5 3 1

Mixed Sources
Product group from well-managed
forests and other controlled sources
www.fsc.org   Cert no. TT-COC-2139
© 1996 Forest Stewardship Council

Stephen Clarke lives in Paris where he divides his time between writing and not writing.

His first novel, *A Year in the Merde*, originally became a word-of-mouth hit in Paris in 2004. Since then it has been published all over the world, and earned Stephen a nomination for the British Book Award for Best Newcomer. The follow-up, *Merde Actually*, went to number one in the Bookseller chart. In 2006, he published his guide to understanding the French, *Talk to the Snail*, which he divided into ten 'commandments' or chapters that include 'Thou Shalt Not Work', 'Thou Shalt Not Love Thy Neighbour' and 'Thou Shalt Not Be Served'.

During his research for *Merde Happens*, Stephen was interviewed by the American Police twice, found one real pistol, was told to 'have a good one' 127 times, and became allergic to cranberries.

His latest book, *Dial M for Merde*, will be published by Bantam Press in August.

You can find out more about Stephen Clarke and his books on www.stephenclarkewriter.com

www.rbooks.co.uk

'If my melodies have found a place in people's hearts, then I know I have not lived in vain.'

Robert Stolz, Austrian composer.

1968, what a great year that was ;)

'I'm told that America has more lunatics than any-where in the world.'

De la Démocratie en Amérique,
Alexis de Tocqueville, 1840.

Contents

Acknowledgements

I would like to thank all the Americans I met during my frequent visits to the States over the past eighteen months for being so American.

I would also like to say an especially big thank-you to the car-hire company who let me drive their valuable vehicle away after I'd just said, 'I've never driven an automatic before. How does it work?'

I would, however, like to request that Americans turn the air-conditioning down a bit. New York sounds as if it's about to take off, and Las Vegas is basically a giant vibrator.

And finally, a big hello to all the pelicans out there. No, you don't need a face-lift – a triple chin is what makes you a pelican.

Stephen Clarke, Paris, May 2007.

An Appetizer

THE DRIVER WHO PICKED me up at JFK that February morning was a young Sikh, and as he bounced his taxi out of the airport, he started talking over his shoulder in Punjabi or some other Asian language.

I was just about to explain that I spoke only English and learner's French when I realized he wasn't addressing me at all. He was speaking into his phone, and kept this up for the whole journey. Maybe, I thought, he was moonlighting with a call centre, maximizing his time spent in traffic by doing computer after-sales service.

I wasn't offended, though. I didn't need conversation about the weather or why I'd come to America. I was happy to settle back in my seat and enjoy the thrill of arriving in New York.

Even the traffic jam was exotic – squadrons of yellow taxis jostling for position with black Lincoln limos and chrome-nosed trucks, all breathing out white clouds of exhaust into the freezing winter air. The spine-crunching bumps in the road did nothing to detract from the fun of it.

After an hour of this, the highway suddenly rose above street level and there it was, the world's most famous skyline, a silver silhouette against the hazy blue of the sky. Through the spider's web beams of a suspension bridge, I could make out the angular spire of the Empire State and the rocket-cone Chrysler building.

I gripped the edge of my seat.

When we'd crossed the bridge, the skyline loomed even bigger out of the left-hand side of the car, then started to recede.

Soon Manhattan was completely out of sight behind us.

Hang on, I thought, that can't be right, can it?

PARIS AND LONDON

Do I Have a Dream?

1

THE SEEDS OF DISASTER HAD been sown the previous autumn, when I opened an English tea room just off the Champs-Elysées in Paris. Almost immediately I was visited by a language inspector from the Ministry of Culture, who warned me that I could expect 'the severest consequences' if I didn't translate my menu into French.

He had been well chosen for the job, a power-mad bureaucrat who refused to believe that even the most linguistically challenged Parisian could understand 'sausage' when the label was standing in front of a plate of long, meat-filled tubes.

He also alleged that my customers were being traumatized by the fear that their 'cheese salad' might contain a chair (*'chaise'* in French). I mean, chair salad? What brand of poisonous Gallic tobacco had he been smoking?

I stayed calm and pointed out that plenty of English food names, like sandwich, cake, iced tea, toast and bacon had passed directly into the French language, to which his only reply was a dismissive 'pff'.

Sensing that I had him on the defensive, I followed up with the clinching argument that the English labels were educational for my customers.

'Hah! You think all French people must be forced to learn English?' he trumpeted, and huffed out the door, leaving me – I assumed – to get on with the serious business of running a café.

But no, his revenge arrived about three months later. It was a piece of sheer bureaucratic sadism – a letter saying that the tea room had been revisited incognito, found guilty of continuing to operate with an untranslated menu, and therefore sentenced to pay an obscene amount of euros in penalties.

'*How* much do we owe?' I asked.

I was at the tea room with Benoît, the son of a sneaky Parisian entrepreneur called Jean-Marie Martin, to whom I'd sold a fifty per cent stake in the business. Jean-Marie had bought this share in a desperate attempt to get Benoît off his student backside and into the real world. It was an astute move – I'd let Benoît take over as manager, and he'd quickly blossomed from a rich-kid slacker into a skilled raker-in of euros. He was making a real go of the tea room. Or so he thought, until the fine arrived.

Benoît read out the amount again, and I slumped forward to cool my aching forehead on the glass serving counter, right above the half-empty plate of what had to be the costliest sausages ever grilled.

'I can solve the immediate problem,' Benoît said in French. 'I'll translate the labels, re-do the blackboard, and I've ordered new takeaway menus. The inspector's coming back tomorrow.'

'But I haven't got that kind of money,' I moaned. It was a huge sum – enough to take me around the globe in business class or buy me a mid-range sports car. Tragic to think that it was probably going to finance some ministerial brochure explaining how to persecute English-speakers.

Benoît tutted sympathetically. He was thoughtful enough to hide his relief that the fine had been incurred for something that happened before his father bought into the tea room. Legally, the money had to come out of my empty pocket. 'You could—' he began, but I cut him off instantly.

'Sell my share to Jean-Marie? No way.' I knew that Benoît had plans to open another branch, and I had no intention of selling up just before the brand started to go global. If the Latin Quarter counted as global. 'No, I'll get the money,' I told him.

'You have to pay within six weeks, or it increases again.'

'What?' I straightened up and looked Benoît in the eye. If it had been his dad or his sister Elodie, some part of them would have been relishing my pain, but Benoît's expression was one of genuine concern.

'The French legal system shows no mercy,' he said. 'They've stopped guillotining people, but they cannot resist the temptation to slice off a businessman's—'

'Thanks, Benoît, I get the picture.'

I left him re-labelling 'sausage' as '*saucisse*' and 'salad' as '*salade*', and went off to try and save my financial bacon. Or '*bacon financier*' as I was probably obliged to call it.

2

I was in shock. Not only because of my money troubles, but also because I had just heard the scariest words in the English language.

No, not 'This might hurt a little', 'There's something I've been meaning to tell you, darling' or 'Did you realize that your credit-card number is being used simultaneously in Moscow, Shanghai and Bogotá?'

This sentence was much, much scarier. It was 'What do you want to do with your life?'

When someone asks this, I usually feign sudden deafness or an attack of the runs. But when it's your girlfriend who says it, you can't ignore her. You have to stop watching the cliffhanger ending of the murder mini-series you've been following for weeks, and answer her question.

'Pardon?' I said, forcing myself to look away from the TV and into Alexa's (admittedly gorgeous) face.

'What are your dreams, Paul?' She laid her head on my shoulder and put the TV on mute so that I wouldn't be distracted by the detective explaining exactly how the murderer had bamboozled Scotland Yard's finest for the past three episodes.

I could tell that I was in for a treat. Just like a lobster knows it's going to have fun when it feels that first gust of steam rising from the cooking pot.

It was eight hours since Benoît had told me about the fine. Alexa and I were cocooned together under a fluffy white duvet in her enormous apartment near the Bastille.

In one corner of this pine-floored palace was a mezzanine bedroom. We were huddled in here because the underfloor heating downstairs cost about a month's salary per day to turn on, and on top of all my other worries, I was temporarily between salaries. As was Alexa, whose only income came from the sale of her photos. She'd recently had shows at the Centre Pompidou in Paris and London's Saatchi Gallery, which had generated plenty of kudos but not much cash.

The apartment belonged to her dad, who had gone to live with his new *amour* in Copenhagen. I'd moved in with Alexa just after Christmas, and this was the first time we'd watched TV in bed. I didn't see it as a sign that we were less thrilled to be there and needed entertainment outside of each other's nakedness. I just wanted to watch the last episode of the mini-series.

But Alexa was an arty French girl, and French intellectuals regard TV mini-series the way crocodiles look at soya rissoles – not meaty enough to merit their attention. This was why she'd decided that it was perfectly OK to talk over the ending.

'My dreams? That's a tough one,' I said. 'I'd need to think about it.'

'But you must have some ambitions. That's why you started your tea room, isn't it?' Her English was so good that you could hardly hear a French accent at all.

'Yes, exactly,' I agreed, congratulating myself for getting out of trouble so effortlessly. My finger hovered over the mute button as the detective mouthed revelations that were making all the other characters gasp in amazement. Five seconds of silence from Alexa and I'd take it as tacit agreement that I could turn the volume on again.

'But you sold half the business, so you must have other dreams, too.'

Damn. I was going to have to buy the DVD to find out whodunnit. I switched off the TV and snuggled up.

'Oh, I have great dreams,' I said. 'Last night I dreamed

you were lying naked in a hot tub and then I got in and—'

'No, Paul, don't joke, please. I'm being serious. What do you want to do with your life?' Her all-seeing blue eyes drilled deep into my brain. 'I dream of making a film about the French lifestyle,' she went on, 'of building a career in photography. What do *you* dream of, apart from watching the end of your murder series?' Which was one dream she'd just murdered. 'It's great being in Paris with you, Paul, but right now I'm getting a bit . . .' She trailed off.

'A bit what?'

'Bored.'

'Bored?' There's something about being in bed with a woman who says you're boring that makes certain parts of a guy go limp.

'Yes. It's no coincidence that this problem of the fine has hit you now. You have gone soft.'

'Soft?'

'Yes, *tu te laisses aller*, you have let yourself go. For a month now, you've done nothing. You almost never go to the tea room.'

'Benoît doesn't need me.'

'You spend most of your time watching DVDs, looking at stupid websites or sitting in cafés.'

'Or curled up in bed with you.' It sounded like the ideal lifestyle to me.

'But that is not enough. You are a guy with energy and imagination. You can't waste it like this. You must be more creative. I am scared you will sell your other half of the tea room to pay your debt, and then you will have even less than nothing.'

I got the message. It was caveman time. I had to go out and brain a mammoth to prove that I was a real male. Even the most feminist women get like that occasionally. They demand that a guy explores his feminine side, but now and again they need to feel the rasp of a five o'clock shadow on his chin.

And deep down, I knew she was right.

Sitting in a Paris café was still a thrill – people pretending to read books while checking out the other coffee-drinkers, couples in conversations so urgent they looked as if they would change the world, teenage schoolkids chain-smoking in an attempt to belong to this adult society. It was always entertaining.

But recently I had been feeling a slight unease as I sat over my fourth espresso of the day. I had caught myself drumming my fingers on the marble table-top, as if I was waiting for somebody or something. And I couldn't put all my fidgetiness down to caffeine poisoning. It was a kind of dissatisfaction, lodged deep in the soul where the coffee, the champagne and the love (and body) of a good woman couldn't reach. Part of me was looking for something else. A dream, perhaps.

'No, I'm not going to sell my share of the tea room,' I told Alexa in my best cave-dweller voice. 'I'm going to get the money. And I think I know how.'

'Yes?' She raised an eyebrow.

'Yes. I got an email a few days ago offering me a job. I dismissed the idea at the time because it sounded too wacky, but now . . .'

'What is it?'

'You've seen *Thelma and Louise*, right?'

'Yes?'

'And *Easy Rider*?'

'Yes?' Alexa's brow was knitted. She wasn't bored any more.

'And *Alfie*?'

'Original version or the remake?'

'Does it matter?'

22

'To me, yes.' Parisian girls think remakes of 1960s movies are as big a blasphemy as Californian champagne.

'OK. Original version?'

'Yes.'

'Well, this was a job offer that would combine them all.'

'So, you will have to drive across America, talking like a Cockney, and you will get chased by the police because you have two dangerous women in your car?'

'Just one French woman, I hope,' I said. 'How dangerous can that be?'

Alexa smiled and planted a kiss on my shoulder. If I hadn't yet brought home a mammoth, at least I'd hinted that I might know where hairy mammals hung out.

3

Two days later, I was in London with my best suit on my back and my whole life printed out on a sheet of A4.

The building where a taxi had just delivered me was at least ten storeys high, all blue-tinted glass except for the white marble staircase leading up to the entrance doors. At the top of the stairs, an ecosystem of exotic-looking shrubs was growing in an immense granite sarcophagus. Perhaps they'd bought an Egyptian mummy and let it germinate, I thought. Though I wondered why they hadn't planted roses and apple trees, because the building was supposed to be selling Britishness. It was the brand-new headquarters of a brand-new organization called (and I quote) Visitor Resources: Britain. These were the people who, via a head-hunting company, had sent me my job offer.

After a cursory interrogation by two bored security guys, I took the lift to the sixth floor and went to sit in a corridor with a carpet the colour of lightly-grilled toast. The walls were baked-bean orange. All that was missing to complete the English-breakfast theme was a set of light fittings in the shape of fried eggs.

There were no signs or sounds of life anywhere.

Until, that is, the lift doors opened again and a female voice flooded the corridor with the soundtrack to a nervous breakdown.

'No, I can't take your fucking dog for a haircut,' she was wailing. 'Well, not before six, anyway.'

She tripped out of the lift, a gangly, curly-headed thirty-something in clothes she must have bought from a charity shop specializing in mismatching outfits. Floppy rainbow jumper, tartan mini-skirt, vertical-striped tights and ancient suede moonboots. In one arm, she was clutching a heap of files that looked as if she'd dropped them ten times that day already.

'No, *you* fuck off, George, just like you always do. Oh.' She saw me and hung up.

'Hi,' she said, holding out her phone for me to shake. 'Sorry about that, you're early, come in, oh shit where are the sodding keys, hold this, bugger.'

She dumped the files in my arms and suffered a second bout of Tourette's syndrome while she rummaged through her suede shoulder-bag. All the while she was giving me the kind of frank, top-to-bottom examination that you might give a girl in a pole-dancing club. Not that I've ever been to one. Well, not in Europe, anyway.

'They wouldn't let me park outside, the bastards. I mean, who's got a permit on their first day, here they are, shit how do you open this fucking . . . ah there we go, oh brilliant, it's been delivered, sit down, coffee, oh no I don't suppose there is any, fuck it let's just start OK?'

She ripped the tape off a large cardboard box that was sitting below a tinted window.

'Ah, we'll try this first, shall we?' She pulled out what looked like a legless Alsatian dog and threw it at me. When I caught it, I realized it was a busby, a Guardsman's bearskin hat. Was this a culture test, I wondered – Name That British Object? Next I'd be asked to identify a deep-fried Mars Bar and a Charles and Camilla tea cosy.

'Well?' she said. 'Stand up. Put it on.'

The hat flopped down over my eyes and tickled my ears. Through a fringe of fake fur I saw her take a photo and then head for her Pandora's box again.

'Ah, yes, what about these?'

This time I had to fit a scratchy lace collar round my neck and grin while she snapped me in Beefeater headgear.

'A bit young, but what the hell,' she said. 'Ooh, I know what we have to do with you – oh, sod it.'

She was on her hands and knees, her whole torso jammed into the box. A plastic crown flew over her shoulder, followed by what looked like a jester's codpiece with little bells on it. At least I was to be spared that indignity.

'Oh well, nothing for it.' She stood up and started to undress. 'Get your trews off,' she said.

Wow, job interviews have changed since I was last un-employed, I thought. Was I about to be asked to shag for England?

'You're not shy, are you? Come on, we see lots of bodies in our business. I bet it's not the first time you've seen a girl in tights, either.'

It wasn't, and the experience was as unpleasant as ever. Sorry, ladies, but it's a law of nature that women's under-wear, even a thong, cannot be squeezed inside coloured nylon and stay sexy.

'The kilt hasn't been delivered, but mine'll do for the test shots. Sorry it's only the tartan of the Marks and Spencer clan.' She gave a loud snort, a kind of clearing out of her nasal passages, which I guessed was her laugh.

At least there was to be no sex involved, just a photo of my tartan-framed knees. I pulled off my trousers and put on the skirt. Luckily – or unluckily – it had a buckle waist, so I had no problem adjusting it to fit, widthways at least.

It was only as I stood there allowing my knees to be immortalized in pixels, and listening to this basket case going on about how 'there'll be a real kilt for the actual brochure', that I realized this whole fancy-dress party was probably unnecessary. I hadn't come about a brochure at all. She had the wrong guy. And come to think of it, I definitely had the wrong woman. I was due to see a man called Tyler. I'd assumed this was his assistant. No, truth be told, I hadn't assumed anything, I'd just obeyed instructions and let her make a fool of me.

'Er . . .' I tried to interrupt, but she was jabbering on as she walked back to her cardboard box.

'Have you got your portfolio with you? You done any big campaigns recently? Oh, poo.'

Her phone was ringing. She checked out the caller's number and then picked it up, making a 'sorry, I have to take this' grimace at me.

'What? Pregnant? Again? Holy shit. Just a sec.' She put her hand to the mouthpiece. 'Sorry, dear, it's my sister. Can you just wait outside for a mo?' Gripping my elbow, she guided me to the door. 'Who's the father?' she said into the phone. 'Shit, so he was lying about the vasectomy? Bastard!'

I found myself standing in the corridor in a mini-skirt, hoping to hell that no one would come along and see me.

'Ah, Mr West I presume?'

I was sorely tempted to say no.

4

A plump man in a grey suit was staring at me over gold reading glasses. He was at least fifty, but he had a full head of longish, floppy grey hair. He bared his teeth at me, not in a smile but so that he could lick them as if cleaning away remnants of his breakfast.

'Jack Tyler,' he said, holding out his hand. He had obviously decided that it wouldn't be polite to draw attention to my naked legs. An old-school civil servant.

'Paul West,' I confessed. 'Er, about the skir—'

'Do go in.' He gestured towards the office next door to the mad stripper.

Tyler's office was exactly the same as the one next door, except that the shelves had been half filled with files and coffee-table-sized books. There was also a computer on the desk. This guy had been in residence a whole day longer than his neighbour, it seemed.

We sat down on opposite sides of his desk.

'I should explain,' I said.

'Are you a Scot?' he interrupted again. His voice was smooth and posh-sounding.

'No.'

'You're not a transvestite, are you? Not that we have anything against them. The British government is an equal-opportunities employer.' He said this as if reciting it straight from the manual.

'No, no, it's just that your colleague next door has got my trousers.'

'I see.' He looked at me indulgently, like a shrink whose patient has just explained that he's really a giant tomato.

'Not that she's wearing them, of course. We didn't exchange clothes.'

27

'No?'

'No. She asked me to take them off for some photos.'

'Really?' He stared at the wall as if he might be able to see all the kinky things that went on next door.

'What I mean is, she needed someone to pose for photos in a kilt – some kind of tourist brochure, she said – and the model hadn't turned up, and I was in the corridor, so she asked me to step in.'

'Ah.' He seemed to have got the picture at last. 'So it was out of the breeks and into the breach.'

'Pardon?'

'Breeks. Scots word for trousers.'

'Ah, yes, good one.' I managed a polite laugh. 'She's on the phone and asked me to wait outside. I'll get my trousers back when she's finished.'

'Yes, yes, it's all par for the course,' he said, licking his teeth. 'It's chaos around here. New name, new headquarters, bloody ridiculous if you ask me.'

'New name?' I asked.

'Yes, Visitor Resources: Britain was the good old Tourist Authority until some trendy twit in the government decreed that it sounded too *yesterday's generation* or whatever. Anyway.' He shuffled some papers to gather his thoughts. 'Enough about us. Tell me what you've been doing recently. In France as well as England, I see.'

I took him through my time in Paris, most of which I'd spent setting up the tea room, and gave him the bare bones of how I'd then gone to London to market a deranged French chef. Tyler asked a few questions, but none of them took me into the dangerous territory of why I'd ditched two jobs in a year.

'OK. Good. So-o.' His tongue shot over his teeth yet again, and it took all my mental resistance not to do the

28

same. His tic was addictive. 'Do you have any questions you'd like to ask me at this point?'

'Well, yes, actually. Quite a basic one.'

'As in?'

'As in, what is the job exactly?' I mean, the headhunters had given me enough info to get me interested, but they'd refused to be specific. Top secret, they'd said.

'Ah!' It was a laugh, but it sounded as if he'd just been shot. 'Typical,' he grunted. 'Outsourcing. You pay someone else to do the job and you still have to do it yourself. Visitor bloody Resources. Visitor outsources, more like. We don't even own the building, you know. Can you imagine how much of our budget goes in rent?' He'd said most of this to the ceiling, but he now came back down to earth and slurped his gums at me. 'What was your question again?'

'The job?'

'Ah yes. How much do you know?'

'Well, all the recruitment people would tell me is that I'd be touring the USA promoting Britain as a tourist destination, and that there was a competition involved.' With, they had assured me, a fat bonus for me if Britain won.

'Yes, that's it,' he said. 'In about a month's time, the first ever World Tourism Capital will be selected. And the winner of the contest will host the World Tourism Fair next year.' I looked suitably impressed. 'Winning would attract not only millions of extra visitors,' he went on, 'but also a very healthy chunk of WTO money. You know the WTO?'

'The World Trade Organization? Yes, though I think it just changed its name to Global Business Solutions.'

'What? Really?'

'No, I was—'

'Ha. Good one. Exactly. Right on the ball. Or nail. Or something.'

'But you say the vote's in a month. So this job is pretty last-minute, isn't it?'

'Yes. There have been some, er, logistical problems.' He didn't seem keen to expand on this.

'And who else is competing?' I asked.

'Good question. Very good question. Who the hell is competing?' He scrabbled around on his desk and finally started squinting at a small booklet. 'The other contestant nations for this first competition are . . .' He put a finger on the page, and read, 'China, France and the USA. I know you'd have been good for France, but we already have someone on the ground over there, which is why we thought you could cover America.' He waved at the window in what he probably thought was a westerly direction.

'But doing what exactly?'

'Ah yes. Well, some details are, I must admit, still being worked out. But basically – I do hate that word, don't you? There must be a better—'

'In a nutshell?' I prompted.

'Yes, in a nutshell – thank you – the successful candidate would be organizing a series of promotional events in the key cities.' He smiled and licked his teeth. This time I couldn't resist a quick flick of the tongue across my own top set as well.

'The key cities being?' I asked.

'Oh. Yes. I honestly have no idea. Here, you look.' He slid the booklet across to me. I opened it at a page headed 'Participating Cities, USA', but all it said was 'Cities subject to confirmation.'

'Have they been confirmed yet?' I asked.

'Yes,' he said. 'Probably. I'll find out. We got that booklet months ago.'

'And I was told I'd be driving across America?' In my

30

mind, I was already there, out on the open highway, one foot on the accelerator (or gas pedal), the other hanging out of the window catching the Wyoming sun. Yes, I could stick my leg out of the window as well as my arm because the car would be automatic.

'That's right, in a Mini.'

'Pardon?' It was a shock to find myself back in a sunless English office. 'A Mini? But I have legs. And I'll have luggage.' Not to mention my girlfriend. 'I was imagining something a bit bigger. A London taxi, maybe? There's nothing more British than a black cab.'

'No, no. We did a *survey*.' When he licked his teeth this time, it was as if to swab away the bad taste of the word he'd just used. 'And taxis were found to be too black.'

'Too black? Why not paint one?'

'And too old-fashioned. Don't ask me, I didn't even get to fill out the survey form. But if I remember rightly, Minis are colourful and fun, stylish but not snobbish. Something like that. You know. What did they use to call it? Cool Britannia.'

There seemed to be one little problem with this.

'Aren't Minis German these days?' I asked.

Tyler took off his glasses and let his fringe flop down over his eyes.

'Do I take it,' he asked, a touch of exhaustion in his voice, 'that you are not convinced that this, er, mission is accomplishable?'

'No, no, I'd love to give it a go.' Correction – I *had* to give it a go if I wanted to pay my fine. 'It sounds a little disorganized,' I said, 'but as you can see from my CV, I'm used to turning hopeless causes around.' He didn't need to know that my last job had ended when the French chef had tried to suffocate me with a grated courgette salad.

'OK, good. Well,' Tyler groped for his mouse and clicked

tiredly on his computer, 'in that case, I have a few questions for you. A *survey*.' He put on his glasses and read from the screen. 'Now then, number one. "What is your opinion of American Homeland Security?"'

'Pardon?'

'It's meant to reveal your attitude towards your trans-atlantic hosts. My advice is, try not to sound too much like a terrorist.'

'OK. Well, how about, "I'm all in favour"?'

'What?'

'"I'm all in favour of a secure homeland."'

'It's a bit brief.'

'But what else is there to say?' I wasn't going to blunder into a speech about what a good idea it is to stop people taking toothpaste on to aeroplanes.

'If you insist.' He typed it out two-fingered, and began to read again. '"What is your view of the current renaissance . . ."' He seemed to run out of energy in the middle of the question, but took a deep breath and pressed on. '"Of the current *renaissance* in American religiousness?" Religiousness? Is that even a word?'

Wow, from one trick question to the next. I shaped my reply as carefully as a French patissier moulding a chocolate truffle.

'Well, if I can quote George Michael, who I think is Greek Orthodox . . .'

'Yes?'

'"You gotta have faith."'

'Pardon?'

'"You gotta have faith." It's the words to a song.'

'You want me to write that down?'

'Yes, please. But maybe you should leave out the George Michael bit. And make it "got to" instead of "gotta".'

Tyler simply shook his head and typed.

'And, last one, I promise,' he said. ' "What is your view of American foreign policy?" '

He saw my look of horror and nodded. Oh yes, this was the nuke.

' "Like all Brits," ' I finally said, ' "I'm really grateful that the Americans came into World War Two and helped us liberate Europe." ' And my gran says thanks for the silk stockings, I thought.

Tyler shrugged and typed my answer into the hotline to the Pentagon or wherever this was going.

'Well, that seems to be that,' he said. 'If you're successful, I'll be in touch. Or someone will be. That's probably been outsourced, too. Ha!'

I laughed, shook his hand and leapt for the door before he could inflict any more of his manic-depressive humour on me. It was time to get my trousers back.

5

'Inspire that atmosphere!'

My American friend Jake suffered from what was, as far as I could tell, a unique linguistic condition, namely that he couldn't speak any languages at all.

No, that wasn't quite true. In fact he spoke two languages simultaneously – French and English – so that you needed some kind of stereo listening system in your head to work out what he was talking about. What was worse, he often pronounced French words with an American accent and vice versa.

So what he actually said was, 'Inspire that atmos-fair.' Luckily, I spoke enough French to know that '*inspire*' meant 'inhale'.

Between the lank curtains of his chin-length blond

hair Jake was beaming a smile of pure pleasure as he breathed in a deep lungful of the air around him. Well, I say air, but the atmosphere was mainly damp and smoke. There was precious little room for molecules of oxygen.

It was about ten at night. I'd called Jake as soon as I'd arrived back in Paris, and he'd told me to join him on his roof. We occasionally came up here to get away from the world and talk nonsense, usually with the aid of a bottle. As long as it wasn't raining or icy, it was relatively safe to climb out of the skylight and on to the flattish area in the centre of the roof. Providing, that is, you didn't trip over one of the ridges where the zinc plates overlapped and plummet into the street six floors below.

I was sitting on the bone-chillingly cold metal roof with my spine pressed hard against a warm chimney stack. It was a popular place to hang out. The chimney was pockmarked with cigarette burns and chewing-gum fossils, and there was a grinning cat graffiti'd on the plaster, as if to make the spot more homely.

There was a good reason for this popularity. From my centrally heated outdoor vantage point, I had a spectacular view over the anarchic jigsaw of Paris rooftops. The apartment buildings that look so grey and uniform from the street show all their individuality at skyline level, with wildly different slopes, skylights, and illicit rooftop terraces. On one building, the top-floor residents had colonized the zinc with a square of AstroTurf and a fake palm tree. Two plastic loungers faced west to catch the sunset.

The sun was long gone, but now the distant Eiffel Tower began to sparkle as if a billion sexually aroused fireflies had just jumped off the summit. Every hour on the hour, from sundown to one in the morning, the tower's illuminations go disco for five minutes, and the throbbing golden light-show that I was now watching would have made even the most blasé of electrical engineers go 'ooh!'

Jake, though, wasn't interested in this display of French lighting technology. He was hugging a shiny metal tube that curved up on to the roof from the central courtyard of the building. It was the outlet for the air-conditioning system in the café on the ground floor.

'Inspire that,' he repeated, standing on tiptoe to get his nose as close as possible to the mushroom-shaped nozzle. 'Pure Paree.' Yes, he was actually sniffing the waste air from a Parisian café, a mixture of gases only slightly less toxic than a fire at a tar refinery. And at the same time he was puffing on a Gauloise.

This had to be the only explanation for his success with women, I thought. When he wasn't wearing the black Paul Smith suit that he'd borrowed from me three months earlier and had never returned, he looked as if he'd dressed in the dark after a scarecrows' orgy. So there had to be something irresistible about his boyish grin and his ability to behave like a total dork.

He had recently discovered a rich new seam of dorkish behaviour – France had announced that smoking was to be banned in all public places. And even though it seemed unlikely that Parisian smokers would actually obey the law, Jake wanted to get his fill before the world came to an end.

'Virginie, she wants me to stop smoking already,' he said. 'She won't permit me to smoke in the apartment, man, like, not even with my head outside the fenêtre.'

Virginie was a film student with whom Jake had been living since around the time he'd borrowed my suit. It was his longest relationship ever, and pretty well the only one he'd had with a Frenchwoman during his ten-year stay in Paris. Since arriving here, he'd been living out his project to sleep with, and then write poetry about, every nationality of woman living in the city. With Virginie, though, for once he actually seemed to be after something more than a poke and a poem.

'Do you write poems about her?' I asked.

Jake eyed me suspiciously. He often accused me of 'not respecting his posy'. By this he meant not flowers, but his '*poésie*' – his poetry. He was wrong, though. I respected his poems a lot, in the same way that I respected pit bull terriers – meaning that I tried my best to avoid close contact with them. Once you've had to listen to fifty unrhyming couplets about exactly what Jake did with a drunk Iranian interpreter and a jar of caviar, you're not exactly hungry for more.

'Yeah,' he said. 'In fact I do. All the days I send her an erotic posy in a texto. Good, no?'

'Yeah, wonderful.' I took a long swallow from my glass of Chenin Blanc to calm my stomach.

Jake sat down next to me.

'You think you will accept this American proposition?' he asked.

'I'm not sure they'll accept *me*.' I listed a few reasons why I was likely to get a rejection letter, including my evasive answers to the trick political questions and my accidental excursion into transvestism. 'It turned out that this woman was auditioning models,' I told him. 'It was an open audition so she didn't know who would show up, and she naturally assumed I was waiting for her.'

Jake nodded as if this was a perfectly normal mis-understanding, which was heartening. I was rehearsing my excuses for when I broke the news to Alexa, who was down south filming some kids for her documentary on the French way of life. She wanted to ask them why it was an integral part of the lifestyle in the Marseilles suburbs to set fire to forests every summer and cars every winter.

'The whole set-up was so chaotic,' I said. 'I think I just stopped taking the job seriously at some point.'

'It is a damage,' Jake said. I translated this as a shame ('*dommage*'). 'Where will you get the money for your almond?'

It took me a few seconds to work out that he meant *amende*, the French word for fine.

'I have a few other job leads,' I said. 'And one of my ex-girlfriends works in a bank. She might be able to get me a loan. But that wouldn't solve the problem of me being Mister Boring for Alexa.'

'You must surprise her, Paul. You know, buy a Superman costume, maybe? Then invite her to make love on a trapeze.'

'Yeah, neat idea, Jake.' As usual, his advice concerning women ought to have been stamped with a mental-health warning.

'I'll go to America soon, you know,' he said. 'To my mom, in Nevada. And I thought, we could meet ourselves.'

'Meet up? Yeah, except that even if I get the job, I'm not sure I'll be going to Nevada.'

'Me neither.'

'What?'

Jake sighed deeply, and proceeded to wrestle his garbled way through a story about buying a plane ticket, then spotting a cheaper fare and cancelling, only to get hammered so badly with the cancellation fee that he barely had enough left over for a dirt-cheap charter to Orlando. All in all, it was like listening to someone who'd received a baseball bat in his Christmas stocking and then spent all day hitting himself on the head with it.

'But it's no problem, man,' he concluded. 'I'll trap a greyhound.'

'What?' He was planning to ride home on a dog?

'You know, the bus.'

'Oh, right.' Of course, '*attraper*' was 'to catch' and greyhound was, well, Greyhound. He'd actually used the right American word for once.

'I'm really – how d'you say – waiting with impatience?'

'Looking forward?'

'Yeah. I'm really, you know, waiting forward with impatience or whatever, to go to America, except for one thing.'

'What's that?'

He inhaled. 'The smoke, man. My friends in New York told me smoke is already extinct as the dodo there. Even at a rock concert, the atmos-fair is *clean*.' He grimaced. He was a big fan of Paris rock gigs, where – for the moment at least – the air was so thick with cigarette smoke that you could hardly make out the huge 'no smoking' signs on the walls.

Jake took a long pull on the stump of his cigarette and pointed to a modern building across the street.

'Regard,' he said as the silhouette of a woman appeared at a curtainless window on the top floor. 'Sometimes she does the cuisine in her lingerie. I'm sure she knows that people see her, but she takes off her clothes and she does the steak-frites.' He laughed. 'Smoke and lingerie. Vive Paree. Who needs l'Amérique, uh?'

6

There are girls who let you rest on your laurels. Not Alexa. Telling her you loved her wasn't an open-ended contract meaning that you didn't need to say it again. It was more like buying yoghurt – your vow of eternal love only stayed fresh for a few days before it had to be renewed.

Similarly, you couldn't just say 'I love you, darling,' and hope that this would distract her when you announced, 'Look, I think I cocked up the job interview, so I really don't hold out much hope of living the American Dream in the near future.'

So on the night Alexa returned to Paris from Marseilles, I met her at the station and whisked her off in a taxi to one of her favourite restaurants.

During the twenty-minute cab ride, I delivered a carefully edited account of my time in London. 'How could they expect me to give coherent answers off the top of my head?' I pleaded. I knew that a French girl would sympathize with anyone having to answer silly questions from the US Government. Wasn't it a French pilot who, when asked at JFK what he had in his suitcase, told an airport security man something along the lines of 'A bomb, stupid.' I think he's due out of Guantanamo soon.

To my surprise, she laughed at my one-liner replies.

'Well done, Paul,' she said. 'Who wants to go to America, anyway?' Which came as a bit of a shock. She was the one who'd wanted me to dash off on some manly quest for adventure in the first place. 'You will find another job,' she went on. 'As I told you, you are an inventive guy. Do you feel inventive this evening?'

She gave my trousers a playful, and only slightly painful, pinch, and suddenly I was no longer in the mood for a long drawn-out banquet.

'Are you sure you want to go to the restaurant?' I asked, my voice a half-tone higher than normal.

'Yes. Didn't your mother tell you that you must feed a girl before you—' she pulled my ear close to her mouth and whispered.

'No, she never mentioned that,' I said. 'Mum used to tell me to scrub my fingernails before a date, but that's about all.'

'Ah, you Anglo-Saxons, you think it is more important to be hygienic than romantic. Anyway, you have not asked me how I did in Marseilles. Does my work interest you so little?'

We were back in yoghurt-renewal territory again.

I got the driver to drop us off on the Boulevard Bonne Nouvelle, part of the network of wide avenues that were carved through medieval Paris in the nineteenth century to allow troops to march around the city and quell rebellions.

A few yards down a side street was a traditional Parisian dining hall, where the food was OK rather than spectacular, but where getting a table on a Friday night, even for an early dinner at around seven thirty, took all our self-assertion skills. The restaurant was set back from the street in a courtyard, most of which was taken up with a typically Parisian mixture of queue and riot. Things were even more congested than usual because a large group of tourists had arrived just as two people were looking around for a safe place to leave their pushbikes.

Parisians always assume that they take priority over groups of tourists, so Alexa and I shoved our way through to the bright lights around the restaurant's revolving doors, where the maître d', a middle-aged guy in a blue suit, was putting on his show.

'*Une table pour quatre!*' he announced.

At this point it was up to the first group of four in the queue to speak up and lunge forward. Two Parisian couples in thick woollen overcoats did just that, leaving a foursome of American tourists frowning about whether they had let themselves get bypassed.

A bearded, middle-aged guy in an Austrian-style green feathered hat was hovering by the door. 'I called to reserve,' he said discreetly.

'You called to reserve?' the maître d' guffawed. The whole crowd listened expectantly. 'Not at this restaurant, Monsieur,' he went on. 'We don't reserve. Maybe you called the McDo on the boulevard?'

There was laughter and applause.

'How long for a table for two?' I asked. I'd always found that it was best to introduce yourself to the guy in charge. You were less likely to lose your place in the queue if he'd seen you. It also meant that for the time it took to ask the question you were semi-legitimately at the front of the line.

'*Dix minutes,*' he said. At any other restaurant, this could mean anything up to an hour, but here we knew that the staff kept things moving.

The maître d' stepped back inside for a moment, and through the partially steamed-up windows we saw him barracking a table-load of backpacker types, or rather hassling the waiter in charge of their section of the restaurant.

'*Allez,* dessert, coffee, bill! We don't charge enough to let them sit there all night.'

He came back outside. 'Where do they think they are?' he asked his audience. 'La Tour d'Argent?'

This earned more laughter from the crowd. La Tour d'Argent is the kind of restaurant that gives credit-card companies indigestion.

A waiter gave a signal from inside and the maître d' called out again.

'Six! Who asked for a table for six?'

There was a cheer from the middle of the scrum and a bunch of people moved forward. The maître d' counted them as they approached.

'Wait, you are only five.'

'Yes, the sixth is on his way,' a woman said, giving him the full benefit of a glorious lipstick smile.

41

'Sorry. Full tables only. Any more sixes? No? Who doesn't mind sharing? A four and a two?'

'Two,' I said, thrusting my arm around Alexa's shoulder to prove that we were both here.

'*Allez, les deux amoureux*,' the maître d' said, and we were in.

My first impressions were of a warm, gratin-cheese fug and a contented hum of conversation. We marched down the aisle with that warm feeling of having been admitted into an exclusive club. There were at least a hundred tables – all of them occupied – arranged in long lateral rows, like a canteen. Quite a canteen, though, decorated with high framed mirrors and a bizarre romantic mural of a classical French garden that was being buzzed by a World War One aeroplane.

We squeezed into the two seats nearest a low wooden partition, and a few moments later we were joined by the American foursome who'd been overtaken in the queue earlier. They nodded and wished us '*bonsoir*' as they took off their whitewater rafters' anoraks. It was easy to see which couple was which – one pair had let their hair go grey, the others were clearly sharing the same bottle of jet-black dye.

Alexa and I ordered an aperitif of two *coupes de champagne* and came to a tacit decision to speak French together to ensure a little privacy.

'Look at them reading their guidebook. I bet they don't even know which country they are visiting,' Alexa said.

'I think they probably do. All this French food on the menu . . .'

'You know what I mean, Paul. They think that Paris is France, and that France is full of artists and champagne bottles.'

I didn't dare remind her that she was a photographer who'd just ordered a glass of the house bubbly.

'So you really are not sad that I have no more American dreams?' I asked.

'Oh no, I don't want to go there and condone their corrupt system. And I know you'll find a way of paying your fine and keeping your share of the café.'

We clinked glasses and drank to her optimism.

'Er, excusez? Nous sommes American. Vous, er? Translate the menu pour nous, si voo play?'

We turned to see four sets of perfect transatlantic teeth glinting at us.

I intervened before Alexa could growl out some jibe about cultural colonialists being unable to decipher menus that didn't have pictures of hamburgers on them.

'How can I help?' I asked.

'Oh, you speak such wonderful English,' the grey-haired woman said.

'Sank you,' I said, remembering I was supposed to be French.

'Where did you learn it?' she asked.

'From ze Ollywood feelms,' I improvised.

'Wow, that's amazing.' The jet-black woman flapped her heavily made-up eyelashes at me.

'Yes, any-sing zat is a line from Ollywood feelm, I say wiz ze perfect accent. Go ahead punk, make my day. You talkin to me? Hasta la vista, baby.'

Signs of scepticism were emanating from the grey-haired side of the American table, but the jet-blacks were totally sold on the idea of Hollywood as an educational tool.

'And where does that line, "How can I help", come from?' asked Mrs Jet.

'Austin Powers Deux?' I hazarded.

'Oh, Paul,' Alexa interrupted. 'He's English.'

This got a huge laugh. Whether it was at my joke or

simply that the notion of being English was inherently comic, I don't know.

To my astonishment, Alexa then proceeded to run the Americans through the starters and main courses, patiently explaining how each item was prepared, and warning about the possible inclusion of garlic or strange animal parts. I helped out whenever Alexa's explanations got a bit too technical, and when the waiter returned we were all ready to order. He scribbled his notes directly on to the paper tablecloths, and disappeared again.

'Merci, Mam'sell,' the jet-black guy said, making Alexa flinch slightly. You don't call a French feminist '*Mademoiselle*'.

'You're welcome, Sir,' she said, with only the tiniest clenching of her teeth.

'Paris is the most beautiful city in the world,' the grey-haired guy announced.

'Except for Venice,' his wife disagreed.

'And Sydney,' the jet-black woman suggested.

The grey-haired guy valiantly kept his smile in place, but his eyes were hinting that maybe the wives should have been left in America.

'It's definitely Paris for me, too,' the jet-black guy said. 'You see, you mustn't imagine that all Americans are anti-French. It's not true.'

'At our golf club, we got French patisseries on the break-fast bar instead of Danish,' his wife reminded him.

'Not that we have anything against the Danes,' the grey-haired guy chipped in. 'Europe's the most beautiful continent in the world.'

'Except for Asia,' his wife pitched in.

The food came, and we returned to the privacy of our own conversations. I asked Alexa – in French – why she'd been so helpful towards our globalizing neighbours.

'Oh, as individuals, Americans can be the nicest people on earth,' she said, 'and these ones seem to be willing to learn about French culture. There is a lot to learn, of course.' Her implication being, compared to the superficiality of American culture. 'From the sound of it, the most complicated cookery technique they know is lighting the barbecue.'

'I think that is—' I couldn't think of the French word. 'Un peu . . . unfair?'

'You know what I mean, Paul. They don't really respect other cultures except as tourist attractions. All they care about is defending their own culture. Their globalization is—'

Her political speech was cut off by a buzzing in my pocket.

'Sorry, I should have switched it off,' I said. I pulled out my phone and saw that the call was coming from a London number. 'Probably bad news about the job.'

'Well, answer it, then,' she said.

'Hello? Mr West?' asked a woman with a strong Yorkshire accent.

'Speaking.'

'Oh, hi there. Lucy Marsh from Visitor Resources: Britain. Am I disturbing you?'

'Well, I am in a restaurant . . .'

'Sorry, I know it's late, but I've stayed on myself because I need to get your file complete before the weekend.'

'My file?'

'Yes, Mr Tyler omitted to ask you a few questions during your interview. He should have given you the Britishness test.'

'What? But I *am* British, it's written on my passport.'

Alexa was staring at me with a mixture of amusement and

alarm. It must have sounded as if I was about to lose my nationality.

'Yes, but there are a few questions we need to ask you if you're going to represent Britain abroad. Have you got five minutes?'

'Five minutes?' I said this more as an apology to Alexa than to the woman in London. Alexa shrugged, why not? 'OK, but maybe I'd better nip outside.'

I clambered into the aisle as I fielded the first question.

'Can you name the two sons of Prince Charles and Princess Diana?'

'Of course,' I said. 'William and Harry.'

'Right. Good. Can you name the Prime Minister?'

'Depends, is it the same one as yesterday?' I said, squeezing past the maître d' into the courtyard.

'*Oh, vous abandonnez votre table?*' he asked.

'*Non, non, une minute,*' I assured him.

The courtyard was totally jammed with people now, so there was nowhere I was going to get some peace and quiet. Anyway, wasn't this conversation pointless? Hadn't Tyler told everyone I was a cross-dressing subversive?

I named the PM anyway.

'Right, good,' Lucy said. 'Can you explain the basic rules of cricket to an American?'

'No way.' I'd tried this before with French people, but it was like explaining how to yodel underwater. They didn't see the point.

'Well you've got to give it a go, just so I can tick the box.'

'OK, how about, cricket is like baseball except that there are two batters and two pitchers on the field at any one time, and cricketers don't wear silly knickerbockers.'

A couple of French guys in the queue were listening in and started to mime incomprehension.

'Fair enough,' Lucy said. 'Maybe I'll pretend I didn't

hear the bit about the knickerbockers, though. Now can you sing the first verse of the national anthem?'

'Why? Is there a second?'

She laughed. 'I guess there must be, but God knows what it is, so just the first will be OK. And I'm afraid I need you to sing it – not recite it.'

'So you're only hiring people who can sing? Aren't you discriminating against the tone deaf?'

'We need to be sure that you won't make a fool of yourself if you have to sing the national anthem,' my examiner told me. 'You know how terrible it looks when they do close-ups of football players before an international and they don't know the words.'

'But you're making it sound as if I'm actually in with a chance. I thought I blew it with Mr Tyler.'

'Oh no. He may have seemed a little . . . subdued. It's because of –' She broke off and I got the impression she was looking over her shoulder to see if anyone was listening '– his medication. That's probably why he left your file incomplete.'

'Ah.'

'And from what I can see, you're on a shortlist of one. Sing for your supper and you've got the job, I reckon.'

There was a moment when I almost chickened out. But I've never been one to deliberately screw up a job interview, and I really needed the money, so I closed my eyes and launched into the opening line. Pretty softly, I must admit, so that only the two guys who'd been teasing me about cricket began to wonder whether I was having a mental breakdown.

But then I heard someone joining in. Behind the two Frenchmen, there was a clutch of studenty Americans in ski jackets and woollen hats.

'God Bless America,' one of them was crooning. Of course, in 1776 they kicked out our government but they kept the tune of our national anthem.

I had to raise my voice. 'Send her victorious,' I demanded, just as the two French guys struck up the opening words of the Marseillaise. 'Happy and glorious,' I boomed, as loudly as if I was trying to bring Queen Victoria back from the dead. 'Long to reign over us, God save our Queeeeen.'

I got a cheer from a British contingent at the edge of the crowd, and suddenly felt the hairs stand up on the back of my neck. What is it about national anthems? At that moment there was nothing in the world I wanted more than to go out and give the Yanks and the Frogs a damn good thrashing at cricket. An especially appealing prospect given that they didn't understand the rules.

'Ooh, loovlay,' Lucy in London cooed as the other national anthems fizzled out for lack of people willing to make public idiots of themselves. 'I think you're on your way to America.'

NEW YORK

Merde in Manhattan

1

THE EMPIRE STATE BUILDING disappeared over the horizon, and the taxi bumped down off the highway into a neighbourhood of small red-brick houses. It was a zone where some enterprising salesman had apparently started a fashion for coloured awnings – whole streets of houses had sunshades shaped like car bonnets over their windows. They were primary red, royal blue or moss green, and suggested that in summer this place must bake. Now, though, many of the awnings had a fringe of icicles.

'What is this neighbourhood?' I interrupted the driver's phone conversation. 'The Upper East Side?'

'Kind of,' he said. 'It's the Bronx.'

'The Bronx?' To a middle-class Englishman like me, this conjured up images of gangsta rappers emptying Uzis at each other. Or possibly at me.

'Yeah.'

'But why are we going to the Bronx?'

'That's the address you gave me, man.'

I looked again at the printout that I'd shown him at the airport. The address of the B&B had been emailed to me a couple of days earlier by Visitor Resources: Britain. It hadn't said 'the Bronx', though. It had just included an NY zip code. And like a dork, I'd assumed that NY always meant you were within ogling distance of the Empire State.

'The Bronx? That's brilliant, Paul. Much more typically American than touristy Manhattan.' Yes, Alexa was along for the ride. Less than ten minutes after my job-clinching rendition of 'God Save the Queen', she'd given up accusing me of collaborating with the colonialist enemy and seized the prospect of an American road trip as if it was the best idea since putting jam in doughnuts.

It was impossible for her to finish her documentary on the French lifestyle at this time of year, she declared. There were so many scenes she needed to shoot in spring or summer. Filming the USA in winter, on the other hand, was a much better idea. It would, she said, 'take the Hollywood veneer away' and let people see the place as it really was. It would allow her to get below the surface and reveal 'the rotten heart of the world's most menacing country'. A good thing Visitor Resources hadn't inter-viewed *her*, I thought.

I was pretty astonished that they'd re-interviewed me, and frankly amazed that I'd got the job. But then I remem-bered what Lucy Marsh had said about being on a shortlist of one, and I'm ashamed to say that I took full advantage of the situation. You're a matter of days away from the start of the campaign, I'd said, and Jack Tyler couldn't even tell me the names of the participating cities. This wasn't a job, it was a mission. It merited danger money.

Lucy was a practical, straight-talking Yorkshire lass, and we cut a deal there and then on the phone. The salary they had been offering was transformed into a much more lucrative consultant's fee, the bonus if I won the competition went from fat to borderline obese, and – the icing on the cake – she said that if things went well, there was a job in it for me. Head of promotion at their Paris office. A kind of roving tourist ambassador whose duties would include plenty of wining and dining of French bigshots, as well as regular trips back to the motherland to try out the top English hotels and spas. Another tough mission, but I was willing to take it on, I told her.

So here I was in New York with not only a good chance of paying off my debt to France, but also a girlfriend who thought I'd turned into a magician. Out of my hat I'd suddenly produced the money I needed, plus a trip across America and the prospect of endless luxury hotel stays and seaweed massages. English seaweed rather than French, perhaps, but she wasn't one to look a gift seahorse in the mouth.

'You know, Paul,' Alexa now said, 'your guidebook has a section about how the Bronx is regenerated, with a chic area near the university and the best Italian restaurants in New York, but I am sure that is only the partial story. There will be many people who have been excluded from this regeneration.'

Yes, I thought, and they're going to be really pleased if a young French woman with an expensive camera comes and rubs their noses in the fact.

Our taxi juddered on due north away from the Statue of Liberty, past blackened, leafless trees and shopping streets populated only by steam-puffing people in inflatable ski jackets.

We passed below a clattering overhead train. The subway came out this far, then. I began to console myself that we were only in New York for a couple of nights. All I had to do here was pick up the Mini for our drive to Boston, where my first event was planned. We could go into Manhattan whenever we wanted.

'This is it.'

The cab driver had pulled up outside the largest building in a row of well-kept Victorian villas with bright white mortar holding the russet bricks together. It had baroque plaster mouldings above the windows, with a tiara-like flourish of decoration in the centre of the flat roof line. Beside the saffron-yellow front door was a sign saying 'Noontide B&B', with a smiling sun and a large 'WELCOME' in capital letters.

'Hmm.' Alexa didn't look too pleased. I guessed she had been hoping for something with a bit more grit. I was relieved at the friendliness of the place, though. I was here to do a job, not to pretend I was a homie from the hood.

The landlady was a pleasant, middle-aged hippy with ginger plaits and floppy wooden earrings, who introduced herself as Lorie and was 'so glad' we'd found the place OK. She humped Alexa's rucksack up the narrow stairs without showing the slightest sign of muscle strain, and chatted all the way to our snug little room. It was as bright yellow as the B&B sign. The house's colour scheme seemed designed to make up for the winter chill. Perhaps she re-painted it snow-white in summer, I thought, to take the edge off the heat.

'Oh, one thing,' Lorie said as she swung Alexa's bag on to a luggage stand. 'You are married, aren't you?' She asked this with the same beaming grin she'd worn since opening the door, but I guessed it was a deeply serious question.

'Yes, of course,' I lied.

'Good,' Lorie said, embracing us both in the warmth of her approval. 'Only . . .' She held up her own ring finger, which was adorned with a chunky diamond engagement ring and a gold wedding band.

'Oh yes, we don't wear them when we travel,' I said. 'Our rings are much too precious to us. They're locked up in a safe at home.'

'Ah.' Lorie blinked at me as if this was the most touching thing she'd ever heard. 'Come down and have some tea,' she said, and smiled her way out of the room.

'Are you crazy?' Alexa whispered to me when we were alone. In French, I was glad to hear. 'Why should you lie? It's not illegal to sleep in the same bed if you're not married.'

'No, but she prefers to think we're married, so why not? The important thing is that we're together, isn't it?'

'She needs to face up to the realities of life.'

'But it's this lady's house, a B&B, not a political . . .' I couldn't think of the French word for workshop or in-doctrination centre.

'The whole world is political, Paul,' Alexa said, but smiled to show she was joking. Well, half joking.

An earthenware teapot with three matching mugs, a milk jug, a plate of lemon slices and a sugar bowl were laid out in a stiflingly heated glass conservatory that had been built on to the back of the house. The walls and French windows were almost invisible behind a mass of tropical foliage.

Lorie was waiting for us in a yellow-painted wickerwork armchair, and motioned for us to sit facing her on the other side of the coffee table.

'So, tell me who you are,' she said.

Alexa obviously thought this was a weird way to phrase the question, but she was happy to talk about her on-the-road documentary.

'It will be about the *reality* of America,' she said. 'I think it's important for people to face reality, don't you?' She aimed a challenging stare at Lorie.

'Alexa also does photography,' I added quickly. 'Portraits, mainly.'

'That's wonderful,' Lorie said. 'And who are you, Paul?'

I followed Alexa's example and talked about my job rather than my innermost workings.

'And where will your journey take you?' Lorie asked.

I was glad to be able to reply. I'd finally received the list of cities from Jack Tyler. 'From here to Boston, down to Miami, across to New Orleans, and then we keep going west until we hit the Pacific. The final ceremony is in Los Angeles,' I said. 'Hollywood.' Alexa and I exchanged a smile of anticipation.

'Hmm, Hollywood,' Lorie grunted. Not a movie fan, it seemed.

'I'm looking forward to getting down south in the sun,' I said. 'But this is great. So warm.' I held up my arms in tribute to her indoor jungle.

Lorie brightened instantly. 'It's for Joey.'

'Joey?' I looked around for a parrot.

'Yes.' Lorie gave a little wave in the direction of a thick branch above Alexa's head. On cue, the branch opened a beady eye and gave a flick of its long spiny tail. It was some kind of miniature dragon. Although three feet long is a pretty big miniature.

Alexa leant back, effectively offering her throat to the beast, and screamed. The monster opened its jaws.

'He's only one of God's creatures, my dear, don't be fearful,' Lorie said, as Alexa dived for shelter behind my seat.

'It looks pretty fearful to me,' I said. 'What is it?'

'He's an iguana. My husband works at JFK and we rescued him from some smugglers. Joey has a lot more to fear than we do, you know.'

Alexa didn't look convinced. We swapped chairs, and Alexa kept her eyes fixed on pal Joey's softly breathing belly.

'Now, let's have tea,' Lorie said, and began pouring. 'Lemon? Milk? Sugar?' When all the cups were ready, she gave her warmest smile yet and said, in a perfectly matter-of-fact tone, 'I think we should thank God for this tea and the way that we have all come together safely today, don't you?'

She closed her eyes and held her hands above the table to say grace. 'Dear Lord, we would like—'

'Excuse me.' Alexa stood up and left the room.

'She has a mild reptile allergy,' I told Lorie. 'I'll just go and see if she's OK.'

'We're not staying here,' Alexa hissed, sounding eerily like Joey. She was sitting on the bed in our room. 'She's got a Tyrannosaurus living in her house and she's a dinosaur herself. *Are you married? Let's thank God for this tea.*' Alexa did a cruel impression of Lorie's slow, benevolent voice.

'It's only for two nights,' I said.

'No, I refuse to thank God for my tea. We should thank the Indian woman who picked it so that she can feed her children who are hungry because Americans push the world tea price down. Thank God? Huh!'

I'd forgotten just how deeply atheist the French can be. To Alexa, even singing a Christmas carol was like kissing a bishop's backside.

'What difference does it make?' I asked. 'Just come down, let her say grace and we'll have a cup of tea.'

'No, she will not impose her opinions on me.'

'If we were in Africa, you wouldn't mind people carrying out their rituals. You'd think it was *folklorique*, as you French say. The Americans are more religious than you, that's all. Remember what I said at my interview? "You gotta have faith." That's what they think over here.'

Alexa refused to budge.

'You are my boyfriend, Paul, you should respect my feelings before hers, OK?'

'I do respect your feelings, Alexa, it's just that . . .' I didn't
know how to tell her diplomatically that she was creating a
storm in a teacup.

'There are lots of Bed and Breakfasts here.' Alexa was
flicking through our wrist-thick USA guidebook.

'You really feel so strongly that you want to leave?'

'Yes. Where's your phone? I'll call some places.'

But I had a better idea. I began scrolling down my list of
American contacts, looking for a guardian angel who'd
solved an accommodation crisis for me in the past – a girl
who'd offered me bed and breakfast and everything in
between.

2

It took me a while to work out how Elodie had changed
since I had last seen her in Paris.

She was still blonde, she still wore her hair back in a
short ponytail, and her way of speaking and looking at
people still suggested that she had either just finished, or
was just about to start, having sex. Or maybe both.

She wasn't tarty at all, just incredibly knowing. I'd seen
her in action. She'd catch the eye of a guy, exchange sexual
data with him for a microsecond, then instantly classify him
– hung up, sexy but gay, gauche but maybe worth the effort,
or hmm, not bad, if he makes a move I'm definitely
interested.

All this at the age of twenty-four. It says something for
the French education system.

I wasn't spared her analytical gaze as she strolled into the
diner on the Upper East Side of Manhattan where we'd

arranged to meet. She and I had had certain, let's say, physical dealings in the past, and she was obviously checking me out to see whether I'd improved with age or was on the way downhill. But I didn't pick up her conclusion because she saw Alexa, and seemed to switch off the radar out of respect for an old female friend.

We all kissed and hugged, and Elodie loaded her jacket on to a straining coat-stand.

That was when I realized what was different about her. In Paris, she would usually dress in chic American or Italian brands. Here, she could have been the French fashion ambassador. A chestnut-brown Agnès B jacket, orange Coq Sportif sweatshirt, Chevignon jeans. She seemed to be playing the Typical French Miss, which I suppose she was, on a year abroad as part of her Paris business course. A year to learn all about American business practices, then go home and watch them founder on a reef of French strikes and monopolies.

'Oh Paul, you never call me unless you have housing problems,' Elodie said. I'd originally met her when I was working for her dad, Jean-Marie. I was looking for a place to live in Paris and could only find temporarily broomless broom cupboards.

I updated her on where Alexa and I were at, and why. We'd fled the B&B, found the nearest subway station, which was above a stretch of waste ground next to a Dunkin' Donuts, and waited fifteen minutes in the searing cold for a train. For at least ten stops everyone seemed to be asking themselves, did these two tourists take the wrong train at JFK or what?

'It sounds like you need a hearty American breakfast,' Elodie concluded. 'Choose what you want, everything here is good.' Along with her new French look she'd adopted an American accent and a loudness of voice which suggested that every word she said was of vital importance.

My body clock couldn't work out what I wanted to eat. While I was trying to decide between porridge (or oatmeal, as they called it), a double cheeseburger with shoestring fries or a hot-fudge sundae, a small guy in the diner's logo'd white shirt came over and filled our water glasses. This was supposed to be a Greek diner, but all the staff were Mexicans in whose faces you could still see Inca heritage.

'I would normally let you stay with me,' Elodie said, 'but it's a bit delicate. I house-sit for a guy and he's home right now.'

'You house-sit even when he's there?' I asked.

'Yes. It's a big apartment. It belongs to Clint Highway.'

'Who?'

Alexa and Elodie laughed, and explained that he was one of the old French rockers who'd started their careers by changing their name from Jean-Claude Dupont or Jacques Leclerc to something vaguely American and singing covers of English-language hits. Clint's first record was, they told me, a French version of 'Strawberry Fields Forever' called 'Je Suis Une Tarte Aux Fraises', – 'I Am A Strawberry Tart' – a title which proved that either the French translator was crap or that he'd been taking the same drugs as John Lennon, but in much greater quantities.

'Whatever happened to Clint? He just disappeared,' Alexa said. 'Thank God.'

'Well, he still makes records, but, yes, he is invisible these days. He had an, er, accident.' Elodie looked embarrassed for her host. 'You'll see. I'll take you there so we can get your hotel sorted out.'

In the end, I splurged on oatmeal, a double cheeseburger with shoestring fries *and* a hot-fudge sundae. I felt my stomach expanding inside me like an aeroplane life vest.

None of the other people in the place were eating as vast

a meal as me, I noticed. One of the waiters took an order from a group of four skinny women who were dressed as if they'd just got out of a designer aerobics class.

'Sesame bagel, toasted, with cream cheese,' a dark-haired gym queen said, talking at one word per minute as if the guy was a total moron.

'Can I get a *latte*?' her friend asked, looking up expectantly at the waiter as if this amazing breakthrough in coffee drinking might not have spread to this part of town yet.

Neither of them said 'hello' or 'please'. Maybe, I thought, New Yorkers are so insistent on their rights as consumers that they don't think politeness is necessary.

Elodie saw me staring.

'They all come here to network after their gym class and then they go home to watch the babysitter give the bottle to their kids,' she said. 'They are the Upper East Side's Native American tribe. Come, let's go and find your hotel.' She held out a hand as if to grab the coffee pot from a passing waiter. 'Check?' she said.

I half expected him to answer, 'No, Mexican actually, but thanks for asking.'

3

Elodie led us out on to the teeming avenue, sunlit now beneath a cloudless sky. This was the New York I'd been hoping to see. Shabby brick buildings with chic stores on the ground floor, tall apartment houses with air-conditioning units poking through the windows like a vanload of small fridges that had been hurled at the facade by Superman. There were people everywhere, probably in even more of a rush than usual because of the cold wind that was trying to chew their noses off. Half of the world's taxis were rushing southward in a panicky exodus, as if they hoped it might be warmer downtown.

We wheeled our bags towards Elodie's apartment, and she showed us how the USA, or this part of Manhattan anyway, was being recolonized by France, two hundred years after the French sold their last territories in America to the fledgling republic.

In the space of three blocks, we saw two French fashion chains, a French brand of kids' clothing, a French hairdresser, a French bakery and a French chocolaterie, with boxes of sweets laid out like sculptures in a modern-art museum (at similar prices to modern-art exhibits, too). This was not counting two small galleries with Matisse and Picasso in their windows.

'You see,' I told Alexa, 'America's not the only country that's globalizing.'

'Yes, but France does it with Matisse instead of McDonald's.'

The Americans I met in Paris and London always tried to tell me that theirs was a classless society, but Elodie's building was several million social strata above the tenements we'd passed coming in from the Bronx. It was within sight of the misty treetops of Central Park. There was ornate art-nouveau stonework running up the facade, and a long green awning stretched from the doorway to the edge of the sidewalk. You were meant to arrive in a limo, not dragging your luggage, as we were.

A uniformed doorman rushed to open the heavy brass-framed door. He was middle-aged, with a greased-back Elvis haircut, and examined Alexa and me as if we were young squatters planning to sleep on the shiny white marble floor of his lobby.

Elodie swanned majestically past him, pausing only to ask if he could help Alexa with her rucksack.

'Give him a dollar when we get to the lift,' she told me in French.

Elodie's apartment on the fourth floor was, as she had said, 'quite big'. The wood-panelled lounge had a half-size cinema screen on one wall, and the dark corridors leading off it seemed to go all the way to Brooklyn.

I was just about to ask how on earth she'd wangled this fantastic house-sitting deal when a gnome appeared and answered all my questions. He was about two hundred years old, five feet tall, with a face like a polished walnut and a blond wig as convincing as a Chinese bottle of 'Channel Nomber 5'. This had to be the rock star Clint. He was dressed as a Napoleonic general – presumably a French translation of the Beatles' look circa 1967.

''Allo, beb,' he croaked, and Elodie bent forward to allow him to insert his tongue into her mouth. I exchanged a look with Alexa. We'd both figured out what the 'house-sitting' deal was. The house was probably not the only thing she was sitting on.

Clint nodded indifferently up at me, but Alexa seemed to ignite some kind of firework under that wig of his. He flared his nostrils at her and trotted over.

''Ey, beb. You lahk pardee?' he slobbered.

'*Non*, Clint,' Elodie said in French. 'She is not—'

'Ah.' Clint pouted in disappointment. Another of Elodie's household tasks seemed to have been explained. She procured party partners for him.

'My friends need a hotel,' she told him, sticking to French. 'That room your record company keeps for you. Could they have that?'

'Record company?' Clint frowned, adding a few extra

wrinkles to his wrinkles, in an attempt to remember where he'd heard this phrase before.

'Yes. They have a room at the Chelsea.'

'Ah, the Chelsea? Yeah, man. Less go pardee!' His tongue seemed to want to go on ahead and get the drinks in.

'No, Clint. They're just *amis*,' Elodie said. 'They need a place to stay. No party, Clint. Don't worry,' she told me. 'We'll sort it out. You know, the Chelsea is where English rock stars kill their girlfriends. It will be perfect for you at the beginning of your American stay. Now tell me some more about your new job.'

She sat us down in her railway-station-sized kitchen and I talked her through my insane interviews, the World Tourism Capital competition and my chance to relive *The Italian Job* right across America.

'And which cities will you visit?' she asked.

I told her, and she repeated the list to herself.

'And what are these promotional events that you must organize?'

'Ah.' This was where my story ran out of steam. The one thing London hadn't been able to tell me was exactly what I'd be doing in each city. Details were still being finalized, they said, but not to worry. I didn't have to set the events up from scratch. I'd be co-hosting them with local partners, and I'd be getting all the necessary info well in advance of each event. Although forty-eight hours seemed to me to be cutting it fine for Boston.

'They are Her Majesty's secrets, are they, Paul?' Elodie teased.

'For the moment,' I lied.

'Well, when you feel free to reveal all, maybe you can send me some invitations. I'd love to come. Especially to Miami – it will be wonderful at this time of year.'

'OK, great.' I was flattered by this show of solidarity, especially from someone who was theoretically on the opposing team.

Elodie made a couple of phone calls and told us that the room would be ready after lunch. Seemed there had been a bit of a 'pardee' there the night before, at which Clint had been a star guest, and the wreckage was still being cleared away.

She said we should leave our bags at the apartment – unlocked in case Clint tried to shoot the lock off. He'd already been sued by a couple in the next building, she told us, because he'd used a Magnum on the stubborn door of the refrigerator and the bullets had pierced the wall and taken out the neighbours' collection of fish-shaped serving dishes. And this was just to get at a bottle of champagne. If he thought there were drugs in our cases, he'd probably use a grenade launcher.

We arranged to meet at the Chelsea later on. Elodie was heading up to Columbia University, she said, for a seminar. It was part of a course she was taking, a Masters in 'emergency and disaster management'.

'To help refugees from floods and hurricanes?' Alexa asked.

'Yeah, kind of,' Elodie said in her most American accent. 'You know, refugees from any sort of disaster, they're the biggest captive market you can imagine. Federal government isn't really interested in taking care of refugees, so there are some great business openings there.'

There was no mistaking Jean-Marie's opportunist genes powering that brain of hers.

We accepted Elodie's offer of a lift uptown. I had to go to Harlem, which was on her way. And Alexa decided to go to the university so that she could interview some students on 'their awareness of the damage done to the outside world by American foreign policy'. Oh well, I thought, if she gets arrested for subversion, at least there'll be more room in the Mini for my luggage.

The vehicle that pulled up outside Elodie's building was a black limo – not a stretch but a Lincoln all the same – with a dark-suited chauffeur.

'I charge them to Clint's account,' Elodie said when I whistled my appreciation. 'He can never remember when he took a bath, never mind a car ride.'

On the way uptown, she told us Clint's tragic story.

Until ten or so years ago, like all ageing French stars, he'd been able to make a fortune out of chat-show appearances, the kind of programme that is inflicted on French audiences every Saturday night, in which a hysterical male presenter shows clips from old TV shows and then gets the half-dead stars to mime their hit song or read an anecdote from the autocue.

But then Clint had got big ideas and decided on a comeback tour of France, which was where it all went wrong. During an encore of 'Je Suis Une Tarte Aux Fraises', some nostalgic members of the audience had held up their cigarette lighters and begun to wave them in the air. Opinion was divided on what happened next. Some said that, blinded by his sunglasses and the drugs, Clint had tripped and fallen head-first into the crowd. Others were sure he had tried a stage dive. Either way, he'd flown into the audience, the cigarette lighters had set his wig on fire, and his terrified fans had tossed him around the venue like a lighted match until he finally landed back on the stage to be extinguished by the roadies. He had only been saved from third-degree burns because his pancake make-up had baked solid and protected his skin.

However, when they peeled off the charred hair and solidified foundation cream, he looked like a pickled walnut. And even French TV doesn't invite pickled walnuts on to its primetime shows. So now, Elodie said, he recorded the occasional song, but mainly he just lived, very comfortably, on the royalties from all the plays of 'Je Suis Une Tarte . . .' on French radio. Luckily for him, it seemed that strawberry tart really was for ever.

4

I was disappointed to see that the Harlem address I'd been given didn't lead me to a car showroom with polished display models glinting under neon lighting.

In fact, the address didn't seem to lead anywhere at all, because the building had vanished. In its place was one of those typical American parking lots, a demolition site that was now so crammed full of parked cars that you'd need to be an expert at Rubik's Cube to extract one. In the middle of this tapestry of vehicles was a wooden hut.

I looked inside. It was a tiny, brightly lit living room, complete with a velvet easy chair, a radiator and a TV. In place of family photos and vases, there was a poster of a girl only just managing to stop her enormous breasts falling out of her bikini top, and several equally huge bunches of car keys.

'We full.' The guy who had come up behind me didn't seem to like having someone peer into his lounge. He was an African American, with a camouflage parka and a battle-worn expression. The hood of his parka ringed his face with fluffy fur but it didn't make him look cuddly.

'Sorry, I wasn't actually looking for a parking space, I was hoping you'd be able to tell me where I might be able to find the Mini I'm due to pick up tomorrow.' I was halfway through this sentence when I realized that the guy couldn't understand what the hell I was on about. We southern Brits think we speak 'pure' accent-free English, but of course there's no such thing. Everyone who opens their mouth has an accent. And the car-park attendant was totally bewildered by my middle-class English tendency to express what I want by apologizing for being a nuisance rather than just getting to the point. This was probably why people in New York limited their questions to barked monosyllables like 'latte?' and 'check?'

He replied with a strong (for me) Harlem twang, which he probably thought was totally accentless too. I saw that we were both equally confused by our conversation.

'Fa di da ra la tata ha ha Mini?' I had asked.

'Bang lang a nang bo sang karang Mini,' he answered.

'Er, popo froofroo looloo Mini?' I pursued.

'Cum a hum dum muthafuggin boondong Mini,' he concluded, and made it clear he wanted to get inside his hut and out of the cold.

'No, look, this is the address.' I read it out to him from my piece of paper.

'Oh, yeah, back there, see?' He pointed to a door at the rear of the lot.

'Ah, thanks,' I said, but I was talking to the closed door of his warm log cabin.

There was, I now saw, a kind of trail through the maze of cars, leading to the back of the lot. It ended at a dark-red sliding door with orange light filtering out underneath it. There was a smaller entrance cut into the door. I knocked, and opened it very slowly indeed. Again, my ooh-I'm-in-the-ghetto prejudices kicked in. What kind of things went on in a workshop at the back of a demolition site in Harlem, they wanted to know.

Dismantling stolen cars? Discount gun sales? A crack factory?

I'd never actually seen a crack factory, but I didn't think that the equipment on display in this place was drug apparatus. It would, for example, have been fiendishly clever to hide a crack oven inside an electric-blue convertible Cadillac. And it would have taken a long time to smoke one of the fat black tyres stacked against the wall. This was, it seemed, a car-conversion workshop, a cluttered, oily, paint-smelling garage that was currently rocking to the beat of a rap record and hammer blows.

'Hello?' I called out.

The hammering and the rapping stopped and a small, stocky Black guy with goggles around his neck emerged from behind the Cadillac.

'Hi,' I said. 'My name's West. I'm looking for – er, sorry, can you understand what I'm talking about?'

'Dunno,' he said. 'What *are* you talking about?'

A good question, I realized, and spoken in an accent I understood.

'Sorry, look.' I gave him the piece of paper where I'd written his address. He frowned, no doubt distracted because the most legible writing on the paper was 'Join our Air Miles scheme and win two free nights at a luxury hotel.'

'The Mini ordered by Visitor Resources: Britain?' I said. 'For Paul West?'

'Oh yeah.' He laughed, clearly relieved that this foreigner wasn't inviting him to share a luxury room for two nights. He introduced himself as Dwight. 'Sorry, Paul, but your Mini ain't ready yet. I didn't know what to paint on it. I only just got the confirmation.'

'Paint on it? I thought you were just giving it a service before I picked it up?'

'No, I gotta paint an English flag on the roof. They was

going to send me a colour scheme and all. I didn't get it till this morning.'

A mental picture of Jack Tyler flashed into my head. He was giggling manically at a website called AMillionWaysToPissOffPaulWest.com.

'Shit.' I was supposed to be driving to Boston in the Mini in less than forty-eight hours' time.

'Hey, no problem,' Dwight said. 'I'll start on it as soon as I'm done with the Caddy. It'll be ready on time. You just want the paint job?'

'Yes, I think so.'

'Oh, 'cause I could do some other English stuff for you. How about I cover the doors with AstroTurf, stick some cricket balls on there? Or no, I *embed* the balls in the door like you've just been hit by them.'

'You know about cricket?' I asked.

'Oh yeah. I come from Brooklyn. West Indian guys got a cricket club there. Every summer they beat the hell out these English teams come over to play.'

'You understand all the rules?'

'Nah,' he said. 'But I do know, some of them fellas from the West Indies, they just *love* throwing hardballs at English guys. What did you do to them back in the colonial days? Oh man, they'd sure like to embed your head.' As far as I could see, he'd understood the rules of international cricket perfectly.

5

The Chelsea loomed above me like a blood-red gothic mansion. I'd heard about the hotel where Hendrix used to stay and where Sid Vicious allegedly knifed his girlfriend to death, but I didn't expect it to be quite this forbidding.

The shops on the ground floor of the building seemed to hint at the eccentric activities within – a vintage guitar shop, an acupuncturist, a tattoo parlour, and, bizarrely, a fishing-tackle store.

On plaques by the hotel entrance there were quotes by or about some of the famous literary residents. One read: 'Dylan Thomas sailed out of here to die.' Very reassuring.

In the lobby, the first thing I saw was a fat lady hanging from the ceiling on a swing. She was not one of the eccentric guests but an almost-lifesize sculpture. The whole lobby was an art gallery, its lurid yellow walls hung with modern portraits and abstract splashes. Adding a period touch was a pair of gothic urns on a mantelpiece, implying perhaps that being dead didn't exclude you from hanging out at the Chelsea.

People (most of them alive) were hunched in armchairs, computers open on their laps. There was no sign of Alexa and Elodie, but that was probably because I was on time and they were French women.

I took off my scarf, gloves, hat and three or four layers of outer clothing and went to wait in one of the armchairs. No one bothered me, although the laptoppers seemed to be confused as to how I was managing to email people with no visible computer. I considered pretending to type on to my shirt sleeve just to freak them out that their laptop might not be the latest model, but finally contented myself with slumping low in the chair and closing my eyes.

Next thing I knew, Alexa was grinning down at me, running a video camera along my body.

'And here is the typical position of the dynamic Englishman who has crossed the Atlantic to follow his dream, and instead he is fantasizing about English beer and naked women on the beach. Where is the car, *chéri*?'

'It's not quite ready yet.'

'And when will it be *quite ready*?'

'Before we go to Boston.'

'And have you found out about the Boston event?'

'No, that was next on my list.'

'After your siesta.'

'After my closed-eye brainstorming session, yes.'

When we'd dumped our bags, Elodie took us across town for a drink at a revolving bar. By that, I don't mean a mini-bar that swivelled when you tried to grab a glass. No, this was one of those panoramic places that give everyone a perfect view of the city, if they can wait long enough for the view to come round. A posh, mobile version of Jake's rooftop on the fifty-somethingth floor of a hotel.

The bar took an hour to do a full circuit, and as we drank we got two looks at the most famous skyscrapers – one just before sunset and another when the night sky was black and the multicoloured, multilayered jumble of city lights seemed to splash like electronic surf against the tower we were sitting on.

Alexa was as bubbly as the Long Island sparkling wine, which was better than a few real French champagnes I've tasted. She was telling us about the filming she'd done at Columbia, and the cameraload of idealistic young American students who shared her views on the big NATO bogeyman. She'd even found a few who, to her astonishment, were actually left-wing and believed in the redistribution of wealth and other such un-American things.

'In France, we think all Americans are capitalists at birth,' Alexa said. 'We don't believe that socialists even exist here.'

'Oh yes, there are lots of socialists in the USA,' Elodie said. 'Around a hundred in New York, fifty in Seattle – the

71

eco-socialists – and probably one at Harvard in the political science museum.' Elodie's view of politics was coloured by her father's total lack of any principles except self-advancement.

'How is Jean-Marie doing by the way?' I asked.

'Ah, that is a funny thing!' Elodie laughed and almost inhaled her glass of wine, though I didn't think my question had been quite that witty. 'I called Papa this afternoon,' she said when she had cleared her lungs of bubbles, 'and he told me all about your problems with the French government. Is it true that you might be going to prison?'

Alexa looked at me as if I had been hiding something from her.

'No, that's bollocks,' I said as categorically as I could manage. 'I've just got a stupid fine to pay, which I'll be able to do with the money from this American contract.'

'But it is a *lot* of money,' Elodie said.

'Yeah, but I'll get it.'

'Why don't you borrow it from Papa?'

I almost spat my peanut down her cleavage. Borrow from *him*? I would rather have owed it to a Russian loan shark. Jean-Marie was truly like a shark – all smile, but with teeth that could pull off your limbs. Before he bought his stake in my tea room, he was my boss at a Parisian food company, and if I'd learnt one lesson from the experience, it was that you did not get into debt – financial or moral – with Monsieur Jean-Marie Martin.

'No need, I'll pay the fine,' I repeated, hoping to kill the subject.

'But if I understand correctly, you actually have to win this competition to get enough money, no?' As I'd foreseen when I was with Benoît that day in the tea room, behind Elodie's sympathy was a perverse desire to twist the knife and watch me squirm.

Alexa observed me carefully as I replied.

'Sure,' I said. 'If Britain wins, I'll be able to pay everything off at once.'

'But you still haven't heard what these promotional events of yours are going to be?' Elodie said.

'No, but I will, don't worry.'

'Maybe you should call and ask,' Alexa said, inadvertently joining in the game of Let's Hassle Paul.

'I'll call tomorrow morning,' I said, with Dalai Lama-like patience.

'Why don't you call now?' Elodie suggested. 'You can leave a message for them to send you a text first thing in the morning.'

'Excuse me, ladies,' I said. To avoid yelling something unpleasant about French bosses' daughters sticking their cute noses way too deep into other people's business, I headed for the refuge of the men's room.

When I got to the bright lights of the gents', I realized that I was surprisingly drunk, on a head-spinning cocktail of alcohol and jetlag. I wasn't so bad that I felt the need to pee on my, or someone else's, shoes. I was just tipsy enough to have a conversation with the toilet door.

I should explain.

I know this isn't sexy, but when I'm drunk I sometimes sit down to pee. It's safer for all concerned. You have no aiming problems, there's no risk of accidentally flashing someone, and there's the added advantage that it takes the weight off your feet.

In this hotel, sitting down was even more inviting than usual because they had disposable toilet-seat covers. I had to work out how to get them out of the dispenser, which way round to put them on the seat, and then how to punch a hole in them without thrusting my fist into the water below, but after only four or five attempts and a bit of swearing I finally got the seat cover sorted out, and it did make sit-down peeing a much pleasanter business than in some bars I've been to.

Trouble was, as soon as I was seated, I noticed that the toilet door had been sawn off at the knee. Anyone under five feet tall could have looked under it and seen what I was up to. What was the idea of that, I wondered – some American need to 'share your restroom experience'? The toilet version of a group hug?

And then I noticed that a grey-haired, denture-baring couple was grinning down at me. They were in formal evening wear and were ballroom dancing. This wasn't, I realized almost immediately, personal in-restroom entertainment. It was a framed advertising poster on the back of the door, demanding in large blue letters, 'Are You Experiencing ERECTILE Issues?'

'No, not yet,' I told the door. 'But if you keep staring at me like that, I don't think I'll ever get a hard-on again.'

'Are you OK in there, Sir?' a deep male voice asked.

Below the door I could see a pair of sturdy ankles in shiny black shoes.

'Go away,' I told the feet.

'Sir?' Now he was actually knocking on the door.

'Isn't there some amendment to your Constitution about a man's right to a few minutes' peace in the toilet?' I asked.

'Are you alone in there, Sir?' the voice demanded.

'Just bend down half an inch and you can see for yourself.'

'I beg your pardon, Sir?'

'I said yes I am and I intend to stay that way.'

'OK, I'll just wait in the lobby,' he said, and the shoes disappeared. Thank God for that, I thought.

When I came out of the gents', there was only a security

guard standing there, a chubby guy in a maroon blazer with a walkie talkie on his lapel. I thought of mentioning that there was a weirdo cruising the men's room, but before I could explain, I was distracted by the distinct absence of Elodie and Alexa in the bar. They'd disappeared.

The security guy must have seen that I wanted to tell him something, because he moved forward as if to speak to me, but I waved him away and went to ask the two women sitting in Elodie and Alexa's seats what they thought they were doing.

'Hi,' I said.

'Hi,' one of them answered. They both had long, wavy hair, and were dressed up for a glitzy night out in New York.

'You're not Alexa and Elodie,' I said.

'No, I'm Lynda – with a "y",' one of them answered.

'With a "y"?'

'Yeah.'

'And I'm Lisa,' the other one said.

'With a "z"?' I guessed.

'No, with an "s".'

'Ah.' We were getting somewhere, but I didn't know where. 'What happened to Alexa and Elodie?' I asked. They consulted each other blankly. 'Alexa's my girlfriend, you see,' I told them. 'And Elodie – well, she's a sort of ex-girlfriend. I used to live with her in Paris. But now she lives in New York. She's, well, I suppose she's a kind of live-in party girl for this French rock star hobbit guy. Anyway, she's got us a room at the Chelsea where the rock star has his groupie parties, and we're meant to be going back there after we've had dinner here, so I really need to find—'

'Excuse me, Sir.' The security guy, who'd been listening to our conversation, was now standing right behind me.

'This man is making improper suggestions,' Lisa told him.

'No I'm not, I'm just looking for two girls.'

'Get your coat, Sir. I'm going to escort you from the building,' he said. His hand was hovering within an inch of my shoulder, as if he didn't want to touch me but would if he had to.

I looked around the bar for moral support. Which was when I spotted Elodie and Alexa sitting about ten tables away, chatting like old buddies, their foreheads almost touching. 'Ah, look,' I told the security guy. 'Those two girls over there.'

'Come with me, please, Sir.' The hand was now clamped on my shoulder, rather painfully, too. Pinching a nerve. He began steering me towards the exit. 'This kind of behaviour may be acceptable in Europe, Sir, but here in America we have standards.' His face was flushed with moral outrage.

'Unhand me, I am a representative of Her Majesty,' I informed him, and to prove that we Brits don't take attacks by foreign powers lightly, even if they are our allies, I shook myself free and made a dash for liberty.

I was only a few yards away from Alexa and Elodie when they suddenly soared upwards, along with all the other tables, and I found myself getting mouth-to-mouth resuscitation from the carpet. There was also something or someone on my back, puffing unpleasantly hot breath down my neck.

'Paul?' A new voice was added to the clamour around me. 'Yes?'

'Why have you got a security man on your back?' It was Alexa.

'You know this gentleman?' the security guy asked.

'Yes,' Elodie said. 'He was with us. He just went to the bathroom.'

The pressure on my back eased off, and while Elodie and

Alexa explained who I was, I got slowly to my feet. On the way up, I noticed the shiny shoes.

'Hey, this is the guy who was trying to look under the door into my cubicle,' I said.

But for some reason, neither Elodie, Alexa, nor the security man were interested in this invasion of my privacy. They seemed to come to an agreement, and I was allowed to accompany the girls to their new table.

At which point, the golden haze of Long Island wine in my brain lifted for a moment, and I saw where I'd gone wrong.

It was obvious, really. The central hub of the building, where the lifts and the toilets were, stayed stationary, and only the outer section of the bar revolved. So if you were away from your seat for several minutes, like I had been, your table had moved round a few degrees from where you left it. And if you weren't drunk and jetlagged, you probably figured this out as soon as you saw that your friends had vanished.

'Paul, bad things happen when you drink too much,' Alexa lectured me. 'I want you to promise you won't do it again on this trip.'

'I promise,' I said, but I might have slurred the 's' a little.

'God Save the Queen,' Elodie said, raising a glass of American champagne to Britain's chances of winning the World Tourism contest with such a geographically challenged drink-driver at the wheel.

6

It was four o'clock in the morning and I was wide awake, wondering why I wasn't being served a reheated omelette by an air hostess.

The radiators were hissing and puffing, generating enough heat to bake bread. The traffic was growling past in the street below, and the rain falling on the air-conditioning unit was amplified by the metal casing so that it sounded as if a rock drummer was rehearsing outside the window. There was no way I was going to get back to sleep.

Alexa had thrown off the covers and was slumbering soundly, lying on her side, naked and unaware of my gaze. I took a few minutes to enjoy the curves of her, the soft cusps of flesh clutched between her arms, the deliriously rounded arch rising up from her waist, over her hip and down to her outer thigh. The small shadow that looked like an arrow pointing between her legs.

I was tempted to film her so that she'd discover the footage while viewing her politically active students.

But no, that would have been an abuse of her trust in me. And I didn't know how to work the camera, anyway.

Lying there in the semi-darkness, I remembered why I'd gone into the revolving hotel's bathroom. It had been to get away from Elodie's merciless questioning about the pro-motional events. But she was right, I now decided. I really needed to know, at least about Boston.

I calculated transatlantic time differences and went to sit on another toilet.

'Hello Mister West Visitor Resources Britain Serena speaking how may I help you?' It came out as one sing-song sentence.

This was a hotline number I'd been given by Jack Tyler. I'd never actually met this phone operator whose job it was to guide me through the next phase of my life. We'd spo-ken once, emailed three or four times. To me she was just a name, Serena. Serena Hart. A cute name and a pleasant, silky voice.

'Hi, Serena. Yes, you can help me. I'm really hoping

you'll be able to give me the details of the Boston event.'

'I sent you an email with a local contact number for the gentleman who is co-organizing it with you. Didn't you get it?'

'No.' Oops. I'd been too busy drinking to read my mail. 'I haven't been able to get online recently. So what's the event, then?'

'A tea party.'

'You're joking. A Boston tea party?'

'Yes.'

Whoever said that Britain had run out of original thinkers?

7

Alexa announced the next morning that she wanted to devote the day to socialism. Not to redistributing wealth or nationalizing America's banks, which would have taken far more than one day, but just to finding some socialism.

We'd eaten pancakes and bacon at a diner on the corner of Twenty-Third Street, and emerged full of the goodwill that a massive breakfast always brings.

Right there on the corner, standing in the weak sunlight, was a woman of about fifty. She was wearing a thick duffel coat, a balaclava and enormous mittens, all in shades of red. She looked like a giant raspberry. She was shaking a cash box and holding a large placard which showed men huddling in a doorway against the cold.

'Spare a thought and a dollar for your fellow man? Give some cash to the less fortunate?' she was asking passers-by. It sounded pretty socialist to me.

Alexa and I each stuffed a dollar into the tin.

'Can I interview you for a film about the American lifestyle?' Alexa asked.

'Why, yes,' the woman said, suddenly looking less frozen.

Alexa opened up her camera and pointed it into the woman's face.

'You are wearing red and collecting money for the poor. Does this mean you are a socialist?'

The woman looked as if the red was going to drain out of her duffel coat.

'A socialist? You mean a communist? No!'

'In that case, why are you collecting for the poor?'

'Out of Christian charity, of course. Helping my fellow man. I'm a volunteer at the shelter over on Twentieth Street.'

'But is it not better to change the system so that they can help themselves?'

'The system? What system?'

'The capitalist system.'

Again, the woman blanched. It was as if 'capitalist' was a rude word that you couldn't say in polite society.

'Why, no, it's not the rich people's fault that the home-less are homeless,' she said. 'There are some wealthy people who make very generous donations to the shelter, you know.' She gave her money box a shake.

'But if the rich weren't so rich, maybe the poor would have more money, and a home and a job?'

'Oh no.' The woman smiled at the absurdity of the idea. 'A lot of these people can't hold down a job. They have drink problems, mental problems. We had a discussion at the shelter the other day. Someone was saying maybe there's a homelessness gene.'

'A homelessness gene?'

'Yes, you know, maybe some people are genetically predestined to end up on the streets. They're inclined towards alcoholism and mental instability, so they're naturally more liable than others to end up homeless.

So all we can do is make their life more comfortable.'

'Maybe you can give them genetically modified soup?'

'Pardon?'

'Soup that will cure their genetic problem, so they can become rich entrepreneurs.'

I realized that Alexa's film was going to be a lot more fun than I'd thought. The woman was staring at her, trying to work out exactly how much irony was floating around in the air between them.

'Are you mocking me, young lady?' she finally asked. 'Because if you are, you're being very uncharitable. Very un-Christian.'

'Oh no,' Alexa said, looking positively angelic. 'I have just arrived here and I am trying to understand America. It's a fascinating country, isn't it?'

The woman's cheeks glowed as red as her balaclava.

'Oh, yes, it's the greatest country in the world.' She smiled and began shaking her cash box again.

As we walked away, Alexa declared the interview a total success. She'd even managed to get the woman to sign a release form allowing her to use the footage on TV.

'What's all that stuff about America being fascinating?' I asked her. 'You were taking the pee, weren't you?'

Alexa laughed. 'Oh no, it is a technique I got from Michael Moore. You know, the documentary maker? He criticizes America, says it is totally corrupt and stuff, and then every few minutes he says "It's a great country, isn't it?" and everyone is reassured and they let him say what he wants. If they think you are anti-American they will stop talking to you.'

'But aren't you anti-American?'

'Oh no, it's a fascinating country.' She giggled all the way to the subway station.

8

Early the next morning, during the taxi drive a hundred or so blocks north, I observed the New York drivers whose road space I was about to share. As so much of their driving was done in long straight hauls, it seemed mainly to consist of lane-swapping, a sort of inability to stay in a monogamous relationship with the line of cars in front of you. Is the lane on the far side of the street moving half a mile an hour faster? OK, as soon as there's a two-inch gap I'll pull across and get honked at. They were conditions that favoured the Mini, I figured. A short, nippy car would be ideal for queue-jumping.

My fingers were twitching to get hold of the wheel.

Dwight the mechanic was there as arranged, buffing up the impossibly scarlet doors on the Mini that was crouching in the middle of his workshop. It was ready to spring out of the door and into action.

'Beautiful, ain't she?' Dwight said.

'Wow, yes, she is,' said Alexa.

'Oh shit,' I said.

'What's the problem? You didn't want a convertible in this weather, did you?' Dwight was inviting us to laugh with him, but it was a nervous laugh. He could tell that something major was up.

'What's that flag?' I had to go and touch it to make sure it was really painted on. Surely he was going to peel it off and tell me it was a joke? But no, it was a perfect paint job, with the stripes of colour spreading across the whole car roof. Only trouble was, they were the wrong stripes. He had painted an American flag, but with a minuscule Union Jack in the top left-hand corner instead of the stars.

'It's the Union Flag, just like they asked for,' Dwight said.

'That's called the Union Flag?'

'Yeah, the *Grand* Union Flag, in fact. Kind of neat, joining up the English and the American flag like that, huh?'

'But I'm not supposed to be doing any joining up. I'm supposed to be Team Britain. You might as well have put the French Tricolor in the other corner and dotted a few Chinese stars around.'

'Hey, man, I just did what they told me to do.' Dwight ducked into his office – a windowed compartment at the far end of the workshop – and returned with a sheet of paper, a printout that he'd grafitti'd with phone numbers and a shopping list of paint colours, but which was still legible enough for me to see that he was right. Serena had sent him an email asking him to paint a Union Flag on the roof instead of a Union Jack. And *I* was the one who'd had to take a Britishness test.

'Does it matter?' Alexa asked. 'It is a good symbol. The small Englishman in one corner of the USA.'

'Yeah, that's right,' Dwight agreed, with all the excess enthusiasm of a man who doesn't want to re-do a paint job.

'Excuse me, there's someone I have to shout at.' I was already speed-dialling Serena.

'Hello Mister West Visitor Resources Britain Serena speaking how may I help you?'

'Nyaarrgh.'

'Sorry?'

'What I mean is, how could you ask for the wrong flag to be painted on top of the Mini?'

'The wrong flag?'

'Yes. Why didn't you just send over a picture of the flag we wanted?'

'He said he was going to find it on the internet.'

'He did find it on the internet. And he found the flag you told him to find.'

'So he found the right flag?'

'Yes, but it was the wrong flag.'

'Sorry?'

'You told him to find the Union *Flag* when what we needed was the Union *Jack*.'

'Oh my.'

'I'm going to have to leave the Mini in New York and get to Boston some other way, OK?'

'OK,' she said, sounding bemused by these new developments.

'Look, Serena, I know you're probably dealing with Jack Tyler, aren't you?'

'Yes.'

'And am I right in saying that he's not always there when you need him? Not *all* there, if you get my meaning?'

'Well . . .'

'Perhaps you should have a word with Lucy Marsh.'

'Who?'

'Lucy Marsh. You don't know who she is?'

'No.'

'Holy dingbats, how big is that new building of yours?' But I was breaking the first rule of self-assertion, which is, of course, stick to the bloody point. 'In a nutshell, this is a major cock-up. And I can't afford cock-ups, or I'll be in the merde in more ways than you can imagine.'

'In the what?'

'It's French. Didn't you learn French swearwords at school?'

'No, we didn't do French.'

'What? I thought all schools did it. You can't ignore French, you know. I did, and that's what got me into this merde.'

'This what?'

'Nyaarrgh.'

BOSTON

Digging for Victory

1

I SOMETIMES THINK THAT WE Europeans have a patronizing view of Americans' grasp of history. It's not really
our fault, though – we're basing our opinion on TV shows
in which King Arthur talks like a cowboy and war films
which suggest that the Battle of Britain was won by a bunch
of USAF pilots who destroyed the whole Luftwaffe in an
afternoon.

Deep down, we're convinced that Americans have no real
concept of what went on before 1945, and that they see
British history like this:

Stonehenge–1776: A time of castles, kings 'n' shit.

1776–1945: Crushed by the loss of its American colonies,
Britain gradually shrivels up until it is so powerless that it
almost loses a war to a vegetarian with a silly moustache.

1945–present: Saved from destruction by the USA,
Britain becomes a trusted ally, as vital to the balance of
world power as, say, Bermuda.

Meanwhile, most French people, especially the

politicians, are sure that America views France like this:

Jurassic period–1940: An area of the planet devoted solely to the production of wine, cheese, prostitutes and body odour.

1940–present: Supposedly a friend, but in truth as reliable as the wedding guest who sleeps with the bride.

In fact, though, many Americans have an acute sense of history. For instance, they can tell you what happened in America on practically any day between 1775 and about 1790. Which goes some way to explaining what happened when I tried to put on an event in one of the country's most history-conscious cities.

2

'Oh!' Alexa gave a typically French puff of outrage, as if a complete stranger had just walked up to her restaurant table and helped himself to her slice of foie gras.

I looked round to see who could be causing such fury. We were at Penn Station, two implausibly expensive train tickets to Boston in our hands, and had just arrived down on the platform.

'The train,' Alexa huffed. 'It is a TGV! They say it is their new American high-speed train and it's French.'

She was right. The blue and silver locomotive, like a snobbish snake looking down its nose at you, could have been the Paris–Marseilles express.

'Even more French globalizing,' I said.

'Only because they need our technology. What is better? Globalizing with fast trains or fast food? In fact, France is giving America aid.' Alexa had forgotten her outrage and was now looking insufferably smug.

Inside, the train had been adapted to American tastes.

Amtrak was obviously keen to kid us into thinking we were about to leave the ground. The carriages had overhead lockers, reclining seats, and business-class amounts of legroom. A little leaflet tucked into the seatback by my knees explained that our maximum speed was likely to be 165mph.

When we pulled out of the station, though, the aeroplane fantasy was dispelled – our initial speed was less like a Jumbo than an elephant. At first I didn't mind this at all. Crossing the East River, we swung past a classic poster view of the distant Manhattan skyscrapers impaling a low-slung canopy of cloud. The train was so much quieter than a plane, too. Totally silent, in fact, when it ground to a halt ten minutes out of Penn.

We were perched high on the tracks above a depot full of gleaming red fire engines. A wave of unrest rippled along the carriage. Alexa and I looked at our watches. The meeting with my Boston contact was scheduled for two. We were due to arrive at one thirty. It would soon be time to start sending out distress signals.

Right on cue, a voice came over the PA system, informing us that there was an electrical fault with the locomotive, and that the driver just had to reset it. It sounded simple, like rebooting a computer. But the guy sharing the foursome of seats with us didn't look so sure. He hummed mournfully, as if to say, 'Don't you believe it.' He was around sixty, with frizzy grey hair slicked back over a high, deeply wrinkled forehead, and had a naturally hangdog expression. His jowls could have been transplanted from a bloodhound.

'Do you think we'll be held up for long?' I asked.

'Hmmm.' This could have meant anything from 'Yes, hours,' to 'Sorry, my dentures are stuck together so I can't answer.'

'At least they tell you what the problem is,' Alexa contributed. 'In France, we can wait for hours with no information.'

'Hmmm,' the old guy repeated. 'Here the problem is different. You try to get on a train to Montreal and they tell you that there's no service because the windshield is cracked. Or that the train hasn't been shipped down from Albany yet. They're very informative, it's just that the information is so much bullshit.'

Something about the way he said this made us all laugh, and we introduced ourselves.

He was Joseph, a semi-retired furniture wholesaler, and he was on his way to Connecticut to meet up with some hunting pals.

'Not to blast the heads off coyotes with an M-62,' he said. 'We're real woodsmen.' He took a magazine out of his bag, a kind of suede fetishists' monthly full of ads for tasselled jackets and crotchless chaps. 'We get into costume, head up into the woods, and then it's just us and the animals. You get one shot with your musket, and if you miss, that's it. Nothing for the campfire. And if you wing the animal, you have to track it and finish it off with your knife. It brings out the marksman in you.' It all sounded very romantic in a bloody kind of way. 'It wasn't only Washington's army that got rid of the English, you know, it was the woodsmen. People forget that. And we owe a lot to the French, too.' He smiled at Alexa as if she personally had helped to kick the redcoats into the Atlantic all those centuries ago. 'Some Americans say that France is ungrateful to us for liberating them in 1945. But we ought to remember, the French helped to liberate *us*. Back in 1781, your fleet captured an entire English army at Yorktown.' Now that his teeth were unglued, he couldn't stop them opening and shutting, or so it seemed to me.

The train began to hum, then jolted into movement.

We still didn't get many of those 165mph we'd been promised, but at least the short surges of acceleration were sending us in the right direction. Soon we had left the city behind and were whirring past wide, sunlit bays with frosted reed beds, clusters of clapperboard houses and narrow sand beaches. Scandinavian-looking towns came and went, some of them looking as if the old whaling fleets had only just left. It was incredible, these open seascapes and drowsy harbours so close to the frenzy of New York.

'How far you going?' Joseph asked.

'Boston,' Alexa said.

'Bunker Hill!' Joseph pronounced the name as if it was a military order. 'June seventeen, 1775. Colonel William Prescott and his small band of resistance fighters held off the massed ranks of the English, and all thanks to good marksmanship. A few brave men, almost no ammunition, but they knew how to use a musket and the English got their asses shot off whenever they tried to storm the hill. That's where they coined the expression "Don't shoot until you see the whites of their eyes." '

'So if they'd been wearing sunglasses, you would have lost?' I asked. I hoped my own visit to the city wasn't going to be quite such a debacle.

'Hmmm.' Joseph opened his magazine again, and began to examine an article on the best way to gut a moose.

3

Boston's South Station was an airy, well-lit place compared to the subterranean Penn. Standing by the concourse bookshop, as arranged, was a tall blondish guy, about my age, but with longer, thicker sideburns and a two-day beard.

The kind of bloke they choose to model chunky knitwear in catalogues. This was my Boston contact, Mike.

'Paul, Alexa? Hey.' Mike shook our hands and gave us a huge smile. The one he extended to Alexa was all welcoming, but mine wasn't 100 per cent proof, I thought. Mixed in there was a small percentage of amusement.

'Sorry we're so late,' I said.

'No worries. You're Europeans, so you won't mind walking a short way?' he said. 'We could get a taxi, but with the big dig it'd take hours to get where we're going.'

'Big dig?' Alexa asked.

'Where *are* we going?' I wanted to know.

Mike took Alexa's rucksack and answered her question first.

'The big dig, yeah, for the last ten years at least, the city's been trying to dig tunnels to relieve the gridlock downtown. But the engineers were too ambitious and the foundations are unsuitable, and basically it's just made driving around the city a nightmare for a decade. Good time to get shares in a construction company, though – they still got years of work in their order books. Even more since the fire.'

'Fire?' Alexa asked.

'Yeah.' We were crossing part of the inner harbour, a still, brown canal, and he pointed to the next bridge down, which was blackened and swathed in scaffolding. 'Hit by lightning. That was the museum wharf, too. The site of the original Boston Tea Party. You know all about that?'

'No,' Alexa said, only just preventing herself from adding, 'Fill me in, you fascinating hunk.'

'Well,' Mike continued, 'on the night of December sixteen, 1763, Bostonians decided they'd had enough of paying English taxes on Indian tea and emptied three shiploads of the stuff into the harbour. This was more than ten years before the revolution took hold. It was kind of the spark that lit the slow-burning fire.' His eyes were aiming sparks at Alexa. He probably did pouty calendar photos as well as knitwear catalogues. 'One of the ships, the *Beaver*, was preserved here as a permanent reminder of their heroism. But it's all burnt out now.' Manfully, he held back the tears.

'So your *Beaver* was hit by lightning? Ouch.' My low-grade quip made Mike twitch, and then his smile returned, with the percentage of mockery a little higher this time, I noted.

He led us across a complex mud trail of roadworks and between shiny, medium-sized skyscrapers. The streets were short and at European angles, and took us over a low knoll.

'So where are we going?' I asked again.

'Not much further,' Mike assured Alexa. We dropped down past a bustling square with what looked like a Greek temple in the middle, and then suddenly we were in an English pub.

Well, no, there was one major thing that differentiated it from an English pub, and that was the group of three men in long waistcoats, neckerchiefs and knee breeches, and two women in thick woollen dresses, lacy skullcaps and shawls. New York fashions hadn't quite reached here, it seemed.

'Hey guys,' Mike greeted them. 'This is him.'

'Hey!' They all broke off from their loud, laughing conversation to come and say hello. They, too, had that friendly but amused look in their eyes.

'So, you want to organize another Boston Tea Party,' one of the men said, a dark-haired giant whose ponytail looked real.

'Yes, though we won't be throwing any of our drinks into the harbour,' I said.

'And you're planning to do it like your friend Serena said, are you?' Mike asked.

'Er, yes.' Though something in his voice made me suspect I ought to say no.

'An outdoor tea party, by the river, in February?'

'Outdoor?' I asked. 'Are you sure?' Serena hadn't mentioned that. I could see that a picnic in sub-zero temperatures might not be the best way of attracting visitors.

'Oh, yeah.' Mike and the knee-breeches crowd had a good laugh at this. 'An English tea party, on the site of the original Boston Tea Party, where America first rebelled against English rule. You don't think the city's opinion-makers might see a kind of historical insult in there? Like holding a British barbecue on the site where Joan of Arc was killed?' He flashed a smile of complicity at Alexa, who was starting to look at me the same way she'd done when I got lost on my way back from the toilets in New York.

'But we're all allies these days,' I tried to object. 'A lot of tea has flowed under the bridge since 1763.'

'Allies, right.' Mike laughed. 'Did Serena really think that the best co-organizer for your show was the vice-president of the Boston–Eire Association?' Mike pointed a thumb at his chest. 'I mean, Paul, some of our older members still haven't forgiven the English for the potato famine. And you thought we'd give the OK to help publicize England as a tourist destination?' I got the distinct impression that he'd been practising his barbed speech in the bath. 'Believe me, you're lucky the site of the Tea Party was hit by lightning. At least it gives you an excuse to hold yours indoors. So I suggest you have a glass of great Boston beer, and then get on with organizing your event. You've got twenty-eight hours or so to do it.'

This earned him a small cheer from his historically challenged friends.

'So do I take it that you're backing out of the agreement to help me with this, Mike?' I asked.

'Well, I wouldn't say there ever was an agreement,' he said. 'I mean, at first we said send us details, so we could find out what all this business with the tea party was, but then your people seemed to assume we'd agreed to help, and the faxes and the emails just kept coming. So I thought the least I could do was meet with you and explain what was going on.'

'Yes, thank you for that,' Alexa said, giving me a stare as if to remind me of my manners.

'Yeah, thanks, Mike, you've been more than helpful. Excuse me, I just have to go and yell at someone.' It was fast becoming my catchphrase.

'Hello Mister West Visitor Resources Britain Serena speaking how—'

'I'm in Boston,' I interrupted.

'Good.'

'No, not good at all. Mike, our contact here, isn't going to help me set up the event.'

'What? But he—'

'And anyway, what on earth were you thinking of, organizing an English tea party in Boston? An *open-air* one, too. Don't you read the weather forecast before you arrange events?'

'Yes, of course. If I remember correctly, on Boston's own city website it said that the minimum January daytime temperature is fifteen degrees.'

'Yes, *Fahrenheit*, Serena. That's below freezing. Don't you know—' I broke off in mid-sentence. An awful thought had occurred to me. I'd just realized what had been

94

bugging me all along. The fact that she didn't know Lucy Marsh. The screw-up with the flag. Not learning any French at school. There was something about her voice, too, her way of speaking. 'Serena?'

'Yes? How can I——?'

'What colour are the fish in the pond outside the Visitor Resources building?'

'Pardon?'

I repeated my question.

'Gold?' she answered.

'There is no fishpond, Serena,' I said, suddenly feeling as if I was making up for missing that murder mystery on TV. There was no fooling West of the Yard. 'Where are you really?'

'Oooh.' Serena made a noise like a kid who's just blotched ink on a new pair of jeans.

'I know you're not in London. And I bet your name's not Serena Hart, is it? What's your real name?'

For a few moments I heard only the swishing of the satellite that was relaying our fraught conversation, and then she whispered, 'Suraya.'

I asked her to spell it out for me.

'Pleased to meet you at last, Suraya. And where exactly are you?'

There was another radio silence. 'Please don't tell anyone you know,' she finally whispered, her voice wobbling. 'But . . .'

'But?'

'We're in Chennai.'

'Wales?'

'No, Chennai. You know, the new name for Madras.' She pronounced it 'mut-raas'.

'India?'

'Yes.'

'Visitor Resources: Britain has outsourced its national tourism campaign to a foreign country?'

'Yes. We already handle all their phone enquiries.'

'What, even a question like, What are the opening times of the Aberdeen Museum of Wet Fish Processing?'

'Winter or summer?'

'Pardon?'

'Sorry, I am joking. But yes, everything. This is why you have perhaps had the impression that things are being organized from rather a long way away.'

'From the Moon, yes. The dark side.'

'I am sorry, but it is difficult for me when the management in London communicates information late, and some of them do not agree with the outsourcing policy, so they deliberately hold up information.'

'Right, so you're saying I have to distrust practically everything you tell me in case it's late or misinformed?' Suraya's silence spoke volumes. 'I mean, Suraya, what must the mayor of Boston have thought when he received an invitation to an outdoor English tea party in winter? He has been invited, hasn't he?'

'Yes, of course. The mayor and the director of tourism, and journalists from the local press.'

'And none of them reacted strangely?'

'No.' There was a pause. 'None reacted at all, in fact. Not to anything that I sent them. I am sorry, but I am also dealing with the events in China and . . .' She started to sob.

Oh well, I thought, the one consolation about being in the merde is that the only way is out.

Although, come to think of it, there was a second way to go – deeper in.

4

Mike, Alexa and I had some Boston Creme Pie – not a pie at all, but a skyscraper of a custard-filled layer cake – and a soothing quantity of Sam Adams beer. And as the beer soaked in, I began to get philosophical.

There are times, I reflected, when it's best to accept humiliation and play for sympathy. Mike and the people in woolly underwear weren't really malicious – they just thought my arrival in Boston was a big joke. Which, of course, it was.

So I milked the story of the Bronx iguana and the Mini with the wrong flag, and got them laughing with rather than at me. The fancy-dress group were official Boston guides, it turned out, and they started to brainstorm on places in town where I could hold a party at short notice.

'The trouble is,' the giant with the ponytail said, 'so many places have anti-British historical resonances. I mean, there was the Boston Massacre here in 1770. I bet you don't know about that, do you?'

'No,' I confessed. 'When I was at school we didn't tend to spend much time on British massacres.'

'Your troops panicked and fired into a crowd of innocent civilians, killing five,' the giant said.

'Huh, call that a massacre?' Mike pitched in. 'They killed twenty Irishmen on Bloody Sunday.'

'And the whole French nobility at Agincourt in 1415,' Alexa added. 'Many of them after they had surrendered.'

'That's not all, though,' the giant went on. 'We have the Old State House, where the Declaration of Independence was read out. And the battleground at Bunker Hill, where our men were told, Don't fire until—'

'You see the whites of their eyes,' I chorused with the

other guides. We clinked glasses and drank a toast to the whiteness of English eyes.

'You see,' Mike said, 'this whole city is a tourist trail of anti-English revolt. It'll be like setting up a tea party in a minefield.'

It might be simpler to do just that, I thought. At least I wouldn't have to do any washing up.

Alexa and I took a taxi (we were going along a straight, non-dug-up route, Mike said) to our B&B, which turned out to be a funky little place in a cool-looking part of town. It was in a street of brownstone houses, the ground floors and basements of which were taken up by tattoo parlours, bars and punkish clothes shops. There was even a store selling nothing but condoms.

The B&B had thick carpets, efficient heating and a young Korean receptionist with fluorescent pink streaks in her black hair and dangerously low-cut jeans.

'I'm me,' she said. A very Asian thing to say, I thought. We're all me in our own way.

'Hello, you,' I said.

She giggled and pulled at a lock of pink hair. 'No, it's my name. M-I, Mi. If you need anything, just ask for Mi.'

I laughed until I caught Alexa eyeing me with a 'Why do you always have to act the idiot with attractive girls?' expression on her face.

Mi showed us up to our room, which had refurbished gothic furniture and a view over a tiny service alleyway of parked cars and huge dustbins, the kind where bodies get dumped in American films.

'OK, the view sucks, but it's quieter than in front,' Mi said. 'It gets, like, crazy out there at night.'

Which suited me a lot better than having the craziness *inside*, as we'd had in the Bronx.

'You don't have any idea where I could organize a tea party, do you?' I asked her on an impulse.

'A what?'

I explained the problem and gave her my phone number in case.

'If you have any brainwaves, just call me, Mi,' I said, and we shared another laugh.

'You gave her your *number*,' Alexa said when Mi had gone downstairs with a generous tip nestling in her tiny jeans pocket.

'Yes.'

'Do you give your number to any girl who smiles at you?' Her eyes were shooting icicles at me.

'No. I'm in a crisis here, Alexa. In a strange city, with a tea party to organize and absolutely no support from the people – including your friend Mike – who were meant to be helping me. So yes, I gave her my number.'

'There's no need to be so aggressive.'

'I'm sorry, you're right. It's not your fault.'

We both stood silently for a few moments, letting the bad vibes dissipate.

'I'm sure if you asked Mike again, he would help you,' Alexa said.

'If *you* asked him, you mean. He'd set up a leprechaun cull if you fluttered your eyelashes at him.'

Alexa didn't answer.

We went across the street to a bookshop/wi-fi café so that I could check out a list of function rooms, tea shops and restaurants in the city – anywhere that could hold a party. I also wanted to read up on Boston's history in the hope of avoiding any more Anglo-American conflicts. I now had only twenty-six hours to put things right. I wasn't going to get a second chance.

The shop was the kind of place where you could find ten different books on Taoist pet care and no thrillers. Its café smelt of cinnamon and pesto, and had waitresses with more earrings than eyebrow hairs. It was full of studenty types working together, flirting together or both.

I hooked up to the wi-fi and did a search on Boston, while Alexa read through the guidebook. I soon found a website that gave a leaf-by-leaf account of the Tea Party. Apparently it had involved a group of Americans who wore disguises to fool the English into thinking that their tea crop had been destroyed by Black slaves and Indians. But their get-up was so amateurish that one of the English sailors wrote that 'about eighty men came, some of them dressed and whooping like Indians'. So much for revolution – it was a belated Halloween party.

The website said that the Brits could have saved their tea if they'd been a bit sharper at business. The English government had tried to force the American colonies to buy their tea exclusively from the motherland, and pay tax on all imports, even though the Bostonians usually got it cheap from France and Holland. Knowing this, the English offered to undercut the black-market imports, but stupidly they let it be known that even the new lower price included a nominal tax, so the Americans still went ahead and emptied the cargo into the harbour. If the Brits had just shut up about the tax, the Tea Party – maybe the whole revolution – would never have happened. Perhaps that was the real reason they kicked us out, I thought – we were such bad capitalists.

I was about to share this irony with Alexa when my phone rang. A waitress glared down at me for disturbing the karma, so I hurried out into the cold to answer. It was Suraya.

'I think I have found something for you.' She sounded excited.

'Found what?'

'A place for your party. Indoors, of course. And heated.' She was positively buoyant. 'I have a male colleague, you see, and he lives in the same street as me, and we both come on scooters to work, so we often ride together . . .'

'Yes?' I tried to scoot her along. My fingers were already starting to turn blue.

'I told him about our problem, and his father's best friend has a restaurant in Boston.'

'An Indian restaurant?'

'Yes. They often hold wedding parties there. And I just called the owner and he is definitely willing to hold a tea party for us.'

I mulled this over for a second or two. An English tea party in an Indian restaurant?

'Suraya, you're a genius,' I told her.

5

Alexa and I went downtown on the subway, which Boston calls the 'T', probably just to provoke British tourists. It was basically an underground tram, and like a tram it seemed to make a designated stop about every hundred yards, so that our three-station ride took a matter of seconds.

The restaurant was down at Quincy Market, the building I'd noticed earlier that looked like a white Greek temple. In fact, it was a temple to American food. Inside the city's old market hall, there were stalls selling everything from hot dogs and ribs to health food and chocolate-dipped straw-berries.

Around the building was a big cobbled square – a pedestrianized zone, too – that was ringed by cafés, restaurants and boutiquey shops. The Indian restaurant was here, on the south-facing side of the square that was catching the pale afternoon sun. Even now, on a cold workday afternoon, there were plenty of people milling about. The square was a magnet for passing trade, the ideal place for my party.

The restaurant was called the Yogi Mahal, and a blazing electronic sign across its facade advertised 'world-class Indian, Bengali, Pakistani, Sri Lankan, Vegetarian and Halal cuisine'. The owner clearly didn't want to alienate anyone who might once have enjoyed a curry somewhere. This was the spirit of enterprise that had been missing from my campaign so far.

Inside, the restaurant was the usual mix of maharajah's palace and velvet wallpaper factory, with incense and faint Bombay disco completing the sensory overload.

A white-shirted Indian waiter greeted us and I asked to see the owner, Mr Randhawa.

Seconds later, a short, hyperactive guy in a grey suit came bustling in from the kitchen. He held out a large hand with two hefty gold rings weighing it down, and flashed a smile that looked as if it had been moulded in finest porcelain. Business was pretty good, I guessed.

'Paul? Ma'am? Siddown, please. Have some tea with spices, our best chai. We can also make normal English tea, of course. Vijay, chais here!' His accent was mid-Pacific – Indian with sudden incrustations of American.

Over an excellent milky spiced tea, we quickly got down to business. The tea party could take up the whole restaurant, Mr Randhawa said. At five in the afternoon, they didn't have many other customers, anyway. He could provide so much tea at such-and-such a price, source so many English-style cakes and sandwiches, and lay on six staff – his sons and nephews, who helped out when they weren't studying for their science degrees. He even promised to get in touch with the mayor and a few key people, and make sure that the event got enough notable visitors to ensure a write-up in the press.

'I will call a friend at WBFM to get the party announced on the radio. I will print some posters for the window. I will call the mayor now, and I am playing golf with him at eight tomorrow morning, so he will not forget.' Mr Randhawa was a guy who'd come to America to make as many decisions as he could in as short a time as possible, it seemed. He chortled happily and spun his gold elasticated watchstrap around on his wrist.

I watched him and fell in love with his optimism.

'So shall we say five hundred dollars now and the balance after the party?' he said, still chortling. You don't get big watches and a smile like that just by being optimistic, I realized, and reached for my Visitor Resources credit card.

The only problem we hit – apart from a short and terrifying delay getting permission for such a big debit on the card – was what to call the party. For historical reasons we obviously couldn't bill it as a British or English tea party.

'How about Friendship tea party?' I suggested, but that sounded too much like a religious sect.

'Peace party?' Alexa said.

'Americans hate pacifists.' Mr Randhawa was dismissive. 'No, I know. We must call it a "we love America" tea party. They will come to that.' At first I wanted to laugh, but he was serious, and carried on brainstorming to himself. 'A big poster saying, "We heart America, come to a free tea party offered by the government of our British allies." How about that?'

It was stunningly cynical, but brilliant.

6

While Alexa went off to do some filming, Mi very kindly let me make some local calls from the reception desk at the B&B, and even helped me look up the numbers on the internet.

She seemed to be really excited about the project. She said she'd love to come and work at the party and wear a 'GB heart USA' T-shirt, as long as it wasn't too loose. She preferred her T-shirts short and tight, she told me, like the low-cut black one she was wearing now. She pulled open her jacket to show me, and I was able to confirm that her T-shirt was indeed very tight, and yes – when she stood up – quite short, too. Though it would have needed to be abnormally long to reach down to the top of those waist-band-less jeans.

'I'll take my jeans off,' she said. I gulped. 'I've done some waitressing, and they usually prefer me to wear a skirt.' A very short one, it seemed, that came down to an imaginary line which she traced with a forefinger across her thighs and around her bum.

'You OK, Paul?' she asked.

'Yes, it's just the air in here. My eyeballs seem to have dried out.'

'Yeah, it's really dry with this heating on. I have to use lip balm the whole time.'

She pulled a small honey-scented tube from her jacket pocket and began kissing it passionately.

I ground the heel of my left shoe into the toes of my right foot. Intense pain was the only way to get my mind and body back on the job I had to do. If I hadn't known better, I'd have said that Mi had been hired by the French to seduce me away from the goals of my American tour.

*

To be fair, though, at least one French person seemed to be backing my bid for victory.

Elodie rang, concerned that she hadn't heard anything and wondering whether I'd driven the Mini into Long Island Sound. I updated her about our enforced TGV ride, and described the excellent venue for my tea party.

'An Indian restaurant?' Elodie scoffed, clearly not appreciating the closeness of Britain's ties with its ex-colonies.

'Yes, it's perfect.' It struck me now that the restaurant was far better than anywhere Mike would have found. He'd have set things up in a corner of an Irish pub. 'I can't see any signs that there's a French event planned here, though,' I said. 'You don't know if your fellow countrymen are doing anything, do you?'

'No. But I read in *Le Monde* about a group of French engineers on some kind of official visit to Boston.'

It was my turn to scoff. French engineers? *Engineericus Gallicus* has to be the world's least sexy species, instantly recognizable because of its bad haircut, unmatching shirt and tie and the body of a man whose only exercise is calculating concrete stress levels. No way were they going to attract hordes of excited Bostonians as they toured the city.

'*Merci*, Elodie,' I said. 'You just made my day.'

Next morning, things were still looking good. I picked up the T-shirts I'd ordered (including one XXS for Mi) and went to check in with Mr Randhawa, who now insisted that I call him Babar. His wife's nickname for him, he said. I didn't like to ask which bit of his squat anatomy resembled a cartoon elephant.

When I got to the restaurant at about eleven, he was talking to a large White guy who didn't look as though he was ordering a spicy chai. 'Sorry, I know, you're right,'

Babar was saying, but the guy kept ranting on at him in a foreign accent. Italian, maybe. Not Sicilian, I hoped.

But no, Babar told me when the guy had gone that he was the manager of the wine bar opposite. And he wasn't too pleased about this sudden tea party clashing with his happy hour. Usually the bars and restaurants warned each other in advance of special events.

'It's OK,' Babar said, waving his ringed fingers in the air. 'I told him you had been let down by the Irish-American Association and that the whole city seemed to be against you.'

'The whole city?' Had there been some new disaster?

'Oh, I was just dramatizing. You know that everything in America must be larger than life. Don't worry. Have a cup of tea.'

He was right. When I sat down and warmed myself with his milky chai, my worries floated away like the steamy breath of the people walking past the restaurant window. Several of them, office-worker types, stopped to read the posters and look inside.

Babar dropped a stack of paper on my table.

'Labels,' he said, peeling off a small rectangular section from the top sheet. 'For the cakes.'

'Pardon?'

'We must write labels for the cakes. I have ordered portions of hazelnut cake, and we will have to serve each one on a small paper plate, with a label saying, "Warning, may contain nuts".'

This, I declared, had to be a joke.

'No,' he insisted. 'We could get sued if someone with a nut allergy eats the cake, or if someone chokes on a piece of nut. It is best to write the labels.'

'But of course hazelnut cake contains nuts. That's why it's called hazelnut cake,' I argued. 'Why not just write "May contain cake"?'

'You have never done business in America, my friend,' he said, placing a pen in my hand.

Writing my lines took me back to school punishments for passing love letters to girls in class. It also reminded me of Benoît, translating labels for the cakes and sausages back in Paris. Both of our tasks were absurd, but they might just save me from financial disaster. I knuckled down and got on with it, while Babar kept me amused by describing his golf game against the mayor, which, as usual, he had lost by one hole, thereby making the mayor feel good enough to promise that the voting committee for the World Tourism contest would come along to the tea party.

'I will call city hall and ask if any of them have food or tea allergies,' Babar said, completely earnest.

When I got back to the B&B, Mi was at reception, and stood up to show me her thighs. Well, I'm not sure if that was her exact intention, but she told me she had already got her waitress's skirt on, and when she showed me the tiny black garment, I just happened to notice that it left a lot of thigh open to the elements.

'Tell her she should put some tights on or her panties will freeze. If she's wearing any,' said a French voice behind me. Alexa had come in from the street and was scrutinizing Mi's legs even more attentively than I was.

I grabbed the room key and told Mi we'd see her later.

'All of her, probably,' Alexa felt obliged to add.

'A bad morning's filming?' I asked as we climbed the stairs.

Just for a micro-second, Alexa blushed, a sign that she didn't want to talk about something.

'No, no, it was great,' she said. 'This is a really cool city. There's an area of old houses around Boston Common that reminds me of the Marais. And the Old Souse Meeting House is fascinating.'

'The Old Souse Meeting House?' She made it sound like an alcoholics' hangout.

'Sou–tha,' she articulated. 'South' was one of the few English words she had problems with. 'It's where the people met before the Boston Tea Party. It's a beautiful old church, all white inside.'

' "A beautiful old church"?' I reminded Alexa that she was usually violently opposed to religion and all its earthly manifestations.

'Yes.' She blushed again.

'Did you interview some Americans about their faith?'

'No, I did some filming of different ethnic groups and their attitude to being American. You know, in France we try to encourage all ethnicities to integrate completely, but here people stay in their ghettoes, and I am not sure it is a good idea.'

'Which ethnicities did you film?' I asked.

'This morning?'

'Yes, this morning.'

'Oh, the Irish,' she said.

'Ah. *All* the Irish, or just the tall hunky male section of the population?'

'Well, yes, I did have lunch with Mike, as it happens. He is an important member of the Irish community here.'

'Right. And how does he feel about inter-ethnic relations? Is he in favour of closer Irish-French ties, for example?'

This had a predictable effect.

'Honestly, Paul. You are such a hypocrite. You stare at that girl's body like it was a piece of sushi and now you criticize me for interviewing someone for my film. *Je suis une grande fille*,' she said – a big girl. 'I can have lunch with a man and not jump on him. You are not quite the same, I think.'

She pointed an accusing finger at me, a finger that was

designed to thrust me back in time to two occasions in the past when I'd sinned against her – inadvertently, I might add. Once under the blinding influence of French alcohol, and once when a woman had decided to invite herself into my bed when I wasn't looking.

There is only one thing to do with a woman who is in the right. You squeeze her in your arms and tell her how right she is, adding a few extra degrees of rightness so she feels proud enough of herself to forgive you for whatever she's right about.

'Yours are the only thighs I'm interested in,' I told her when she'd stopped resisting me.

'Oh, and the rest of me doesn't interest you?' she asked, so I felt obliged to carry her into our room and prove her wrong.

7

It wasn't until just before six that things started to go belly up.

The party had been going well. Lots of home-bound office workers had popped in for tea and a piece of cake, and not one of them had threatened legal action or fallen to the floor in allergic spasms.

Mi's T-shirt was attracting plenty of attention to our 'GB heart USA' message, especially from a reporter who'd come to cover the party for the city's biggest newspaper. He was studying the heart as if there might be some hidden meaning in its position over the cleft between Mi's breasts. Alexa, meanwhile, was alternately studying Mi's chest and my eyes, to check whether they were interacting in any way.

Alexa was getting her share of stares, as she usually did, and was having plenty of success signing people up for the

Win a T-shirt prize draw (and subsequent spam email campaign). Everything was cruising along nicely.

Then at around quarter to six, our ship hit its first minor iceberg.

'More labels,' Babar said, sidling up to me.

'Pardon?'

'For the cups,' he added out of the side of his mouth. 'I forgot that we need to put labels on the cups. "Warning, may contain a hot beverage." My son is writing some now in the kitchen. Meanwhile, please warn everyone verbally. And make sure you have an independent witness.'

So for the next ten minutes or so, Alexa and I worked the room together, asking if everyone was enjoying themselves and slipping into each conversation a short warning to the effect that tea can on occasions be hot. I was relieved that Babar hadn't asked us to get everyone to sign a disclaimer.

Then, almost on the stroke of six, when it was dark outside and our hub of light and warmth seemed to be attracting more people than ever, there was a palpable rise in the buzz level. I turned to see a small group of men and women in smart overcoats and chic scarves cutting a spontaneous V through the crowd as they entered the restaurant. Babar was over there instantly, holding up his arms and welcoming them as if they'd crossed continents to be at the baptism of his first-born son. The reporter, too, unstuck his eyebrows from Mi's heart and made for the new arrivals.

These, I gathered, were the local dignitaries. Time for me to earn my bonus. I had to go and schmooze with them individually, and then make my rousing speech about why Britain loved Americans so much that it was inviting them all to come and holiday – or 'vacation' – there.

But as I tried to make my way through the crowd towards them, a new tidal flow seemed to push against me. The noise level rose yet again. Someone seemed to be chanting over by the entrance.

'No to the English colonizers! No to English tea!'

Across the heads of the crowd I could make out a couple of triangular black hats and several very artificial-looking ponytailed wigs.

'No to the English colonizers! No to English tea!'

The tidal wave got stronger and a few people started to panic, including the dignitaries, who were looking over their shoulders as they got shoved up against the long table where the food was being served.

'No to the English colonizers! No to English tea!'

I could see all the gate-crashers now – five guys in eighteenth-century costume. I didn't recognize any of them from the group of guides in the pub, though, and there was something different about their outfits. They were less coarse and woolly, more like formal wear for a ball. They looked like hired party costumes.

Some of my tea-drinkers were laughing, thinking the demonstration was part of the show. Others were panicking slightly, holding their cups aloft to avoid spilling the tea. They'd obviously taken the warnings about hot liquid to heart.

'No to the English colonizers! No to English tea!'

Babar pushed forward and held out his arms in a gesture of appeasement.

It did no good. The invaders shoved their way to the table, spread out along its width, and upended everything on to the floor. One of Babar's sons threw a punch, but was pushed back by a burly guy whose brown wig fell off to reveal a dark buzz cut.

The party distintegrated in a chorus of shouts, screams, bouncing cakes and smashing crockery. The invaders gave a last defiant cry of their slogan, and surged out of the door.

'What the hell was that?' I asked Babar, who was apologizing profusely to one of the dignitaries, a frowning man in a cashmere coat that had taken a hit from a cup of milky tea.

'It was the bastards from the wine bar across the road. We were disturbing their happy hour.'

So it was just like the original Tea Party – the rumpus was all about money.

Babar barked something in an Asian language at his sons and nephews, who were guiding guests across the wet, cake-covered mush on the floor. At once, they all abandoned their charges and headed for the exit.

'What are they going to do?' I asked. 'We can't get into a fight. This is an international friendship party. A peace party.'

'No, it's not. I told you, America hates pacifists.' Babar followed the younger troops towards the door.

'Wait – didn't Gandhi teach you anything?' I pleaded.

'Screw Gandhi, this is war.' And he was out in the street.

Oh well, I thought, I'd better go and make sure no one gets killed in the name of British tourism.

The night air was painfully cold after the hot crush in the restaurant, but jogging to catch up with the two gangs of potential combatants kept me from suffering frostbite anywhere except my fingertips, nose and ears.

The costumed impostors were heading towards the pub we'd gone to with Mike. The army of white-shirted Indians were around twenty or thirty yards behind them. The reporter was jogging with the Indians. Babar, meanwhile, had given up the chase and was leaning against the window of a clothes shop.

'You've got to stop them,' I said. 'We don't want any violence.'

'It's my restaurant,' he panted. 'I can't let them get away with this.'

I didn't see how a heart attack was going to help his cause, and told him he would do better to return and protect his base camp.

Suddenly Alexa sprinted past, filming the pursuit with her camera held out like a relay baton. I set off after her.

Soon we were in the Italian district, where every other shopfront was a restaurant. I wished I could stop and get myself a steaming plate of pasta, or just warm my hands in the pizza oven. But I had to catch up with the others before civil war broke out.

The chase turned down a side street, and we all ran past an old red-brick church, with the Indians yelling some decidedly un-Christian things at the costumed vandals. We climbed a small hill to an old cemetery. I leapt over a sign that said 'No alcoholic beverages', and wondered briefly whether the dead were meant to stay eternally teetotal in this Puritan town.

We jogged down the other side of the hill and hung a right on to a spooky-looking metal bridge, its skeleton looming eerily over the river. Alexa stopped on the bank to film us all running across. Our feet clanged loudly and made the old bridge shudder. I didn't like to think what would happen if the flimsy metal walkway collapsed and we all went for an unplanned swim in the freezing water below.

The journalist began to laugh.

'I know where they're heading,' he said. 'This is great.'

'Where?' I asked, but in reply he only accelerated. Trust me to invite a fit on-the-spot reporter and not some over-weight desk-blob.

We began to jog – painfully now – up narrow streets lined with cute little clapperboard houses. There was no traffic, and the only sounds I could hear were our rhythmic steps, the occasional shout of defiance from one of the two sets of runners, and my own hoarse breathing.

'I was right,' the reporter said as we came in view of a tall white obelisk.

'What is it?' I gasped.

'It's Bunker Hill.' Alexa had drawn level with us, and was checking out light levels in the gloom. 'I filmed here this morning with Mike.'

'You did?' I was keen to enquire further about this – she had only said she'd had lunch with him – but I was distracted by the journalist, who was laughing again.

'They're reliving the battle,' he said. 'The Boston Tea Party and Bunker Hill all in one day. They'll be declaring independence before the night is over.'

This didn't sound too promising as far as my British PR campaign was concerned.

The fake guides had climbed over the low black railings into the park around the obelisk. The Indians were considering their next move.

'Let's go and whack the bastards,' the tallest of Babar's sons was saying.

'No,' I told him. 'Let's not. They've caused some trouble, but your dad knows who they are and he'll sort it out peacefully. He'll sue them.' Americans' ultimate threat.

'Yes,' Alexa said. 'Violence is not the solution.'

'Huh. Let's take them out,' one of the younger sons growled. 'They look like a bunch of pussies.'

So much for Europe's appeasement skills.

We all scaled the pointed railings and made our way cautiously up a flight of steps towards the obelisk. We could hear the others taunting us from the brow of the hill. At the top of the steps, we sheltered behind the statue of Colonel William Prescott. This, I remembered, was the guy who defended the hill against the English. A courageous man, I thought, because if the sculpture was historically accurate, his only defences had been a very short sword and a pair of inhumanly tight trousers.

In the glow from the streetlamps we could make out the costumed men, who were standing round the base of the obelisk and urging the Indians to come on and make a fight of it.

Babar's eldest son, Vijay, stepped forward. He'd brought a broken teacup with him, and launched it towards his tormentors. The cup smashed spectacularly against the obelisk, provoking a growl of fury from the defending army.

Heartened, the Indians cheered.

Another brother had brought a weapon – a vicious-looking shard of china plate.

I tried to stop him, but he stepped forward and drew back his arm to launch his missile. He threw it with all his strength and then collapsed like a starfish. A dark shape had flown out of the shadows and hit him squarely in the chest. It rolled away from his squirming body, leaking frothy beer, and I saw that it was a bottle of Sam Adams. A truly Bostonian weapon.

The downing of their comrade enraged the Indian army.

'Don't retaliate,' I told them. 'Your dad'll sort this out.'

But as Babar had predicted, this continent was no place for pacificism. They raced into the attack. History really was repeating itself – the Whites and the Indians were fighting again. Although this time, Columbus's geographical mistake had been corrected. These were real Indians.

As always, the Europeans seemed to be gaining the upper hand. The waiters were lithe and had some neat martial-art moves, but the White guys were bulkier and were using American-football-style clinch tactics to disable the Indians' scything arms and legs.

I suddenly noticed that Alexa was missing. Oh no, I thought, had she been hit by the friendly fire that modern Americans are so notorious for?

But no, after a long minute of calling her name, I found her safe and well with the reporter. They were in a huddle behind the tight-trousered statue, apparently in negotiations about film rights to the battle. To her credit and my relief, Alexa seemed to be saying no.

'This isn't really news, is it? The fight's not worth an article,' I told the hack. 'We don't want to cause inter-ethnic trouble in the city.'

'You kidding? I got to go and talk to those guys. This is a hoot.'

'What? I invite you to my tea party and now you're going to publicize the blokes who disrupted it?'

His nostrils flared with journalistic indignation. 'You Brits against the freedom of the press or what? We win our independence and now we're meant to bow down to you *again*?'

Which was pretty damn unfair.

'Hey, none of this is my fault,' I told him. 'You think this is what I wanted to happen? I try to give a few people a nice cup of tea and end up provoking a colonial war.'

Even as I said it, I realized that that just about summed up the history of the British Empire.

8

My troubles in Boston weren't over, of course.

I'd flirted with disaster in this city. I'd even taken disaster out on a first date, found that she was too scary and ended the relationship, trying my best not to hurt her feelings. But no, she'd come back with her two brothers

– cock-up and catastrophe – and they'd put the boot in.

After the battle, I was in such a gloomy mood that I started having a go at Alexa. How come, I wanted to know, she'd only told me she'd had lunch with this Mike character when it was obvious that they'd spent the whole day together, doing the tourist sites?

She erupted into instant fury. How dare I be so suspicious? Hadn't I invited Mi to put on the shortest mini-skirt in human history and join our party? And had she, Alexa, accused me of anything?

'Not in so many words,' I said. Though she had made a few cutting remarks. 'But anyway, there was nothing to be suspicious about. You saw her at the restaurant. She was flashing flesh at everyone, not just me. She's been watching too many rap videos, that's all.'

'OK, so nothing happened with her, and nothing happened with Mike.'

'Yes,' I conceded, 'but you must admit you were a bit evasive when I asked you about your filming. Besides, how did you arrange it all? You had a go at me because I gave Mi my number, and you'd already given Mike yours?'

'No. He gave me *his* number.'

'Right. Big difference.'

'Oh!' She made one of her outraged puffing noises.

We were wandering back down the hill into the city centre, and the reporter was just behind us, interviewing the Indians. The two armies had disengaged pretty quickly after the initial skirmish, and the only real casualty was the young brother who'd got hit by the bottle. He was holding his ribs and being half carried along by Vijay, who had given him a scalp-like wig as a trophy.

Alexa waited for them to catch up, and began to talk reprint rights with the reporter.

*

Next morning, the city's bestselling paper ran a double-page spread about how a visiting Brit had made a mockery of the Tea Party and then been deservedly routed in a new Battle of Bunker Hill. The reporter joked that the rebels had been heard to say, 'Don't fire until you can see the whites of their teacups.'

The article was illustrated with grainy, shadowy pictures that looked like real war photos. And these images were all copyrighted to Alexa, who showed not the slightest guilt about selling out to the enemy. Flicking through the paper, she even looked pleased with her first excursion into news photography, which had proved to be very well paid, too – each still from her film had earned her several hundred dollars.

She and I were having breakfast at the bookshop café, and my pancakes weren't looking fluffy enough to tempt me, even with a double squirt of maple syrup and a stack of organic strawberry slices.

'You wanted war, you got it,' she told me.

War? Hers was a very French version of warfare, I thought bitterly. They don't take any part in the fighting, but step in to make a profit afterwards.

Although in this case my jibe wasn't quite accurate. As it happened, there had been some direct French involvement in the hostilities.

The reporter had done a solid job on the article. He'd made sure that he interviewed all concerned, including the manager of the wine bar opposite the Indian restaurant, the guy who'd been threatening Babar – one Denis Lefèvre, aged thirty-one, a green-card holder from Toulouse. The accent I'd heard wasn't Italian, it was southern French. Yes, as in the original colonial war, France had helped to shaft the Brits.

And worse news was still to come. In the business section

I found an article outlining the French government's promise to provide a team of its best engineers, free of charge, to advise Boston on its 'big dig' problems. The mayor was pictured shaking hands with a typical French engineer, a flat-headed guy whose wardrobe had surely been chosen by a practical joker. The flathead was grinning lopsidedly at the camera, but I instantly saw that I'd been wrong about him and his ilk – some people find Gallic engineers very sexy indeed. The mayor was staring with open-mouthed adoration at the Frenchman as if he smelt of the most erotic aroma ever concocted by a Provençal *parfumier*. It was all too obvious where Boston's vote would go in the World Tourism contest, and it wouldn't be to the organizer of abortive tea parties.

Oh well, I told myself, it was just one battle, not the war. Miami was bound to be more pro-British than Boston, which was after all the heart of the revolution. Same went for Las Vegas. We Brits are such huge gamblers that there had to be some fellow feeling there. And if things looked really bad by the time I got to Vegas, I could use some of my budget to buy a few roulette chips and win enough to repay my fine. The bulldog spirit would triumph in the end.

'When you've finished,' I said to Alexa, 'we ought to head off to the railway station. The Mini waiting for us in New York.'

'Leave Boston, Paul? But we are having so much fun here. Don't you want your breakfast?' She leaned across and forked a strawberry.

Despite her protestations of anti-Americanism, she seemed to be adapting pretty damn well to the land of opportunity.

NEW YORK TO FLORIDA

Seriously South

1

'NOW *THAT'S* AN ENGLISH FLAG.' Dwight the mechanic was pointing his two index fingers at the freshly painted roof of the Mini like a bull about to gore a matador.

'It certainly is,' I confirmed.

'You can throw away your passport. Everyone'll know you're English as hell.'

'You're right there.' I mimed frisbeeing my travel documents into the far corner of the workshop.

'You drive this baby past Buckingham Palace, the guards are gonna salute you.'

'Yes, they'd probably open up the gates and let me park it in the palace courtyard.'

'Yeah.' Dwight had good reason to be proud of his paint job. The Union Jack was so bright it was probably visible from space. But I sensed that he was overdoing the self-congratulation because he'd seen that I wasn't entirely happy.

He was right. It wasn't his fault, though. I'd noticed

something new about the car. Something I should have spotted before. It was, as its name suggested, very mini.

The headroom was fine, and to get enough legroom I just had to push the seat back so that only a legless passenger could sit behind me. No, like a studio apartment, the crunch came with storage space. There was absolutely no way I could fit all our luggage into the Mini's rear compartment. It was like trying to stuff an elephant suppository into a mouse.

'You want a real trunk, you should get a real car,' Dwight helpfully suggested. 'This thing's cute, but it's for going to Midtown, not to Florida. It's like, for ladies on the Upper East Side that don't wanna take a taxi to the hairdresser's. Only time they use the trunk is when a valet puts a shoebox in there.'

'I've seen guys driving them,' I said, less to defend my own image as a future Mini driver than to pre-empt Alexa before she let rip at him for being sexist and shoppingist. Instead, she expressed her frustration by heaving her rucksack one last time at the boot. It stuck there and hung out as if the Mini had sprouted a snub bulldog tail.

'There must be a way,' I said, pulling her bag out and getting a closer look at the problem. 'No one designs a car to hold one shoebox. And if it was made for shopaholics, they must have thought of a way of making space for the dresses, coats and handbags.'

No sooner had I finished speaking than I found the catch that lets you fold the back seat down and create a whole new luggage space.

'*Voilà*.' Triumphantly, I slotted Alexa's bag and my own inside the car and closed the boot.

'What happens in a car park?' Alexa wanted to know. 'We will leave our bags and our laptops in view so people know it is a good idea to steal everything?'

'We'll just have to keep our valuables with us at all times,' I said. 'And if we stop for a pee we'll go separately. Ladies first, of course.'

With the boot closed, the lipstick-red doors open and the rooftop flag glinting in the harsh light of Dwight's work-shop, the Mini looked irresistible. Dwight patted it on the roof and said that even if he'd made a few jokes about her stature, he'd be sad to see the car go.

'She's like my wife,' he said. 'Small in body but plenty big in character.'

After that, for a few delicious minutes, everything was wonderful. The engine started first time, the heating turned the Mini into a snug cocoon, and I got the car out of the maze-like parking lot without taking any chunks out of the paintwork. Then – with a bump – we were on the road to Florida, heading for the sun.

In theory, at least.

'This is Canal Street,' I said.

'Yes.'

'So we're back in Manhattan.'

'Are you sure?'

'Pretty sure.' In fact, I was *very* sure, and so was Alexa, because we'd just driven through the Holland Tunnel for a second time, passing several million signposts informing us which bits of Manhattan were waiting for us on the other side. 'Unless Jersey City also has a Canal Street, a West Broadway, and –' I nodded to our right '– a Brooklyn Bridge.'

OK, that last one was a really cheap shot because I couldn't see the bridge at all, but Alexa made no comment except to give a Parisian shrug, the most profoundly felt gesture of indifference and/or ignorance so far developed by Western civilization. If the universe had decided we were meant to be back in Canal Street, she was implying, then who was she to argue with the greater forces of the infinite cosmos?

There wasn't really much she could say. With her in charge of the road atlas, we'd followed Dwight's directions down the riverbank to the Holland Tunnel, dived under the Hudson into New Jersey, and then somehow ended up back in Manhattan again.

'Doesn't the atlas tell you how to get us from the tunnel on to the New Jersey Turnpike?' I pleaded.

'No.'

I was half willing to believe this. I'd found our road atlas in a forgotten corner of a giant supermarket-style drugstore in Manhattan, next to some curled-up postcards and a yellow-paged book of crossword puzzles.

'Is this detailed enough for a trip down to Florida?' I'd asked the uniformed girl at the counter.

'Dunno, I never been there,' she said, which was fair enough.

Still, I figured, it couldn't be that difficult to find something as big as the Atlantic Ocean.

Wrong, it transpired, for a reason that Alexa now revealed.

'I can't read a map,' she said matter-of-factly as we said hello again to Broadway.

'You can't read a map?' We stopped at some traffic lights, and I took time out to stare at her in horror.

'No, not at all.'

'Can't you try?'

'No. They discovered it at school. I have no sense of two-dimensional orientation.'

'Of what?'

'Of maps. And atlases.' She shrugged again – this handicap was the fault of the great French engineer who'd designed the universe.

The light turned green and we headed even further away from New Jersey.

'But Alexa, how can you be such a female stereotype? It's the biggest gender cliché since the footballer's wife.'

'Please don't moralize to me, Paul. You're not my father.'

'See what I mean? In a minute you'll be getting at me because I'm male and never ask for directions.'

'Why don't you ask, then?'

'Because I know exactly where the tunnel is – we just came out of it,' I said, neatly combining my tiff-winning argument with a left turn that would enable me to back-track west. 'I'll find a place to stop and you can drive. I'll do the map-reading.'

'Oh no, I can't drive an automatic,' she said. 'I've never driven one.'

'It's easy. You just press the accelerator when you want to go, and the brake when you don't. It's like a toy.'

'You want me to learn a new way of driving in the middle of New York? No way. I will crash the car and your tour of America will end at the beginning, and people in England will shout at you. Or people in India, anyway.'

This, I gathered from a quick side view of her smile, was a really amusing joke.

'OK,' I said, accelerating needlessly fast around a corner into the westbound lane of Canal Street. 'Forget the atlas, let's try to read the signposts together.'

Which was easier said than done.

2

French road signs are polite – 'If you'd like to stay on until Paris,' they tell you, 'it's 122 kilometres straight ahead, but if you'd prefer to leave the autoroute and go to Rouen, then feel free to turn off at the next exit, yes this one just coming up now, which, incidentally, will also take you to the villages of this and that, and, if you go far enough, Belgium.' They shepherd and coax you to your destination.

By comparison, American road signs are like riot police. 'Hey you,' they yell. 'Yeah, you! Where you think you're going? Don't know, huh? Well get off the main drag now, yeah, *now*, exit 21, interstate 95, highway 17. Whaddya mean you don't know the number of the road you want? Get off this mudderfuggin highway right now, where it says exit only, yeah there, get outta here, ya dumb fuck.'

What I mean is, you're driving away from New York, you think you're heading more or less in the right direction on the right road and then a sign appears ordering you to get off the highway. It doesn't tell you what will happen if you stay on the highway, whether you'll be heading for New Jersey, New Orleans or New Delhi. It just tells you to exit now for some Aztec-sounding town like Secaucus or Warinanco, and you think, My God, Mexico already? I'd better exit or I'll end up in Patagonia. Next thing, you find yourself spinning down a swirl of motorway ramps into the Jersey wasteland of cranes, pylons and railway tracks.

On our second attempt, though, it did look as if we'd escaped the magnetic attraction of Manhattan. We crossed a giant bridge that didn't take us to Brooklyn, then passed an airport that was neither JFK nor La Guardia. And after a couple of wrong exits and hurried re-entries on to the main drag, I learnt a simple lesson about American highways. You just stick with the road you're on until you absolutely have to get off it – which sounds like the chorus of one of the many country songs we had to listen to before finally tuning in to a decent road-trip classic rock station.

Besides, sticking to the straight-ahead lane soon turned out to be the only viable policy because, contrary to what

I'd expected, American drivers were even more deadly than the French. What was all this bullshit I'd heard about low speed limits and hardline highway patrols? These New York and New Jersey drivers had absolutely no problem with slaloming around me at a hundred miles an hour to get where they wanted. I could be tooling along in the centre lane at the speed limit, overtaking plenty of trucks and stragglers, and cars would come careering up to within a yard of my compact rear end, then veer randomly either right or left. They'd overtake me and then swerve back across my nose, often without taking the trouble to indicate.

If I dared to stay close to the speed limit when there was neither a veer-right or veer-left option for someone tailgating me, then suddenly my whole rear-view mirror would be full of the glowering headlights and growling radiator of a high-slung 4×4.

It was obvious that these guys had grown up with computer games. They were flinging their heavyweight vehicles around as if, after a fatal multi-car pile-up, they'd just start a new game with a brand-new car and ten more lives. What's more, they were free to take on any identity they wanted, because practically every 4×4 had windows tinted darker than a film star's sunglasses. There was no way I could see the faces of the maniacs who were trying to shunt me off the highway. For all I knew they could have been wearing masks and living out Darth Vader fantasies – 'You don't know the power of the dark outside lane, Obi Wan Mini-driver. So fuck off and let me pass.'

The worst of the intimidators were the truckers. A typical American truck looks just like an antique Samurai helmet, with the wide cowl, slit eyes and bare-toothed grin of a ruthless killer swordsman. When you see one of those coming at your rear windscreen from the seat of a knee-high Mini, you start looking for a place to hide. Especially if you've got a Union Jack painted on your roof and you look like some kind of beach towel.

But despite all the heart-stopping moments, it felt great to be on the road south, the New Jersey Garden State Parkway, which certainly lived up to its name. It was a straight highway running through a tree-lined park. Not a house in sight. I wondered if anyone actually lived in New Jersey, or whether it was just some kind of drive-through entrance lobby for New York.

'Hey, we should give the car a name,' I suggested.

'A name?' Alexa frowned at the idea, as if I'd said we should call her rucksack Gerald.

'Yeah, something that sums up its personality. How about Mini Me?'

'I'm sure she would be very flattered,' Alexa said icily. It took me a second to work out why. Of course, being an arty French woman, she had never seen *Austin Powers*. I cleared up the misunderstanding, but she still seemed convinced I had some subliminal thing for our Korean receptionist.

'No, come on, Alexa,' I told her. 'You're The One. You're the girl I gave everything up to be with. You're my *elle éternelle*.' Normally I hate making declarations like that, but being able to stare straight ahead out of the windscreen helped me to pile on the romanticism.

'*Merci*, Paul,' she said. 'No one has ever called me their *elle éternelle* before.' She gave my elbow an affectionate squeeze. 'How about Thelma?'

'Thelma?' I said, trying it out.

'From *Thelma and Louise*.'

'Yes, great, I like it. Thelma. Sassy, knows how to have a good time, a little bit dangerous.'

'You'll just have to make sure you don't drive her into a canyon, like they do in the film.'

'I don't think New Jersey is known for its canyons,' I said.

Alexa pretended to check for gorges in the atlas.

'Why are we going down this Parkway?' she asked, suddenly serious again. 'Didn't Dwight say we should go via Washington?'

'It's more direct.' Apart from the fact that the knot of highways heading through Philadelphia, Baltimore and Washington looked like perfect traffic-jam territory, I'm a coast-road type of guy. 'Look.' I prodded at the map where the green land joined the blue ocean. 'We go down to Atlantic City, which is bound to be deserted at this time of year, then nip over the Cape May ferry and we're practically in Virginia.'

Instead of being thrilled about my scenic – and, I hoped, quicker – route, Alexa was mad with me again.

'You decided this without consulting me? And you accuse me of being a gender stereotype?'

The trouble with French feminists is that although they might be sexier than their foreign counterparts, they're also more intellectual. A deadly combination. You let slip one lazy remark that might conceivably be gender-biased and – if they're in the mood – they'll pounce. You've put the grenade in your trouser pocket and they'll pull the pin, explaining sexily why it's your own stupid fault that your balls are getting blown off.

'When did you plan all this?' she demanded, pouting beautifully.

'Last night. Did you think I was just watching the European football highlights? Men can watch TV and read a map at the same time, you know.'

Unexpectedly, she garrumphed in defeat. I'd out-stereotyped a French feminist. It had to be a first.

'Are you sure this isn't just a summer ferry?' she asked, clearly reduced to looking for minor weak spots in my unassailable defences.

'Yup. I checked on the internet. Even in winter they run till six o'clock. We stop over in Virginia tonight, then Jacksonville next night, and in forty-eight hours we'll be swimming on South Beach.'

Alexa admitted that this sounded cool.

'Wake me up if you need me to ask directions for you,' she said. She closed the atlas and reclined her seat for a nap.

3

Jake had made me promise that when I was in the USA I would visit his favourite pancake chain. I'd find them at plenty of malls and highway exits, he said, and they had ten different sorts of maple syrup.

I mentioned this to Alexa. She was awake again, but drowsy after an hour of semi-jetlagged dozing, and in need of a coffee.

'Ten sorts of maple syrup?' she said. 'That's very sophisticated.'

'What do you mean?'

'Well, I suppose they have different syrups from Ontario and Quebec, perhaps a vintage one, you know, a 2005 Vancouver Red or something.'

I had to laugh at the sheer Frenchness of the idea.

'No, Alexa, this is America. So they're going to be sugar-free, low-fat, salt-free. Probably vitamin-enriched, fibre-added and non-stick. And definitely cranberry-flavoured. Everything in America gets cranberry flavoured at some point in its existence.'

Alexa thought I was being very patronizing, and we had a bet. If there was a cranberry-flavoured syrup, she would learn to drive Thelma in the restaurant car park.

It turned out, though, that we'd have to wait for our bet,

because when we reached the service station it was a modest, central-reservation job with a gas station and a café, and a parking lot in between.

'Food and fuel,' the sign said, sticking to the essentials.

'I'm sure a man invented that sign,' Alexa said.

I had to admit that she was probably right. Jake once told me about a shop near his summer camp, a place called Beer, Bait & Ammo. As the name suggested, it sold everything a guy could wish for on a trip into the woods. The French would probably have called it Tout Pour l'Homme.

Sticking to the rules of our luggage-guarding strategy, I offered Alexa the chance to go visit the service station first, but she insisted that I go in and bring out a coffee for her.

I jogged through the damp chill of the car park into a kind of sauna with deep-fried air. I'd expected something more grandiose with a real American flavour to it. Instead, it was a lot like every other service station I'd ever been to, except for a couple of roadside places in Thailand. There was dull brown tiling on the floor, fake panelled walls, a meagrely stocked news-stand on one side of the entrance, a candy and drinks store on the other. I quite fancied a chocolate bar myself, but the only ones on sale were giant, instant-obesity packs, and I decided to give diabetes a miss for today.

After exploring the restrooms, I ventured into the main part of the service station, where the atmosphere smelt of hot caramel, as if the whole world was being sugar-coated. A long open workshop was churning out giant cinnamon buns, sugar-glazed cowpats, each one of which must have contained the daily intake of carbs and calories for an average African school. They looked great. I bought two.

I then went to queue at the coffee-chain stand, where customers were taking a full minute each to reel off the blend of coffees and flavourings that they wanted. I ordered two single shots of espresso and, in a spirit of discovery, a mango and banana chocolate mocha slushie.

'Twelve, sixteen or twenty-four ounce?' I was asked.

'Small, please,' I said, pointing to a beaker the size of a fire bucket.

I sat in the car and snacked while Alexa took her turn in the restrooms. On her way back, she stopped to press the toe of her shoe on to a puddle of water that was covered in thick brown ice.

'Are you sure the ferry will go tonight?' she asked. 'That ice is very solid.'

'Yes, certain,' I said. 'It sails at six o'clock.' Though I was beginning to wish that I'd written down the phone number of the ferry company, and maybe even called them before heading down this one-way road. What was that Alexa had said about men not asking for directions?

4

The trees had thinned out. The Garden Parkway had become the Bog Parkway. My thoughts were getting pretty boggy, too.

The highway was now snaking between flat areas of marshland that were patched with residual snow. Then suddenly, the marsh opened out into a lake surrounded by frosted reeds. I felt the wind swipe the Mini up on to its toes.

'Look at that,' Alexa said. 'Look at the ice.'

'It's only a pond,' I said. American ponds had to be ten times bigger than European ponds, right? 'It's probably fresh water. Everyone knows seawater doesn't freeze.'

A couple of miles further on, we soared over a short but steeply curving bridge, like the parabola of an arrow fired into the sky. From the summit we got a clear view of the distant Atlantic shoreline – high-rise hotels, water towers looking like sputniks waiting for blast-off, grey shadows in the fading daylight. And between us and them was a gigantic, white expanse of ice.

'Must be fresh water,' I said, anticipating a comment from the passenger seat.

'I'm not sure,' Alexa said. 'On the map, it looks like it's a kind of, how do you say it, *lagon*. You know, open to the ocean.'

'Oh, so now you can read a map?' The satisfaction of scoring conjugal argument points was almost totally cancelled out by the realization that she was right – further ahead, the ice met the horizon at a point without any trace of high-rise, or even low-rise, buildings. The lagoon seemed to open out into the sea. It was almost certainly part of the ocean. And it was frozen.

But no, be optimistic, I told myself. This is America. Don't give in to French defeatism. In France, everything is potentially crap. The French will tell you why your idea won't work, and say, OK, if you want to make a fool of yourself, we'll give it a try. And then they'll be so late and half-hearted that of course it fails. In the USA, though, anything is potentially brilliant. They say, Let's go for it, and they really go for it.

I pressed hard on the accelerator. Fifteen minutes later, the terminal loomed ahead of us, a floodlit blue metal archway. Beyond, I could see two white ferries apparently hovering in the freezing fog.

'Look, no queue, brilliant,' I said with American-style positivity as I weaved through the empty approach lanes.

I could feel Alexa eyeing me sceptically.

A man in a yellow fluorescent jacket stepped out of a toll booth and pointed up at an electric signboard. He read the glowing words for me, in case I was illiterate, blind or stupid. I felt a little of each.

'All ferries cancelled due to freezing weather, Sir.'

'Ah,' I said. 'When do you expect them to restart?'

The ferryman puffed out a foggy laugh. 'Sir, if I knew when the thaw was coming, I'd be getting my back yard ready for planting.'

'So you have no idea at all?'

'No, Sir.'

'How thick is the ice, then?'

'Why? You thinking of skating across, Sir?' He got a laugh from Alexa.

'No, I mean, it's seawater, isn't it? It can't be that thick. Seawater doesn't freeze properly, does it?'

'No? You never heard of the North Pole?'

'Ah, but isn't that ancient fresh water? I saw this TV show about how they were drilling into icebergs and getting pure drinking water.'

The ferryman's frown told me that we might be straying slightly off the subject. And by this time, the sub-zero fog was beginning to make both of us blink painfully. So I thanked him for the info and reversed away from the toll booth.

'What are we going to do now that we have come two hundred kilometres down an *impasse*?' Alexa asked.

'Let's get a hotel for the night and have a rethink. There are bound to be some near by. Cape May's a seaside resort.'

'Oh, excellent. You mean we don't have to wait until Miami for a swim? And maybe we can go ice-skating on the waves.'

She kept up the sarcasm all the way into town.

5

'Stephen King,' Alexa whispered. Being French, she pronounced it 'Steffen', but I knew what she meant.

The streets were dark and misty. Gothic houses loomed, their wooden turrets and pointed rooftops in spooky silhouette against the pewter sky. They had shuttered windows and rickety stairs leading up to empty porches deep in shade, perfect hiding places for madmen – or madwomen – to lurk in wait for their victims.

That was it. I realized what they reminded me of – *Psycho*. This was a whole town of guesthouses where knive-wielding wackos lived with their mum's corpse. I was almost glad that they all seemed to be posting 'no vacancy'.

We cruised the criss-cross of streets looking for an open B&B, but there was no sign of activity except for the occasional flap of a flag in the wind. There were Stars and Stripes outside practically every house. It felt as if they were saying, 'Ye non-Americans, do not dare to enter here,' or something similarly doom-laden.

'Let's go,' Alexa said. She had switched the light on in the car and was studying the New Jersey page in her atlas. 'We can turn back towards Atlantic City and then go into Philadelphia and get the highway.' It seemed that the urgency of the situation had cured her two-dimensional map allergy.

On cue, our headlights picked out a 'vacancy' sign.

We stopped and stared at it. A varnished board carved with daisies (or were they bullet wounds?) was hanging by two small chains from a post shaped like a gallows. The word 'vacancy' was painted on in black, and the slot where the 'no' could be slid in was empty.

'Should we try it?' I asked. The timing did seem a bit too

convenient, like that scene in *Rosemary's Baby* when the pain in Mia Farrow's tummy is so bad that she decides to get a scan. Immediately, the pain stops and the devil's spawn is free to carry on its evil growth. Was the town luring us back into its clutches the instant we'd decided to leave? 'I'll go and check whether it's a mistake,' I said. 'Maybe the "no" just fell off.'

'I'll come with you.' Alexa was gazing up at the purple-and-green-painted house. She didn't seem too keen to stay out here alone.

'Look, if I don't come out in two minutes, or you hear a blood-curdling scream, just drive away and leave me. Oh, I forgot, you can't drive automatics.'

'Huh, I will ask, Mister Macho,' she said. Next second, she was striding up the stairs on to the porch.

The front door opened before she could ring the bell or knock. A white-haired, white-faced woman appeared in a pool of yellow light. Her mouth opened and shut, but no sound came out.

Of course, once I got the car window open, I could hear slightly better.

'. . . dollars a night,' the woman was saying. 'Just one night?'

'Just one night,' Alexa said.

'Go to the end of the block, turn left, pull into the second driveway, not the first, and keep going till you come to a back yard. I'll come round and let you in.' The woman said all this in a slow, trembling voice that really did sound as if she'd just been aroused from the dead. You kind of wondered how many of her resuscitated relatives would be waiting in the back yard with cleavers. Or at least you might have wondered something like that if you hadn't been a steely-nerved, stiff-upper-lip Englishman like myself.

We drove towards the corner as instructed. In the mirror, I could see the lady watching us, as if checking the street for witnesses to our disappearance.

6

The hall was decorated with a framed photo of a large lighthouse, a poster of laughing tourists on a sunny beach, and a watercolour that was either a cloudy sunset or two seagulls in a bloody mid-air collision.

The landlady was only about sixty, rather than the six hundred or so I'd imagined. She was swathed in a long bottle-green cardigan, the same colour as the columns holding up her porch outside. The cardigan had a high collar, so that her tightly permed grey hair looked like the ornate cork on a perfume bottle.

She asked us the usual questions about where we'd come from and where we were going. Fortunately, she didn't put the two together and ask why the hell we'd ended up here. We explained our strange accents, and she told us that she lived with her sister, who would be putting some coffee out in the hall at eight fifteen the next morning.

'You don't do breakfast?' I asked.

'Oh no. Coffee at eight fifteen.'

'Is there anywhere we can get some dinner?'

'Oh yes.' She gave us a couple of leaflets for places that were open all year. One of them, a pub, looked promising.

'Can we walk there?'

'Oh yes, they're all within ten blocks of here.' She seemed to start every sentence with 'oh', as if life were full of surprising questions, although she must have been asked the same things by every single guest. Perhaps she'd forgotten them all since the summer season ended.

'Do you have internet?' Alexa wanted to know.

'Oh sure. But the computer's switched off. You can use it in the morning.' She frowned, as if thinking 'If you survive the night, hahahaha!' Although she was probably just trying to remember how to turn on the computer.

Our room was morgue white, with an old metal-framed double bed, a modern-aircon/heating wall unit and a large fridge with a long notice taped to the door about what not to put in it. I didn't check whether 'guests' severed heads' was on the list.

The room was icy cold, but our landlady – who appeared silently behind us – switched on the heater and said it would be cosy by the time we got back from dinner. She gave us an absent smile, as if associating us with the word 'dinner' had set her tastebuds fluttering.

If ghouls and monsters were regulars at the pub, they'd decided to boycott it that night. The place was full of dis-armingly normal people. Middle-aged, middle-class couples, a group of baseball-capped fishermen types, an ageing hippy and even a few twenty-somethings.

It was so normal that when Alexa and I walked in – two obvious outsiders – the conversation didn't drop a single decibel, except maybe for the people nearest the door, temporarily paralysed by a lungful of freezing fog.

The pub looked surprisingly English. It had high wooden seats running along the bar, a chequerboard floor, and mugs hanging from green beams on the ceiling, as if put there to catch a hundred leaks.

We sat at a table and started to read the dinner menu.

'Hi, can I get you folks something to drink?' A young, shaven-headed waitress with four earrings in each lobe was smiling at us.

'I see you have New Jersey wine,' I said.

'Yeah, we have a Chardonnay, a Merlot and a Riesling.'

'This is produced near here, not just shipped in and bottled?'

'Oh yeah, sure.'

Alexa looked dubious – the French are willing, at a pinch, to acknowledge that Californian wines might be good enough to drink rather than pickle gherkins with, but offering her a New Jersey Riesling was like asking her to drink crop spray. Even so, she agreed that we should try one glass of Merlot and one of Chardonnay.

The waitress then did something astonishing. She asked to see our ID.

'You're carding us?' I couldn't believe it. I'd been over twenty-one long enough to have forgotten the hangover the day after my party, and that was one unforgettable hangover. And Alexa was twenty-four, and had that European sophistication that gives a woman her full maturity.

'Er, well . . .' The waitress was hesitating. Perhaps my surprise had added a few wrinkles to my forehead.

'No, please, look,' I begged her, fishing in my pocket for my passport. 'You have no idea how flattering this is. I haven't been paid such a great compliment since my doctor told me I have a beautiful appendix.'

Alexa groaned. Oops, I thought. I'd forgotten about not joking around with women under the age of ninety.

The waitress pretended to study my passport.

'It wasn't really a compliment, Sir,' she said. 'We can't be too careful. Some people age prematurely.' Was I imagining things, or did I really see her wink at Alexa? In any case, Alexa's groan mutated into a grin. Womankind one, manhood a resounding zero.

Alexa had a misnamed *filet mignon*. *Mignon* means cute,

but this would have been like calling a brontosaurus cute. In fact, it might well have been a whole brontosaurus buttock. Even so, she chomped through all of it, along with a shipwreck-sized portion of fries.

I had an 'ocean burger', meaning that it was topped with shrimp and cheese. Shrimp on a burger? Maybe they had too many and were trying to find ways to offload them. Shrimp and vanilla ice cream, coffee with a shrimp on top. It went down nicely with the New Jersey Chardonnay, though, which had a slightly metallic aftertaste but made the world seem a warmer, friendlier place.

We walked back to the B&B on a cloud of alcohol-based bravado, defying any nutcases to come out of their gothic lairs and cleaver us. I apologized to Alexa for causing our day-long bickering session about maps and asking directions.

'I was a bit nervous driving on these roads in such a tiny car. But I've learnt how you do it now. All you need to know is what number road you want, and whether you're heading north, south, east or west, and the rest is easy. Pretty soon we'll be on 95 south, and we'll just stay that way till Miami.'

'And tomorrow, I will learn to drive Thelma *en automatique*,' she conceded. 'I will look sexy in a Mini, no?'

'You'd look sexy inside one, outside one, on top of one, anywhere.'

'On top of a car? You imagine me in a bikini in a car magazine?' It sounded tetchy, but her eyes had lost the slightly steely look that they'd had all day. She pulled down the scarf and rollneck jumper she was wearing and – just for a second – bared the tops of her breasts at me.

It looked as though I'd been forgiven for my screw-up in Boston, and would soon be getting an even closer look below that neckline. I said a silent prayer of thanks to the grapes of New Jersey.

*

Our room was now so well heated that the only option was to go to bed naked. This did our mood of reconciliation no harm at all, of course, and we snuggled down under the thick duvet and began to make the most of each other's closeness.

The only thing was, I wondered whether Alexa shouldn't turn the volume down a bit. She kept asking me, rather loudly I thought, and in very understandable English, what I was intending to do with her body now that it was naked and 'vulnerable to caresses'. I didn't want to inhibit her, but apart from her voice, the whole house – no, the whole town – was eerily silent. I decided it was best not to spoil the mood, and instead of mentioning the volume problem, I simply kissed her hard on the mouth, so that my skull acted as a kind of sound insulator.

Meanwhile, the floorboards seemed to have detected the variations in weight distribution and were starting to creak like a mountain just before an avalanche. I hoped that the landladies were fast asleep, deaf, or out haunting somewhere.

I clenched every muscle in my body and operated a strict go-slow policy that French workers would have been proud of. Even so, my ferociously disciplined tantric antics were making the metal bedframe rattle, and Alexa was squeaking like a ticklish mouse.

Then she reached up with her arms and calves and clutched me down on top of her, and all attempts at noise limitation were blown to pieces. The floorboards bucked and squealed in agony, the bedhead hammered holes in the wall, and the springs twanged like a piano falling down a liftshaft while the two of us performed a duet for gibbon and grizzly bear. Never mind the landladies, I'm sure the guys out at the ferry terminal cocked their heads and began to prepare for a hurricane coming in from the east.

In the subsequent calm, we lay there and giggled into each other's ears.

'Her!'

We both held our breath and listened.

'Her!'

There it was again, a voice so clear that I even bent down to check that there was no one under the bed.

'Her!'

It seemed to be accusing someone of something. But who? And what?

'Her, her!'

I finally realized that it was a woman coughing in the room below us. Not very violently, either. The ceiling was so thin that we could hear her as if she was standing beside our bed.

Alexa and I shared this thought mutely, our eyes wide and staring at the floor. Then Alexa laughed.

'Don't worry, Paul,' she whispered. 'They have a B&B. In summer they hear this from every room, every night. And no doubt every morning, too. They are probably happy to hear the sounds of summer again.'

Which was one way of looking at it. The other was that an old lady had been lying down there, alone in bed – or, even worse, in bed with her sister – eavesdropping on my sex life. Not exactly a turn-on.

Until, that is, Alexa said that *she'd* like to have a go at making the whole house creak again.

'Lie on your back,' she told me in French, 'and hold on to the rails of the bedhead with both hands. Now relax, and don't move . . .'

When a guy has a French feminist girlfriend, sometimes he just has to grit his teeth and do what she says.

7

Next morning, I was all for leaving before the eight-fifteen coffee-pot deadline. We'd already paid, and it would avoid an uncomfortable conversation about who had slept well. Or not.

Alexa, however, reminded me that the sisters were going to switch on their computer for us. 'You think there is another place to read your emails in this dead winter town?'

At eight fifteen prompt we tiptoed down into the hall. A tall black flask and a pair of transparent plastic cups were standing on the top level of a drinks trolley. We pumped out two coffees and went to knock at the lounge door.

One light tap did the job. It was as if the two sisters were permanently lurking behind doors. Or under bedrooms. The woman who opened up was obviously the second sister – her cheeks were splashed bright pink with blusher and her high-necked cardigan was purple, the second colour on the facade of the house. The two women were like part of the building.

'How'd you like my coffee?' she asked.

'It's great,' I said, though so far it had been much too hot to taste. American coffee and tea are always way too hot for at least twenty minutes after you buy them. It's the only country in the world where water can be heated beyond boiling point.

'Oh good. Her!' It was the cough. This was the woman who'd had to put up with two sessions of bedspring-twanging the night before.

'Could we use your computer to look at our emails?' I asked her.

'Oh sure, come in. I'll turn it on. Her!'

She ushered us into a square room that had more un-necessary furnishings than anywhere I'd ever seen. It wasn't only that there were three cushions for every seating place. The easy chairs had arm covers, cushion covers, headrests, headrest covers, and even some of the covers had covers, all in different colours, like slices of cheese, tomato and onion on a hamburger. And below all the superficial covering, the chairs and sofas were swathed in woollen rugs, throws and wraps, so that the sisters themselves probably had no idea of the original shape of their furniture. In fact, there might well have been a third sister under there somewhere, a lost sibling who'd got in the way of a throw or wrap one day and had never been seen since.

'We crochet a lot,' the sister said. 'Her!' Perhaps, I thought, she was allergic to wool and didn't know it. She pointed to a laptop that was folded shut, with an apricot-orange doily on top of it. 'Well, you help yourself, I'm sure you know how it works.' She motioned Alexa towards the desk. 'You can sit and drink your coffee and watch TV while you wait for your wife to finish,' she told me.

The TV was tuned in to the public channel, and was showing a documentary about studying the effects of global warming via the analysis of moose droppings. I dug a hole for myself in a mound of cushions and sat down.

'No,' Alexa said. 'Paul, you look first. You can read your emails then go and get us some breakfast, eh, *chéri*?' she said.

'OK.' I switched the computer on and hooked up to my mail. Apart from an offer to extend my 'Pen1s' by three inches, a security warning about my account from a bank I'd never heard of, and an anti-French joke from a friend of mine, there were only two new messages. I opened the one from Benoît first, praying as I typed that he wasn't going to give me bad news about my legal worries. Perhaps he'd omitted an acute accent from one of his labels and the inspector had doubled the fine.

But no, he simply reassured me that the inspection had gone OK, and that the fine was still fixed at its previous – albeit heart-breaking – amount. I thanked him for his good news and begged him not to forget to translate the *sandwich du jour* on the blackboard every day. Maybe, I suggested, he should even do away with the free English newspapers. The Ministry might demand that he translate those, too.

The second email was from Jack Tyler in London. A personal, direct message, no less, cutting out Suraya the middle woman for once. It was headed 'Imperative!'

Oh no, I thought, don't tell me he needs more photos of me in a busby or a kilt.

Actually, I was pretty close. It said, and I quote: 'Imperative you convince chair of Miami Scottish Dancing Society that your campaign will have knock-on effect for Dunfermline.'

'What the fur?' This was a combination of me starting to swear and the sister in her armchair cutting me off with a cough. It was a pretty accurate description of how I felt, though. What the fur was he on about?

8

The morning was bright, but judging by the way the air dived down my throat and tried to anaesthetize my tonsils, I didn't think there had been enough of a thaw to clear the way for the ferry. Even so, I could tell we'd come south since Boston. It was the damp chill of a dungeon rather than the bite of a freezer cabinet.

In daylight, of course, the houses looked much less ghostly than they had at night. They ranged in size from dark, squat cottages to sprawling mansions. Even the biggest houses had a temporary feel, as if they might get suddenly washed away. They were made of painted planks, with dainty columns holding up the porches, and the wood-work under the eaves looked as though it had been crocheted from coloured wool by my two landladies. They were painted in soft but often startling combinations – spinach and custard, sunflower and gunmetal, crimson and blue. In the summer, full of holidaymakers, the town must feel like an immense doll's house store.

I found a sunny, sheltered street corner and phoned Suraya. She listened to my question about Dunfermline and burst into tears.

What the fur?

'I am doing my best,' she sobbed when she'd calmed down enough to be coherent. 'Everything is late, every-thing is difficult, and then they tell me everything is –' she lowered her voice '– fucked.' We gasped together at her swearing. 'I don't care if they do record it,' she snapped at someone. An admonishing colleague at the call centre, I guessed.

'Calm down, Suraya, and tell me exactly what the problem is.' Amazingly, I actually felt as if I was the one in control.

She sniffed and, to a certain extent, explained. I still knew considerably less about my job than about moose droppings, but I finally managed to piece things together from her long, jagged sentences.

My contact in Miami was to be a guy from city hall called Jesus (pronounced 'Hay-zooss', she stressed) Rodriguez. We were due to meet at eleven a.m., just over forty-eight hours away. There was no exact venue, though. I'd fix that up with him. And then there was the Dunfermline stuff.

My next gig was a dancing show organized by the Miami Scottish-American Society, or MSAS. I didn't have to organize anything – I just needed to latch myself on as a sponsor and scatter our tourist literature about. However, the previous day, the MSAS had sent an email threatening to pull out because they had discovered that the Visitor Resources: Britain campaign was publicizing only one Scottish city, Edinburgh. They had said, Add in Glasgow, Stirling, Skye and Dunfermline or you can stick your Scottish dancing show in your sporran and smoke it.

'Why Dunfermline?' I asked.

'It's stupid,' Suraya said. Apparently, Dunfermline – which was just northwest of Edinburgh, she told me – had been included in the demand because it was the birthplace of the current MSAS chairman's grandfather.

'Stupid's not the word for it,' I said. 'It's deranged,' and Suraya burst into tears again.

'It's not fair,' she sobbed. 'My scooter was stolen and my father won't lend me the money for a new one, and I have to walk three miles to work because he won't let me ride with my neighbour – you know, the guy who suggested the restaurant for us – and I get hassled by the taxi-drivers and nearly die of heat exhaustion every day.'

'Heat exhaustion? It must be awful.' After ten minutes phoning in the open air, my fingers and nose were all in danger of dropping off on to the glistening sidewalk. 'Sorry, but I've got to go, Suraya, I've got to go. To Miami, remember?' I interrupted another outburst of sobs with a prod of my last moveable finger.

I found a store, waited for two bagels to be sliced open and slathered with cream cheese, then took a wrong turn and found myself down on the ocean front, a blond beach that was being slapped by dark, frothy surf. There were flecks of ice along the tide mark, and the waves were moving sluggishly, as if carrying a weight on their backs.

I called the ferry company and got a recorded message that sounded almost as grief-stricken as Suraya.

'We apologize that all ferries are out of action until further notice,' it moaned.

The numb-looking seagulls began a chorus of heckling laughter. In league with Alexa, obviously.

9

'One thing I *can* do,' Alexa said, 'is read manuals.'

'Next left up ahead. You should see a sign for the forty-nine,' I told her.

'Maybe it is more prestigious to read atlases, but it is very *practical* to read manuals.'

'It might tell you to head for Millville,' I added.

'And even more practical to look at the writing on your – what do you call it?'

'Gear lever. Don't take the forty-seven. It's the forty-nine we want,' I warned.

'Yes, gear lever. If we'd done that, maybe we could have continued to Philadelphia last night.'

'Last night was fun, though, wasn't it?'

'*Oui*.' She took her hand off the gear lever to stroke my arm.

Alexa had worked out that the car could be switched over from automatic to manual, and now she was driving us towards highway 95 and, ultimately, Florida. Her right hand was constantly clamped on the gear stick. Except, of course, when she needed to stroke my arm. And she did occasionally steer as well.

She wasn't what I would call a smooth driver – she'd learnt in Paris, after all, where there are traffic lights every fifty yards or so, and where the longest stretch of straight acceleration is along the Champs-Elysées if you're lucky enough to get a series of greens. But Paris driving had made her a fearless lane-changer, so with me reciting the road numbers and telling her to aim right or left, we successfully skirted Philadelphia, sliced through Baltimore, and suddenly we had crossed all of Delaware (not difficult) and made a major dent in Maryland. We were heading seriously south.

'You've really bonded with Thelma,' I said as she cut up a dawdling luxury saloon.

'Yes, she is Thelma, I am Louise,' she said. She waved at the driver of the saloon, who had sped up and was pulling level with us again.

I was amazed. If I'd cut him up like that, he'd have been trying to run me off the road, but now he was grinning and nodding approvingly at the combination of beautiful woman driver and funky red car. Alexa replied with a smile that would have had him following her to Miami if she'd been alone.

An hour later, Alexa's smile of enjoyment had turned into full-blown hilarity.

She thought it was 'sooo funny' that I, the master of the map, the atlas artist, had directed us down the wrong highway.

'You are Supermap,' she said. 'Batmap.'

The thing was, I'd foolishly decided that we might as well leave highway 95 and take a slightly more direct route between Baltimore and Washington, and then get back on to the 95 just north of DC. But when we hit the relevant junction, I saw a combined sign for the 95 and another highway, and—

I tried to explain, but Alexa simply shook her head and accused me of trying to blind her with numbers. The inescapable fact was that I'd sent her straight into downtown Washington.

'No, I know. You're Spidermap.' She enjoyed that one,

engrossed as I was in the web of roads leading us into – and I hoped out of – Washington.

'Have you ever seen the White House?' I asked her. 'We can drive right past it.' And although the French love of puns could have kept her adding the word 'map' to the names of superheroes for several hours, this set her thinking.

America's capital is – appropriately enough – the perfect drive-thru city.

'How clairvoyant of the original George W. to plan it like that,' I said as we cruised past the White House, getting an admittedly distant view of the famous railings.

'No, it was designed by a French architect,' Alexa said.

'Well that explains why you supported them in the War of Independence. It was another of your engineering deals. You help them out, but only if they give you a building contract afterwards. It's like the whole Big Dig stitch-up in Boston. France hasn't changed much in two hundred years.'

Alexa smiled, proud of her country's talent for engineering-based diplomacy.

We passed some grey administrative buildings and a few groups of shivering tourists, and then we were out in the open, gazing up at the immense white needle of the Washington Monument. Although it's more of a six-inch nail than a needle. Despite France's close links with revolutionary America, the monument seemed to be an attempt to tell Paris, 'OK, you've got that little Egyptian obelisk on the Place de la Concorde, but this is the real deal. This is an American obelisk. A megalisk.'

'Oh, the buildings have disappeared,' Alexa said. She was right. Although we were now, theoretically, in the epicentre of Washington, we were also in the middle of an enormous park. Lawns, lakes and wintry trees undulated away as far as we could see. It was as if Paris had demolished every building between the Sacré Coeur and the Arc de Triomphe and turned the Champs-Elysées into a pond.

In the distance we could see the immense white Capitol Building, like a caricature of St Paul's Cathedral. We turned towards it, driving past the museums of history, natural history and art, and it kept on growing to increasingly mammoth proportions. When we finally got right up in front of it, it was almost freakish. The gigantic dome was big enough to be a parliament building on its own, and the facade was like Buckingham Palace after a course of steroids. One thing was for sure – the colossal Capitol was sending out an explicit message to the world. This was a government that took itself very seriously indeed.

We doubled back and went to see Abraham Lincoln. His memorial was the only monument that had not been designed for the drive-thru or drive-past visitor. We couldn't see him at all from the street, especially through the small windscreen of a Mini. So we were obliged to stop and feign engine trouble while we took turns to puff up the steps and visit the white giant on his cubical armchair.

Despite the cold, Lincoln had quite a few fans milling around, taking in the murals and the Gettysburg Address, or just standing expectantly at his feet, observing him through camera lenses. I understood why they wanted to gaze at him. With his hands on the arms of his seat, big Abe looked as if he might suddenly lift himself up and sprint across the lawns to the Capitol. He'd heard that it was built for giants.

10

It was when we hit North Carolina that Alexa gave me the bad news.

Ever since the daylight had begun to fade, she'd been in the navigator's seat, poring over the mileage map at the end of the atlas and doing mental arithmetic.

It sounds pretty sexist, but I almost wished I'd left her to languish in her ignorance of everything map-related. Now all she seemed to do was use the atlas to batter me with unwelcome facts. She was a like a born-again New Ager who discovers Feng Shui and can't stop rearranging the furniture.

'If we drive non-stop and respect the times on the map, we will arrive in Miami at six fifty in the morning. Your meeting is at eleven, no? So either you call and – what do you call it? – push off the meeting.'

'Put it back. No, not a good idea. Things are disorganized enough as it is.'

'Or we drive non-stop and if we arrive early, we have time for a rest in the hotel. Or a swim on the beach.'

I took all this in. Dusk, I find, is the most tiring time to drive. I can't judge distances, and the dimming light seems to lull my senses to sleep. In any case, the interstate 95 was turning out to be one of the most soporific roads in the world. With its anonymous white surface, paved in blocks so that our tyres drummed out an endless, hypnotic badum-badum, badum-badum rhythm, and its non-stop fringe of woodland, it was like an infinite driveway to a chateau that never appears.

Only the changing registration plates gave us any idea where we were – the thinning out of Virginians, the growing mass of Carolinans, the rising number of migrating Quebeckers, and the increasing urgency of the speeding Floridians as they got closer to home.

The radio had also lost some of its appeal. I'd now heard every single rock record made between 1963 and 1980, and after the fourth or fifth play of 'Hotel California' I could sing every note of the guitar solo. Even the local ad segments had begun to drag. When you drive right through a state, you end up knowing all its best places to buy paint, and who to contact to get great new deals on car insurance. You start to talk along with the ads as well as singing the hits.

This was why the idea of another twelve straight hours on the road was even less of a turn-on than our coughing landlady of the night before.

'What will we do? Divide it up into two-hour stretches?' I said.

'Hmm, I am not sure. The problem is, Paul, you are certain that if I drive alone, I will get lost and take us to Canada.'

'That's not true.'

She held up the atlas to silence me, as if it contained the proof of her allegation.

'I am also very tired, like you,' she said. 'I have done half the driving today. Or more. And it is, after all, because of you, because you took us to Cape Moose—'

'Cape May.'

'Whatever. You took us there without having consulted me, and made us stop there for fourteen hours. And then you took us to visit Washington.'

'I thought you enjoyed that.'

The atlas was solemnly raised again.

'OK, but it put on two hours to the trip.'

'So?' I could feel there was a major 'so' coming up.

'So, even if I am prepared to do some driving tonight, I think it is not fair if I do half. If you fall asleep and I turn the wrong way—'

'You can't turn the wrong way, it's just straight south on the same road.'

'Ah, no.' This time the atlas was actually opened for me at chapter and verse. 'I have understood the numbers written next to the roads. The little blue ones are the *sorties*, the exits. And the numbers start again in every state. And from the moment we enter Florida, there are three hundred and eighty exits before Miami. Three hundred and eighty possibilities for me to go wrong.'

Bloody atlas, I thought. I should never have bought the stupid thing.

'And if I turn the wrong way,' she went on, 'you will be angry and say it is my fault you are late, when it will be fundamentally your fault. And so I think that you must *assume*.'

'Assume?'

'Yes, how do you say it? Accept your responsibilities. This is what feminism is about, Paul. Equal rights and respect for women, but also equal responsibilities for men. You must *assume*. In this case, you must assume more of the driving.'

'Oh, come on, Alexa, we're in this together, aren't we?'

'It's your job, Paul, you're the one getting paid. Perhaps you should have come with a professional driver.'

A professional driver? I thought about this, and realized that my American journey was teaching me a hell of a lot about life. Before that conversation, I'd never imagined that there really would be occasions when you wished your girlfriend was a trucker.

'But if I drive all night, I might kill us both,' I said.

'Well, it won't hurt me. I'll be asleep. Goodnight.'

MIAMI

Go Ahead, Merde My Day

1

THE FIRST RAYS OF MORNING sunlight were hitting the hugest Stars and Stripes I'd seen on the trip so far, and that was saying something. This one was big enough to be the bedspread for a pair of humpback whales.

The flag was hanging from a taut cable that stretched the length of a car sales lot. Each star was at least a foot tall, and the stripes had been elongated to give a kind of red-and-white-toothpaste effect.

The car lot covered a whole block that ended in a set of traffic lights. As I stopped for the red, I squinted up at the glowing stars on the gigantic American flag, and even this cynical Brit was filled with a sudden desire to spread the message of democracy across the un-free world. Or at the very least buy a Chevrolet. Too bad that the cars lined up beneath the flag were all Korean.

It was something that I hadn't yet got my head around. Americans are so patriotic when you talk to them, but offer them a Korean car that's a few dollars cheaper than an American one and they don't hesitate for an instant.

We were in the low-rise outer suburbs of Palm Beach. I'd turned off the main highway a couple of hours earlier to avoid falling asleep in the sense-deadening twilight. This road running down the east coast of Florida seemed to have been conceived in an attempt to get into *The Guinness Book of Records* for having the world's longest series of traffic lights, but at least the constant stopping and starting gave me something to do.

The lights also gave me a crick in my neck that was turning into a full-blown muscular spasm. The Mini was designed by Europeans for our low-hanging, street-level traffic lights. In the USA, home of the overhead light, the car needed to be fitted with a periscope.

'It's green,' a half-awake voice mumbled beside me. Parisians are genetically programmed to sense the microsecond the light turns green, even when they're asleep.

'*Bonjour*,' I said. 'I was going to wait till the car in front pulled away before I accelerated, but thanks for letting me know.'

Alexa was too groggy to react to anti-Parisian irony.

'Maybe you can find a place for breakfast?' she said.

The Stars and Stripes seemed to have had an effect on her, too. Subliminal appetite enhancement.

'Can't you hold on till we get to Miami?' I asked. 'It's only an hour or so away.'

'But your rendezvous is not before eleven. It's very early, no?'

'True.' I quite fancied a cup of coffee or five myself. I found that I needed three bladderfuls of the typical American brew to get the same hit as a double espresso.

A mile further on, we found a mall that was decorated with the usual batch of lollipop-like signs for drive-thru everything – pharmacies, doughnuts, banks. Soon there would be a drive-thru plastic surgeon here. Sit back in your seat while we pump in the silicone and suck out the fat. You don't even need to undo your seatbelt.

Though in reality this was a fairly downmarket mall. Not the kind of place for a plastic surgeon. Between a discount shoe shop and a shuttered drugstore there was a small window with signs telling people that they could pop in, cash cheques and 'avoid foreclosure, keep your home'. Not everyone in South Florida spent their days golfing, fishing and getting boob jobs, it seemed.

The car park was pretty empty, but like the American driver I'd become, I wanted to reduce wear and tear on my legs to a minimum. I also thought it wise to keep my eyes on our luggage while we were away from the car, so I drove along the front line looking for a spot right outside the shops. The first available space was beside a gigantic black pick-up – a dusty, flat-backed 4×4 with wheels almost as tall as the Mini. Standing together, the two vehicles looked as though a toddler and a basketball player were comparing shoe sizes.

We got out, stretched, and took off lots of clothes. It felt like an English midsummer dawn. As Alexa pulled off her sweatshirt, she was staring up at the giant truck.

'Huh, the driver of that monster must stop at every single gas station on the road,' she said.

'You can ask him how many miles to the gallon he gets if you want.' I nodded as discreetly as possible at a couple who were staggering straight towards us.

They were tangle-haired, ghost-white, and wore jeans and sleeveless T-shirts that hung off their bony frames. Their arms were graffiti'd with smudgy black writing, and the man had a clumsily inked spider's web pattern on his upper chest that made him look as if he'd been

160

squirted while trying to kiss a terrified octopus.

'Hey, wotchoo doon tar fuggen truck?' the woman shouted. She obviously couldn't see the Mini beyond her skyscraper of a vehicle.

The man lifted his sunburnt skeleton face towards Alexa and me, but didn't react.

'They tranna steal are fuggen truck!' the woman yelled at him. She had what sounded to me like a Deep South accent, though this was no Scarlett O'Hara. Unless Scarlett had spent the last century or so on a diet of booze and smoking materials.

'No, no, we're just parking our car.' I gave her my poshest English accent. In my experience, no American would believe that a member of the royal family could be a car thief.

'Oh *yeah*?' From the aggression in her voice, I guessed she wasn't a royalist. 'Well yalkan gitcher fuggen hands offenar fuggen truck thin.'

They were now within kicking distance of us, and close up they didn't look too appetizing. Dental hygiene had not been one of their priorities in life. And the whites of most people's eyes usually have some white left in them, rather than this scarlet and yellow marbling effect.

'*Putain, elle est folle*,' Alexa whispered, telling me in French that, fuck, the woman was nuts. Not that I needed to be told.

'Waddat bitch jess sayda me?' the woman spat.

I moved out from behind the Mini and, rather gallantly I thought, put myself between Alexa and her conversation partner.

'We're just stopping for a cup of coffee, folks,' I assured them. 'We've been driving all night.'

'Waddat fuggen bitch jess sayda me?' The woman did not want to change the subject just yet. The man dumped a flatpack of beer in the back of their truck and came to put a comforting arm on his partner's bony shoulder.

'C'mon babe,' he cooed. ''Sokay. She's *Canadian*.'

He had obviously perfected his technique for calming his wife or girlfriend over many years of confrontations. The woman's tense body relaxed almost immediately. She glowered one last time at Alexa, called her a 'fuggen bitch' again, then appeared to forget her completely. They climbed up into their truck and it rattled away with a farewell belch of grey smoke.

Alexa stood and watched them with open-mouthed shock. Not because of the woman's aggression. It was the first time anyone had ever accused her of being a Quebecker, and it hurt.

2

Alexa was probably the first person to read the whole diner menu since the guy who wrote it. Even the printer would have glossed over most of it, but Alexa was browsing through the entire selection of goodies on offer.

'Low-fat omelette,' she read out. 'Only three eggs with low-fat cheese and sour cream. *Only* three eggs? With *only* French fries? And *only* a chocolate milkshake? Oh, and there is a scary kids' breakfast. *Junior* French toast, with eggs, fries and blueberry-flavoured pancakes. Wow. You eat that every morning and you will be obliged to buy one of those enormous trucks to carry you.'

She then undermined her social comment by ordering a breakfast twice as calorie-stuffed as anything she'd just read out. A wildly misnamed 'short' stack of pancakes that would probably satisfy a whole French family at Mardi Gras, one side order of fried bacon, another of wheatmeal toast, and a fried egg that she ordered just for the pleasure of saying 'sunny side up'. I'm sure it made her feel as if we really were living out *Thelma and Louise*.

This diner was not a movie set. The waitresses were small Hispanic women wrapped in uniforms of beige nylon. There weren't many customers at the equally beige tables, and the women spent most of their time in a huddle by the counter, chatting softly in Spanish to a pair of guys who were making pancakes and slicing meat. The only décor in the place was a row of chrome-framed posters advertising the various big-brand drinks on sale. Even the music was boring – a dim jangly sound suggested that somewhere there was a radio playing guitar music, but it was too far away to tell what style exactly, let alone what song.

Two large white mugs of coffee arrived on our table just as the sunlight suddenly broke into the parking lot outside. Car roofs shone like coloured pebbles in a pond, and even the scattering of scrawny trees 'landscaping' the tarmac looked somehow more tropical and luxuriant.

I did my best to soak up the enlivening effects of both coffee and sunlight. I knew that down in Miami I was going to need not just physical energy but diplomatic strength, too. I mean, even the Dunfermline tourist office doesn't talk about Dunfermline. It tells visitors that they've got lost and should go back to Edinburgh.

A painful sense of foreboding took root somewhere behind my eyeballs. If I wasn't careful, the Miami Scots were going to give me as many headaches as the bolshy Boston Irish.

'Why do they hate us so much?' I asked Alexa.

'Who?' she said.

'The Scots and the Irish. What have they got against the English?'

She stopped piling bacon on to her toast and looked at

me as if I'd just asked her why the French love croissants.

'You really need to ask? It's like Mike said – you starved lots of Irish people to death. And I think you massacred plenty of Scottish people, and took their farms, no?'

'True, true. But that's ancient history. These days, I think the real problem is that we English don't form clubs like they do. Why are there no Anglo-American dancing societies in Florida? We could have had a display of Morris dancing.'

'Morse dancing?' I understood why Alexa looked confused. In French, '*morse*' means walrus.

No, I explained, Morris dancing did not usually feature aquatic mammals. I did my best to reconstruct childhood memories of bearded men, flowery hats, bells on knees, and hey nonny no's around a ribbon-tressed maypole.

Alexa chewed meditatively on her bacon sandwich, trying to picture what I had described.

'From what you say, Paul, I personally thank God that there are no Morris dancing societies in Florida. I have never heard of anything less sexy in my life. If you do one of those dances, I will never have sex with you again. Ah, thank you.'

She held out her mug to a tiny waitress who had come by with the coffee pot. The young girl gave no sign that she'd heard – or understood – Alexa's threat to me. It was as if she was moving through a parallel universe whose only physical contact with our own cosmos was via empty coffee cups. She filled both of our mugs and resumed her slow, blank tour of the tables.

'That reminds me,' Alexa went on. 'You think they have whiffy here?'

I smiled. One day I was going to have to tell her how to pronounce 'wi-fi'. Not yet, though.

'How does not having sex with me remind you that you want to check your mail?' I asked.

She blushed. 'It doesn't.'

'But you just said it did.'

'I didn't.'

'You said, "I will never have sex with you again. That reminds me, you think they have whiffy here?" So there seems to be a link somewhere in your subconscious between the internet and me not being shaggable. Have you become addicted to online sex?'

I thought I was teasing, but Alexa took me seriously.

'It was only a what do you call it? A thing of speech. Like "by the way" or something. And I don't know why you are so aggressive with me just because I want to read my email.'

I apologized. Of course I didn't think there was really a link between a lack of sex with me and her emails. Being on the road together, so close for so many waking hours, had made me hypersensitive to what she was thinking and feeling. I went to ask the waitresses about wi-fi.

Unsurprisingly, our beige diner wasn't hooked up, but one of the girls told me in heavily accented English that if we went a mile down the road and parked outside a certain chain hotel, then we could surf for free. We wouldn't even need a password, she said. All her friends did it, so they could chat to their families back home.

I was impressed. These new immigrants were getting the most out of modern America, just like those first pilgrims who discovered that the continent offered unlimited free turkeys.

3

The hotel was bright pink, as if it had spent all its life lying by the highway getting sunburnt. I tucked the Mini into a corner of the parking lot as far away from the reception doors as possible, alongside four other vehicles with one or two people gazing intently at their laps. It was the internet version of Lovers' Lane.

As if to confirm this, Alexa announced that she was going to get in the back with the luggage. I asked her why she didn't just sit beside me.

'I will bump you with my elbows when I type,' she said, and set about digging herself a foxhole in the heap of stuff back there.

I flipped open my laptop and logged on.

'Welcome, valued guest.' The hotel's website invited me to have brunch on the poolside patio. Hypocritically, I accepted their welcome and logged on.

My first email was from Jake, a quick note telling me that he was 'coming in America very soon' and asking, 'Can you please pass me your coordinates for when you will be in Florida.' My coordinates. It was classic Jake. I knew that he wasn't trying to find me with his satellite location system. He wanted my 'coordonnées', my address and contact info. He was going to need some English lessons before coming back to his homeland, I thought, otherwise no one would understand him. Except perhaps the golfing Quebeckers.

I replied, truthfully, that I had no idea where I would be staying. My contact in Miami was setting it all up. I looked at my watch. It would soon be time to call my man Jesus. I'd phoned him the previous day and he had been annoyingly laid back about where to meet. He said he never knew where he was going to be before he got there, making himself sound as trustworthy as a blind taxi-driver.

Next on the list was a message from Elodie in New York. She'd decided to come down to Miami to see a friend of hers who was marketing director of the local Alliance

Française – a French language school and cultural institute. She wanted to know exactly when I would be arriving in the city, and what my event was. I gave her as many details as I could.

Finally, there was an email that had me groaning as if Alexa and I had parked for a more traditional reason.

My old boss in London, Charlie, had forwarded a link to a gay website called Men in Skirts. Why he thought I'd be interested in that, I didn't know. But his curt message said, 'as dark horses go you're jet black paul my son', which made me curious enough to click further.

A few seconds later, my groaning – along with a fair bit of swearing – began. Because there, filling the screen, was one of those photos that your best man hands out to cause maximum embarrassment during your wedding reception. The drunken idiot leers at the camera with a beer can superglued to his penis.

I hadn't been drunk at all, and there were no beer cans involved, but it was almost as bad.

The fact that there was a perfectly logical reason why I was wearing a tartan mini-skirt was no consolation. Neither was the banner headline announcing that I'd been voted the website's 'undercarriage of the month', a title I didn't understand until I looked closely and saw that the madwoman's kilt had been so short that there was a distinct bulge of white underpant hanging below my hemline. As bad luck would have it, I'd been wearing tight jockey shorts that day instead of boxers. But at least I hadn't done things the genuine Scottish way and worn nothing under the kilt.

And the worst thing was that, judging by the list of forwardees at the top of Charlie's message, the link was already doing the rounds of corporate England. I'd never be able to show my legs in a pub again.

'I can explain,' I wanted to reply, but it would have done

no good. The evidence was there – Paul West likes to dress up as some kind of kinky Scottish waitress and flash for the camera.

The question was, how the hell had this photo escaped from the London madwoman's camera into the wilds of the web? The site didn't elucidate. It just said that here was one Englishman who was willing to give his all for his country, and begged browsers to send in my email address, or better still my phone number, so they could post them alongside the photo.

I replied to Charlie that if he forwarded the Men in Skirts link to anyone else he would lose various key parts of his anatomy, and then fired off an email to Jack Tyler begging him to have all photos of me erased from every camera and computer in the land. My laptop told me 'message sent' and I slumped back, suddenly exhausted again.

'Are you OK?' Alexa asked from the back seat.

'Er, yeah, fine.' After her jibe about unsexy Morris dancers, I didn't think the time was right to show her my knobbly-kneed alter ego. 'Get any interesting messages?'

'No. You?'

'No, nothing.'

We'd both spent a long time reading and replying to nothing.

4

As Alexa drove us even further south, I made my call.

'Rodriguez,' a Hispanic man answered.

'Hi, it's Paul West.'

'Uh?'

'Paul West? We're due to meet up this morning?' I felt

that adopting the American way of giving out information as a series of questions might help the message get through. Especially because, as far as I could hear, I was competing for his attention with a massed salsa band.

'Oh, yeah. Hey, no problem. You in Miami?'

'No, about an hour north,' I yelled above a trombone solo. 'Where do you want to meet up?'

'Oh. In an hour? Wow.' Looking that far into the future seemed to be as painful as getting a nipple pierced. 'Which way you coming in?'

'From the north?' I pronounced this as a double question, as in, didn't you hear me using the word 'north' earlier, and if you did, do you understand it?

'Right. But you gonna go via downtown or drive along North Beach?' Which was also pronounced as a double question – are you stupid or do you just think I am?

'Oh. I don't know. North Beach sounds good.'

'OK, meet me in South Beach. You know Ocean Drive?'

'No, but I can find it.'

'OK, see you there.'

'Great. What number?'

'I don't know.'

'You don't *know*?' This conversation was starting to make my undercarriage ache.

'I'm not sure. There's a couple places I hang out. I'll be somewhere between fourteenth and tenth. Look out for a yellow Porsche Cayman S. You know the Cayman S?'

'No. How many wheels does it have?'

'Uh?'

'No, I don't know the Cayman S. Doesn't it look like all other Porsches?'

'Oh no, dude.' With the salsa band as a backing track, he went on to describe his car's distinctive curves, its horse-power, its price, and the kind of women it attracted.

'So you'll be sitting in the car?' I interrupted.

'Ha, no, dude.' Apparently, now that we'd steered the conversation on to cars and women, we were *dudes* together. 'I'll be hangin at one of the cafés there.' By his testicles from the ceiling, I hoped. 'You in a Mini, right?' he asked.

'Yes.' I was flattered he'd remembered that much about me.

'Cool. What engine she got?'

I guessed a plausible number of horsepower.

'Wo. Cool. She's fast, uh?'

'Yes.' I invented a top speed that would have got me deported from America if I'd tried to use it.

'Way to go!' This seemed to excite Jesus more than anything I'd said so far. 'What colour is she?'

I gave a description of the car's red-blooded body and proud-to-be-British roof, trying to be more accurate than I had been with the horsepower.

'You pay extra for the flag?'

'No,' I said, wishing we could end this shouted conversation about our respective vehicles, which was making Alexa sneer as women do when men start showing their testosterone in public.

'I never saw one with a flag before. Least you be easy to spot. Later, dude.'

We cruised along the coast with the sun rising higher to our left and the flow of vehicles getting heavier at every junction. But to a northerner, even a minor traffic jam feels like heaven when the sun is out and everyone's driving in their shades. The Mini had been an interloper on the northern highways, but felt totally at home down here – Thelma was a sunshine girl, not a fog-dweller.

The road signs pointed to some intriguing places. What could there be at Hypoluxo, I wondered, a Greek brothel?

Gumbo Limbo Nature Center sounded like an elephants' yoga park, and Boca Raton was obviously a hideous new name given to a town to discourage anyone else from moving there.

But I could understand why people were flocking to Florida. Every other town was called something beach. Boynton Beach, Pompano Beach, Dania Beach. The road signs kept trying to entice us to turn and make for the ocean.

It was after we did so, following the sign for Miami Beach, that we hit trouble.

'*Merde alors.*' Alexa braked suddenly, slowing to the pace of the dense traffic ahead of us. She started to laugh.

I wanted to cry. The whole horizon was a mass of Minis. Solid-tops and convertibles, new Minis with their raised rear haunches, old ones looking like egg boxes on toy wheels, Minis of every colour in the paint-spray spectrum.

'What the fur?' I began, before seeing a banner that answered my question. One of the flood of Minis ahead was flying a flag which informed us that our path was blocked by the 'Miaminis', obviously some kind of car fan club. They were hooting and swerving with self-delight, as if this might attract even more attention to them than the mere fact of being the biggest collection of small cars on the American continent. I wondered what the collective noun for this gathering should be. A nip of Minis? A buzz? No, I decided, a hobbit. It reminded me of a scene from one of the *Lord of the Rings* films, the army of hobbits rushing through a forest of giant trees – the trees here being the towering hotels that had sprung up beside the highway. We were now just one block back from the beach.

'Here is who should organize your event,' Alexa said,

smiling across at the woman driver of an orange convertible Mini who was nodding her appreciation of our paint job.

We were sucked into the herd, or hobbit, and in true American style, everyone was being overwhelmingly friendly. Drivers were waving, grinning, giving the thumbs up, all deliriously happy about being together.

Alexa was right – these people would definitely have been more pro-English than my Hispanic Porsche driver. But if, as I suspected, they were planning to keep up the celebrations right down through South Beach, poor old Jesus was going to get one hell of a surprise. He'd be looking out for a single 'unmissable' Mini and would end up staring over the heads of a tribe of them. Knowing my luck, the Mini parade would meet up with the Yellow Porsche Owners' Club, and we would be totally screwed.

'Can't you speed up a bit and overtake them all?' I begged Alexa. One lane of the wide boulevard seemed to have been reserved for people who wanted to drive straight and slightly faster between bouts of swerving around.

'Why not?' she said, and hit the accelerator.

With Parisian effortlessness, she careered over to the right-hand lane, causing only three or four Mini drivers to slam on their brakes. Staying in the (relatively) fast track, we started to move past the pack. As we did so, drivers of the usual gigantic American personal vehicles flashed their lights in mock fury as they waited to get out of hotel car parks, and a pair of old, bearded rabbis stared as if we were a visitation from either heaven or hell.

We drove this way for a couple of miles, and my maps and guidebook suggested no way of branching off and getting ahead. It was one straight run along the boulevard to South Beach.

'We're going to have to pull off and let them pass,' I said. 'I'll call Hay-zooss and tell him to ignore the first hundred Minis he sees.'

Suddenly a break in the tower blocks appeared on our left. It was a large car park set between two high-rise hotels. Alexa did some more French swerving and got us in without causing a major pile-up. She found a space, turned the engine off, and we sat back, letting the cool ocean breeze wash over us.

'Hey, bro,' a voice said through my open window. I turned and looked into a hole. Fortunately, seeing a hole in mid-air was no more surreal than getting caught up in a hobbit of Minis, so I didn't faint when I realized that the hole was the barrel of a gun.

A gun? A real, live gun? No, I couldn't believe it. It looked like a strangely shaped TV remote. It was the same silvery colour, and had similar stylish curves. It appeared much smaller in real life than the ones you see in the films, too. But then, I reasoned, so does Tom Cruise, and he's scary enough.

'I want you car, bro,' the gun-owner said, his voice soft and calm. He was a handsome young Black guy with pilot's sunglasses and smooth, light skin.

'Our car?' I asked.

'Yeah. Get out the car now.'

I looked across at Alexa, who was gazing into the barrel of the gun with exactly the same expression of shocked disbelief as me.

We got out, keeping our hands in view like they do in the films. Even the intellectual Alexa would have to admit that she'd learnt something useful from American crime movies.

'I can't believe you want this little car,' I said. 'Isn't it more profitable to take Hummers and Porsches and that kind of thing?'

'Paul, please shut up,' Alexa hissed.

The dark sunglasses seemed to X-ray me.

'No way, bro,' the gunman finally said. 'No one want that big shit no more, Hummers an shit. They use too much gas, you know wham sayin? Price of gas juss kill that muthfuckin bidness. Small cars and them new hybrids, they the way to go, you know wham sayin? No one want that big shit no more.'

'Right.' I felt I ought to thank him for this lecture on eco-trends in the carjacking trade. 'No chance of keeping our backpacks, is there?' I asked. 'British passports probably aren't worth that much on the black market.' His gun seemed to flinch. I definitely did. 'Er, not that *black* market is in any way—'

'Paul, please shut up.' Alexa didn't care about the colour of markets. She just wanted to survive.

'Yeah, listen to your girlfriend, bro. Shut the fuck up. I'm getting patient here.'

I guessed that he meant '*im*patient', but I wasn't going to quibble about his accent.

'Right. Sorry. There's not much petrol – I mean, gas – left, but—'

'Shut the fuck up, bro.'

The carjacker was just about to take possession of his new vehicle at last when a mournful wailing sound cut through the blustering wind. All three of us turned as the sound grew stronger, and we two males uttered a simultaneous 'Holy shit.' We even – I think – bonded in a moment of shared bemusement.

Like the cavalry ambling confidently over the horizon in an old Western, a column of hooting Minis was advancing slowly towards us between the rows of parked cars. The 'Miamini' banner was flying high above a gleaming blue Cooper S. One of the cars in the front row was identical to ours – red with a Union Jack roof – but a vintage model. The father rescuing his lost son.

The carjacker looked from the oncoming Minis to me, from his gun to the oncoming cars again. 'Fuck dat shit,' he said. He sprinted away across the parking lot and jumped into a black 4×4 that immediately screeched off north. The carjacker hadn't extended his eco-principles to his getaway car, I noted. Presumably for getaway cars the priority was power rather than fuel consumption.

Our backs were slapped, our hands shaken, and Alexa received a hug from the woman who had been driving the orange convertible. We were assured that the police would be called, the 'no-good motherfucker' would be caught, and that Florida wasn't usually like this.

'Except for the sun, that is,' a guy with a neatly clipped beard chipped in. He was wearing a T-shirt with an English pound note on the front. He introduced himself as Tony, the president of Miamini. 'Like Blair, right?' He said this with a huge smile on his face, as if it was the best thing in the world to share a name with a British politician.

'A 1968 racing-green Austin Mini saw you were in trouble and we all came back to help out,' the orange-convertible woman said.

'What a great year that was,' I told her.

Standing in the wind tunnel between the two big hotels, Alexa and I told our life stories, retraced our route from New York, and pleaded ignorance about the age and exact model number of our car.

'It's not a standard model, though, right?' Tony asked me. 'That flag, I mean?'

He was stroking his chin like an antiques expert who's found suspiciously new-looking hinges on a supposedly medieval trunk.

'No, we got it painted on in New York.'

'You'd have done better getting the standard flag livery.'

'You can get it standard?'

'Oh yeah. Didn't you know?' Tony said, pleased to impart this vital information.

Another bloody cock-up by Visitor Bloody Resources Bloody Britain, I thought. Well done, Tyler.

'Yours is wrong, see,' Tony said.

'No, it can't be. I had to get it repainted because they did it wrong the first time.'

'Sorry, but it is. You have to look at the flag from the viewpoint of the driver as he gets in the car. That's when it should be the right way up. But yours is upside-down when you go to open the driver door. Look.' As if to show me, he bent down and gripped the door handle, gazing theatrically across the painted roof as he did so. 'Upside-down. You're a Brit, surely you noticed that?'

An audience of three or four other Mini-drivers nodded and hummed at his wisdom. Of course, like 99.9 per cent of Brits I have no idea which way up our flag should be. How typical, I thought, that Britain should have the only flag in the world that can provoke an argument about whether it's the right way up or not. Even the Australians don't have that problem, and their whole bloody country's upside-down.

'Maybe they painted it that way because I'm English, and they expected I'd be driving from the passenger seat,' I said.

They all laughed at the eccentric notion that cars should have steering wheels on the right, and then the police turned up and things got serious.

The cops were two surprisingly skinny White guys with crew cuts and the cleanest uniforms, shiniest belts and biggest guns I'd ever seen in my life. They wore walkie-talkies clipped high on their shoulders as if they needed to be in constant contact with their collar bones.

They talked Alexa and me through our meeting with the carjacker. Their questions made me feel as if it was our fault for leaving our windows open. And when they heard that we hadn't reserved any accommodation in Miami, I thought they were going to take us up to the state line and dump us in Alabama.

'Can I see your passport, Sir? Madam?' cop number one asked. He looked exactly like his buddy except that he had a short pink scar on his cheek and bigger biceps.

'What is the motive of your visit to Miami, Sir?' asked cop number two.

Motive, I thought. Now they really think we're criminals.

'I work for the British tourist authority,' I said. 'I'm here to do a promotional event.'

'But these are tourist visas,' the one with the scar and the biceps said.

Both sets of police eyebrows were raised. They'd got me now.

'I'm not getting paid dollars or anything,' I said. 'I'm not working for an American company and taking an American's job.'

'But you're working on a tourist visa.'

It's not my fault, I wanted to say for the umpteenth time on this trip. Tyler had told me that I didn't have time for the hassle of getting a work visa. And now, thanks to him, I was going to get deported and lose everything.

Luckily we had back-up. The other Mini-owners were there to plead for clemency, offer us and our car places to stay, and give contact details in case the cops needed help identifying the carjacker.

After half an hour, we were told we were free to go. I felt as if I'd been acquitted of murder.

Though by this time I was afraid Jesus would have given

up on us. No problem, Tony told me. He went over to his car to make a phone call, and a couple of minutes later he returned with his beaming smile covering half his face.

'Yellow Porsche Cayman S parked up on the corner of Ocean Drive and Eleventh,' he said. 'Owner has been identified and informed of your imminent arrival. There will be a cream 1980 Clubman in a slot two cars behind the Porsche. As you approach, it will move away and leave you free to park.'

This guy should have been organizing not only my event in Miami but the whole tour of the USA, I decided. He'd have written me a schedule accurate to the last millisecond. I'd tell him the exact size of soundproofed bed I wanted in each town, and the room would be found. In fact, he was so much more pro-British than any Englishman I'd ever met that he deserved to have my job. I really ought to call Suraya and tell her I was outsourcing myself.

5

I took over the wheel for our final mile, and as I drove into South Beach with my escort of excitable Minis, my first thought was, hey, they've painted my Great Aunt Caroline's building a funny colour. She used to live in a block of flats near Wembley Stadium, the only Art Deco building in a sea of suburbia.

This, though, was a whole Art Deco *city*. Practically every building looked like the upper decks of an ocean liner stranded on the beach. What's more, they'd raided the paint catalogue and splashed colours about with no regard for matching tones and subtle combinations. It was Cape May on cocaine. Purple porticos above blood-orange doors, coral-pink window frames curving around deep-blue corners, green plaster waves etched into yellow facades. And those were just the small hotels. Beachside, the same themes were repeated on ten- or fifteen-storey towers, making the oceanfront look like a display of gigantic coloured meringues.

It was no lifeless architecture museum, either. Everyone and everything seemed to be in 'look at me' mode. The proportion of open-top cars and customized pick-ups had suddenly shot up. Hip, tanned people stepped out of the Art Deco buildings and looked around as if they were expecting to be filmed. Tightly clothed butts of both sexes swayed along the sidewalks. You could almost hear the daiquiris being mixed in the hotel bars. This place, I decided, was going to be fun.

'*Franchement*, Paul.' Alexa was shaking her head.

'*Franchement*', or 'frankly', is France's most serious way of expressing disapproval. If someone lets their dog poo on your new Chanel shoes, '*franchement*' is what you'll say before you kick the dog and smear the merde on the owner. It implies total disbelief at their lack of *savoir vivre*.

'*Franchement*,' she continued, 'we were almost shot because of you.'

Ah yes, the gun and all that. The buzz of arriving in sun-drenched South Beach had almost made me forget about the bad things in life. And we hadn't actually set eyes on the ocean yet, so it was lucky she'd reminded me now. I knew from experience that as soon as I spotted my first blue, swimmable wave, all negative thoughts would be washed from my mind.

'Sorry,' I said. 'It was just my way of panicking.'

'This country, it is all so . . . so *precarious*.' 'Precarious' is another of France's worst insults. The French are so used to jobs for life and general prosperity that anything precarious scares them to death. Whereas of course *every* job in the

USA and the UK is so precarious that we take instability in our stride.

'I thought you were starting to like it here?' I said.

'Yes. Yes.' She nodded, apparently envisaging her most recent short stack of pancakes. 'I was starting to feel at home, but I forgot. Under the surface, it is, it is so . . .'

'*Franchement* precarious?' I suggested.

'I forgot about the guns, the crime.'

'They steal tourists' cars in Paris, too, don't forget.'

'Yes, but not with guns.'

No, I thought, they just loot the contents and set light to the vehicle.

'And we have a lot of gun crime in the UK these days,' I said.

'Not as much as here, I think.'

'That's just because knives are cheaper.'

'Paul, how can you joke? Do you think this will be good for your campaign? The British tourist ambassador is attacked in Florida, so vote for England?'

This hadn't occurred to me, but it sounded like a pretty damn good idea. I'd have to get Suraya on to it.

'Sorry,' I said yet again. Well, they do say it's an Englishman's favourite word. 'It must be the shock. He was pointing it at *my* head, you know.'

'Yes.' She put a comforting hand on my arm. It was cold, I noticed. She was suffering from shock. She needed a good old English cup of tea.

I wondered why I felt so calm and anger-free about the whole nearly-getting-killed business. And what I saw, felt and heard around me held the simple answer. We were stopped in traffic outside a bright-purple hotel with parasols soaking up the sun on its café terrace. A short-skirted, silky-legged waitress was standing on the sidewalk waiting for customers, her head and body slowly rocking to the Latino beat that was oozing out of the building. Death or the threat of it just did not exist. This was life.

'We have to try and forget what *might* have gone wrong,' I said. 'We got out of it safely, and he didn't steal Thelma. That's all that matters. Besides, I'm more worried about what's *about* to go wrong.'

I turned on to Ocean Drive and began looking for the yellow Porsche. I was distracted, though, by the view on my left. Beyond a line of palm trees and the low hump of a dune, there – suddenly – was the wind-whipped ocean. I whistled as a bricklayer might do at a mini-skirt passing his building site. This was one sexy sea. I hadn't seen water that blue since they used to tint postcards of Bournemouth to make the English Channel look like the Indian Ocean. Two days ago I'd been looking at grimy ice, and now this?

'Paul!' Alexa forced me to look roadwards again, just as I was about to hammer into the back of a little Mini estate with fake wood panelling on its rear doors. A 1980 Mini Clubman. This was our rendezvous.

Our escort of five or six Miaminis filed slowly past, and we waved and smiled our gratitude to all of them. Last in line was Tony's car. He stopped and lowered his passenger window.

'See you later, Paul. Alexa. Give me a call if you need me.'

'Thanks again, Tony,' I said. 'You saved our lives.' For once it wasn't an empty phrase.

6

Jesus was sitting under a fake-palm-tree parasol. He had his legs spread wide, a phone jammed against his right ear and sunglasses pushed up like a hairband on his ultra-dark, short curls. His eyes were apparently trying to hypnotize every passing woman into admiring the large Porsche keyring on his table. He was thirty, maybe thirty-five, and clearly spent most of his life toning his muscles, topping up his tan and staring at himself in a mirror.

'Yeah babe, yeah babe, I be dare. Six o'clock. I be dare babe. Ciao.' He flipped his mobile shut, and I wondered why he had such existential problems pinning himself down to meet me at a certain time and place, but no trouble at all promising to see someone tonight. The answer was obvious. I wasn't a babe.

'Hay-zooss?'

'Yeah?' He looked up warily.

'Paul West.' I held out my hand.

It took him no more than five seconds to remember who the hell I was.

'Hey, Paul. Wassup, dude!' He stood up, grabbed my hand, pulled me against him until our nipples were rubbing, and slapped me heartily on the back. We must have been army pals in a former existence. 'Wo, how was your drive down, man?'

'Oh, fine.' I didn't feel like going into the carjacking story.

'That your car? Cool. There's mine. What you think?'

'Cool,' I told him.

'Yeah, cool, dude. Siddown.'

'This is Alexa.' He'd already noticed her, of course, and had run his eyes over every inch of her body.

'Hey, Alexa, great to meet you.' He shook her hand formally, bowing like a prince at a garden party, and then looked away as a girl in a bikini top shimmied past. I could see the affront in Alexa's eyes.

'You had breakfast?' Jesus pronounced it almost as a French person would – 'brek-fass'.

'Yes,' I said.

'No,' Alexa said, no doubt wanting to punish the guy by ordering something at his expense.

Jesus laughed and turned towards a tall, coffee-skinned girl in a white shirt and short black skirt who was keying something into the café's ordering system.

'Hey, Yooliana, we get some menus?' Jesus called out. He gave the girl his most loving smile. She finished her keying and ambled over with a small sheaf of menus. Her hips swung so far from side to side that I was sure she was going to slam the tables over as she walked. The only stable part of her seemed to be her pierced belly button. If this was the general standard of waitresses in South Beach, I thought, I'd be spending my whole time here eating and drinking.

The café was as sexy as its waiting staff. It occupied the forecourt of yet another Art Deco hotel, a long, sky-blue four-storey building with what looked like a bright-pink air-traffic-control tower poking up in the middle of its facade. The name was written down the sides of the control tower in purple neon lettering, unlit for the moment. Clearview, it said. An accurate description – from up there you would see nothing but blue Atlantic.

Jesus asked us about the trip so far, but kept flipping his phone open every three seconds to make sure he hadn't missed any calls or messages. In between flips he scanned the horizon for signs of female life. If any specimens came close enough, he called out a 'hey' to try and strike up a conversation. Alexa quickly gave up talking and glowered at him over the bagel and milkshake that she'd ordered.

'So, about the Scottish dancing?' I tried to lead the conversation towards practicalities.

'Hey, Clara!' Jesus called out to a small, curvy woman, who looked as if she was trying to save the world's fabric resources by buying clothes three sizes too small. Though by the look of her upper body, she had used up a fair chunk of the world's silicone stocks. They *had* to be false. Even so, Clara was, I had to concede, what most men would class as a babe. She had certainly been stocking up points on her loyalty card at the beautician's – her legs were as smooth and shiny as the paint job on a brand-new car. She stopped and smiled at Jesus.

'Come siddown,' he begged her, pulling up a chair. She obeyed coyly. 'This is Clara.'

Clara shook hands politely, frowned at the rumpledness of my clothes, and embarked on a long conversation with Jesus. It was in Spanish, but I understood all of it because it was also in the universal language of 'You never called, yes I did, no you didn't, OK I'm sorry let me make it up to you, OK you call me, yes I promise, mwa mwa, goodbye.'

As she shimmied off down the sidewalk, Jesus looked very pleased with life.

'About the dancing?' I reminded him.

'Oh yeah,' he said. 'We see them here tomorrow for brunch, OK?'

'Tomorrow? But the event is tonight, right?'

'Oh, no, iss tomorrow, dude, not tonight. No problem, man.'

This news was shocking enough to distract Alexa from her glowering and bagel-eating. 'Tomorrow?' she gasped. 'But we hurried—'

'Hey, Maria! Maria, yo!'

Jesus had lifted himself half out of his chair and was waving at a tall, light-skinned woman on the other side of the street. She had a barbed black tattoo around her bare white waist.

'Maria!' He mimed a prayer that she would stop, but she seemed to be out of the range of divine intervention.

Jesus sat down again, not in the least put out.

'So the event is tomorrow?' I reminded him.

184

'Yeah. One here, one close by and another, uh, somewhere else.'

'Three events?' I tried to work out whether this was good
or bad news. Pretty good, I decided. No, actually it was
astonishingly good. Three shows, three audiences, three
operations to report back to London, and all put together
by this guy who seemed unable to concentrate on any event
not directly related to his dick. 'So did the mayor's office set
all this up?' I asked.

'Uh? Mayor's office?' Jesus looked at me as if I'd
sprouted feathers.

'Yes, I understood that events here were being co-
ordinated by city hall?'

'City hall?' Now I had wings and a beak, too.

'You don't work for city hall?'

'What? No!' I had finally revealed my true identity as a
species of talking flamingo.

'Who do you work for, then?'

Grinning at the absurdity of my line of questioning, Jesus
produced a business card from the breast pocket of his
florid shirt. It was thick-grained, and had as much gold on
it as the bath taps at Buckingham Palace. Its embossed
calligraphy read, 'Jesus H. Rodriguez, Vice President of
Development, Golden Beach Realtors.'

'What's a realtor?' I asked. The opposite of a fake one, I
guessed, but that didn't help much.

'You donno?' Now I was a dunce even by flamingo
standards.

'No.'

'Real estate, man. We buy, we sell, we develop. This is
Miami, man. Welcome to the realty world.'

As his laughter cackled out across Ocean Drive, I
wondered why my events here were being organized by
an estate agent, a breed that usually comes just below

serial killers in the straight-talking and reliability charts.

'Everything here organized by the Cubans and the realtors,' Jesus said. 'And you lucky, you got yourself a Cuban realtor.' He gave us his cackle again. 'Don worry, man. We invited the people you want, the ones who suppose to vote for you.' At least he had some idea what the contest was about. 'And a realtor tell a politician to come to a party, he comes, man. He comes.' He flashed a con-spiratorial smile at Alexa, who met it with her full arsenal of Parisian disdain.

'Where are we sleeping?' she asked. 'I need to change my clothes and take a shower.' She stretched, taunting Jesus with a double eyeful of her straining T-shirt.

'Here.' Jesus poked a thumb over his shoulder towards the Clearview sign. 'Ask Yooliana, she show you your room. You go put on your bikini, catch some rays, yeah?'

'Jesus, baby!' A suntan on legs was swaying towards our table. She had long blond hair that hung in spikes as sharp as her stiletto heels, and was wearing (but only just) a halterneck top and skintight white jeans. She had three-foot-long eyelashes, and was carrying a pink leather handbag that looked barely big enough to hold a mini-vibrator. Jesus saw her, and leapt to his feet.

'Wow, baby,' he cooed. 'You incredible.' He took her hand and kissed it as if it had just written him a cheque for a billion dollars. 'I give you the honour of meeting Anna, my fiancée.'

I only just managed to stop myself laughing. *Fiancée*, I thought, did I hear right? Jesus was actually planning to stop chatting up other women long enough to say 'I do'?

'Nice to meet you, Anna,' Alexa said, giving the poor girl such a look of pity that she turned to check herself out in the hotel window to make sure her hair hadn't fallen out.

'Come, Paul, we must leave the happy couple alone. Jesus has been *so* impatient to see his fiancée.'

'Aw.' The lucky lady groaned with delight and slobbered kisses all over Jesus's face. America, least of all Miami, just wasn't the place for French irony.

7

Inside, the Clearview didn't immediately live up to the promise of its chic facade. Unless this was some new trend in Miami minimalism, the hotel was a construction site. None of the rooms we passed had doors on them. Most had bare electric wiring poking from the walls, and one had only half a ceiling.

'You having some work done?' I asked the picturesque pair of black-skirted buttocks that I was following along a wide, bare corridor.

Juliana (as her staff badge called her) laughed. She had thick black hair piled up on top of her head, and Cleopatra's face, with a comma of eyeliner giving her a permanently amused look.

'We're having the *works*,' she said. She spoke as slowly and liltingly as she walked. 'Hayzooss is pimping our ride.'

At the end of the corridor, we came to an entrance that actually had a door in it. Juliana pushed it open, and looked surprised to see that the room beyond had a tiled floor and fitted light switches.

'Your dressing room,' Juliana said.

'Dressing room?' Alexa asked, crinkling up her nose at the decorating smells.

'Yeah, you're dancing, right? Gonna be a good party. Free whisky cocktails and all. You Scotch?'

'We're not *dancing*.' Alexa looked at me sternly, inviting me to confirm this as soon as possible.

'No, we're not *dancing*,' I said. 'We're the . . .' I didn't know how to describe our role here. 'A Scottish group will be dancing while I schmooze with the people from city hall, and hand out literature about Britain's tourist attractions.'

'So you're a kind of ambassador?' Juliana asked.

'Yes, a kind of ambassador.'

'Cool. I never saw an ambassador in shorts before.' She gave my legs a flirtatious look, handed me a key and shimmied out the door. I'm sure my legs were blushing as brightly as when they'd worn the kilt.

'You have a thing with hotel receptionists, Paul,' Alexa said. 'First Boston and now here.'

'She's not a receptionist,' I protested.

To my surprise, Alexa agreed. 'No, because I am not sure this is a hotel.'

Our room was actually a studio apartment, with a newly fitted kitchen. It looked as though no one had stepped inside the place since the furniture had been delivered. There were no cups, no cutlery, the fridge was empty, and there wasn't even a coffee machine.

The balcony, though, was equipped with one of the best sea views I'd ever seen. Straight ahead was the line where the blindingly blue sky sliced into the sunlit ocean. Down a few degrees was the creamy white surf rolling in towards an almost empty beach. Closer still, in the shade of the sway-ing palm trees, a bunch of people dressed in only swimwear and sunglasses were playing volleyball, or rather showing off their perfect bodies while leaping around on either side of a net. The whole scene was a hymn to hedonism.

There was only one thing to do.

'I'm not sure an ambassador is supposed to do *that*,' Alexa said, as I shed my shorts and began making diplomatic advances towards her. 'And I don't think I am in the mood after what happened.'

It took me a second to work out what she meant. Oh yes, she was still harping on about nearly getting shot. It seemed so long ago, and so absurd compared to the sheer vibrancy of what was happening now. It was as though whatever happened to you before you arrived in South Beach didn't matter. Everything was here and now. The hedonism rubbed off on you, and you felt an urgent need to rub it on to someone else.

'No, Paul. Can't we wait till later?'

But Alexa was, after all, dressed only in a sleeveless T-shirt and a pair of shorts that could have been bodypaint. Gently, using all the tact required to restore amicable Anglo-French relations after the trauma of recent events, I continued my advances.

As usual, the softly-softly approach towards France paid off, the greater good of the Entente Cordiale won the day, and soon we were giving the brand-new mirrors on the fitted wardrobe their first sight of what was probably going to be a long career of voyeurism.

With the open balcony doors letting in a mix tape of distant surf, volleyballers' laughs and café salsa, we got into the South Beach mood.

8

Several hours later, I found myself sitting up in bed, wondering where I was. The light had faded. The room was empty except for the sound of the street below.

'You were dreaming,' Alexa said. She'd been sitting on our balcony. 'You were saying, "I'm sorry, I'm sorry." '

'I usually am,' I said.

As soon as I'd gathered my wits, I called Suraya to find out what was what. She wasn't there, naturally enough, because it was the middle of the night in India. Instead, I got through to a guy who called himself Harry. His real name, he eventually admitted, was Hemang, and he was ecstatic to know that I was in Miami.

'Hey, I gotta cousin there,' he said, sounding more American than most of the Americans I'd met recently. 'He's a Dennis.'

'A Dennis?' Was this some codename for honorary US citizens? When you got your temporary visa you were a John, and if you got your Green Card you were a full-blown Dennis?

'Yeah, don't you say that in England?'

'No, we just say you're a naturalized citizen.'

'Uh?' Hemang was confused, and so was I, so I retorted with an 'Uh?' of my own.

'I mean he's a Dennis, like a dennal practitioner, orthodennic surgeon or whatever.'

'Oh, a den-tiss-tuh,' I enunciated.

'Yeah!' Now he was ecstatic again.

'OK, that's wonderful. But the thing is, I really need you to help me with something.'

'Shoot,' he said. I could imagine him with his feet up on his desk, his earpiece and chin-mic askew, his hands free to pump at the PlayStation on his knees.

I told him I'd like some info about the set-up between Miami city hall and these realtors (a word I didn't have to explain to Hemang). I also asked for the names and contact info of the Scottish dancers we were going to meet. Plus, if he had them, more details about the three events tomorrow night.

'OK, I'll get back to you with all that,' he said.

'Soon?' I asked.

'Gimme twenny minutes,' he said.

Amazingly, he got back in only ten, and with some startling revelations. The realtors were, he told me, the sponsors of the events. They'd paid to take them over from Visitor Resources. Why a firm of estate agents in Florida would want to sponsor a display of Scottish dancing I didn't know. It was outsourcing at its most extreme. I just hoped that a chunk of my bonus wasn't being outsourced to the realtors if they helped us to win the competition.

Of course, as is the way with outsourcing, the people who originally commissioned the service knew absolutely nothing about the actual service provided at the end of the line, so Hemang had no information regarding the three events planned.

'Maybe the info got zapped when they changed their computer system,' he suggested.

'What?'

'Yeah, that new building in London came with a whole new computer system. Cost millions, and crashed straight away. They lost tons of info. Suraya didn't tell you about that?'

'No.' It was lucky she hadn't, I thought – my confidence in Visitor Resources was low enough already.

'Oh man, she tells us everything about *everything*.' I got the impression that all Suraya's workmates were suffering with her over the scooter problem. 'You know,' he went on, 'you Brits should let us Indians handle your IT, not just your call centres.' He had a good laugh at that one.

I rang off and tried to sort things out in my mind. It was getting harder and harder to fathom – the British tourist authority wanted some Scottish dancing in Florida, so they got a firm in India to organize it via a Cuban bloke called Jesus who spent his days ogling women from a café terrace.

And my job was to watch the chaos unfold.

191

9

The sky was splashed with clouds so wispy that one of them could have been a thinly sliced cucumber. It was the first time I'd ever seen a green cloud. While sober, anyway.

The colours of the Art Deco buildings were even wilder than the sunset. Neon lights were coming on everywhere, long strips of colour that turned grey or white hotels into glowing pools of purple, pink and blue.

'You certainly go well with the décor,' Alexa said. Faced with the avalanche of snowballed-up clothes that had fallen out of my bag, I'd splurged on a new shirt in one of the discount stores near the hotel. Well, it was more a tableau than a shirt. It was silky turquoise with a motif of smiling golden cherubs. Although 'motif' is perhaps not the right word. They were more life-size portraits, fat golden babies flying up towards my nipples. So what? I thought. If you can't be kitsch in Miami, you can't be kitsch anywhere.

Alexa was not quite so enthusiastic. 'You look as if you have had twins,' she told me. 'Now it is time for their milk.'

'Just because Parisian guys refuse to wear anything but black or jeans doesn't mean the rest of us have to conform,' I defended myself.

Alexa and I strolled up the boardwalk, crossing paths with half-naked joggers (male, unfortunately), departing sunbathers and one guy on a bike pulling a surfboard on which his little white dog was balancing. We watched him head down to the beach, paddle out into the gentle waves and then surf back in with the dog balancing on the tip of his board. Whether the dog loved surfing or was there as a decoy in case the guy was attacked by sharks, I didn't know.

From the boardwalk we could also see the pools and gardens of the hotels on the oceanfront. Some were quiet teak-and-spa luxury, others in loud beach-party mode. All had fences guarded by security men to keep out the home-less people who were sitting aimlessly in the dunes.

It began to feel suspiciously like cocktail time, and we went on the lookout for a beachside place to kick off the night. But if they all had security men to keep out non-guests, we weren't going to get within ordering distance of the bar.

'The guards are not for us,' Alexa said. 'We are White, we are dressed OK' – she frowned as if to apologize to the concept of OK-ness for associating it with my shirt – 'so we are acceptable to middle-class America.'

She was right. When we walked confidently up to the security gate of a chic hotel, the uniformed guard simply stepped aside. We were in.

A tall, white-suited woman walked us to a table on the lawn that looked out towards the darkening ocean. She asked us in an Eastern European accent whether we would like something to eat.

'Yes, please, we'd like an aperitif snack,' I said, trying to remember whether I'd ever used the term 'aperitif snack' before. Yes, surely. I'd lived in France for over a year, after all.

We ordered a couple of glasses of American sparkling wine and a plate of roasted Mediterranean vegetables. No sooner had I put down the menu than a guy came over with a tray and flourished a pair of serving tongs at us.

'Allow me to introduce our signature breads,' he said. 'Poppadom, sesame baguette and black olive.' We were a very long way from the roadside diner where we'd had breakfast, I realized. Even in France they don't do 'signature breads'.

Revived by the surprisingly good bubbly and our snack, we felt ready for more. Indoors, we decided, because the sun had gone down behind the hotel and it was getting slightly chilly in the breeze. Not as chilly as Boston or Cape May had been, of course. In the space of a few hours we'd driven to a world where totally different standards applied.

We went one block in from the ocean to check out the bars on the city side. It was hard to choose. Everywhere seemed to be moodily lit, full of slim shadows acting out courtship rituals. The avenue pounded with the competing sound systems of cars and bars. Finally, we saw a hotel with cool-looking security guys in black suits and shades, and headed up its sloped driveway as if we'd just left our Lamborghini round the corner.

Inside, the décor was so hip that I couldn't work out how to sit on any of the seats. There was a velvet armchair with a ten-foot-high back that tapered down to a cushion no wider than a baby's buttock. A mattress had been dumped (or, more likely, placed according to Feng Shui principles) in the middle of the room. A few people were perched around its edges, wondering how to stop their drink spilling every time someone got up or sat down. There were also rows of stools that looked like giant pulled teeth, with four bobbles on the crown, as if they had been designed for people who wanted to give themselves a public anal massage.

The clients were just as strangely designed as the furniture. Many of them had clothes the same fluorescent white as their teeth and squat noses that had all come from the same surgeon's catalogue. Only by looking very closely could you tell if someone was twenty or fifty.

Bizarrely, in the midst of this millionaires' fashion set, a group of T-shirted, bulge-bellied guys in baseball caps were gurgling beerily around a pool table. I wondered for a moment whether they weren't part of an art installation designed to show the fluorescent-teeth crowd how the other half lived. But no, the two worlds seemed to cohabit, happily ignorant – or tolerant – of each other's existence. It seemed to sum up Miami Beach, which managed to be chic and tacky at the same time, and not give a damn. I loved it, and had forgotten all about gunmen, Scottish dancers and realtors.

My amnesia was helped by a zingy Daiquiri and a dark, heady Mai Tai. I now began to understand the need for the cushions that were scattered about the place. It was comforting to know that you could fall in any direction and land on something soft.

'Paul, I hope you're not going to get drunk,' Alexa said. 'Remember the bar in New York.'

'You're forgetting my aperitif snack,' I told her. 'I'm taking precautions tonight.'

Out by the pool, we lounged on a cushion hillock of our own construction and began to feel seriously relaxed. Waiters and waitresses in black pyjamas hovered. As soon as I'd drained my Mai Tai glass and nibbled the mint leaf, a waitress was by my side.

'Are you good?' she asked.

'I try my best,' I replied. But all she wanted to know was whether I needed a refill. Which I did, of course. I also sensed that I needed more food to accompany all this alcohol.

Alexa agreed, and asked the two women sitting beside us if they could recommend anywhere to eat. Dinner was quickly forgotten, though, when Alexa revealed that she was French and the women went into a state of hysteria. They both, it seemed, *adored* France, and went there *every* year for inspiration.

Their style did look kind of Parisian. One of them, Japanese maybe, had very muted make-up compared to most of the women I'd seen here, and her black hair was pulled back and held in place by a red pencil. Her friend, who was European-looking, had bright lipstick and a baroque hairdo but wore very discreet jewellery and classic French-style stilettos.

'What sort of inspiration?' Alexa asked.

The Oriental girl said that she was a floral designer.

'You design flowers?' I asked.

No, she replied, she designed floral arrangements for weddings and dinner parties, and *adored* French gardens. I doubted that she'd been inspired by the scrubby fenced-off lawns near Alexa's place in Paris.

The European girl said that she was a personal shopper.

'What a great idea,' I said, swallowing the first tasty gulp of a fresh Mai Tai. 'Alexa drinks gallons of mineral water, and I have to hump it up the stairs. Kills me.'

No, she answered, she focused on *clothing*. If a woman needed help with her image, she escorted her to the shops. She eyed the cherubs on my shirt as if I might need help myself. If someone was too busy to shop, she went on, the personal shopper was there to stock the wardrobe with things that would suit the client. If the woman was going on vacation, she'd even pack the necessary outfits for the climate and style of resort.

'Oh wow, you do packing?' I asked. 'You should have a go at the stuff on the back seat of our car. It's like a dog's basket in there.'

At which point they all went off in a women-only conversation, leaving me to stare up at the inky sky and wonder whether anyone was staring back at me from a distant planet. I ordered another cocktail to help me decide.

Next thing I knew, we were entering a restaurant, which if I wasn't mistaken had a grass floor. Yes, I checked. An indoor lawn.

'Get up, Paul,' Alexa said, sounding very much like a French schoolteacher.

'It's real,' I said, showing her the green blade I'd picked.

'It's tantric,' the Oriental girl said.

'What, you shag on it?'

No, she explained patiently as I climbed to my feet using Alexa's leg as a banister, the lawn was a sensual experience designed to heighten your awareness of the meal you were about to eat.

I seemed to be the only one who didn't have a clue what this meant.

'You're drunk,' Alexa said. She was always a perceptive girl.

'I told you I needed food to soak it up,' I said. 'Do they have food here? Apart from the grass, I mean?'

'May I show you to your table?' The maître d' was standing with a clutch of menus in his arms and a forced smile on his face, waiting for our discussion to end.

The menu was as confusing as the lawn. It wasn't in Spanish, it was just that there were so many *words*. And unlike diner menus, which were long lists of different meals, this was a series of essays about each dish. You had to wade through three paragraphs to work out what would end up in your mouth. And by this time my eyes weren't focusing quite as well as they had been earlier in the evening.

'What do you recommend?' I asked the European girl. I'd been told their names, but couldn't quite remember them.

The trouble was, instead of saying 'the fish' or 'the beef', she launched into an essay of her own, telling me the tantric value of one thing and how chewing something else very slowly would be the food equivalent of a shiatsu massage. All I wanted was something to *eat*.

'I'll have what Alexa's having,' I decided. This went down well with our new friends – it would bring tantric harmony.

197

Though Alexa wasn't looking at me at all harmoniously. She seemed to be miffed again. Perhaps it was because I'd asked the waiter for another Mai Tai, 'Straight, not tantric, please.'

She looked even less harmonious when my phone began vibrating in my pocket and I practically took off my trousers in an attempt to retrieve it.

'*Bonsoir*, Paul. How are you going?' How was I *going*? There was only one person in the world who spoke like that.

'Jake!' I said, a little too loudly. 'Where are you?'

'At Miami. And you?'

'Yeah, at Miami, too. Let's meet up. Did you bring Virginie with you?'

'No, man. I'm strictly solo these days.'

'Oh, too bad. Hey!' I'd suddenly had a brilliant idea. 'Alexa and I are having dinner with a couple of *femmes*. They're both really *belles*.' Now I was speaking Jake-style Franglais. 'And one of them . . .' – I lowered my voice – '. . . is Japanese, I think. You still doing your one girlfriend of every nationality thing?'

Judging by the decidedly un-tantric look on the three women's faces, I hadn't lowered my voice enough. And the Oriental girl was giving me an especially acid stare.

'On second thoughts,' I whispered into the phone, 'I think she might be Korean.'

MIAMI TWICE

Dirty Dancing

1

I OPENED MY EYES and waited for it to hit me. Any second now, the hangover was going to swing down from the ceiling and land on my face like a bag of cluster bombs. I could remember when I'd started drinking but not when I'd stopped, which is always a very bad sign. Even worse, I had no idea when or how I'd got to bed.

But no, nothing hit me apart from an awareness that if I didn't start swallowing water within the next minute my tongue was going to shrivel up like a raisin and roll down the back of my throat.

I couldn't understand it. Usually if I drink a lot on an empty stomach, I'm half-dead for a week. But now I felt almost zero pain. Amazing. I turned to share my relief with Alexa, and moving my head hardly hurt at all.

This, though, was when I realized that I hadn't got off scot free.

'Come bodge.' A blond guy was sitting up in bed, leaning over me. I recognized that permanently dishevelled look and the tobacco deodorant. It was Jake. But what was I doing in bed with him?

'Uh?'

'Come bodge,' he repeated, as if this meant something.

'What?' Did he want me to get up? *'Bouger'* is 'move' in French.

'Combo *chien*,' he said.

I closed my eyes. This was getting worse and worse. Now he was talking about a dog.

'She's combo *chienne*. Cherry, the Japonaise in the restaurant, man. She's not Japonaise, she's Cambodgienne. You know, of Cambodge.'

'Cambodia.'

'Yeah.'

'So?'

'So I – you know – I foot myself. Damn, how do you say? Je m'en fous.'

'You don't care about what?'

'That she has no envy to sleep with me. I already slept with a Cambodgienne. Anyway, Cherry and Gayle, they're, you know, a couple.' He pronounced it 'coopul'.

Miraculously, without the use of alcohol, Jake had managed to bring on a vicious hangover. My temples were beginning to throb as if I'd sniffed a gallon of ice-cold vodka up my nostrils.

'What are you on about, Jake? And what is that you're smoking? It smells like donkey shit.'

'Cigar, man.' He grinned and puffed a cloud of animal odours into the sunlit air. 'Civilized city, Miami. They love to smoke.'

'But why are you smoking that in my bed? And where's Alexa?'

'Justement,' he whispered. 'After we met ourselves last night, Alexa went to sleep chez Cherry. Here.' He held a dark object in front of my face. I dragged it into focus. It wasn't the cigar. It was a phone, my phone.

'What the fuck?'

'Alexa is on the line, man. Here.' He shoved the phone half an inch closer to my nose.

'She's on the . . . ? Well why the fuck didn't you tell me before?'

'I was trying to give you the situation.' Jake shrugged his despair that the world never seemed to understand his motives. 'Your girlfriend passed the night chez a lesbian Cambodgienne. It's the sort of thing a man must know before he talks to her on the phone.'

It suddenly struck me that he was right. Alexa had dumped me here and gone off to sleep with two girls? Something was very wrong somewhere.

'Alexa?' I put on my brightest voice.

'Oh, you are awake? I thought you would sleep until next week.' She sounded simultaneously sulky and carefree. Not like her at all.

'Where are you?'

'Didn't your friend Jake just tell you? I'm with Cherry and Gayle.' I didn't like the way she said 'your friend'. It made it just a tad too clear that he wasn't *her* friend.

'What I mean is, why aren't you here?'

'Ha!' From the way she laughed, the answer was all too obvious.

'OK, so I was a bit drunk. It must have been that glass of American bubbly. Not as pure as French champagne.'

'Huh!' My attempt at diplomacy had fallen on deaf ears. 'Maybe you are forgetting the ten cocktails you had as well? You were impossible, Paul. You don't remember what you did with the oysters at the restaurant?'

'No.' And by the sound of it, I didn't want to know. 'But I can't have had *ten* cocktails. I haven't even got a hangover.'

'You want a medal? Anyway, we brought you back to the hotel to find your friend Jake, and we left you there. *Franchement!*' There was that word again.

'Sorry.' Apology delivered, conversation ended, I hoped. No such luck.

'Honestly, first you try to force Cherry to eat your oysters, then when we arrive at the Clearview you announce to the whole terrace that she is going to have tantric sex with your friend Jake. *Merde*, Paul!' Now she was really angry. And I kind of understood why.

I groaned. 'Oh God. I must be allergic to rum.'

There was a worryingly long silence. 'You don't take anything seriously, do you, Paul?'

I gave this a moment's thought and decided that I took one thing very seriously indeed.

'OK, Alexa, so I got drunk and acted like an idiot. But I wouldn't have had so much to drink if we'd gone to dinner when I said, instead of hanging around to chat up your two friends. And you – you went off and slept with, well, slept *chez*, or maybe with, a couple of, you know . . .' Jake gave me a thumbs up. Now, it seemed, I was asking the questions that mattered.

'So?'

'Look, Alexa. I'm sorry. I know I can be a total dickhead when I'm drunk. But I'm sober now. So will you come back home? Let's talk about this.'

There was another long silence, then a sigh.

'I need some time to think,' she said. 'Anyway, the reason I called was because it is time for your brunch. You must go and see your dancers.'

'Holy fuck.' I leapt up so fast from under the duvet that I tipped Jake off the bed.

'Alors, did she?' he asked just before his head hit the floor. But I was already in the bathroom, pulling back the shower curtain. It came as some surprise to find that the hot and cold taps I was reaching for were dark nipples, set just below the centre of two golden-brown breasts.

'Juliana, right?' I said when I finally looked up at her face.

'Yeah, hi.'

2

'She's Puerto Rican,' Jake explained when I went back into the bedroom. 'Well, her maman is.'

So Juliana was part of his plan to sleep with one of every nationality in the world.

'What happened to Virginie?' Somewhere deep in my memory of the previous night there was a conversation about him breaking up with his French girlfriend.

Jake's brow furrowed. This was a delicate subject. 'Oh man, that Virginie, she blessed me so much.' In Jake's case, I knew that 'blessed' was not a good thing. He was using the French word 'blesser', meaning 'hurt'.

'What did she do?'

'She had no respect for my posy.' His usual gripe against the world. 'I had the custom to send her a poem by text all the mornings. I told you before.'

'Did you?' I must have blocked out the horror of what he'd put the poor girl through. His poems were basically gynaecological reports with the romanticism taken out.

'Yeah, and you know what? I discovered that she was effacing them.'

'Deleting them?'

'Yeah, man. Incroyable, no?'

'Yes,' I said, thinking, no, it was very, very *croyable*. Deleting his poems was as natural a defence mechanism as closing your eye when a mosquito tries to headbutt your cornea.

'Yeah, I ask her to see her phone so I can copy them for myself, and she said she effaced them. So I larg'd her.'

'You larg'd her?' That was a new one for me. I just hoped that it didn't involve violence. 'And what are you doing in Miami? I thought you were going to get straight on a Greyhound at Orlando airport?'

'Yeah.' He looked pained. 'I depensed all the money.' Meaning he'd spent it. 'I only had enough to get to Miami. I was thinking you can maybe take me to Nevada in your car?'

'In the Mini? But there's only just room for Alexa, me and our luggage. And I'm not going to Nevada, anyway.'

'Yes, you said you're going to Las Vegas.'

'Las Vegas is in Nevada?' It was funny. I'd never thought of Las Vegas as being in a state. It was just Las Vegas, like Washington is just Washington.

'Yeah, man.' Jake took a satisfied suck on his cigar. He seemed to think he'd earned his seat in the car by explaining the city's location.

'I'll have to talk to Alexa about it,' I said. If she ever came back, that was. 'Now can you go and see if it's safe for me to take a shower, please?'

When I got outside into the sunlight, with my hair wet and my T-shirt sticking to my soggy back, Jesus was just walking on to the café terrace. He was wearing a bleached white suit and a pastel-blue polo shirt, looking as though everything about him, including his skin and hair, had just been freshly dry-cleaned.

'Dude,' he said, a touch less manically than usual.

'Hi, Jesus. Where are the dancers?'

'Aagh.' He gave a sigh of disgust and flopped down into

a chair at the large table that had been laid out for our brunch. 'Fucken headcases.'

'What's wrong?'

'They give me some shit about Dun-firm-witch, Dun-witch-farm . . .'

'Dunfermline? Yes. I was going to talk to them about it.'

'Whatever. Forget it, man, they all losers, anyway.' He flicked his hand across the table like a king dismissing a bunch of boring courtiers.

'What do you mean?'

'I mean, this is great exposure for them, right? They dance in public, everyone sees them. And they want *me* to pay *them*? Then they start busting my balls about this Dun-shithole. Forget them, man. I fired their asses.'

'So we have no dancers? Christ, Jesus.'

'We find some dancers. Miami's full of dancers.'

'Not Scottish dancers.'

'What's the difference? It's all dancing, right? Just different music. Hey, babe!' He forgot instantly about my troubles as a girl glided past, doing what looked like a solo tango.

Understandably, at such short notice, Suraya couldn't put her finger on a Scottish dancing group nearer than Nova Scotia. She seemed to have problems concentrating, anyway. Her neighbour had offered to lend her his scooter while he hitched a ride to work with a friend, but she wasn't sure it was wise to accept the loan. And she was far more interested in my view of her moral dilemma than in my panic at not having an event to put on.

Shit, I thought, I was going to have to drive around South Beach with a megaphone, calling for volunteers.

Which gave me an idea.

I was just about to make the necessary call when

my phone began buzzing. The screen showed an American number. Alexa, maybe, calling from *chez* her new friends?

'Alexa?' I said, but all I heard in reply was some male laughter. I hung up.

A couple of seconds later, a tall, suntanned guy with a low-cut sleeveless singlet and an obviously waxed chest was grinning down at me out of the sun. He was carrying a laptop like an open book, and held it out for me to see.

It was tough to make out details in the strong sunlight, but I saw enough to make me close my eyes and want to slip into a nice, comforting hangover.

'It's you, right? Paul? We love your photos.' He pointed to a small guy sitting at a nearby table. The friend had a short-haired dachshund on his lap. Both man and dog were wearing black-leather waistcoats and collars. The guy waved with one hand, and wagged the dog's paw at me with the other.

'No, it's not me,' I said, trying to close the laptop and usher its owner away.

'But we just called the number. You answered.'

I opened the computer again. There, beneath the photo of me in my frilly collar and kilt, was my phone number. The worst had happened. The Men in Skirts website had got hold of my name and number. Someone in England was going to die for this.

'What is *that*?' Jesus was looking over my elbow at the screen.

'He's famous,' my admirer said. 'It's Paul, the under-carriage of the month.' He pointed to the part of the picture that had earned me my title.

The next five minutes felt like watching myself get circumcized. Jesus alternated between croaking in pantomime horror and screaming with laughter. He summoned Juliana – who was now dressed and at work – and practically everyone else at the café to admire my knees.

Beyond the palm trees, a flight of pelicans skimmed above the shoreline. I prayed for one of them to come a hundred yards inland and crap on Jesus's head, but fate had turned against me, and no birds answered my call.

3

'Tony!' I called out.

This was the rescue call I'd eventually put in, and as before, the leader of the Miaminis had come up trumps. A mere half-hour after I phoned him, he was stepping out of his Mini and giving me a thumbs-up.

I was at the brunch table with Jesus and the two kilt fans, Sven (waxed chest) and Greg (dachshund man). Jake had come down to join us and was chewing meditatively at his cigar.

Tony was accompanied by a gangly, heavy-breasted woman called Birgit whom he introduced as a keen Scottish-dancing fan. She was as tall as I was, and dressed in a shapeless T-shirt and profoundly unsexy draw-string trousers, but I fell in love with her as soon as she sat down and told me that she had two women friends who were also Queens of the Highland Fling.

'The math is simple,' she said. 'We need at least four men and four women to put on a convincing display.'

'Sorry guys,' Tony said. 'I'm a driver, not a dancer.'

'Hey, you've done more than enough lifesaving over the past two days,' I told him. 'Looks like I'll have to dance, after all.' The two kilt fans clapped. 'Jake, if you don't dance you're going straight on a plane back to Paris.' Jake blew a smoke ring in mute agreement. 'Jesus, how about you?'

'Me?' Jesus refused point blank to do any dancing that didn't involve rubbing his groin up against a woman.

'We're in,' Sven said. Greg nodded.

So we had the full male complement. All we needed was one more woman.

'Yooliana!' Jesus beckoned, and Juliana came over.

'You like to dance, huh, babe?' Jesus cajoled.

'Ye-ah?' Juliana sensed that there was a plot against her. It wasn't difficult, because six men and one woman were gaping expectantly at her.

'OK. You learn some Scotch dances this afternoon, you do the dancing shows tonight, I make sure you get pay plus share of tips, OK?' Jesus might look like a brainless himbo, but he knew how to pitch a deal.

''Kay.' Juliana didn't need to think twice about it.

Against all odds, it looked as though we were game on.

All I needed now were some costumes. Pursuing his role as saviour of lost causes, Tony offered to guide me to a hire place, and we set off straight away in a minor Mini convoy, the two cars nipping through the late-morning traffic towards downtown Miami.

As we crossed the bridge to the mainland, I caught my first sight of all those waterside homes you see in the celeb mags. Set along the shore of the circular island in the bay there were Italian palazzos, Spanish haciendas, colonial mansions, and a fifty-room tropical log cabin. Each had parking space for a yacht and a powerboat. But from the road you could practically gaze into their living-room windows. And these supposedly dream homes looked out on to a smoke-belching line of moored cruise ships apparently waiting for a sea-lane traffic light to change. Beyond the smoking ships was a container port, which was colourful – a sort of 3-D Mondrian painting – but surely not worth paying millions to look at.

The two Minis criss-crossed the modern high-rise office blocks until we came to a warehouse underneath a soaring flyover. A neon sign on the roof said 'Partys R Us'. Three mannequins dressed as a fairy-tale princess, a vampire and a conquistador were standing out front on the sidewalk. I pulled up alongside Tony, who gave me his signature thumbs-up – a double one this time.

His magic worked again, and we emerged twenty minutes later with eight sets of approximately Scottish clothing, consisting of reddish kilts (made in Guatemala, no doubt the tartan of the McGonzalez clan) and loose white shirts. I'd had to guess at sizes, but the kilts were adjustable, and the shirts roomy enough to fit anyone, even though the diminutive Sven was probably going to look as if he'd been swallowed by a giant pillow.

I'd almost made it back to South Beach – alone this time – when my phone lit up on the car seat beside me. It was a message from Elodie. As soon as I stopped at a red light, I called her back.

'I am in Miami,' she said. 'At the airport. Can you come to fetch me?' What? I thought. Didn't her dad's wildly overgenerous allowance and Clint Highway's credit card cover an airport taxi?

Elodie must have changed out of her winter clothes on the plane. She was looking almost as undressed as when she was my flatmate in Paris and used to wander about our apartment in nothing but her knickers. Her flowery top was more revealing than most bikinis and, although it seemed barely possible, her skirt was even shorter than the one I was wearing on the website. With her in the passenger seat of the Mini, you regretted that the car wasn't manual so you'd have a frequent excuse to look down at those slim brown thighs.

'Oh, Paul, this car, it is so *cool*,' she said, jiggling around in the seat as if trying to find the best position for a bit of drive-thru *amour*. She smiled approvingly at everything around her. The highway signs directing us to South Beach, the rush of cars heading into town, even the scraggy backyards of the poor housing we could see from the airport road. Miami was doing its sunny magic trick, making the winter feel like a good place to be. It certainly made a change from Alexa's recent bouts of grumpiness and sarcasm.

'So you haven't seen her since last night?' Elodie asked, with her usual mixture of sympathy and relish.

'No. I've left at least three messages since, but she's not answering.'

'Give her a few hours. She is a woman. She needs to decide for herself when she will forgive you. I will call her as soon as I get to the hotel.' Elodie had booked herself into one of the posh oceanfront places.

'So are you here just to visit your friend, or are you doing some business?' I asked her.

'Oh, just to see my friend. I will help her with her show at the Alliance tomorrow.'

'Show? What kind of show?'

'Oh, pff.' She threw up her arms dismissively. 'A fashion show.'

'What, Chanel dresses and stuff?'

'Oh no, lingerie.'

I almost crashed into the back of a school bus.

'Lingerie? In a language school?'

'Yes. Not very sexy lingerie, probably. Just ordinary French underwear. I will be modelling some of it myself. Afterwards, we will sell the underwear.' I presumed she meant they'd have supplies of the lines they were modelling, though I didn't put it past Elodie to auction off the actual knickers worn during the show.

She turned to look at the heap of costumes in the back of the car. 'Are you really going to dance yourself?'

'Yes.' I tried to sound enthusiastic. 'Just to help out. They were one man short.'

'So all the others are authentic Scotch? A professional dance group?'

'Oh yes, totally authentic, and totally professional.'

What is it they say? If you're going to tell a lie, go for the big one?

4

There was a noisy crowd filling the Clearview's terrace and the sidewalk beyond. The purple neon made everyone's teeth and eyeballs shine, and the high proportion of white clothing gave an ultraviolet glow to the bobbing, chattering mass of people.

My own white shirt and almost equally white legs were glowing too as I moved amongst them, handing out *Visit Britain Now You Lovely Yank Bastards* (or something like that) booklets, none of which acknowledged the existence of winter sleet and sub-Miami temperatures. Here, at dusk, it was so warm that iced whisky cocktails felt pleasantly refreshing. Back in England, they would only have accelerated the onset of hypothermia.

I kept an eye out for Alexa – who, thanks to Elodie's intervention, had promised to be here for the first show – and for anyone who looked at all like a politician in need of schmoozing. On both counts I drew a blank. I did, though, meet plenty of people who were delighted to shake my hand, pat me on the back and welcome me to Miami. Lots of them wanted me to autograph the booklets as if I'd written them myself. And a few even asked me to sign myself as undercarriage of the month. Yes, word had got round and, to judge by the number of booklets that people hung on to rather than ditching in the nearest bin, it looked as though Scotland was soon to see a sharp upturn in visits from Floridian kilt fans.

Still, I wasn't happy.

'There's absolutely no one from city hall, is there?' I asked Jesus, who was in the indoor lounge, rubbing his nose on a woman's neck.

'No worries, my frenn,' he said, not removing his nose from the neck. 'They will come, you will schmooze them.'

I left him to it and went to inspect my troops, who were giggling nervously in one of the unfinished bedrooms upstairs. Kilts were being re-adjusted, sleeves rolled up, and shirttails tucked in to give the right degree of bagginess. They looked a pretty mismatched army, and several of them had obviously been getting Dutch courage out of a Scotch bottle.

As promised, Birgit's two friends had completed our line-up. They were called Shweeanna and Mary. Shweeanna was a history teacher who'd done her Master's dissertation on the clearance of the Highlands by my evil forefathers, but she seemed to have forgiven me. Mary was a small woman of about forty with a boy's body and – amazingly – an authentic Scottish accent. So I hadn't told Elodie a complete lie, after all. Mary was originally from Clydebank, where her dad had been an unemployed shipbuilder. She and Birgit had spent an hour pre-show running us through the basic steps. Birgit's large chest bouncing on Mary's head looked like a small boy trying to knock coconuts out of a tree, but we'd got the basic idea. It seemed to me that if you just kept twirling, you couldn't go too far wrong.

Seeing that we were in America, I felt we had to do the communal prayer thing.

'Huddle up, team,' I said, and we linked arms, bowed heads and bonded. 'For what we are about to do, may the Lord of the Dance forgive us,' I said, and we whooped. Even more so when Sven spun me on my heels and began giggling at my back.

'Look guys,' he laughed, and gathered the dancers behind me. They all joined in the hilarity and began pulling at my shirt.

'What are you up to back there?' I asked, and they started to hand me a colourful harvest of Post-Its with names and phone numbers. It seemed that my website fans had come prepared.

'OK, you start now? We got three shows to do, people.' Jesus burst in, clapping his hands like a true theatre manager. He high-fived us as we filed out the door.

I felt a wave of butterflies come up the stairwell and hit me in the stomach. Oh well, I thought, you're a long way from home. None of these people will ever see you again, apart from Jake, Alexa and Elodie. If Alexa's even here. I breathed deeply and headed down towards the Scottish accordion music that was wafting in on the Atlantic breeze.

When we got outdoors into the purple neon night, I sensed the banks of digital cameras and phones pointing at me, waiting for my undercarriage to show. As I reeled and jigged, there was a collective intake of breath and a flutter of hopeful camera flashes every time I lifted a knee. When – only once – I fell over, the lenses pointed towards my raised kilt like a swarm of rectal thermometers.

The others were doing a valiant job. Sven and Greg tended to put too much ass-bumping into the traditional Scottish dances, though at least for once the Gay Gordons lived up to its name. Jake was almost totally lacking in rhythm, which explained a lot about his poems, but he was motivated by the chance to grab hold of a multinational group of women, and performed gamely. Juliana was a natural dancer, and she and Shweeanna swung their hips in a way that would have repopulated the Highlands in no time.

And then, after three dances, any remaining nervousness changed to laughing euphoria when half a dozen people from the crowd joined in and turned our display into a party. By the end of our half-hour show, there were almost as many people dancing as watching. Tables had been pushed aside, and Birgit was calling the steps rather than massaging people's heads with her chest. During the final Strip the Willow, I was delighted to cross arms with a breathless, smiling Alexa, followed by her new friends Cherry and Gayle. I was, though, less delighted to see a male face I knew from somewhere. I couldn't quite place him, but I was aware that I didn't like him for some reason.

Jesus finally killed the music, took the microphone and began to thank everyone for coming. However, instead of encouraging them all to go and spend their tourist dollars in the UK or, if it was in their power, to vote for Britain in the upcoming election of the World Tourism Capital, he started explaining that the Clearview was no longer a hotel, that it was being refurbished to the highest standards of Miami interior design, and that a whole variety of ocean-front condos would soon be going on to the market. Tonight, he said, was their chance to get in early with a downpayment and qualify for a 5 per cent discount. What was more, they could, if they wanted, get a preview of one of the studios that had been completed early. He raised an arm and pointed towards the only source of light on the upper floor apart from the neon. Our room.

'A representative of Golden Beach Realtors will be happy to show you around and explain our mortgage plans,' he said. He then proceeded to make the same speech in Spanish.

What the fuck was going on?

Before I could ask, a woman with pasty make-up, giant pearls and an unseasonal-looking trouser suit grabbed me by the left bicep and started to drag me away.

'We gotta get to the next show,' she said. 'Hi, I'm Angela, by the way. Business Development Assistant with Golden Beach.' She smiled and held out a hand with glittery pink talons in place of fingernails. I shook it, being careful not to impale myself on her claws.

'But—' I had a million objections, none of which seemed to interest her.

'The next show is due to start in ten minutes. There's a barbecue,' she said, as though I personally was going to spoil the sausages if I kept her waiting.

She shoved me into a minibus, where my fellow dancers were already waiting in air-conditioned comfort. They were all high on their success, reliving the best moments of the performance, oblivious to my worries about the condo-voting-Alexa-unknown-bloke turn that the evening had taken. Little Mary put a Coke bottle in my hand and I took a slug, immediately gagging it up all over Jake's kilt. It was neat, warm whisky.

I might be able to dance like a Scot, but I couldn't drink like one yet.

5

When we arrived at the next venue, the Latino music on the PA system was immediately replaced by the wail of bagpipes, and we emerged from the minibus like rock stars coptered in backstage at a festival.

This, though, was less Woodstock than woodpile. The sound system had been set up in front of an old, half-ruined bungalow made of unpainted, very porous-looking grey stone. It had a fenced-off yard full of builder's refuse, and tarpaulins draped across the roof. It stood a few yards back from the street behind a parking area that was to be the venue for our dancing and barbecuing. On either side of the bungalow, there were small Art Deco apartment buildings, and I couldn't see why this house had survived the prettification of the neighbourhood. Maybe, I thought, it had belonged to an eccentric millionaire or a mass murderer.

'Oh wow,' Mary said, as if the tumbledown shack was a French chateau.

'Don't tell me,' I said. 'Gloria Estefan was born here.'

'No, it's a coral rock house.'

I caught Jake's eye. He was as unimpressed as I was.

'It's like *eighty* years old,' Juliana said.

I laughed. Hell, in France, some of the cars aren't much newer.

'That's a really long time for us,' Shweeanna the history teacher explained. 'This was one of the first houses on the island, when it was just a dune.'

'Look, same old promises,' Mary said. She pointed to a sign hanging from the fence. It had originally announced that the house would be opening as a museum in December. This missed deadline had been crudely painted over with 'April'.

'Yeah,' Shweeanna said. 'They been trying to pull these down for years. Put up some more condos.'

'Hey, guys! Showtime!' Angela was beckoning with her

claws. 'After the dance you can get a bite to eat.' She pointed over to the barbecue that had been set up next to the fence on one side of the bungalow. Meaty smells were beginning to escape, attracting quite a crowd. I recognized lots of people from the Clearview show. It seemed we already had tour groupies.

The bagpipes changed to accordions, and we did our dances again. Fewer of the crowd joined in, no doubt because of the rival attraction of grilled sausages, but the half-hour went by quickly, and at the end of it we trooped over to the barbecue. At the far end of the food table, I could see Alexa talking to Elodie. I interrupted their conversation with a kiss on Alexa's bare shoulder.

'Sorry about last night,' I said, not for the first time in our relationship.

'I see you weren't too ill to get Elodie from the airport,' she said. I detected a note of disapproval.

Elodie looked on, smiling mischievously. She had changed out of her beachwear into a jungle-patterned dress that seemed to be massaging various key parts of her body into shape. It was a good thing, I thought, that Alexa didn't know exactly what had gone on between Elodie and me when we were sharing an apartment.

Jake came over. '*Ça va?*' he asked Alexa.

'*Oui, merci,*' she replied frostily.

I introduced him to Elodie, but he lost interest as soon as he heard she was French.

'Hey, Paul, I had an idea,' he said. 'To make more space in the car, I can attach my baggages to the roof.'

Alexa suddenly became even more frosty. 'You have invited Jake to come in the car?'

'No,' I corrected her. 'He asked to come along, and I said I'd talk to you about it.'

'But you didn't say he couldn't come?'

'What? No. I mean yes.' I wasn't sure I'd understood the question.

'*Franchement*, Paul, I can't believe it.'

'What's the problem? I said I'd ask you, that's all. What's wrong with that?'

'You must choose. It is him or me.'

Jake, who had provoked a few female outbursts in his time, put a hand on my arm.

'C'est bon, man. I have caused you too many ennuis. I will take the bus.'

I thanked him and offered to lend him the money, but even this didn't placate Alexa. Maybe, I thought, she was afraid the bus would break down and we'd find Jake blocking the highway with his thumb sticking out.

I turned to Elodie for support. That was when I noticed that someone else was observing our conversation. And suddenly I was the one turning frosty. I hadn't recognized him before, because he'd had his blond hair cut and had changed out of his heavy winter clothes into a loud Hawaiian shirt. But I knew that Irish 'you're in the shit, Brit' grin of his. It was the bastard from Boston.

'What the fuck's he doing here?' I demanded.

'Who? Oh, Mike?' Alexa asked with innocence as clumsy and unconvincing as my Scottish dancing. 'He comes to Florida every winter.'

'Oh, really?' I was getting flashbacks of that innocent expression of hers. I'd seen it quite a few times recently. Like when she was being just a little too keen to read her emails. Shit, was that why she'd kept asking about 'whiffy'? 'So when did you two have your big reunion, then? Last night?' I asked.

'What are you saying, Paul?'

I didn't need to say anything.

'Huh, you accuse me,' she said. 'But one could say that

you have brought an ex-girlfriend to Miami. She has told me *everything* that happened between you two in Paris.'

Elodie shrugged 'Sorry' to me, though her smile was anything but apologetic.

'But it didn't—' I heard the cliché alarm ringing in my head, but I had no choice but to press on. 'It didn't mean anything really, did it, Elodie? And it was before Alexa and I even met, right?'

'I don't know. When did you two meet?' Elodie was wearing a lost-little-girl look.

Alexa, meanwhile, was as grim as ever.

'Look, Alexa,' I said. 'Let's talk calmly about this, away from everyone else. If you say you didn't sleep with the Boston strangler last night, I believe you. And I certainly didn't ship Elodie down here to relive the old days.'

'But you are coming to see my underwear tomorrow, right?' Elodie asked. What the hell kind of sabotage was she up to?

Suddenly Jesus was beside me, trying to dislocate my arm. 'You got to dance the last show, dude.'

'I'm not doing the last show,' I told him. 'I've got this Irish jig to sort out.'

6

The last show was a twenty-minute minibus drive north.

Jesus had press-ganged me into coming by telling me that the mayor and various city officials were being wined and dined at a big restaurant just out of town. The host was Jesus's boss, the big realtor. He and the mayor often got together, Jesus said, but this was a more important occasion than usual because certain major decisions were about to be taken, and Jesus's boss was keen for the decisions to go the right way. Not, of course, that any money would change hands. No way. If things went well, the boss would make sure that Miami would also take the right decision concerning the World Capital of Tourism. Jesus gripped my shoulder as if he needed to squeeze the point home.

By this time, I was almost beyond caring whether London, Paris or Chernobyl became World Capital of Tourism. Fuck world tourism, fuck international diplomacy, I was thinking, some foreign bastard is trying to shag my girlfriend. Three foreign bastards, if you counted the girls. I tried to call Alexa, but she didn't answer. I left a message saying we needed to talk at the hotel later on.

There was one thing about the competition I did want to ask Jesus, though.

'What was all that about condos back at the Clearview?' I said. 'You didn't mention my campaign once.'

'Hey, I got to do business, man.' He was completely unapologetic.

'If I'd known I was dancing to help sell your apartments I'd have asked for commission. Or an apartment.'

'You want a condo? I'll give you the best price,' Jesus said. 'Your friend Elodie, she is taking one.' For some reason this didn't surprise me at all.

We pulled off the highway into a gigantic parking lot and stopped beneath a Godzilla-sized plastic palm tree with fairy lights twinkling up its unnaturally straight trunk.

'Less dance,' Jesus said, sounding like a Latino David Bowie.

From here on, things got a bit too complicated for my shellshocked brain.

I was introduced to a big, laughing man who thanked me for doing such great work for his firm over the past year. Jesus's boss thought I was one of his underlings. The boss bracketed Jake, Juliana and me in his sweaty arms and escorted us over to nod politely in the direction of a long table at which a dozen or so dishevelled men were getting drunk. These, it seemed, were the mayor and the dignitaries.

It wasn't until someone hung a collar of flowers round my neck that I noticed the surprising number of indoor palm trees and stuffed parrots decorating the room, and that the waiters and waitresses were all wearing grass skirts. We were in some kind of Pacific Paradise-themed restaurant. The lighting was low, and groups of diners were sitting in intimate, leafy booths around a central stage that was fitted out to look like a camp fire, with loudspeakers hidden in the log piles and a varnished plastic pig grinning on a spit. Soft ukulele music was plinking in the air. It reminded me of the bedsprings in Cape May, and I felt a shudder of nostalgia for the wintry north.

'You gotta get changed,' Jesus told us.

'Changed?'

'You gotta put on the grass skirts.'

'Grass skirts?' we choroused.

'Yeah, they don't want no Scottish dancing here.'

'We're not doing a hula dance, Jesus. My job is to promote Britain to that lot over there.'

I pointed at the mayor's table and suddenly my heart stopped beating.

One of the so-called dignitaries was grinning in my direction. I'd seen his flat head and lopsided smile before. The image in my memory was a black-and-white newspaper photo, but there was no mistaking the man I'd seen shaking hands with the mayor of Boston. So he and his friends weren't dishevelled just because they were drunk. In their case, it was genetic. They were the French engineers. After big-digging my grave up north, they'd come down to shovel merde over me in Miami.

7

Back at the Clearview, I could barely get into my room for people viewing the 'show apartment' where I was meant to be sleeping. Alexa wasn't amongst them. Jake and Juliana came in with a bottle of whisky and started evicting the visitors, so presumably if I wanted to sleep there later I'd have to curl up in the shower cubicle.

I wasn't surprised – nothing would have surprised me by then – to find Elodie down on the terrace, having a drink with Jesus, who had recovered his composure after I'd stormed out of the hula club and demanded to be driven back to the hotel.

'Dude, have a whisky cocktail. We got lots left over.' Jesus was eyeing Elodie as if deciding which bit of her to drink.

'Did you know those engineers were coming down here?' I asked her.

'No. What are they doing here?' she said.

I tried to scan her brain for signs of complicity, but she could be totally inscrutable when she wanted.

'I asked one of them,' I said. 'They're here advising on hurricane protection.'

'Good guys, protecting the real estate.' Jesus raised his glass in salute.

'But what has that to do with your competition?' Elodie asked.

'Well, who do you think the mayor and his mates are going to vote for? The guys who can save their city from destruction or the dickhead in a kilt?'

'Poor Paul. Have a drink.' Elodie handed me a glass topped with a giant cocktail umbrella and a hunk of pineapple.

'Has Alexa been here?' I asked.

'She came for her luggage,' Elodie said.

'Shit. Was she alone?'

'No, she was with that cute guy from Boston. He has a big Chevrolet convertible.'

'I bet he fucking does.'

'Let her go, dude,' Jesus said. 'They start giving you shit, they never stop.' The rest of his homespun Cuban advice was drowned out by the whooping of a siren. It wasn't the first I'd heard since we got back to the hotel. They all seemed to be close by.

'What's going on?' I asked Jesus. 'A drive-by shooting?'

He shrugged.

'No,' Elodie chipped in. 'There was a problem at the barbecue.'

'What happened?' I addressed my question to Jesus, but again he didn't care to comment.

'One of the trucks that came to collect the equipment crashed into the old house,' Elodie said. 'A couple of people got hurt, right, Jesus?'

'Accident, dude,' Jesus said, a little too emphatically.

'The old bungalow? The coral place?' Doubts and denials started to pound in my head. He wouldn't, would he? There were probably millions at stake, and he was an amoral shit, but would he really be that shameless? Everyone knows that his company is dying to demolish the coral house and still he goes through with his plan to total the place? And uses me as an excuse? No way.

Though watching him fidget in his seat, torn between the need to look innocent and the desire to boast, the conclusion was obvious.

'Where are you going, Paul?' Elodie asked.

'Taking my drink for a midnight swim.'

I climbed over the low dune and marched across the sand

towards the crashing ocean, throwing off my trainers, socks and floppy white shirt. I was way past worrying about the deposit for the Scottish costumes, which I was probably going to lose anyway, given that Jake had worn one of them, which spelt death for any garment.

A sign on the beach informed me that it was illegal to go on to the sand after nightfall, that nude bathing was banned at all times by city law, and that public alcohol consumption was subject to an automatic fine. But what the hell. I pulled off my boxers and was about to whip off my kilt when I had second thoughts. I felt like trying an experiment. Was it true, I wondered, that the sight of a man with nothing on under his kilt could terrify any enemy? Would that include sharks?

It was while I was floating in the middle of my tartan lifebelt that I saw the flames. They were coming from the window just to the left of the neon Clearview sign. My window. I must admit that my first thought was, Shit, my luggage.

When I arrived back on Ocean Drive, there was a screaming crowd milling about beneath the blazing facade of the hotel. With no police or fire officers to hold them back, people were staying much too close to the building. Until, that is, the first of the neon tubes popped, showering hot glass over the terrace, at which point there was a stampede across the road for cover.

Jake cannoned into me. He was wearing a pair of white boxer shorts with little heads of Baudelaire on them. In one hand he was carrying a bulging Army Surplus kitbag, in the other a bottle of whisky that he had presumably saved from the flames.

'Paul, man, let's foot the camp.'

'Get out of here? Why?'

'C'était un accident, man. My cigar, the bed. I mean, what kind of merde do they put in these non-smoking rooms?'

'But my clothes, my stuff – it's all in the fucking room, Jake.'

'No, man. Jesus took out all our baggages before the visits. They were all in the cuisine. Juliana is apporting yours. Come.'

As we ran down the street away from the shrieks and the heat, Jake was trying to ask me something. I didn't hear properly till we got to the car.

'Juliana, she comes too with us, no?'

'What?'

'Juliana. She will have no job now.'

'Well, Jake, maybe you should have thought of that before you destroyed her bloody workplace.'

Juliana came jogging round the corner of the Clearview that was furthest away from the flames, dressed only in her baggy Scottish shirt. She was showing almost as much flesh as when I'd interrupted her shower. The burning bed must really have taken her by surprise. She had my main bag over her shoulder and was clutching the backpack where I kept my passport, driving licence and other valuables.

'Three of us will never fit in,' I apologized.

'Allez, man,' Jake urged. 'She sauved your baggages.'

'But you'll have bags, too, right?' I asked her. 'There's not enough room in the car.'

'I always travel light,' Juliana said, handing over my precious backpack. 'Hey, when you say "car" you sound just like that guy from Boston who was with Alexa. You both say "kah". Funny, huh?'

'No, it's fucking not funny,' I said.

'Sir.' An official-sounding voice behind me cut off the anti-Bostonian, anti-French rant I was planning to start.

'Did you know that it is a contravention of city law to go semi-naked in the street and use obscene language in a public place?'

'You got anything left in that whisky bottle, Jake?' I moaned. I might as well go for the full hat trick of crimes.

To New Orleans

Hubble, Bubble, Toil and Double Trouble

1

'HI, ALEXA, I'M REALLY SORRY, but I have no choice. I've got to get to New Orleans for the next event, and as you haven't answered any of my calls, I've told Jake he can come with me. I wish we were going there together, just you and me. I mean, *New Orleans*. It'd be fantastic to drive there with you – Thelma and you are a team. I'm sure she prefers having you at the wheel. And don't forget we still have our bet going, about those ten types of maple syrup.' I attempted a laugh, which didn't quite come off. 'But it's nine o'clock now, and we have to leave. So, well, we're leaving. If you change your mind, I'll buy you a plane ticket. I'll come and get you at the airport. Just give me a call. I mean, Alexa, *New Orleans*. You'll love it . . .'

I stopped rambling. Long phone messages do no good. They never convince anyone of anything. They just make people think you're nuts or desperate.

'Good one, man,' Jake told me.

'Yeah, and best not to mention me,' Juliana said. She was

right – I'd done it deliberately to avoid misunderstandings.

'More coffee, anyone?' Tony came out on to his patio with a fresh jug of pure Arabica.

The cop hadn't charged us with public nudity, swearing and whisky-drinking. After all, even the sternest law-enforcement officer can understand why people might be upset, lacking clothes and in need of a stiff drink when they've just escaped from a fire. That was what we told him – we'd been sleeping when the fire broke out. I was wet and sandy because in my initial panic I'd doused myself in the shower and then rolled in the ornamental garden. No way had I been disobeying city ordnances and beaching it after dark.

He let us go and went to help out at the fire. I made sure Elodie hadn't been hit by molten glass – I didn't really care about Jesus – and then called Tony. True to form, he had instantly offered to put us up. He'd even driven over to South Beach to escort us back to a leafy suburb called Coral Gables.

So Jake, Juliana and I had slept on his three couches, and Thelma had had her first sleepover with a boyfriend – a whole night in a double garage with Tony's boyish blue Mini. I wondered whether there might be some mini Minis on the way in a few months' time.

Now we were full of fresh fruit, pancakes and coffee, and watching the sun climb ever higher over Tony's tropical back garden. His infinity pool was looking more inviting every second, but we had to leave.

'It's not your foot,' Jake said, patting me on the shoulder.

'What?'

'All this, it's not your foot, man.'

Now I got it – he was pronouncing 'fault' like a Frenchman.

231

'It's not your fault, either,' I told him. 'It's that fucking Mike. I could see he fancied her when we were up in Boston. I bet he was the one who suggested meeting up in Miami. He went all out to seduce her. He even hired a fucking convertible, the bastard.'

'Oh, no, I was meaning the competition. The engineers,' Jake said. Of course, to him, losing a woman was a bit like misplacing a T-shirt. You just went out and got another one. 'It was the French. They bezzed you again.'

'Bezzed?' Tony asked.

'It's French for screwed,' I told him. 'These engineers keep popping up all over the country. They've offered to save Boston from subsidence and Miami from getting washed away. They're blowing my events out of the water.'

'Well, at least now you know your enemy,' he said. 'It's a big advantage. It's like when I got divorced.' He rubbed his freshly clipped beard reflectively. 'I knew my wife wanted the house. I didn't give a damn about it, but I fought like hell to hang on to it, and ended up with this place, my car and even some of my money.'

'Yeah,' Juliana agreed. 'Sure you've had an argument with Alexa, but you two will fix things up. You're made for each other. Anyone can see that. Right now, you got to prioritize. You got to make sure these engineers don't screw you again. From here on in, it's go Paul West, and go England. Whoo!' She gave a kind of cheerleader's whoop, as if her team had just scored the winning points at the World Series Superbowl final or whatever Americans play at.

Normally, the cynical Brit in me would have cringed – it's all very well announcing that you're not going to let yourself be beaten, but when you're a lone guy in a Mini up against the steely might of the French engineering establishment, a whoop doesn't solve all of your problems.

This time, though, I let Juliana's American optimism burst through my natural defences. I think I might even have whooped.

She and Tony were right, I told myself. I'd lost Boston and Miami, but there were three more cities to go. If I won them, I'd win the competition and my all-important bonus. There was still everything to play for. I was going to come back from the dead and stuff the French, who – if I knew them at all – would be getting just a little bit too cocky for their own good. At two-nil up, they'd be tempted to rest on their well-engineered laurels. They'd be off their guard and open to a surprise attack.

It had been a brilliant move on Lucy Marsh's part to make me sing the national anthem, I now realized. I could almost hear 'God Save the Queen' wafting up from the yucca plants.

2

After a fond farewell to Saint Tony – who even kitted us out with a thermos of coffee – and a promise that he could call me anywhere, anytime and I would be there with Thelma to save him, I drove us west across the Everglades.

They were very well named, we decided. They seemed to glade on for ever.

At any other time, I'd have loved to stop off and take an airboat tour through the mangroves, skimming over alligators' heads, but it was one of those days when I was doomed to keep my right foot pressed down and my eyes on the cars and trucks all around me.

It would have been a relaxing exercise, the minor challenges of overtaking and looking out for speed cops keeping my mind off my troubles. The problem was that dark thoughts kept jolting me like potholes in the road. And having Jake in the passenger seat didn't help. Living in central Paris, it had been so long since he'd been in a car other than a taxi that he was friskier than a puppy in a biscuit shop. He poked in every compartment, pressed every button, and seemed determined to try out every radio station on the North American continent.

'If you go to jail, you'd better glue your butt shut,' one chat-show host informed us.

'The Lord inhabits the praise of his people,' yodelled an FM prophet.

'We accept no responsibility for injuries or damage caused by the prizes won on our station,' breathed a woman at lightning speed.

'Jake, can't you just find some music and leave it there?' I pleaded.

'There's no music, man, it's all parler parler.'

'America invented rock 'n' roll, there must be something. I need some road music. Cruising tunes.'

'No, I know what you are needing.' Jake smiled ominously, and began digging in the pocket of his cargo pants. 'You must – how do we say? Get out of your head?'

'Take drugs, you mean?'

'No, no. Sublimate. You need posy!' He produced a small black notebook. 'The posy of boddle air,' he said.

It took me a second to understand what he meant.

'Baudelaire's poetry?'

'Yes. I am traducting them.' He meant translating. 'I will post them on a site internet and educate the Americans to France's posy. Listen. It will help your mood.' He flicked through the pages and I wondered whether it might not be less painful to jump out of the car.

'You know the poem "Chevelure"?' Jake asked.

'No.'

'Exactly. But listen. It is talking about the black hair of an exotic girl, maybe one like you, Juliana.'

'Why thank you, Jake,' she said. But the spell of his gallantry lasted only a millisecond before he began to read his translation.

'Oh fleece, sheeping to the collar,' he intoned. 'Oh curls, oh perfume, loaded with nonchalance. I get ardently drunk on the confused smells of coconut oil, mud and tarmac.'

He stopped. That, apparently, was it. Juliana wasn't looking quite so flattered any more.

'Magnifique, no? Listen to this one,' Jake went on. 'It is named "Venus Belga". I think it is on a Belgian prostitute.' He took a deep breath. I took an even deeper one. 'Here, the breasts of the smallest girls weigh several tons,' he said. 'But I don't need a big soft breast, I need it firm, or I turn into a Cossack.'

'I liked the beginning, but it kind of tailed off at the end,' I said.

'That's what France is supposed to be famous for?' Juliana asked. 'Sorry, Jake, no disrespect, but it's, like, shit.' Which was one of the most accurate bits of reviewing I'd ever heard. 'Paul needs something soothing, Jake.' She leant forward between the front seats, keyed in a radio frequency and found Lauryn Hill singing about dumping her man. Fantastic voice, great tune, but touchy subject.

'Paul? You want me to take over the driving?' Juliana asked.

'No, I'm fine, thanks.'

'But you've got your eyes closed.'

Juliana had been behind the wheel for three straight hours. American women clearly had no problems 'assuming' the driving. We were making good time, and were up in northern Florida, in a mist so thick it looked like airborne ice cream.

I was in the back with the luggage, trying to find a comfortable position for my legs, and doing my best to shake off the black cloud that had taken up residence in my soul.

Checking my messages didn't help.

'Bravo Paul,' was all Jack Tyler had to say. He'd obviously heard about the debacle in Miami.

And there was still nothing at all from Alexa.

Perhaps, I thought, because she couldn't get through. My phone was totally clogged up with texts and voicemail from weirdos raving about my knees, thighs, and other bits of my body I would have preferred to keep to myself. By the time I'd deleted them all, my battery was running low – in all senses of the expression.

So maybe it wasn't the best time to call Alexa. And it definitely wasn't the best time for her to answer at last.

'I don't get it, Alexa. What went wrong?' I asked.

'I don't know.' At least she sounded sad about it.

'I would have stayed in Miami, but I have to get to New Orleans. You understand that?'

'Perhaps that's the problem,' she said. 'I thought we would be simply travelling together. You would do your job, I would film, it was going to be – you know – *équitable*.'

'Equal? But it was – is. I never stopped you filming.'

'No, but everything was chaos – the tea party, the dancing. It wasn't what I *dreamed* of.'

'But that's what travelling is all about. The unexpected. It's a road trip, not a guided tour.'

'Yes, I know, and I love that idea, but it was all too . . .'

'Too what?'

I never found out, because the combination of low battery and being encased in a bucket of fog cut us off.

'Shit!' I shouted.

'Oh man,' Juliana said. 'Tonight, we're going to do something about those blues of yours.'

3

Our hotel was on the outskirts of Panama City. No, not the one with a canal. Even with me map-reading the last leg, we hadn't come that far off course. We were on the fringes of its namesake in Florida, up on the Gulf of Mexico.

Juliana had worked in Panama, and drove us away from the huddle of buildings around the highway intersection and into what she called the beach-party zone. The road to the zone made gaudy Miami seem as subdued as a classical French garden. Restaurants disguised as log cabins and medieval castles yelled at us to sample their megalithic portions. Every third shop seemed to be a drive-in beach supermarket selling towels emblazoned with sports team logos, Dixie flags and semi-naked women.

We hit the beachfront strip and cruised by – or sometimes through – the gigantic hotels. Many of them had expanded across the road, or moved their car parks there, and built overhead walkways to ferry their guests into the lobby without the inconvenience of going outdoors. The hotels looked brand-new, as if last year someone had had a brainwave – I know, I'll build a resort – and hired all the world's builders to get it instantly done. Which would explain the difficulty of finding a man to come and look at my folks' leaning garage.

After a mile or so, things got low-rise again, and Juliana pulled into a beachside car park.

'Here?' Jake asked. We were outside a restaurant whose name is a slang word for women's breasts and whose staff are reputedly recruited for their bra size. I knew what Jake meant. I never thought a woman would suggest coming here. If this was American feminism, I approved.

'Sure. I worked here over spring break last year. I want to see if any of my friends are still around.'

The décor was wooden benches and TV screens, the music was fist-pumping rock, and the only male staff were three young guys in T-shirts and baseball caps. They appeared to be doing the cooking, but were, I hoped, only standing in while the real chefs had a menu conference.

Not that the customers came here because of the menu.

The girls were rushing around carrying loaded trays that would have given most men a slipped disc. They weren't sex objects so much as labourers with a cleavage. Some of them were pretty, but they were too overworked to give off any kind of sexual vibe. Except, that is, for a Hispanic with classic beauty-queen features who had been excused tray duty and whose job was to pout at everyone who came in from the car park before showing them to a table.

'Table for three?' I said.

We followed the beauty queen to a bench with a view of the car park, and I noticed what it was that kept all the waitresses safe from sexual harassment. Not a security guard or a notice reminding clients of the penalties for molestation. No, it was the tights. All the girls were wearing flesh-coloured tights under their shorts, a thick coating of sheeny nylon that was about as sexy as a hair net. It was like covering their faces with a bank-robber's stocking. I got an unsavoury flashback of the London madwoman's gusset.

'You used to wear these?' I asked Juliana.

'Oh yeah. It killed me. My skin couldn't breathe.' Her skin was certainly breathing now. Her legs were open to the fresh air as far as the upper thigh, thanks to the leather skirt

I'd first seen her wearing when she was working at the Clearview. 'Does Katrina still work here? Or Dawn? Or April?' Juliana asked our waitress, a tiny blonde with pasty foundation the colour of her tights.

'No, I'm sorry,' she replied, and rushed back into the fray.

We three amigos clinked beer glasses.

'To being alive,' Juliana said. 'We escaped from a fire, remember?'

Jake, the cause of the blaze, looked suitably abashed.

'And to you two, for letting me butt in on your date,' I said.

'I don't know if this counts as a date,' Juliana said.

'Why not?' Jake was horrified at the idea that their evening together might be downgraded.

'I'll just ask if anyone knows where my pals have got to.' Juliana went to talk to the hostess by the door. While she was gone, Jake hit me with a bombshell.

'We're not bezzing,' he said gloomily.

'You're not sleeping together?' I didn't believe him. He'd had several close nocturnal encounters with this incredibly sexy woman – incredibly *sexual* woman – who had a body designed by a team of drooling schoolboys and a skirt as short as an American's summer holiday, and he hadn't slept with her? 'She was in the shower at the Clearview,' I said. 'And the two of you weren't exactly fully clothed when you started the fire.'

'Sure, she is OK to *make out*. But we never . . .'

'Wow.'

'It's the merde, man. I had forgotten. In Paris, it is not like this. You go to the bar, you go to bed. You eat the dinner, you bez. But these Américaines, they want to *date*. And you don't get nothing before the third date.'

'Wow.'

'Is that all you'll say for the rest of the night?'

I laughed. Poor Jake. He was in a worse state than me.

'Why the long face, Jake?' Juliana had returned from her scouting expedition. 'Oh, I get it. You been having a guy talk?'

'Yeah,' Jake confessed. 'Can't we count this as our third date? Allez, Juliana.'

He was direct, I had to give him that.

'Third? I'm still not sure that setting fire to a hotel counts as a second date.'

As we ate fried catfish and a logjam of fries, she explained the complexities of the American dating system. First date, it seemed, was like a job interview. You went out and interrogated each other about your potential.

'Potential?' I asked.

'Yeah, like how much you're going to be earning in ten years' time and how many years you want to work before you have kids. That kind of stuff.'

'Romantic.' It made me think of Alexa's fixation about what dreams I had in life. And worse, it reminded me that unless I won this competition and my bonus, I had no potential at all.

'And what will you be earning in ten years' time?' I asked Juliana.

'Depends how well I do at school.' She licked her lips of barbecue sauce.

'School?'

'Yeah, that's why I want to go to Vegas. Didn't Jake tell you? I been saving up and now I want to enrol for a Master's.'

'In what?' Lip-licking, I would have suggested. She was ready to tackle a doctorate in that.

'Cheerleading.'

I blew it. I was probably supposed to ask 'Classic or freestyle?' But I laughed, and she looked hurt. I thought she was making a joke about her great figure, playing up to male expectations. It was as if a guy had just said he was going to do a PhD in darts.

'My high-school cheerleader troupe won the state championship,' she said, pointing a chicken wing at me. 'And I want to study to be a trainer. It's America's fastest-growing sport, you know.'

'I'm sorry, I didn't know. Will you be majoring in pom-poms or chanting?'

She wondered about giving me a ketchup makeover, but then seemed to decide that it was too much trouble to open all the sachets.

'You don't make fun of a girl on the first date, OK?' she said. 'Not if you want a second.'

'What?' Jake gagged on a mouthful of fish. 'This counts as a date with *Paul*?'

'Stupid,' she said, lobbing an affectionate French fry at him.

'Yooliana!'

'Maria!'

A waitress with a licorice-stick perm was hugging Juliana. The two girls chattered in Spanish, flapping their hands about and apparently getting a year's news into two minutes of breathless speech. Then suddenly it seemed that the conversation had turned to me. This was confirmed when I heard Maria say a Spanish word that sounded familiar – 'men-een-skers-do-com'. She stepped back and looked under the table, as if to check whether my legs were covered, and both girls collapsed in a fit of giggles.

'I gotta go,' Maria said, giving me a huge grin as she headed towards the kitchen.

'Oh man,' Juliana said. 'You know you're famous, Paul?'

Over the next fifteen minutes, our table was visited by every waitress in the place.

'You the kilt guy?' they all wanted to know. They blushed and laughed and asked me to sign their order pads, and I got the impression I could have taken any of them for a ride in my car and – space permitting – got much more than was usual on a first date.

Jake was positively drooling, torn between frustration that he couldn't ask any of them whether they were willing to bypass the American dating system and a vicarious desire to see me take my pick of the goodies I was being offered.

And as each girl came and went, he seemed to sink closer and closer to despair. Because all I could do was smile, say hi, and think of Alexa. For all I knew, she was doing much more than smile at the treacherous Bostonian, but my body refused to give up hope. It wanted to be with her, the woman it had been so cruelly torn away from, not one of these girls it had never met before. And if Alexa *wasn't* cheating on me, as she claimed, then I didn't want to do anything that might make me stop wanting her. I can't stay in a relationship if someone else's body flashes into my mind all the time. Screwing around totally screws up my screwing.

'Bye,' I said as the last waitress left.

'Merde, Paul.' Jake's tongue was practically touching the floor. 'You have a serious problem, man. You can take any of those women into your Mini, and boom.' His hands mimed two bodies colliding. 'Juliana, will you come with me to the car? Please?'

'Jake,' she said, 'you're the one with the serious problem.'

4

I went to call Alexa from the privacy of the parking lot.

The sea was a blanket of shadow. Beyond the lights of the oceanfront hotels and restaurants, a couple of red pinpoints were the only signs that the Gulf of Mexico wasn't completely lifeless.

'*Bonjour, c'est bien le portable d'Alexa . . .*' It was the start of the bilingual message she'd recorded – with my help – back in the apartment in Paris. I cut it off before the end. I didn't want to talk to a phone company's computer. I needed to speak to her.

I saw that I'd had a few texts, none of them from Alexa. Suraya had sent one. 'Pls call asap,' it said. Perhaps I was going to get the boot, not direct from my boss but via the outsourced call centre in India. That was probably how they did it these days. There was also a screenful of messages from weirdo kilt fans. I stopped reading after three and cleared the whole inbox. A man can only take so many requests for a personal viewing of his undercarriage.

Next I phoned Suraya. Might as well get the bloodshed over with, I decided.

She sounded depressed and excited at the same time. She was hopping around from subject to subject, moaning that her dad was pressurizing her to give up work, then raving about Jack Tyler and the national newspapers.

'You're mentioned in the English papers,' she told me, 'and you are on the home page of the *Miami Herald*, too. The picture of you in the kilt.'

'Shit.'

'No, it's good. Mr Tyler has asked us to put a link from the Visitor Resources website to your page on Men in Skirts.'

'But I asked him to zap all photos of me.'

243

'Oh no, he has given us some more. Very cute. The girls here are all fans. So is one of the boys.'

'What?' Tyler must have gone direct to the madwoman who'd interviewed me. He'd got his hands on all the busby and Beefeater shots. And the ones in between, like when I'd put on the kilt but forgotten to take off my Beefeater collar. I must have looked like a pink-stemmed daisy. And this stuff was going on Britain's official tourist website? What kind of image were they trying to promote?

'It's fantastic,' Suraya bubbled. 'Mr Tyler says that some men in Miami have posted a message telling everyone to lobby the mayor to support your campaign. Isn't that great?'

'Yeah, wonderful.' In an indescribably hellish way.

'Imagine if it spreads. You will just need to arrive in a city, show your legs, and the vote will be won.'

'Fantastic.' Although my sarcasm did start to ebb away. What if – just if – she was even partially right? What if I could win Miami after all, thanks to the stupid photos? 'So Tyler's actually pleased with the gay-website fiasco?'

'Yes. It makes the problems in New Orleans seem less important,' Suraya said.

'Sorry? What problems?'

'New Orleans. They sent you a text. Didn't you see it?'

'I zapped most of them. What's the trouble?'

'I told you we're sponsoring a performance of a Shakespeare play there, right?'

'No, Suraya, you didn't.'

'Ah, sorry. Anyway, the Shakespeare should be good. It is on a plantation. You don't have to do anything except show them your Mini – and maybe your legs.' I let her get away with a gratuitous giggle. 'But a problem has arisen.'

'What kind of problem?'

'The best thing is if I email you the number of the organizer there, a man called Woodrow. He will explain.'

'OK, fine. What's the play?'

'*Othello*.'

Great, I thought, a tragedy about a guy who thinks his wife is shagging someone else. Just what I needed.

5

'Holy fur.' I caught myself just in time, remembering that I was in a public place. I was consulting my emails back at the hotel, a semi-chic business place, its lobby decorated with a deep burgundy carpet, shiny leather sofas, and oil paintings of historic American landscapes.

I had already alienated myself from the cleaning staff by handing over a plastic sack of the most rumpled laundry seen in America since a trunk was salvaged from the *Titanic*. They were going to have to wash it as a single asteroid-like blob of material, and see what kind of garments separated themselves out during the spin cycle.

I didn't want to add swearing to my misdemeanours.

The first part of Suraya's long email outlined the problem with the Shakespeare, which was obvious, really. I mean, what idiot had had the bright idea of trying to boost British tourism by putting on a play in Louisiana, the heart of the old slave economy, in which a Black guy kills a White woman? Sounds like typical Tyler, I thought.

Anyway, Suraya said I was going to get an email from this Woodrow guy who was in charge of the event.

'Fur me,' I said when I got to the second part of her message.

It was a list of radio stations and their phone numbers, with each station allotted a ten- or twenty-minute slot throughout the following afternoon and early evening. There were also a couple of newspapers in there. And all of them wanted an interview with the undercarriage of the month. With me.

My fifteen minutes of fame had arrived, it seemed, and because of the different time zones in the USA, they had been spread out over half a day.

There was also an email from Alexa, which I saved till last. I was scared of what it might say.

She needed to 'think about us', she told me. Think about us? What did that mean? She was going to fantasize about me while she was banging her giant leprechaun?

She was 'really disappointed in me', she said. I had chosen Jake, after all. I had left Miami without her, and then called from a car where it was totally impractical to talk. It was proof that I 'didn't care enough about us', she said.

That is 'total bollocks', I wanted to reply. You are being 'bloody unfair'.

All in all, she concluded, it was a good idea to spend some time apart. It had been too 'restricting' in the car, and 'in our case, too much proximity gives too much conflict'.

Oh, yeah, I thought, she was probably getting pretty damn proximitous, or whatever the word was, with that Mike.

6

'Good morning, Ohio.'

It was a phrase that I never imagined having to say in this lifetime.

'Right, yeah, great, Paul. Can you make it, like, a bit more up? Good mo-orning, O-HI-o!' Pete, the guy at the other end of the line, was clearly riding high on a wave of Prozac and laughing gas. He said it like a kid who's just woken up and remembered that last night he lost his virginity.

'Good morning, Ohio.' I sounded more like I'd just lost my sanity, but Pete was happy enough. I guessed he was always happy enough. I imagined a tall guy, all tan and teeth, with a sports car and bimbo waiting out in the parking lot. Of course, in reality he could have been a one-legged toothless anaemic. That's the wonder of radio.

'Perfect. We can get started.'

There was a computer-generated musical whoosh, followed by a gospel choir singing the four letters of the radio station's name to the same tune used for radio jingles all over the known universe, and then Pete started gushing about me.

'He's young, he's English, he talks like one of the princes, and he is over here in America to publicize his sexy website, on which you can see him wearing a Scottish kilt that's so short he would suffer some painful frostbite if he wore it in Cleveland. You know what I mean, ladies, right? Hey, Paul, welcome to America!'

This was my cue to lose my radio virginity, but I didn't know what to say. I was in America to publicize my sexy website? Hadn't someone told him why I was really here?

'Hello Pete,' I finally said, after two seconds of radio silence that even I, the amateur, found painful.

'So, tell us about this kilt of yours, Paul. How short is it exactly?'

'Just a bit *too* short.'

'Yeah, because on this website, apparently we can see more than just your kilt, right? I haven't seen it, but my producer tells me it's *very* revealing.' No way would Pete have clicked on a guy's undercarriage, of course.

'Yes, but it was an accident, you see.'

'You accidentally put on a kilt? That's a pretty freak accident, Paul.'

'Ha, yes – no – I mean, the main purpose of the website is to make Americans more aware of Britain's natural and historical heritage. We have a thousand years of history—'

'Yeah. Talking about history, Paul, there's one thing I've always wanted to ask an Englishman.'

'Yes?'

'Was Princess Diana murdered by the Royal Family?'

The interview went downhill from there. I ummed and erred, producing plenty of whatever the opposite of a soundbite is. Sounddribbles? Soundburps? And then all too soon it was arrivederci Cleveland.

After good morning Ohio, I did good afternoon New England, wake up Wisconsin, coo-ee Connecticut and hola California, some of them live, some of them recorded, but all along the same lines. The interviewers were always surreally friendly, the general tone being, 'Hey, you're in America doing something wacky, entertain us about it.' Everyone was very glad to have me on their show, highly amused by the kilt business, but totally uninterested in the World Tourism Contest and how I was staging British-themed events to attract votes for my country.

Predictably, almost all of them steered way clear of the gay-website issue. Only California broached the subject.

'Are you gay, Paul?' the butch-sounding hostess asked.

'No, I'm English. There is a difference.'

She sounded disappointed.

The coyest of the lot was the host on a station called something like KGOD, who warned me before our interview began that it was live but with a one-minute delay to allow them to censor any immorality that might creep into the discussion. He seemed keen to point out to his listeners the moral dangers of male skirt-wearing, especially when it is part of pagan local folklore.

'You're right,' I told him, 'the kilt is a bad thing. Especially if you're wandering around the Highlands in summer with nothing on underneath. The insects can get right up there and have a free bite at your—'

The interview ended before the insects could get any further.

Still, my half day stuck in the hotel did bring one piece of good news – an email telling me that *Othello* had been cancelled. And I couldn't blame Suraya or Visitor Resources for the bad choice of play, either. It had been picked by this guy Woodrow, who'd written me a stream-of-consciousness message totally devoid of capital letters and punctuation, in which he blathered on about Shakespeare and the need to heal Black–White relations through theatre and sugar planting. Or something like that. A typical sentence (if you could call a group of words with no recognizable beginning or end a sentence) ran like this:

> the teachers vetoed othello and then threw out my second
> choice romeo and juliet on account of it was too sexy i
> guess we would have had to bring forward the marriage
> scene to make it moral enough for them

Exhausting. But, if I understood correctly, now that he'd ditched the *Othello* plan, the Shakespeare show he was going to put on at his plantation would have the approval of the local community, so there was less chance of me taking a midnight swim in the Mississippi with a riverboat anchor tied to my feet.

7

It took us only a short day's driving to cross the remaining wedge of Florida, a sliver of Alabama, and a couple of hours' worth of Mississippi coast. We progressed from idyllic bleached-sand beaches, with villas on stilts built right over the sea, to the anonymous ribbon of the interstate, and finally to a sort of car-borne buzz of anticipation as we approached the cluster of highways leading into New Orleans.

With Juliana at the wheel, the Mini seemed to have found its place in the food chain as the little hustler, the opportunist, a kind of four-wheeler mongoose. It was too small to make the big predators feel threatened, and nippy enough to dart out of trouble if it annoyed anyone. Thelma had learnt how to survive in the ecosystem of the interstate highways. And Juliana had obviously been born there.

As we branched off left and followed highway ten into downtown New Orleans, the heavy winter sunset suddenly lit the sky ahead. The twin bands of highway were like two blue stockings poking out of the pink tutu of cloud.

We crossed the longest bridge I'd ever been on, a causeway so endless that you forgot you were over water, and then we hit more swamp. Low-lying woods and wetlands, glimpses of the vast lake. It was hard to know whether it was the usual state of things or if the area had been flooded by the hurricanes and the water had never receded.

'See that? Bayou Sauvage,' Jake said. He was sitting in the back, working on his Baudelaire translations. 'And have you seen that sign before? *Bienvenue en Louisiane.* The last piece of French culture in America.'

'Of what?' Juliana asked. He had pronounced it 'cool-toor'. I translated it for her. 'All Cajuns do is sing country music with French words,' she said.

Jake grunted in pain. 'The proof – we Americans know nothing of the real French cool-toor that inspired the Cajuns, that is the problem. This is the reason I will change my name.'

Juliana and I both expressed our surprise. This was the first we'd heard of it.

'Yeah, this is why I come to see my mom. I must tell her. I want to change my name to Rimbaud.'

'But he's Italian,' Juliana objected.

Again, I had to translate. Jake was not talking about the character played in the movies by Sylvester Stallone, I explained. This one was spelt differently, and was a French poet.

It was logical, I reasoned. Jake was already a French poet in all but name – he smoked like one, and had a very poetic view of sex in that all his relationships were haikus rather than novels.

'Why don't you change it to Baudelaire?' I asked.

'Oh no. I am not worthy.'

'But mightn't it cause confusion in the bookshops to have two poets with the same name?' I asked.

'Hey man, don't mock my om-ahj,' he warned.

Did he mean his 'homage'? I asked. Yes, he replied, his 'om-ahj', and Juliana backed him up. Turned out it was one of those words like 'herb' that the Americans pronounce *à la française*. 'Erb', they say, making themselves sound like Rasta dealers.

'Well, you've certainly arrived in France now,' I said. 'We just passed the Pointe aux Herbes, herb point, and there's a Lake Born. What's that?'

I handed him the atlas, and he took great pleasure in correcting my pronunciation.

'Born-ya. Lake Borgne. Man with One Eye Lake. Hey, and look, here is Chef Menteur highway – chief liar. It's fun, Louisiane.' He then ruined the newly upbeat ambience in the car by adding, 'They will adore Baudelaire.'

We sloped down off the highway, all of us slightly nervous about entering the city at dusk. We knew that there were neighbourhoods where a Mini and its contents could be seen as very worthwhile prey. We'd all heard about the hurricane damage and the slow pace of regeneration. It didn't feel like the kind of place to get lost in.

But we found the French Quarter easily, and within five minutes we'd got ourselves a luxurious room with three queen beds – all for the price of a windowless cubicle in a London backstreet. The hotel was a converted city mansion, with bare brick walls, French windows, and the faded, flaking glory of New Orleans' ironwork balconies.

We strolled out to a restaurant that featured a guy with a metal glove opening a never-ending supply of oysters. They looked tempting, but I was put off trying any by the legal disclaimer at the foot of the menu – 'Eating raw oysters may cause death.' These American lawyers sure knew how to give you an appetite.

After a seafood dinner as fresh, well-cooked and modestly proportioned as anything I've had in Paris, we hit Bourbon Street and its shouting throng of bars and clubs.

Bars were selling drinks to take away. None of this no-alcohol-in-public nonsense – studenty types were sloshing beer and cocktails over their chins from giant plastic beakers as they staggered along the street, checking out the blast of music exploding from every doorway. The jocks were also ogling and hassling the granite-eyed cuties stand-ing outside the lapdance places, who turned on professional smiles and tried to usher the drunks inside.

I couldn't decide if it was the beginning or the end of the world – primitive life forms learning to stand on two legs, or the last fizz of decadence before they all fell over and civilization became extinct.

Whatever. It was fun.

We paddled upstream through the crowd blocking the entrance to a pub, stared at the vibrating tonsils of a girl shrieking Janis Joplin songs, and then went next door, where three old jazzmen were doing their best to compete with Janis, popping their eyeballs to push their trumpet, tuba and drums to the limit. It was a blast, but the band played one blue note too many for me, and I suddenly got hit by a wrenching sadness that Alexa wasn't here. She thought it was better to spend some time apart rather than come to New Orleans? What the hell could she be doing that was more of a thrill than this? I hardly dared think.

I left the two Js to it and headed back towards the hotel through the empty side streets.

It was on one of the street corners – there was a crossroads about every twenty yards in the French Quarter – that I found an old man propped up against his suitcase, with a small cluster of people gazing down at him from a respectful distance.

He had a boxer's nose and a scraggly white beard. He was wearing a thick brown overcoat, with white trainers on bare feet, and seemed to be holding court beneath the iron balcony of a closed art shop. As I got closer, I saw that the seat he was perched on was a small amplifier, and that he was holding a battered red electric guitar clutched to his chest.

He launched into a blues, and he was astonishingly good. His voice was throaty but clear, his playing chunky and rhythmic. I recognized the song. He was, he sang, standing at the crossroads, trying to find his way home. A classic blues, with hypnotically repetitive words.

For the second verse, he branched off from the original. Now he was '*sitting* at the *fucken* crossroads'. And in the last verse, he was 'sitting at this fucken crossroads, cos I ain't got no fucken home,' which got a cheer from his audience. 'Yeah,' he concluded, 'I got the hurricane homeless blues.' He played a short, searing guitar solo, and stopped.

The small crowd was silent for a moment and then clapped and cheered. The old guy ignored them, and got out a cigarette packet.

I went over, gave him a five-dollar note and told him, 'That was real blues.' But he didn't hear me. He was too busy trying to extract a cigarette from his squashed packet.

Another spectator dropped a note into the open guitar case and said something that made the old guy grunt a bitter laugh. He gave up tugging at his cigarette packet, threw it to the ground, and growled, 'Shit life.'

He seemed to like the sound of this, and chanted 'Shit life' four or five times to himself. This went on for a few seconds as we all waited for him to turn his chanting into a song, but he seemed to forget the crowd, his guitar and his money, and began yelling 'Shit life, shit life!' at the sky.

Standing beside me on the sidewalk was a chic guy, dressed in a sports-branded anorak, crisp jeans and expensive trainers. He turned to his equally chic girlfriend and said, in a strong American accent, 'He's probably got Tourette's or something.'

'No,' I butted in. 'I think he's probably got a shit life. It is possible, you know, even in America.'

8

'Where are you?' Alexa wanted to know. It's probably the most commonly uttered question between girlfriend and boyfriend on the phone, constantly checking up on each other.

Actually it was a good question, because I didn't know the answer.

'In Louisiana somewhere. We've lost the Mississippi.' It might seem difficult to misplace one of the world's mightiest rivers, but we'd managed it. Actually, driving out in the bayou it's pretty easy to do. 'It's great to hear from you,' I said. 'How are things going?' It sounded like a neutral question, but of course it meant a million things. Like, have we spent enough time apart yet? And where exactly did Mike the Bostonian sleep last night?

'Yes, fine, thanks. I'm filming in Miami, but *j'ai un truc à te demander*.' Something to ask me, and in French, too. It had to be serious. She was certainly sounding very stern. '*Mes photos.*'

'Which photos?'

'My photos of you. The ones that were in my exhibition in Paris and London.'

'Oh.' It was unpleasant to be reminded of something so pleasant. Alexa had spent the first months after we'd met taking photos of me unawares. They were mostly shots of me waiting for her to turn up to a date – happy times when I'd been impatient to see her rather than resigned not to.

'Was it you who gave permission to put them on the English tourism website? And how did they get them, anyway?'

'Your photos are on the Visitor Resources website? I had no idea.'

'They're all high-resolution scans. Someone gave them the files. It wasn't you?'

'No, of course not. This whole business with internet photo sites is way out of my control.'

'Well, I've been advised to get a lawyer and sue them. Maybe shut down the website.'

'Sue them?' She was turning even more American by the minute. 'But that'd totally screw up my campaign.'

'Then tell them to take my photos off.'

'But isn't it good publicity for you?'

'It's unpaid use of my photos.'

'Is that the only reason you called?'

'What? I can't hear you? Are you in a tunnel?'

'There are no tunnels in Louisiana. They'd only fill up with water.'

'What?'

'I said, is that the only reason you called?'

'Oh damn, not another one.' Juliana punched the steering wheel. We'd come to a dead end, blocked by the entrance to a petrochemical site. Every time you turned off the main road, you ended up meeting a large sign announcing that some multinational had bought the rest of the bayou.

'Who's that in the car with you?' Alexa asked.

'Juliana. She's driving.'

'Juliana?' Alexa sounded shocked, and I remembered too late that I hadn't wanted to mention that Jake wasn't my only hitchhiker.

'Yes, she and Jake are – you know – dating,' I said.

'Jake? He never *dates*. It's you, you invited her. I said you had a thing for receptionists.'

'For a start, she's not a receptionist, and she's Jake's girl-friend, for God's sake, not mine. I've already got a girlfriend, Alexa – you.' At least I hoped I did.

'You'd better take my photos off that website,' she said, and hung up.

I began to redial, but stopped. There wasn't much point continuing the conversation, I realized. It had to be one of the side-effects of my mini-fame. I was already having relationships like the Hollywood stars. Box-fresh love one minute, legal action the next.

9

It was an American who told me that the toothbrush was invented in the Deep South. Anywhere else and it would have been called a 'teethbrush'.

I saw what he meant. Teeth are what divide Americans. They are the ultimate status symbol. If you've got money, you've got teeth. No cash, no gnash. That, I suppose, is why rappers get their mouths walled with gold. They go from extreme poverty in childhood – and hence extremely bad teeth – to absurd wealth, and hence absurdly expensive teeth. It's why Hollywood actors can't play convincing poor people. As soon as they open their mouths, you can see that they're rich.

I remembered the teethbrush joke as we continued our tour of the bayous.

We were looking for Utopia. Who isn't? you might say, but this one really existed. It was the name of a plantation, and I'd been given directions by its owner, Woodrow. We had to get on the 61 out of the city, cross the Mississippi at Gramercy, then turn west and follow the river until we got to a place called Bienvenue. From there, there would be signposts to Utopia.

It all sounded simple, except that driving around the Louisiana bayous with a road atlas of America was like searching for your contact lens from a helicopter.

Juliana was getting pissed off. Jake, though, was happy enough in the back, reading all the French road signs. We'd seen towns called La Place, La Branche, Longue Vue, and even Vacherie, which means cowshed but also a nasty trick to play on someone. Backstabtown. Jake was writing them all down and, I feared, thinking up words to rhyme.

'Let's ask someone,' I suggested, remembering my

conversations with Alexa about macho men being doomed to stay lost for eternity.

But there was no one to ask except the trees, the reeds and – I guessed – the alligators. The houses we'd seen didn't exactly make me want to stop in a tiny urban car and request help in a foreign accent. Most of them were ancient cabins knocked askew by floods, or maybe simply uprooted and dumped miles away from where they'd originally stood. Sometimes a wrecked house had a fancy car standing in the yard. This had to be the only place in the Western world where people's cars were more valuable than their homes.

We eventually found a sign pointing us back to the high-way and followed the road as far as a small town with a brick-built diner. Its parking lot was inhabited by big-wheeled pickups and rusty saloons. All I could see through the front bay window was a bobbing sea of baseball caps. Oh no, I thought, if any of these guys recognizes me as the Englishman who wears skirts, I am dead.

The interior could have been bought up by a French art foundation and shipped out to the Centre Pompidou, floor stains included. They'd even have bought a few of the customers. The place was spacious, with at least twenty booths, and had been built in the 1960s by someone who loved red Formica and yellow metal tubing. It was like a cafeteria for astronauts. The ceiling lights were solar systems, the fixed booths were mounted on curved rocket fins.

But it had been used and abused by a few generations of landlubbers since. Our table had cigarette-burn craters in its Mars-like surface. On the wall was a poster ad for a lawyer, a well-fed White guy in shirt sleeves and braces who called himself 'number one for industrial accidents' and promised to get you ten thousand dollars per crushed limb. Behind the counter was a man-sized fridge with a bumper sticker on the door saying, 'If the answer is Clinton, it's a pretty dumb question.' And above the serving hatch was a large handwritten notice, in clumsy capitals, saying, 'GORDON IS BANNED FROM THIS PLACE.'

There were about a dozen customers, with, all told, maybe a hundred teeth between them. I knew this because, to my surprise, when we walked in, everyone looked up and smiled.

A small waitress in a black skirt and black leggings was moving from table to table, setting out fresh salt cellars and bowls of ketchup sachets.

'How y'all doin' today?' she asked. She was only about thirty, but she had no top teeth at all. Maybe Gordon had punched them out.

We ordered coffee, and when the waitress came back with three steaming mugs, we asked about Utopia. She shook her head guiltily.

'I ain't from heyuh. Ah'm from Gramercy,' she said. It was about five miles down the road. She called for help from the general population. 'Any you guys know Utopia?'

Immediately, everyone in the diner broke off their conversations and had a debate about how to get to the plantation. They discussed various backroad routes, discarded the more complicated ones, and then came to a consensus about how three strangers could drive to Utopia without getting lost.

A tall man in an oil company baseball cap came over to the table to convey their decision. He seemed slightly better dressed than the others, and had almost all his teeth, too. The local dentist, perhaps.

'You want to visit the plantation?' he asked.

'No,' Jake said. 'There will be a piece of Shakespeare there.'

'A Shakespeare play,' I translated. 'Tomorrow night. We're helping to organize it.'

'Shakespeare?' the man said. I saw raised eyebrows around the room, and had a sudden attack of doubt that people down here would be interested in a bunch of men in tights talking in poetry. Still, I reasoned, selling tickets to the masses wasn't really my problem. I was only interested in the local dignitaries who had a vote in my World Tourism competition.

'You actors?' the waitress asked, a look of wonderment on her face as if we'd beamed in from Hollywood.

'No,' I said. 'We're just—'

'Yes,' Jake said. 'Paul, he is Scottish, he will play Macbeth in a kilt.'

'A kilt?' the spokesman repeated, and I looked around for something to stuff in Jake's mouth and shut him up. A bar stool, perhaps.

'Yeah, I'm from Scotland,' I said, in my gruffest whisky voice.

'Hey, you Cajun?' the waitress asked Jake. 'You gotta weird aksint.'

'No, but I speak French. Do you?' he asked.

The waitress didn't hear his question because she was shouting over to another table.

'Hey, Mee-shell, git over here! This guy tokes Frinch.'

A grey-haired man in a black ski anorak and a faded pink baseball cap that had probably been on his head every day and night for forty years hobbled over to our table, and introduced himself in an accent that was uncannily like Jake's.

He was Michel, he said, and lived in 'Gary-veel'. He was a retired 'feesherman', and was 'heppy' to meet someone who 'tok Frensh'. He didn't really speak it himself, he said, but his parents used to, so he 'got the geest'. He was much easier to understand than Jake, because he didn't use French words.

'You here to teash Frensh?' he asked Jake.

'No, not really. But I hope to teach the Americans about European cool-toor. You know Rimbaud, Verlaine, Baudelaire?'

'Rambo, sure, but the others . . .'

'*Justement*.' Jake shooed Juliana over to my side of the booth, invited Michel to slide in, and started lecturing him in mangled Anglo-French. Michel nodded, understood, and even laughed. Jake looked as though he'd landed in heaven. A place where people listened to what he said without taking ten minutes to translate each sentence into a comprehensible language. He was home.

10

'Woodrow?' I failed to keep a note of disbelief out of my voice. No, more than a note, a whole symphony. I'd done a Google Images on him, and he'd looked as old as the plantation house itself – older even, because the house had fewer cracks and dents in its facade.

The guy standing in front of me was – what? Fifteen? Twenty? Twenty-five, tops. The trouble in America is that lots of men have boyish faces, and you can only tell their age when you get up close and check out the wrinkles. This guy was very close, clasping my hand and smiling into my eyes, and he barely had laugh lines. His hair was the same chocolate brown as the Mississippi, and hung over a shirt collar that was way too loose for him. His wide, florid tie seemed to be preventing the shirt from sliding down off his shoulders. He was a kid dressed in his dad's clothing.

What's more, we were standing in a tiny shack – an ochre-stained shed with a pointed wood-tiled roof. And this was meant to be the plantation-owner's office? It was a garden playshed.

Woodrow explained my mistake. I'd seen a photo of Woodrow Woodrow the Twelfth, his grandfather, and he was Woodrow Woodrow the Fourteenth. He had taken over the management of the plantation on his grandfather's death. Woodrow the Thirteenth had dropped out of line for reasons he didn't go into.

He spoke at about one word per minute, all the time smiling benignly as if he'd just eaten some magic mushrooms and was watching dinky green elephants fly around my head. There were no traces of Deep South in his accent. The family didn't believe in sending their kids to the local schools, it seemed.

'Did you grow up on the plantation?' I asked.

'Yeah, but I went to school in the northeast.' I guessed he meant Harvard or Yale. Or possibly both. 'Hey, before I forget, I got something for you.'

He picked up a yard-long FedEx tube from his cluttered desk. It was addressed to me, care of him. He lent me a pair of scissors to open it, and patiently held one end of the tube while I probed about trying to extract the contents. It was as if he had absolutely nothing else to do for the next twenty years.

'Oh my God,' I moaned when I'd unrolled the three items inside. The first was a small printed note telling me that I'd attracted new sponsors to my campaign and was to attach the enclosed stickers to each of my car doors. The two basketball-sized stickers were what caused me to moan. One was the logo of a 100 per cent German make of car. The other depicted an ejaculating bottle of well-known French fizzy water.

So Britain had outsourced the rest of its campaign.

Transport was being handled by the Germans, and the catering contract had gone to the French.

'Problem?' Woodrow asked with the same carefree smile on his face.

'No, no problem.' No more than usual, anyway.

We drove the twenty yards to the main house on Woodrow's little golf buggy.

The place was smaller than I'd envisaged. It wasn't a kind of White House with thick classical columns and a Greek temple portico. It was a brick-and-wood building painted the same ochre as Woodrow's hut. It had a white balustraded porch and tall French windows with spinach-green shutters. With its high, orange-tiled roof, it was a bizarre mix of American mansion and Provençal villa.

'We can get a tour of the house tomorrow,' Woodrow said, 'if you really want to see portraits of all my ancestors.' He drove us around the back of the house, towards the Mississippi which was lurking half a mile away. The front of the house had been all formal lawns and picket-fenced driveway, but now we were chugging through a mossy, pre-historic forest of trees with green spaghetti hanging from their branches. The air was only slightly less damp than the dark waters of the swamp. Instinctively, I tucked my feet and hands tight inside the buggy in case of ambush by an alligator or a chainsaw-wielding wacko.

'This is the kind of landscape my ancestors cleared when they created the first plantation,' Woodrow said. He stopped at the edge of a wide gooey river channel to let us appreciate the dank, fetid charm of the place.

'Did you have slaves?' Juliana wanted to know.

'Oh, yes, of course,' Woodrow said. 'The family's wealth was based entirely on slave labour.' He said this with such openness that even Juliana couldn't think of a retort. 'The original house was almost certainly built by slaves, and we've found traces of a whole village of slave cabins out in the cane fields. I'm having the site excavated by Louisiana State University, and we're going to re-create a slave village so visitors can see what life was like for them. We'll have actors in costume, a working blacksmith . . .'

'A flogging and branding show at eleven o'clock every morning,' Juliana suggested.

'I want to be honest about the way the South got rich,' Woodrow said, 'so we won't hide anything. You know, in the house we have a portrait of my great-great-grandfather in a blue uniform, and his brother in grey. We have a chequered past. That's why I put on these shows for the local community. I want to give something back. Ah, an alligator,' he added matter-of-factly, as a log hoisted itself on to the back of a fellow log about twenty yards away. 'A small female, I think. They come here to sunbathe.' They'd be better off going to a solarium, I thought. Even out on the open water, the faint rays of sun were barely making it through the soupy atmosphere.

Woodrow started up the buggy again and lurched deeper into the forest.

'I'll show you where you'll be staying tonight,' he said. 'We have a little guest cabin out here in the swamp.'

11

'Toe bay oh natter bay. Thayut is the quiz Chan. Wither tis nobbler—'

'*Nobler*, Denzel, nobler. I told you before.'

'Wither tis *nobler* in the man . . .'

On a wooden stage at one end of a long, white party marquee on the plantation lawns, a teenage rap fan was doing his best to be a Danish prince, but it was a giant leap for a young man. He was frowning at his book as if he had to sight-read a secret code, which I suppose he did.

The teacher sitting in the front row, a forty-something White guy in a tight white shirt and sky-blue tie, looked harassed but resigned to a career of stress.

'Did you read this at home, Denzel?' he asked when the boy ran into a word he couldn't work out. It sounded like 'con-toom-lee'.

'They're going to do a kind of Best of Shakespeare compilation,' Woodrow whispered. 'It's bound to be dreadful, but at least they're up there doing something. Katrina destroyed their homes and wrecked their school.' He made the hurricane sound like a crazy neighbour. 'Hey, maybe you should read a passage or two. They'd love it in your English accent.'

'No chance,' I objected. I didn't know what 'con-toom-lee' was, either.

'Well, I'm sorry,' Woodrow said. 'I had great plans for the show, but they didn't work out. I hope we can salvage something for your campaign.'

For once I was actually glad that the photos of my under-carriage were out there in the public domain. At least now a screwed-up event didn't matter as much. Woodrow had told me that TV cameras were coming out to film me and the car, and that the people from city hall were delighted by all the coverage. It sounded as if their vote in the competition was mine for the taking.

'Tubby or not tubby. Vat is dee quess-tchun.' The teacher was showing the schoolkid how *Hamlet* should be read in authentic British English, and a hideously wrong Cockney accent was floating up towards the roof of the marquee.

'Let's get out of here,' Woodrow said.

He drove me back to the guest cabin, where Jake and Juliana were settling in. Or rather, where Juliana was cringing in a bedroom and Jake was on the porch overlooking a football-pitch-sized lake, reading his Baudelaire translations to the alligators. They were doubtless lying in rows out there in the mist, arguing about which of them was going to have the pleasure of crawling up and silencing him for ever.

'I adore this place,' he said.

'Yes, neat, isn't it?' Woodrow said. 'My father built it. He's always preferred to keep away from all the visitors around the main house. Other people aren't really his thing.' He stared across the lake as if looking for his dad out there in the forest.

'He doesn't mind us squatting here?' I asked.

'Oh no, he has his own place down by the river.' Woodrow nodded into the rapidly growing darkness. 'Hey, you know the movie *Swamp Thing*? Well that was my father.'

'He directed it?' I asked.

'No, he *was* it. He inspired it.' Woodrow laughed affectionately. 'I'll see you in the morning.'

I hoped he was right.

'I'm not staying here,' Juliana said, though she was in bed and gripping a bright-red duvet with both fists as if she'd never let go. 'Go in the bathroom, look in the drawers next to the mirror.'

It was a tasteful, sauna-style room with a large oval tub – a jacuzzi almost – and a mirror that stretched from floor to ceiling. The house might have been built by the Swamp Thing, but Mrs Swamp Thing had evidently had a say in the décor.

I opened the top drawer of a plain wooden cabinet next

266

to the mirror. Inside was a small pile of gun magazines. *Sniper's Gazette, Drive-by Weekly, Firing Squad Newsletter*. Standard stuff.

'So?' I called out to the next room. 'Everyone in America reads these.'

'Next drawer down,' she said.

I pulled the second drawer, which rattled open to reveal a veritable scrap heap of spent bullets. There was a two-inch-thick layer of cartridge cases, ranging from tubes the size of my little fingertip to things that would make holes in armour plating.

'Wow,' I said.

'There's the same stuff in a drawer in the kitchen. And go look in the refrigerator.'

I walked along the low-ceilinged corridor and crossed the open kitchen to a man-sized American fridge. A heave on the door handle showed me what she meant. In amongst the staple foods of a generously stocked guest cabin was a rough-edged hunk of raw meat, as deep red as beetroot and apparently well on its way to putrefaction.

I called Woodrow to explain the problem. He didn't sound put out.

'Oh, just dump it in the lake. The alligators will take care of it.'

I did so, bowling it cricket-style to get the maximum distance between us and an imminent alligator feeding frenzy.

'It's OK,' I told the still-cringing Juliana. 'The meat's gone, and the bullets are just proof that whoever hunts out here clears up after himself. He's an ecologist.' I tried to sound convincing.

'Oh yeah? Look in the bedroom across the hall.' Her wide eyes pointed the way.

I found the light switch and nearly jumped backwards

through the wall. Hanging from the ceiling on lengths of string were two alligator heads, and a garland of small brown hands, severed at the wrist. I moved close enough to check that the hands weren't human. They had knobbly leather fingers tipped with long black claws. They were alligator paws.

'Throw it all in the lake,' Juliana said.

'I can't. This isn't rotting meat – it's obviously part of the décor. Looks like he's just into alligator skin.'

'No, it's voodoo,' Juliana said. 'There's blood and feathers out on the porch. I'm not staying here.'

'Oh, you will march on foot through the maray?' Jake said. He had come in out of the tubercular night.

'Uh?'

'He says you're not going to walk through the marsh, are you?' I translated.

'OK, maybe not,' she said. 'But one of you guys is going to sleep in the same bed as me.'

'Will it count as a date?' Jake could speak perfect English when it was really necessary.

12

I opened my eyes in the pitch darkness. The walls seemed to be shuddering.

'Paul? You hear that?' Juliana whispered from across the hall.

'What was it?'

'Don't know. Sounded like—'

With perfect timing, an explosion shattered the night. The blast rolled around the lake and shook the cabin's foundations. If it had any.

'Merde!' So Jake was awake too.

We listened, the only sounds our breathing and the frogs, who had calmed down and started singing again.

'Well, it seems to have stop—' I began, before a third explosion – much nearer, this time – lifted our beds off the floor. Someone was shelling us. And in the Deep South it was probably legal to fire missiles at foreigners.

'I'll call Woodrow,' I whispered. 'If I can find my phone.'

'Don't turn the lights on!' Juliana gasped. 'Listen!'

We all did so, and I heard. Or felt, rather. The floor-boards were rocking slightly, as if we were on a boat. Above the noises of the night, I thought I detected a wooden squeak. Someone was creeping, very softly, along the porch.

'Did you lock the door?' Juliana sounded totally petrified now.

'No,' Jake answered. 'You, Paul?'

'No,' I whispered. 'It didn't seem neighbourly.'

'Neighbourly!' Juliana didn't seem to care about insulting the locals.

There was a clearly identifiable floorboard squeak close by, and we all froze.

'Is there a gun in the cabin?' Juliana's question was barely audible. Neither Jake nor I answered. Quite frankly, I wished she hadn't even raised the subject. Until then, I'd just been imagining a mud-encrusted madman with access to heavy artillery. Now he had a shotgun, too. I'd already looked down one gun barrel on this trip, and that was enough.

I felt around the floor for my clothes. My phone was in a pocket somewhere. But it was no good in the pitch black-ness – I was grabbing at thin air. I switched on the bedside lamp.

'Paul!' An anguished female hiss greeted the false dawn.

'My phone,' I explained. 'Got it.'

The front door scraped across the floor and then clunked shut. With an intruder inside or out, I didn't know. I speed-dialled Woodrow, and before he'd even answered, I said loudly, 'Hi, Woodrow, it's your *friend* Paul, who's staying as a *guest* in the cabin at your *invitation*.' I think I might have added something about being a hunter armed with a heavy machine gun.

At last, the ringing stopped and a bleary voice said, 'Uh?'

'It's Paul,' I repeated more quietly. 'Woodrow, can you get over to the cabin, please? Now? There's someone trying to get in.'

'Oh shit.' He was suddenly wide awake. 'I'll be there. Don't make any aggressive moves.' And he was gone. Not the most reassuring conversation I'd ever had.

The floorboards creaked again. The stalker seemed to be pacing around, either on the porch or inside the kitchen–living area.

Oh, fuck this, I thought. If I was going to get shot, at least I wanted a chance to talk the guy out of doing it rather than passively getting plugged in my bed. I pulled on my trousers and stepped into the corridor.

'No!' Juliana squeaked like one of the floorboards.

'It's me,' I told her.

'Wait, Paul,' Jake said, and I heard his feet pad on to the floor.

We walked as loudly as possible towards the front door, switching on lights as we went. No one would think we were trying to pull an ambush. As we rounded the corner leading to the living area, I took a deep breath and said a breezy 'Hi'.

To an empty room.

'Là, on the porch,' Jake whispered.

There was a shadow moving back and forth across the mosquito-meshed window.

'Hello?' I called, and the shadow stopped pacing. 'Is that Mr Woodrow?' No answer. 'I'll just come and open the door for you.' I crossed the room in what I hoped was friendly haste, gripped the cold metal of the door handle and pulled.

'Good evening,' I said, realizing as I did so that I had no evidence at all that this was Woodrow XIII. For all I knew, it was just an anonymous swamp-dwelling psycho whose hobby was high explosives.

We squinted at each other in the half-light.

He was standing on the porch, dressed in a hooded green hunter's jacket and jeans that were tucked into heavy working boots. His clothes looked bloodstained, and he held a black rifle in the crook of his arm, pointing – for the moment – at the floor. The pre-dawn mist was rising up through the slats in the porch, making him look as if he had brought along a dry-ice machine. All I could see of his face was that his eyes were dark and blank, as if there was no one at home behind them.

'We're friends of Woodrow. Woodrow the Fourteenth, that is. He invited us to stay the night. Were you looking for him?'

'No.' The guy's voice was hoarse, as if he didn't use it that often.

'Ah. Can we help you in any way?' Other than by dying, I thought.

'I need . . .' He nodded towards the interior of the cabin, and raised his gun barrel a couple of inches.

'Need . . .?'

'Don't let him take Juliana,' Jake whispered in my ear.

So that was it. He wanted Juliana as the centrepiece to some elaborate voodoo ritual involving severed alligator limbs and explosions.

'Vous parlez français?' Jake asked.

'I'm not Creole,' the gunman said, and tensed.

271

Oh no, I thought, Jake has insulted the purity of his bloodline. Now we're going to get a stick of dynamite where it hurts.

'Is this your house?' I asked. 'It's a great house. Fantastic view.' As gently as possible, I swept an arm across the horizon, embracing the whole vista of rotting vegetation.

'Yes. I lived here. Before . . .'

Before he started lobbing mortars at visitors and sacrificing women, I thought. But at least we knew who he was.

'Perhaps you'd prefer us to leave?' I offered. 'We can go and find a hotel.'

'I need you to come outside.'

'Outside?'

'Stand against the rail. Face the lake.'

Oh fuck, I thought, is this goodbye world? It looked as though I'd talked my way out of getting murdered by the Miami carjacker only to be offed by a human form of pond life.

Jake and I did as we were told. Beneath my bare feet, the boards of the porch felt like fillets of wet fish. If I hadn't been about to get shot, I would have worried about catching pneumonia.

'The girl too. She needs to come outside.'

'What girl?' I said.

'The Black girl.'

Suddenly she was between us, clinging on to our arms. She must have crept into the kitchen while we were talking. She was bare-legged, with a long jacket for a dressing gown.

'Face the lake,' he said.

We turned and bowed our heads.

'We're friends of your son,' I told him. 'Woodrow invited us to stay.'

'Don't shoot us, please,' Juliana pleaded.

I listened for the sounds you hear in the movies when someone is getting ready to fire a gun, but all I could hear was frog song, female shivering and various unidentifiable bloops and splashes out on the lake. I gazed into the fog, wondering if the shapeless nothingness would be the last image engraved in my memory before a bullet burnt a hole in it.

'OK, you can turn around now.'

Slowly, Jake and I did so. Juliana stayed facing the fog.

'What the fur,' I said. Juliana whipped around to look, then gave a stifled scream.

Woodrow Woodrow XIII was loping away down a trail that led into the woods. Swinging from each arm was an assortment of alligator parts. A grinning set of jaws seemed to be snapping at his backside as he ran.

As we stood watching the thirteenth generation of plantation owner bolting to his lair, the fourteenth came rolling into view, hunched aerodynamically over his steering wheel, although his buggy was doing no more than five miles an hour.

'Was it Dad?' he asked, dismounting, and apparently seeing nothing strange in the fact that his guests were taking a barefoot midnight stroll in the freezing swamp. 'He was dynamiting the drainage channels. He thinks it'll protect us from flooding.'

'He held a gun on us so he could go and get his voodoo stuff,' Juliana said.

'Voodoo?' Woodrow laughed. 'No, he breeds alligators to make souvenirs for the shop. He probably wants to finish mounting them so we can sell them at the show tomorrow.'

'Well, he could have just asked to come in and fetch them,' I pointed out.

'Yeah. He's great with dynamite and alligators, but he's

273

not too hot on interpersonal skills. Apart from members of the family, not many people come out and stay here.'

I could see why.

12A

'I look like a petrol-pump attendant at the Highland Games,' I said.

A second Fedex had arrived, containing a fluorescent-yellow anorak and matching baseball cap, both of which had large logos of Visitor Resources: Britain and my two new sponsors stuck in strategic places on the fabric. My forehead, shoulders, chest and back had effectively become advertising space. The rest of me was presumably still open to offers. Not my legs, I hoped. Those stickers would be agony when I pulled them off.

The anorak, coupled with my kilt, was how I was contractually obliged to appear for all future media appointments. Including radio, it seemed. The order had come direct from Tyler.

I held out my arms in a crucifix pose and let Juliana take a photo of me with her phone. She and I were waiting for Woodrow XIV to pick us up from the cabin. Jake was already over at the marquee. A Cajun band was setting up, and he'd gone on ahead to try and get them to adapt Baudelaire to music, or something.

An alligator-shaped layer of pink cloud lay across the treetops. There had been a sunset of sorts, but it had given up in the face of unfair competition from my fluorescent outfit. A familiar chugging sound drifted through the twilight, and I made out two riders on the golf buggy. A tall, thin one – Woodrow – accompanied by a smaller, female shape. It – or she – was waving.

When I finally recognized her, I didn't feel like waving back. My brain started to buzz with doubts and suspicions. Her presence here was one coincidence too many.

'Hi,' she said as she kissed me on both cheeks.

'Hi, Elodie. This is a surprise.'

'Yes, it is,' she said. 'You're famous, Paul. Or your legs are, anyway. That's wonderful!'

'Well, thanks for coming a thousand miles to see them.'

'No problem. My pleasure.'

It felt like one of those scenes in a swashbuckling film where two men with rapiers are circling around, swishing their blades and being over-polite before they try to kebab each other. 'So, D'Artagnan, it gives me great pleasure to meet you.' 'Yes, Monseigneur, and it will give me equal pleasure to pluck out your kidneys with my trusty blade.' I was rapidly coming to the conclusion that Elodie deserved a bit of kidney-plucking.

'So how was your lingerie show?' I asked. 'Did the mayor of Miami come and buy your underwear?'

Elodie laughed. 'No. Why should he? It was just a little French soirée.'

'Yes, and he'd already been to another French soirée, hadn't he? With the engineers. Are they here in New Orleans, too?'

'How would I know? You think I am the type to hang out with *engineers*?'

'Well, we all seem to be travelling around America together, don't we? The engineers, me and you. Everywhere I have an event, you all turn up.'

'Surely you haven't forgotten, Paul? I'm doing a Master's in emergency and disaster management. If there's one place that needs help, it's New Orleans.' There was so much sincerity in her voice you could have used it to sweeten your coffee.

'So you've come to help rebuild the levees? Did you bring your rubber gloves?'

'Oh, Paul, you and your British humour. As tasteless as ever. I'm just doing a little thing here with the Alliance.'

'And it has nothing to do with the World Tourism competition?'

'Ah, well, I must confess . . .' She put her hands together as if she were praying. 'Since you told me about the competition, and how you might get a job at the end of it . . . Well, I have been asking myself what I will do at the end of my studies, so I offered my services to the French campaign, yes.'

'And you're organizing events in competition with mine?'

'Not exactly in competition,' said Woodrow, stepping in to defend the lady's honour. Not realizing, of course, that Elodie didn't have any. 'Elodie wants the Alliance to organize an event out here at the plantation to tie in with Mardi Gras. A re-enactment of Revolutionary War battles showing how France helped the US achieve independence.'

Why can't the French and Americans just go back to hating each other? I wondered. We Brits are America's allies, not the French.

'And does your mission include trying to screw up my campaign?' I asked Elodie. I was beginning to suspect that she might be fonder of flat-headed engineers than she admitted.

'Oh Paul, would I do that to an old friend?'

It would have been ungallant to answer.

14

While I was sinking under a flood of unpleasant surprises, Jake was like the proverbial pig in merde. He was sitting at the plantation's open-air café drinking beer with a couple of Cajun musicians in checked shirts and baseball caps. He raised the neck of his beer bottle in greeting as we rattled by on Woodrow's buggy.

The car park was filling fast. Shadows were springing up in headlight beams as people walked across the lawn to the glowing rectangle where the show was about to start. I thought I could hear someone making an announcement inside the tent. 'We've raised the stage a yard,' they were probably saying, 'so you'll be able to take photos up his kilt.'

They were going to see a landscape of goose pimples. The rheumatic evening air was making me wonder how the Scots ever managed to breed beyond the Stone Age. Even down here in Louisiana, protected by boxer shorts, you felt your wedding gear shrivelling up in self-defence, so God knows what it must have been like out on the blasted heaths of Scotland.

I had decided to read a bit of *Macbeth*, and had my script folded up in my anorak pocket. I hadn't bought the book, of course. I'd just gone online and printed out some famous scenes. It was tough choosing what to read, though. There were long chunks that I didn't understand. In the 'Is this a dagger' speech, there was a sentence like 'Witchcraft celebrates pale Hecate's sufferings,' which was as clear as the witches' brew to me. And there was no footnote to explain what a 'dudgeon' was.

I'd toyed with the idea of doing the 'Out, out damned spot' speech, but that was spoken by Lady Macbeth, and I thought that my kilt had caused enough gender confusion already.

In the end I'd settled on the 'hubble bubble toil and trouble' scene. Although in fact, I discovered, it wasn't 'hubble bubble' at all. The line was 'double, double'. I preferred the 'hubble bubble' version myself, but I'm not a bard so I thought I'd better stick to the original.

Within limits, of course. You just cannot perform Shakespeare in the unabridged, uncensored version in America these days. So out, out went the line about 'blaspheming Jews'. And the 'Turk's nose' bit the dust – there might be a restaurant owner in the audience. There was also lots in my scene that I didn't understand – what was a 'fillet of fenny snake'? – but if anyone asked, I'd just say it was an ingredient in the original recipe for haggis.

Woodrow dropped Elodie off to find her French cronies, then veered away from the car park and pulled up at the opposite end of the marquee. It was a sophisticated tent, and even came with a backstage area. This was where the city officials were waiting to meet me.

As soon as I walked through the door – or flap – three people jumped on me with smiles, handshakes and greetings. They were all African-American – one woman and two men called Renee, George and Roland – and were dressed in formal business suits, with fine gold chains around their necks and wrists. They looked like a bride, groom and best man waiting for the priest to show up.

They got the 'I saw you on the internet' stuff out of the way and then huddled around me to spell out bluntly what I had to do to gain their vote. It felt good to be dealing direct rather than through a hustler like Jesus the realtor.

'The French will be doing some good work,' Renee said. She had wonderfully manicured nails, I noticed, like a row of perfect false teeth. 'But their battle-revival thing won't interest all sections of our community, if you see what I mean.' I nodded. Of course, independence for America hadn't meant freedom for the slaves. 'You, though, you'll be tapping into the whole web community and getting us global exposure.'

'Great,' I said, 'though I don't see how reading a speech from *Macbeth* will do that.'

'One moment,' the taller of the two guys, Roland, interrupted. '*Macbeth*? Can I see the speech you're planning to read?'

I handed it over, and Renee carried on explaining how I was going to win New Orleans. She wanted me to drive around the French Quarter in the Mini, filmed by a TV crew. I would park outside some of the big hotels, say how great New Orleans was looking, stuff like that. She would then be able to use the footage on the city's website and sell it to the hotel chains, and probably get a few segments on national TV shows, too. The message would flash across the States and around the world, letting everyone know that the city was up on its feet again and ready to play host to as many visitors as wanted to come. Mardi Gras was just around the corner, and it was vital that the city's hotels be booked up.

'Fine,' I said. 'When do you want me to do the filming?'

'We can start straight after your speech here. Nighttime in Bourbon Street.'

'Isn't Bourbon Street pedestrian?' I asked, but saw from her expression that if she gave the word it would turn into an airport runway. 'What about the French engineers – are they here?' I asked.

'French engineers?' This was a new one for Renee.

'Yeah,' George said. 'Those guys gave the talk about hurricane protection.'

'Oh, yeah.' Renee looked fierce. 'But if they think they can barter help in a crisis for votes in this contest, they're barking up the wrong mangrove tree. People should offer help for help's sake, right?'

'Right,' I agreed. That wasn't exactly what I was doing, but she didn't seem to mind. Suddenly, life was looking brighter. If all I had to do to win New Orleans was read a bit of Shakespeare and then pose in a few hotels, there was a real chance of beating the French in their own historic territory.

'Wait a minute. This speech – he can't do it.' Roland was holding out my script for Renee to read. 'Look, there are *witches*,' he said. 'They're making a *potion*. They're saying a *magic spell*. They say *hell*. You know how much trouble there's been about the Harry Potter books. The city libraries have received more complaints about them than any other—'

'Don't be such a tight-ass, Roland,' Renee said. 'You never heard of voodoo? New Orleans'll love it. Now can you take a photo of me and Mr West here? Paul, will you just lift your kilt a little? It's hiding your knees.'

15

My fake accent would have got my throat slit in Glasgow, but the crowd seemed to be loving it. Flashbulbs were flickering, phones were held high, a couple of TV cameras zoomed in, and I could hear my voice booming across the bayou as loud as Swampie's explosions, drowning out the frogs and the babble of amused gossip that had started up as soon as I appeared on stage.

The kids had finished making poor old Will spin in his grave. One of them had turned Richard the Third's call for help into a fireman's lament – 'mah kingdom for a hose'. A boy and a girl had giggled so much during a scene from

Romeo and Juliet that it really did sound as if they were teenage lovers. And now I was the top of the bill. The kilt guy – now the kilt, anorak, baseball cap and logo guy – hamming *Macbeth* and realizing halfway through that in my bulky lurid top, with spindly legs poking out below, I was probably doing a very convincing impression of that other famous fake Scotsman, Shrek.

As I got to the end – 'By the pricking of my thumbs, something wicked this way comes' – I saw Elodie sneak in at the back of the tent and assume the pose of someone pretending they've been watching the whole show. She was whispering to a tall young guy, hubbling and bubbling trouble as usual.

I came off stage to a hero's farewell and delivered myself into the arms of the waiting Renee.

'We'll just wait for the TV guys to get ready, and then we'll head into town,' she said. 'We'll do Bourbon Street, the riverfront by night and maybe a spooky tour of the cemetery. Couple restaurants, maybe. We'll do the hotels and the riverboat tomorrow.'

'My knees are your knees,' I told her.

I went and asked Woodrow not to lock the gates, said goodbye to Jake and Juliana and adieu to the witch Elodie, and then Thelma the Mini followed Renee's long black town car out on to the road.

I wished that Suraya, Jack Tyler, and the doubting Alexa could see me now. The combined might of France's engineers, the Alliance Française and a French revolutionary army couldn't stop my kilt and my little car winning a battle for England.

As Thelma rushed through the night towards the city, I imagined the voters in Boston telling the French, Sorry, Messieurs, but we're going to follow Miami's and New Orleans's lead. We're going to vote for the kilt guy. Did you see those films he did in Louisiana? Great stuff. We're going to invite him back to the city – staying in a five-star hotel, of course – to do the same thing. No regrets, France, but we're going to vote for Britain, earn Paul his fat bonus, and vive les Hommes in Skirts.

My next stop, Las Vegas, was bound to jump on the bandwagon. I could already see myself cruising along the Strip between the lines of swooning casino hostesses, and flicking a finger at the impotent Eiffel Tower at the Paris Las Vegas resort.

The French were going to be as dead as a dudgeon, as filleted as a fenny snake.

LAS VEGAS

Money Makes the Wheels
Go Round

1

'AIM AT HIS HEART,' the girl told me.

She leant across to lift my arm, and pressed her chest against me, as if to identify the part of the body she was talking about. Her chest was highly vulnerable to attack, its only defences being an alarmingly low-cut red-and-gold halter top and a glossy covering of sweet-smelling cream. Her legs were much better protected, exposing no more than a narrow band of skin between a red mini-skirt and gold thigh boots. She looked like a hostess for a pornographic airline.

'An Uzi is light,' she went on, 'but it might buck a little. If you aim at his chest, the worst thing that can happen is you blow his head off.'

'Blow his head off?'

'Well, this thing fires so fast, it'll be more like chain-sawing it off.' She looked almost apologetic about the damage I was about to do. 'Sweep across his chest, OK?' She snuggled up to me again and gripped my sagging arm.

'That way, if he tries to evade the bullets, you're still gonna hit him. This baby don't give you time to dodge.'

I glanced down at the 'baby'. It could have been a toy except for its drill-like weight and the way everyone seemed keen to stay out of its firing line.

'You gonna shoot the fucker or what?' The large shadow standing a few yards away was more mocking than impatient.

'Just squeeze,' the girl said seductively, as if inviting me to fondle her nearest breast.

I looked my victim in the eye and began to tighten my finger around the slim, hard trigger. Not for the first time on this job, I also started to think, how the hell did I get myself into this merde?

2

Poor Thelma never made it into New Orleans.

I was cruising along, congratulating myself on how I was going to stick it to the French engineers and the French Alliance, and thereby earn enough to tell the French government where to shove its fine, when Thelma just seemed to fall asleep. One minute she was sprinting through the bayou, the next she was catatonic, and no pleading or coaxing could revive her.

It didn't take long for Renee and Co. to realize that they weren't being followed through the oil-black night, and they came back to find out why.

Of course, they all wanted to know what was wrong with the Mini. As if I could tell them. The only car maintenance I ever did was fill petrol tanks and drive through car washes. Which explained why, far from diagnosing the immediate problem, I was having trouble finding out how to open the bonnet, or the hood as an agitated Roland insisted on calling it.

'I don't own a car,' I explained, a confession that halted them in their tracks. Even the frogs out in the woods seemed to stop chirruping in shock.

'You don't own a car?' Roland seemed to be choking on his stripy necktie.

'I've always lived in the centre of London and Paris. I'd just be paying a fortune to park it until it got stolen. When I need a car, I hire or borrow one.'

This, to the average American, was like saying that you can live without your own penis or air-conditioning.

'Let me have a look.' Roland found the hood switch, while Renee called for a tow truck.

I stood at the roadside, racking my brains for helpful suggestions. The car had cut out as if someone had disconnected its life-support system, so maybe it was the spark plugs. But I honestly wasn't sure if cars had spark plugs any more. I kept my mouth shut.

Only ten or fifteen minutes later, a swamp dinosaur emerged from the blackness, its four eyes blinding us as they lit up the forest for half a mile around. The repair truck that pulled in to the roadside was one of those pickups with wheels twice as high as the Mini, and almost as wide, the treads on them like black mountain ranges. Mounted on the back was an extendable hydraulic crane with a cable as thick as a cruise ship's anchor chain. The vehicle seemed to have been designed to wade out into the bayou and pull sunken oil tankers back to land.

The mechanic jumped down to earth. He was a thin, wiry guy in baggy yellow overalls. His baseball cap sat low and tight on his skull, and he had a beard of sorts – a few straggly bristles like blond needles in a pincushion.

He took a cigarette stub out of his mouth and

laughed. 'Ah don't normally fix Rollerblades,' he said.

'It isn't a Rollerblade,' I said. 'The wheels aren't in a line.'

He looked me up and down. 'Yo car?' The small vehicle seemed somehow to compute with the tall foreigner in a lurid anorak and a skirt.

I confessed to this, and he got me to describe exactly what happened.

'Don't seem to be anything wrong with the engine,' Roland said, but the repair man ignored him. He strolled over, threw his lighted cigarette to the ground, and gazed under the bonnet.

'We need to get to New Orleans as quickly as possible,' Renee said.

The repair guy nodded silently, and went to sit in the Mini. He turned the key to check the readings on the dashboard, and sat there motionless for a few seconds. Everyone except Roland was watching him as if waiting for a dove to pop magically out of his baseball cap. Roland was fiddling with his watch, annoyed by all the amateur dramatics.

The guy finally moved, and beckoned to me.

'Come have a look, Legsy.'

'Let me see.' Roland shoved in front of me, bent forward, and immediately moaned as if his team had just conceded a lame touchdown. 'You're out of friggin' gas,' he said. His opinion of me had obviously sunk as deep as a Gulf of Mexico oil drill.

'Out of gas?' Renee echoed.

The pickup guy emerged triumphantly from the Mini. 'Middle of America's biggest oilfield, and he's outta gas,' he said.

'No way,' I defended myself. 'We filled up yesterday. We got thirty dollars' worth just when we crossed into Louisiana.'

There were a few dubious faces in the ghostly light from the pickup truck's headlights.

'I can show you the receipt if you like,' I said.

The repair man knelt and checked under the car. 'No leak,' he said.

The dubious faces turned back towards me. There was no point digging around in my wallet for a receipt. They'd only accuse me of forging it.

'Do you have any petrol – er, gas with you?' I asked.

'Yeah, but you let it run out of gas, you gonna screw up the fuel pump. I better tow it in, check it out. Maybe there is a leak somewheres.'

He gave us the philosophical look of the handyman who is forced to inform you that you are going to pay him lots of money in the very near future.

Thelma was hauled off into the darkness, her rooftop Union Jack fluttering defiantly but powerlessly up at the massive tow truck, and I was loaded into the town car and shipped to New Orleans.

There, on the orders of Renee and a stressed-out TV producer, I smiled at a hotel chain's neon-lit logo, signed in for a room while lying to a manically grinning receptionist that I'd had a great journey to the city, and admired the furnishings of a plush guest suite with a four-poster bed and a bathroom as big as a two-car garage. After a short argument, I also agreed to sink into one of the tasselled velvet armchairs and pretend I was worried that the camera might see up my kilt.

Then it was out of the hotel and into the thumping, shouting night for a stroll along Bourbon Street. I was supposed to banter with the revellers and stop at pub door-ways to listen in on some music, but we gave up when it became obvious that the only bantering I was going to do was say 'Fuck you, too' to the frat boys who were flicking beer over my anorak and expressing very loud doubts about the heterosexuality of my legs.

*

Next morning, Woodrow took me out to the garage, where our repair man gave me the bad news that the pump was indeed 'totally screwed' and would take two or three days to fix.

I called Suraya for advice.

'I need your advice,' she told me as soon as I got through. 'Should I tell my father I am borrowing my neighbour's scooter?'

'What?'

She updated me on her problems. She had ignored her father's wishes, and instead of walking to work or giving up her job, she had accepted her male neighbour's offer to lend her his scooter.

'I don't know, Suraya. What does your dad usually do when you tell him you've done something against his wishes?'

'He threatens to throw me out of the house and deprive me of my dowry.'

'Well in that case, I would either not tell him or I'd take the bus.'

'But my neighbour's so dishy.'

'Dishy?' I hadn't heard that word for a decade or two.

'Yes, he has a brand-new scooter and an *MSc*...' The way she said it, an MSc couldn't be a science degree – it had to stand for something like Magical Scrotum.

'He sounds very dishy. I'm surprised he hasn't got a girl-friend already.'

'A girlfriend?' She repeated the word as if I'd just mentioned some obscure species of Creole shrimp.

'Yes. Make sure he's available before you get thrown out of your house. Now I really need your advice, Suraya.'

'OK, sorry.'

She let me fill her in on the car problem.

'Well, if you wait for the car to be fixed,' she said, 'you'll have no time in Las Vegas before you have to go to Los Angeles for the voting ceremony. And there are some exciting things coming in.'

'Yes? Like what?' I was almost afraid to ask.

'Oh, Las Vegas is going to treat you like a star. It would be a shame to miss out.'

'I'll be there on time,' I told her. 'Just make sure that the credit card is well loaded so I have enough cash to cover the flight and the car repairs.'

'Oh! That's his name!' she swooned.

'What?'

'You said "cash to cover the flight". And my neighbour is called Kashta. It's a pharaoh's name. When he wears his gold crash helmet, he looks like an Egyptian god . . .'

3

That same afternoon, I was hauling my luggage through what I'd originally thought was New Orleans Lance Armstrong airport, but which was of course named after Louis. Sorry, Satchmo.

I was feeling excited and only slightly irritated at the unstar-like way I was being treated before I was allowed to get on a plane. My liquids were confiscated, including a cute little miniature Tabasco. I understood why. A bottle of Tabasco in a terrorist's hands could wreak havoc with a pilot's eyes. Though it might take some time to blind him one droplet at a time.

My bags, shoes, belt and coat were X-rayed, of course, and then they put me – still half-dressed – in a kind of shower cubicle that spat high-pressure air in my face. It was, a security woman told me, removing all the dust particles from the surface of my hair, body and clothes.

'To lighten the plane's load?' I asked, but she refused to acknowledge the joke. Soon, I thought, we'll only be able to get on a plane naked, sedated, handcuffed and drained of all bodily fluids. It's the only way to be totally safe.

It reminded me of when Alexa and I first entered the USA. We'd laughed at those green forms you have to fill out, with tough questions like 'Have you ever been, or are you currently involved in terrorism or war crimes?', 'Are you entering the country with the intention of committing a felony?' and 'Are you a total crackhead?'

I mean, is anyone going to be stupid enough to answer yes to these things? I could just imagine the fleeing dictator, with a fake passport and half his country's GNP in his luggage, chewing nervously on his airline pen and inadvertently ticking a 'yes' box. 'Damn,' he'd think as the customs men dragged him on the plane to The Hague, 'I knew I should have said no to genocide.'

I sat drinking a Coke in departures, and ticked off my own checklist of organizational questions.

Credit-card authorization filled out to cover whatever the car repair ended up costing? Unwise, but yes.

Jake and Juliana provided with enough cash to drive the Mini to Las Vegas? Overgenerous, but they deserved it, so yes.

Promise obtained from Renee that New Orleans would vote for Britain at the World Tourism ceremony, despite all the cock-ups? After a full morning waving from a Mississippi river steamer, pretending to be freaked out by the city's voodoo tombs and helping to load a bright-red truck with boxes of Tabasco sauce, yes. She even got me to autograph some stills from the previous evening's shoot. I was, it seemed, still a star in Louisiana.

My flight was called and I boarded, buckling myself in with undisguised pleasure. We were going to fly over the bayou, the hugeness of Texas and then the classic-cowboy movie landscapes of Arizona, before landing in Vegas at nightfall, which everyone had told me was one of the most exciting things you could ever see from an aeroplane.

The plane was full, and I'd only been able to get an aisle seat, but it had a decent enough view if I leant forward. I checked the battery on my phone to make sure I had enough power to record the views and annoy friends and family later with show-off text messages.

My anticipation was diminished slightly after takeoff, though, when my window-seat neighbour pulled down the shutter and killed my view of the vast green swamp. I looked around, and everyone else seemed to be doing the same thing, shutting out the daylight.

What is it with these people? I wondered. They make sure they get a window seat, but they'd prefer it didn't have a window? Or are they all poker players and need darkness to meditate on the game ploys that they're going to be using tonight?

I was patient. I let the 'meal' service (a soft drink and a packet of tiny choke-proof pretzels) go by and kept my eye on the TV screen that told us where we were flying. I ticked off Dallas, Fort Worth, and places that I'd never heard of like Lubbock and Childress.

I had time to observe my neighbour and try to work out if he was the accommodating 'Sure, I'll open my shutter' type. I couldn't decide. He had an iPod, jeans and an open-necked checked shirt, and he took his trainers off for the flight, so he was pretty laid back. But he'd hardly acknow-ledged my 'Hi' when he sat down, and hadn't taken up the opportunity to chat when I'd seen the size of the pretzels and laughed. And he seemed to be a self-contained traveller, the forty-something who's seen it all (hence the closed window) and always packs everything in the same place in his suitcase. He'd have a spare set of his thin-metal-framed glasses and he'd never forget his dental floss. He wouldn't like outside interference during his journey. Still, I told myself, no need to prejudge the guy, let's wait and see if he opens up.

It was only when I saw Roswell appear on the map that I started to get seriously anxious. Wasn't that where all the aliens land? Wasn't it likely that we were at that very minute being buzzed by a flying saucer, and I was missing it because the man next to me didn't want to be disturbed by the outside world?

From the few windows that were unblocked, I could see that the daylight was fading. Sundown over New Mexico – it seemed a shame to miss that.

'Excuse me,' I said with my politest English accent and my brightest smile.

He pulled an earphone out and I heard a faint jangle of guitar rock.

'Yeah?' He didn't sound unfriendly.

'Would you mind opening the shutter so I can see the view? It's my first time here.' Again, I gave him a smile that said how much I loved his country, and what a privilege it would be to actually see America as I flew over it.

'I prefer it shut,' he said, and put his earphone back in.

And people say the French are the rudest people in the world.

'Excuse me,' I said again, and he took out the earplug with a sigh of desperation.

'Yes?'

'We're going to be flying over some of the most dramatic landscapes in the world, and then landing in Las Vegas by night, and I'm not sure I'll ever be flying over here again, so I'd really like to see the view. How's about we switch places?'

'I'm all set up here.' He motioned to his shoes, his magazine on the tray, his iPod tucked in his lap. 'You want to see the view, you should get a window seat.'

'I couldn't. They'd already been taken.'

'Then you should have checked in earlier, or grabbed a seat online.' He ended his comment with a shrug and the faintest hint of a 'duh', and put his earphone back in again.

Now if there's one thing that really gets my goat it's the 'duh' and all that it implies. The person who does it is a genius, the victim is a dickhead. No subtlety, no middle ground, you're an out-and-out jerk and it's just been proved beyond any reasonable doubt.

'Excuse me.' This time I was polite but a little more assertive than before.

'What?' He pulled the earphone less than half an inch out and held it against his lobe, as if this was going to be a very short interruption indeed.

'If you don't want to look out the window, why do you get a window seat?'

'That's my business. America is a free country and not a police state, thank God. We don't need to explain ourselves here.'

As if having to explain something to your fellow man was a breach of human rights.

'But that's like asking for a seat in smoking and then complaining that people smoke.'

'We don't have smoking sections any more. You don't know what you're talking about.'

The 'duh' was back, with eyes raised to the ceiling this time.

'OK then, it's like asking for a table by an open window in a restaurant and then moaning because there's a draught.'

'Listen, fella,' he said. 'You're in your seat, I'm in my seat. You're bothering me. If you don't stop, I'm going to call the hostess.'

'And get me thrown off the plane? At least I might see a bit of the view.'

'Stop talking to me or I'll summon the hostess.' His finger hovered beneath the button next to his light switch. I knew I'd lost. I wasn't going to see the mountains, the sunset or the Vegas lightshow.

'Yeah, and call your mummy while you're at it,' I said.

He pressed the button, and we heard the telltale ding. He glowered at me as if to say, Gotcha now, punk. I glowered back, as if to say, Dickhead. Well, I probably said it, too.

An aged but resolutely blonde air hostess tottered unsteadily down the aisle. She reached up and turned off the call light.

'Do you have an issue, Sir?' she asked my neighbour.

'No, I have a *problem*,' I said, but before I could explain about the shutter, the guardian of the window butted in and reminded me that he was the one who'd called the hostess, and he had the problem because I wouldn't leave him in peace.

'He doesn't have to open the shutter if he doesn't want to, I'm afraid,' the hostess told me, a kind but sad smile on her pastily foundationed face.

I gave her the spiel about it being my first time here and wanting to enjoy the spectacular scenery. I'd gone to stand by the door for a while, I told her, but the porthole was tiny there, and distorted the view. And I wouldn't be able to stand there for the landing, would I?

'The plane's full, I'm afraid, Sir, or I'd try to move you to a window seat,' she said.

'Look, don't argue with the guy,' my neighbour said. 'Just tell him to keep quiet.'

She exchanged a glance with me. Yes, we were saying, dickhead. But she couldn't insult a passenger.

'I'm sure he won't disturb your enjoyment of the flight any longer,' she said. 'Sorry,' she told me.

'Everything OK here?' It was a steward, a young guy with slicked-down hair and a dimple in his chin.

'Yes, yes,' the stewardess said. 'This gentleman would like to watch the sunset, but he doesn't have a window seat.' I was grateful for her poetic description of my plight.

'Flight's full,' the steward said sympathetically. 'Hey.' A question seemed to flash into his head. 'Aren't you the kilt guy?'

I laughed. 'Well, I'm keeping my legs covered up in this air-conditioning, but yes.'

'I saw you on TV. He was on TV.' He nudged his frail colleague and nearly sent her sprawling in the aisle. 'You were on the news this morning.'

'On the news?' This was news to me.

'Yeah. Those kids giving you a hard time in Bourbon Street. It was a blast.'

'Excuse me.' Now it was my neighbour's turn to say it. 'I summoned for assistance because I was being disturbed, and now you're holding some kind of meeting here.'

Three pairs of eyes met and shared the thought: Total dickhead.

'Sorry to disturb you, Sir,' the steward said with so little irony that it only doubled the implied sarcasm. 'Come with me, Mr . . . ?'

'West,' I told him. 'Paul West.'

'Come with me, Mr West. We'd be honoured to upgrade

you to business class so that you don't miss out on the view.'

'Hey, I'm the one should be upgraded. He was causing the disturbance.' Window man was aghast at this un-justified favouritism.

'Well, you'll be able to enjoy the flight in peace now, Sir,' the hostess told him.

I gathered up my things, and couldn't resist a self-satisfied grin at my neighbour.

'Fuck you,' he mouthed.

'Enjoy the view,' I told him out loud, and mouthed the killer American insult, ten times worse than a mere duh. 'Loser.'

4

Business class wasn't very different, but I got a window, a beer and a sandwich, and settled back in my new dickhead-free environment to watch the sun put on its evening show.

The sky seemed to be doing the impossible, turning a lighter and lighter blue as the angular clouds got darker until they were charred black. The sun melted across the rocky horizon, so that it looked as if the plane was flying into an immense strawberry-mango smoothie.

When Las Vegas came into view, it lived up to the hype. All that was left of the daylight was a jagged slash of orange across the black mountain tops. Below, in the bowl of the valley, it was as if a billion people had laid out candles to guide us in from the darkness. Flickering white lights in a dense, warm circle. At the heart of our target was a pulsing splash of colour. Crystal-like outcrops of gold, blue, red and white, the massive resorts on the Strip vying for attention by emitting enough light to blind astronauts overhead in a space station. And as if that really was the city's aim, a white laser bolt was lancing vertically into the night sky. Calling in aliens, perhaps, to lose a few Venusian dollars on the blackjack tables.

I could see the Eiffel Tower quite clearly now, uncannily close to the Empire State building. We were about to land right in amongst the resorts. Having the airport in the city centre must save time, I reasoned. The planes drop you off practically inside the casino. One of the resort hotels boasted that you could fit a Jumbo Jet inside its atrium. That was probably the original idea. Passengers would step out of the jet straight into their poker chairs. But planning permission was turned down when they realized that the jet blast would melt the hotel across the street.

Of course, since the planes couldn't go into the casinos, they brought the casinos out to the planes. The first sound I heard after saying a grateful goodbye to my steward friend was the electronic blooping of slot machines. A tiny high-rise city of them in the arrivals area, beckoning at me as I walked across to get my luggage. I ignored them, but some of my fellow passengers couldn't resist a premature taste of the thrills to come.

There were crowds of people down at baggage reclaim, but one thing immediately caught my eye. It was a large white board being held by the kind of girl that makes you think, Wow, I wish she was waiting for me. Tall, slim, long black ponytail, and a dark business suit that had been cut back to reveal as much of her body as possible without turning the jacket and skirt into a bikini. And on her board was written 'Paul West'. My first jackpot in Las Vegas.

When I introduced myself, she grabbed my outstretched hand and gave a cry of pleasure. I have probably not been greeted so enthusiastically since the night I was born.

'Welcome to Las Vegas, Mr West. I'm Candy.'

I resisted the temptation to make a cheap joke about having a sweet tooth, and told her how pleased I was to meet her.

'What do your bags look like? I'll have someone bring them to the limo.'

'Limo?'

'Of course.' She speed-dialled a number and said simply, 'He's here.'

Wow, I thought, so this is what it feels like to be a star. Although when I saw a small group of unshaven, combat-ready guys jogging in through the doors towards us, I changed that from 'star' to 'kidnap victim'. One of them was pointing a grenade launcher at me.

As they got closer, though, I noticed that the weapons they were carrying were in fact a TV camera, a hand-held light and a boom microphone. I smiled and waved hello.

'Stop,' Candy said. 'He's not wearing the kilt or the anorak. We'll have to shoot it when he's got changed.'

The limo outside was less of a car than a train. I lost count of the number of windows it had. It was a primary-yellow stretch version of a Hummer, and was as long as some streets in Paris. I strolled past a long winding line of people waiting for taxis and got straight in, feeling all those envious eyes upon me. Not necessarily because I'd got this surreally huge ride, but because I'd actually got transport-ation out of the airport.

Inside, the limo was so dimly lit that it was hard to see right down to the front, but I did take in the neon-lit bar on one side, stocked with enough spirits to keep a rugby team happy across the whole Nevada desert. A bottle of cham-pagne was peeping at me out of an ice bucket. I thought I should go and introduce myself.

First, though, I had to say hi to a guy who emerged from the gloom.

At first I thought he was a TV star who'd hired the limo back in 1975 and got lost in its vast interior. He had on a tight black suit, with large white shirt cuffs poking out of the sleeves, and his head was straight out of the *Dallas* book of hairstyles. Centre parting, long over the ears, and even longer on the collar, curling inwards at the neck. All this framed an unnaturally even tan and what they usually call chiselled features, meaning that his eyebrows, nose, mouth and chin had all been designed with extra-bold strokes of the genetic pen.

He held out a large flat hand.

'Larry Corelli,' he said. 'I'm media relations director with the Las Vegas Development Office.'

'Pleased to meet you, Larry,' I said. Larry Corelli. It sounded like one of those composite names that spammers use. Arthur McArthur, Gordon Warden and the like. Then the 'Corelli' sank in and I realized where I'd seen his look before. It wasn't *Dallas*, it was *The Godfather*. And this 'Development Council' was probably a euphemism for a slightly less public organization. Gulp.

'What a great welcome,' I said, suddenly eager to butt-lick as much as possible.

'Yeah, but you got to get your anorak and kilt on. We can't do anything without the logos. Contractual obligation.'

A porter heaved my bag in through one of the doors, and I changed into my stage costume. As soon as the anorak was on my back, Larry jabbed me on the upper arms, not to vaccinate me against gambling addiction but to add a couple of stickers to my collection. One was the letter representing a famous hamburger restaurant, the other a full-face ad for a pop diva who had taken up residence at one of the resorts and was charging a fortune for twice-nightly run-throughs of her old songs.

'Each time you go into one of the resorts, you'll wear the appropriate baseball cap,' Larry said.

'Right.' Soon they'd be tattooing logos on to my face.

I went to re-enact my arrival for the cameras, hosted by an insanely welcoming Candy, and when I walked back out to the parking area, followed by my entourage of film technicians, she took my arm and pulled me towards the limo. The whole taxi line was watching now. It must have looked as if I was about to get the sort of in-transit service that even the world's sexiest airlines can't offer.

5

At first, I got a Manhattan flashback. I was in the taxi again, leaving the famous skyline behind and heading out to the Bronx.

The tall, pulsing lights of the Strip swept past, and I asked why we weren't stopping.

'Relax,' Larry said. 'We got you in the coolest place in town.'

We drove north for thirty champagne-filled minutes. I reclined my leather seat and listened only half-attentively as Larry and Candy ran through the list of stuff I was going to be doing over the next couple of days. Most of it sounded like a beefed-up version of the appearances I'd done in New Orleans. I just had to put on my uniform and smile for the cameras. Much less stressful than setting up a tea party or doing the Highland Fling.

I was tired now, and let things flow over me. The voices, the hum of the engine, the lights outside the windows and the bubbles in my throat. I thought how stupid it was of Alexa to drop out of all this. If she'd stuck in there with me she'd be riding in the world's longest limo through the city that is a kind of distillation of America. All the neon, the swank and the money concentrated in one place. She wanted to make a film about America and here I was, getting filmed covered in logos. It didn't get more American than this.

And yet she'd chosen to give up and stay with a pair of arty Floridians and an ethnically confused Bostonian. A typically French thing to do, I decided. Duck out when the going got tough, stay cocooned in a safe environment, and miss out on the real action.

Although maybe it was better that way, a logical voice told me. How easy would it be to win the competition with a French girlfriend in tow? She would, at this very moment, be hassling me about her photos on the Visitor Resources website, forcing me to choose between doing what she wanted and going all out to earn my bonus and keep my share in the tea room.

My head was starting to tell me things that my heart didn't want to hear.

The limo turned into a winding driveway and stopped outside a grand hotel entrance, monopolizing the whole valet parking zone. A young guy in a porter's costume came over, wondering which door to open. He took off his sunglasses and tried to peer in through the tinted windows. Finally, Candy solved his problem by stepping out.

I followed her and looked up at a kind of five-storey hacienda, a building apparently designed by a poor Mexican immigrant who struck lucky on the slot machines and decided to unite his whole village in one giant farmhouse.

The doormen ushered me in, but I had to wait for the TV crew to film my delight at setting eyes on the hotel. Like the star I now was, or at least like an exhausted, half-drunk traveller, I let my entourage and the hotel staff flurry around me, and did nothing but smile and say hello until I found myself in the middle of a suite that was bigger than most of the apartments I've ever lived in.

There were doors leading off in all directions, an ocean of deep golden carpet and, as a centrepiece, a table covered in a small banquet. Bottles of wine and beer, a whole chicken, a bowl of fruit, salads, wraps, silverware, and a tankard of iced water with yet another bottle of champagne bobbing there like a giant green iceberg.

How quickly stars get jaded, I thought, as I ignored the champagne and made for one of the three queen beds, pausing only to pop a strawberry in my mouth as a kind of nightcap.

'Don't get comfortable, you got work to do.'

Larry Corelli was standing over me, crooking a thumb towards the door.

6

'Hey, that's not fair,' I said.

From the shocked look on the dealer's face, I could tell that it wasn't the done thing to imply, even obliquely, that the blackjack game was in any way rigged.

'Not fair, Sir?' she asked. She was a small Asian woman with a silky waistcoat and a black bow tie. Her hair was gelled into a helmet around her head, as if to protect her from gamblers who might try to knock her out and steal her rack of chips. She looked towards Larry for support. He was standing behind me, out of camera shot.

'Cut, guys,' he told the TV crew. He put a heavy hand on my anoraked shoulder. 'What's the problem, Paul?'

I showed him my cards.

'I won, right? Twenty. The dealer got nineteen, and these two guys had only sixteen and seventeen. I won.'

'Yeah?'

'So why don't I get all the money? How come the dealer gets to keep their stakes? I won ten dollars but she wins – what was it? Ten each?' I asked the two guys at the table with me, a fresh-faced blond kid who looked so young that he'd been carded before he could order a beer, and an old Black guy with a halo of grey curls and a fistful of rings. They nodded non-committally. Like I said, it wasn't the done thing to argue. 'I won, but I get ten and the dealer gets twenty. It's not fair.'

The hand on my shoulder got heavier, and the voice got huskier.

'Yeah, Paul, but if they'd bet a hundred dollars and beaten you, you wouldn't have had to pay their winnings, right?'

It took me a second to work this out.

'Oh, right.'

'And it's not your money, anyway.'

This was true. Larry had brought a pocketful of chips as props for our filming.

'Still doesn't seem like very good odds, though. Just doubling your stake.'

In reply, Larry simply breathed out noisily, and for once I was glad to be wearing a kilt. Without its celebrity status, I got the feeling I might have been leaving the casino with bootprints on my backside.

'Let's go shoot some craps,' Candy chipped in. 'That's fun.'

She took my arm and led me across the crowded gambling hall. It stretched in all directions, as far as I could see. Dealers were standing at card and roulette tables opposite punters of all ages, colours and sizes, who shared one thing in common – the intense look of someone watching a pair of pandas to see if they will breed. The pandas in this case being their chips, which were in just as much danger of extinction.

In a ring surrounding the tables were terraces of brightly lit slot machines, being fed by gamblers sitting on barstool-type chairs. There was no noise of cascading quarters, though, because this place had been modernized, and the machines took only notes. At one end of the hall was a cinema-like area of seating by a bank of TV screens. Punters were watching every type of sporting activity known to man. Except cricket and pétanque, of course.

Lots of people were smoking, but you couldn't smell a thing.

'The air extractors must be fantastically strong,' I said to Candy as a woman at a slot machine waved her arm in frustration and almost burnt my eye out.

'Yes, and they pump oxygen in,' she said. 'It helps people to concentrate.'

'And stops them getting tired and going to bed,' I added. I had no idea what time it was. There were no clocks, no windows, and the dim light seemed to be set at a permanently unobtrusive level. You could have gambled all night and not noticed that it was pointless paying for a hotel room.

'Uh, Candy?' Larry was just behind us, smiling as if his cheek muscles had been strained in a bubblegum chewing contest. He pulled her to one side and murmured down into her hair. She nodded assent and returned to my elbow.

'Apparently they don't pump oxygen in,' she told me. 'It's just very efficient air-conditioning.'

'Right.'

Seemed Larry had had a discreet word about trade secrets.

'Where in England do you live?' she asked me.

'Paris.'

She laughed and gave me a playful poke in the ribs.

'I love Paris.'

'You've been there?'

'Yes, when I go home I sometimes stop over.'

'Home?' I looked down at her chest. Not to get an eyeful of her cleavage, but to see her name badge. Everyone working in the city seemed to have a badge with their name and home town on, presumably so that visitors could tell if their dealer or waiter was from their own home town and tip them extra. Candy's and Larry's both said 'Las Vegas'.

'I'm from Romania,' she said. 'Foreigners get badges saying "Las Vegas".'

I'd thought her accent was South American. I complimented her on her English, and she told me that she'd come over five years earlier to find a job in a hotel. She'd worked her way up from chambermaid to waitress, and then Larry had spotted her and taken her on at his press office.

'I am buying my apartment, and I have seen a little house I want. You can get on in this country, in this city,' she said. 'All you need is ambition, energy and good communication skills.' In her case, the communication was not only verbal but very visual.

'Where you live in Paris?' she asked.

I hesitated for a moment, wondering if I still had an address chez Alexa. Yes, be positive, I told myself.

'The Bastille, and before that the Marais,' I said.

'The Marais – that's the gay area, right?' She looked down at my skirt.

'Yes,' I said. 'I'd be pretty popular if I went there now.'

She was the only one paying any attention to the kilt, though. There were so many weirdly dressed freaks, and

306

the waitresses had to glam up so much, that one guy with bare legs didn't even warrant a turned head.

I was given a pair of dice and told to throw them. My protests that I didn't understand the game cut no ice with Larry. He placed a few chips for me on the high-sided table and told me to roll. A circle of punters watched me intently.

'Whatever happens, you cheer, OK? You just won a fortune.'

I blew on my hand like they do in the films and threw the dice against the far end of the table. They came to rest amongst the piles of chips, and I cheered. Other people nodded for some reason, and began to bet. A few of them egged me on, though I had no idea what I was being egged on to.

I threw again, the dice bounced and rolled, and when everything settled down, most of the other players groaned. It seemed impolite to sound pleased by their misfortune, but I did as Larry asked and cheered as if my horse had just come in after I'd mortgaged my house for stake money.

'You can edit out the others, right?' Larry asked – or told – the sound guy who had been holding his furry lollipop mic over the table.

'Yeah, we got him separately on a radio mic,' the guy said.

'Good.' Larry picked up the dice and replaced them on the table. 'Get a close-up,' he told the cameraman. He made sure a number was showing. I couldn't see which.

'Did I lose?' I asked.

'Yeah,' Larry said. 'The come-out roll was seven, so the don't bets lost.'

'Of course.' Can't we try the slot machines now? I wanted to ask. I'll be able to understand three cherries.

'What's up next?' Larry asked Candy.

She checked her list and grinned.

'Wax,' she said.

The hairs on my legs stood on end and tried to bolt for cover up my kilt.

7

Maybe it was the high doses of oxygen I'd been breathing, but I was still wide awake when they dropped me back at the hotel at about two in the morning. And my freshly detoxed brain was sifting out all sorts of poisonous doubts about the crap (and craps) I'd been asked to do.

I calculated the time difference and put a call through to Suraya, who had recently had lunch with her scooter-owning neighbour in a chic, dimly lit restaurant and was worried in case her father should find out about her torrid thali session.

I eventually managed to drag her attention back to the job, and double-checked that my recent kilt-and-anorak-wearing activities had been officially OK'd by London. I didn't have any more 'visit Britain' literature to give out, and no one in London or India seemed desperate to send me any.

Suraya said she thought London was 'totally at one with me', but put me through to Tyler anyway. I got the feeling that she needed some quality time alone with her text messages.

Tyler had just got into the office, but he was very chirpy. I wondered whether Visitor Resources hadn't taken to pumping pure oxygen through their air-conditioning. Or cocaine.

'The breakdown's not a catastrophe at all,' he reassured me. 'You don't need the Mini till LA. Everything's going fine.'

'But it's all getting less and less British,' I told him. 'In the past twenty-four hours, I've promoted Louisiana shrimps, Mississippi riverboats, Las Vegas casinos and a nationwide chain of American hotels. The most British thing I've done is kiss the Queen.'

'What?'

'At Madame Tussaud's here. It's set up so you can pose with the waxworks and pretend you're famous. People were snogging actors and dry-humping singers, even the dead ones.'

'You didn't hump the Queen?'

'No. To tell the truth, most people were doing American hugs – you know, where you put your arms around someone and keep your genitals at a polite distance.'

'But even without genital contact, one doesn't hug the Queen.' He sounded in an implausibly jovial mood today. Perhaps it was Ecstasy they were piping in.

'No, I had to kiss her, though. And they told me to put my tongue in her ear.'

'What? I hope you didn't leave it there.'

'No. It tasted of wax. Appropriate, really.'

Tyler almost giggled. This wasn't like him at all. It was downright worrying.

'Don't you mind?' I asked. 'I'm meant to be promoting British tourism, and all I seem to be doing these days is showing off my calves and wearing foreign logos.'

He made a sound like a beer can opening.

'Pfff. We're global now, aren't we? The whole world's going global. Even America.'

'True.' Though America always seems to stay American, despite all the Korean cars and Spanish radio stations. The same way that France stays French, whatever the scaremongers try to say about the invasion of McDonald's and Starbucks. 'But what am I doing here, then? The voting ceremony is in a few days' time. Aren't I meant to be securing Las Vegas's vote?'

There was a slightly embarrassed silence on the other side of the Atlantic.

'I'll tell you what you're doing,' he finally said. 'You're making money. This will be the first campaign we've ever kept in the black, and with the new branded-entertainment deal, we're on target to—'

'Branded what?'

'Branded entertainment. It's what you're doing, apparently. Getting paid to stand about in key places while someone films or photographs you. The logos might be foreign, but the kilt's British. And the money's coming back here.' He blabbered on about creating a new economic model for government campaigns.

'Hang on, though. There's something not quite right here.' My problem wasn't with making money. I'm all for that. But I didn't see how all the logo-wearing tied in with the campaign to get Americans to vote for Britain and, yes, to win me my bonus when we came home with the World Tourism trophy.

I told him this, straight.

'Oh, don't worry,' he said. 'They're all Americans, so they'll vote for the most famous guy. Vegas included. Just think, you might become a waxwork.'

8

I lay back, waiting for a late breakfast to be delivered to my suite. Candy had called and told me I had the morning off, and I was making the most of it in the comfort of a gently bubbling whirlpool bath.

I picked up the bathroom phone extension and decided

to see how things were going down south. I got through to Juliana, who told me they'd fetched the Mini the previous evening and had set off for Vegas immediately. They were already well past Dallas.

'Why didn't you wait till morning?' I asked.

'No way I was going to spend another night in that shack.' I heard her shiver. 'Hey, Jake wants a word with you.'

Jake came on, asked me how things were going, and sounded very pleased with himself. I guessed it wasn't just because the Cajun guys had agreed to set his translations to music.

'OK,' I said, 'answer yes or no. You finally did the deed with Juliana, right?'

'Yes, man, oh yes . . .'

'Hey!' Juliana was protesting in the background. 'I know what you guys are talking about.' She grabbed the phone back. 'Yes, Paul, we did sleep together. And if you add up all the dates and half-dates we had, it easily comes to three, so don't go thinking I'm some woman of easy virtue, OK?' I promised I wouldn't dream of it. 'Oh, and . . . you heard from Alexa?' She sounded embarrassed by the transition from women of easy virtue to my supposed girlfriend.

'No.' The tone of my voice told the whole story.

'Well, hang in there, we'll be with you tomorrow.'

While we were speaking, I'd noticed a red light flashing on the hotel phone, among all the autodial buttons. Seemed I had a message.

Or two.

The first was from Elodie. She was 'in town', she said, as Americans love to do, and was going to meet up with me the following evening. Oh yeah? Not if I can help it, I thought. 'I've cleared it with Larry,' she said, as if

311

LAS VEGAS

anticipating my excuse. How the hell did she know about Larry? And how did she know where to find me? Stupid questions. She knew everything. She proved this by signing off with 'Oh, and congratulations for getting to Vegas. I hear that your Mini didn't make it. You should have chosen a Renault. Much more dependable.'

I took revenge by zapping her, and then almost dropped the phone in the bathwater when the next message kicked off.

'Paul? It's me.'

Usually, the only people who say 'It's me' are your mum and your lover. (And some Korean B&B receptionists, of course.) I honestly don't think I would have dared tell Alexa 'It's me' any more – she might have replied in Cambodian or Gaelic. But she obviously thought it was still relevant to do so.

'Your mobile is on voicemail so I'm trying your hotel. Elodie told me where you are. I'm coming to Las Vegas. Can I stay . . . Can I sleep . . . ?' She swapped to French. It seemed that things were so complicated between us now that there weren't enough English verbs for us to communicate with. '*Tu peux m'héberger?*' she asked, meaning, could she sleep with me, but only in the sleeping sense.

I ducked under the water and let the gurgling jets massage my head.

At this rate, my suite was going to turn into a kibbutz.

9

You can't say you've seen all of human life till you've been to the Strip in daylight. The neon make-up is off and you can see its true complexion. It's the face of a madman. Or a genius. Or both. The whole city is a victory of humankind over nature. And over common sense.

I rapidly came to the conclusion that Las Vegas's planners (if they have any) must be permanently on cactus juice – anything is possible, the nuttier the better. Yes, we'll slot a life-size Egyptian temple inside a black glass pyramid. Yes, we'll build a practically full-size Eiffel Tower straddling the Gare de Lyon and the Hôtel de Ville. Hey, why not have a fake volcano exploding every half-hour? And real live lions in a Perspex cage in the middle of a casino?

As we drove around in the limo, Candy told me that one hotel has a suite with a full-sized basketball court – twenty thousand dollars a night – and that guests can get whatever luxury they want in Vegas, right down to a caviar facial. I didn't like to tell her that having fish eggs smeared over my nose was not my idea of luxury.

Candy and I got married that afternoon. She made a very sexy bride, imprinting her bright-pink lips on my cheek and crushing her whole upper body against me. I was getting treated like a waxwork already. The priest – not an Elvis but a blue tuxedo'd MC – performed the ceremony sitting down. There was no room to stand up because we were in a car. It was a publicity stunt for the wedding chapel who'd provided the limo. That was why the car was so huge – so they could hold drive-thru weddings in it.

'Do you do drive-thru divorces as well?' I asked the MC.

'No, that's my brother,' he answered seriously.

Larry turned up, very appropriately (I didn't like to say) at the Venetian, where Candy and I took a romantic motorized gondola ride on a 'canal' so clear and blue that a real Venetian gondolier would have got vertigo from being able to see so far down into the water.

After our cruise, Larry announced that he was taking me across the street 'to get your dick wet'.

'What?' I thought he might have fixed up some branded entertainment with the city's anytime-anywhere girls. Tyler seemed to have accepted every promotional offer going.

Twenty minutes later, I was looking down at the eerily lapping waters of a harbour, a sea port in the middle of the desert. This was the other side of the city's folly – water. The gondoliers' canal was a mere damp patch compared to the huge hotel swimming-pool complexes and the Bellagio lake, not to mention the millions of gallons needed to keep the golf greens looking like emeralds rather than coal dust. And I was now at one of the wettest bits of the desert – the Treasure Island's pirate harbour, with its hidden wave machines and two full-sized galleons.

I had taken my place on one of the ships, wearing my usual kilt and anorak, plus a black three-cornered pirate's hat. Larry had gone to sit in a bar overlooking the harbour, where I could see him bantering with two security guys. They were being excessively respectful. Candy was with me on the ship, listening intently while a pirate with an eye-patch and painted-on beard explained what was going to happen. Or rather, what he really didn't want to see happen.

'Don't stand here or you'll get your ass fried by a gas flame,' he said. He pointed down to a nozzle hidden in a barrel. 'And smoke comes out of these at high pressure.' He placed a hand on two pipes painted to look like lengths of wood. 'And when the ship sinks, jump in that direction or you might get hit by the falling mast.' He held out a naked arm towards the water. Candy seemed very interested in the arm, and in the torso it was attached to. I was much more concerned about where the arm was pointing.

'"Sinks"?' I asked.

'Yeah. The girls fire cannons at us, we sink, some of the guys do high dives into the water, then we board the girls' ship, the two captains go aloft to make out, fireworks, curtain.'

'You do a high dive?' Candy asked him.

'Nah,' he said. 'I hang on to the rigging and dance.'

'Can't I hang on to the rigging as well? I can do a Scottish dance. Jigging in the rigging.'

'No, best you jump clear.'

I looked down at the dark-blue water. It didn't seem pirate-like to ask whether it was heated.

By the time the show started, neon had flooded the night. The two ships were spotlit, music was making the masts vibrate, and a traffic jam of spectators was blocking the whole section of the Strip.

The crowd didn't seem to notice that one of the male pirates was not dressed in traditional seafarer's garb, although a few of them must have been wondering why the TV crew were pointing their camera at me when there was so much flesh on display elsewhere – male and female.

The show was a pantomime. The goodies were a crew of skimpily dressed girls who kept themselves amused during their long sea voyage by miming to raunchy disco music. The baddies were the male pirates, who also interspersed their skulduggery with bouts of frenetic dancing. The male ship moved threateningly towards the female vessel – very smoothly, I noticed, a sort of boat train on underwater rails. The girls taunted the men, and a battle ensued in which the girls defended themselves by shaking their booties even more provocatively than usual. It was a very effective ploy, because the guys' ship belched smoke and flames and then began to sink.

As the deck tipped away beneath my feet, the pirate

in the rigging yelled at me to jump, and I hit the water.

It was a lot colder than the last time I'd taken my kilt for a swim, in the real Atlantic over in Florida, but this time I had a much more attractive welcoming committee than a Miami policeman. I climbed up a rope ladder on to the girls' boat and was instantly grabbed by a thin woman in a ragged white shirt and black lingerie. She rubbed herself around me like a cat begging for milk, thrust me away in disgust, then propelled herself back into my arms, all the time mouthing the words to a song about what she'd like to do to my body. Finally she squeezed me as if she wanted to wring all the water out of my dripping clothes, and then dragged me through a hidden door as the fireworks whistled up into the night sky.

'You must be the kilt guy,' she said breathlessly when we got backstage. She looked down at the sopping length of cloth hanging between my legs.

'Yeah,' I said, beginning to shiver.

'Can I get your autograph?'

'Sure, when my fingers stop shaking.'

'Good one,' the pirate with the eyepatch said. He clapped me on the back and sent a shower of cold water splashing off my anorak.

Candy was beside me now, and shrieked as she got hit by the spray.

'Let's go for a drink and something to eat,' she said. 'You want to come, too?' she asked the pirate.

'No thanks.' He lifted his eyepatch and examined her with both eyes. 'You're cute but you're not my type.'

'Oh.' Candy looked disappointed.

'Too female.' He winked and covered his eye up again. 'Hey, Paul,' he said, 'the guys' showers are through here.'

10

The shower cubicle was roomy enough for three people, but I had it to myself. The eyepatch dancer also lent me a tracksuit that was big enough for at least two people my size. He told me it had been left there by a giant who had been fired from the show for taking the fight scenes too seriously and breaking off chunks of mast to use as weapons against the girls.

I found Larry and Candy in the harbourside bar.

'Take him back to the hotel,' Larry ordered Candy. 'They got great food,' he told me. 'Sushi, Italian, whatever you want. Then you can go and persuade them to change the odds at their casino.' He chuckled to himself. 'Or maybe you got a system? Think you can beat the cards or the roulette wheel?'

'Yes, I've got a system,' I said. 'Don't bet, don't lose your money. Works every time.'

I was only shaking his tree, of course. I got changed, slurped down some raw tuna, a seaweed salad and a couple of Japanese beers, and went to check out the hotel casino.

It was smaller than the conurbations of gaming tables that I'd seen downtown, but there was still plenty of room for anyone who wanted to play cards, roulette, craps or the slot machines. And there was quite a crowd in, lots of people wearing delegates' badges for a conference.

I tried to watch a poker game, but of course the players were keeping their cards flat on the table and showing no emotion, so it wasn't exactly a spectator sport.

I had a flutter at roulette, which was fun for the time it took for the ball to stop whirring round and rattle into a number slot. Then the wheel proved, four or five times on the trot, that my birthdate, Paris postcode and pin code aren't lucky numbers.

So I went and played a few hands at blackjack, testing a theory that I'd worked out. If you double your stake with each hand, surely eventually you'll win all your money back? The weakness with this theory is that if, like me, you lose four times in a row on a five-dollar-stake table, you quickly arrive at an eighty-dollar hand, panic and decide to keep your remaining cash so you'll have something left for drinks.

I took a bottle of beer for a walk as far as the giant aquarium at one end of the casino, a coral reef alive with fish of all sizes and colours, from blue thumbnail to silver dinner plate. Names of species came back to me from when I'd tried to read a guide to tropical fish on holiday in Thailand – parrot fish, angel fish, puffer fish, suckermouths that were trying to gnaw their way out of the tank, and a few varieties that looked decidedly edible.

I wasn't the only one gazing in at the reef. There was a girl there, too, a blonde who looked as though she might be an off-duty cocktail waitress. Very tall, almost no make-up, her hair hanging loose, kind of hippy style. She had a strong-featured face with a longish nose and real eyebrows, characterful.

I saw she was looking at me, but I decided not to make eye contact. Even though she might only want to ask me the name of the fish with a blue face and a big nose, I didn't want to get into any kind of chat-up situation.

'Don't you think it's spooky they put it so close to the Japanese restaurant?' She was the one who broke the ice.

'I'm trying not to. I just ate there,' I said.

'Are you here for the crime-writers' conference?' she asked. She had a southern English accent.

'No. You?'

'Sort of.'

'Right.'

OK, dead end, I thought. I smiled to show I didn't mind that our conversation had died of natural causes, and took a slurp of beer. Or tried to. I was standing too close to the tank and the bottle clunked against the glass.

'Careful!' She was looking into the tank as if checking the fish for signs of shock.

'I don't think I traumatized them,' I said. 'They've only got ten-second memories, haven't they? They'll get over it pretty quickly.'

'That's not true. Some of them are capable of quite complex learning processes.' She flashed a pair of accusing blue eyes at me.

'I wish I was.' I stepped back from the glass and took a tentative sip from my bottle.

'You're English, aren't you?' she asked. 'On holiday?'

'Yes.' I didn't feel like explaining the truth.

She moved closer and looked conspiratorial.

'I'm here for the fish,' she said.

'The fish?'

'Yes, I'm checking all the different ones they have in their aquariums, making sure there are no endangered species.'

'And do they have any here?'

'No. Though I wonder why they have to have them at all. What's the point of a tropical-ocean aquarium in the middle of the Nevada desert?'

I hoped she wasn't planning to liberate them. I remembered a story about a well-meaning pop star who'd bought all the live lobsters in a French restaurant and 'liberated' them into a river, where they'd died instantly on contact with the fresh water.

'I guess it's just because the fish are beautiful,' I said, and as I pronounced the last word I couldn't help looking at her face and making it sound as if I was talking about her. She was beautiful, so I was perfectly justified in doing it. But even so, it sounded like a tacky come-on.

'Yes, you're right, they are,' she said.

My phone cut into our fishy conversation. It was the hotel laundry, asking for confirmation that the skirt I had given in was under the right room number.

'It's not a skirt, it's a kilt. A men's kilt. Yes, it's mine. Will it be ready for tomorrow?'

The laundry woman assured me it would and I hung up a happy man.

'I thought I'd seen you before. You're the guy with the kilt and the puffy jacket. Paul, isn't it? They've got you doing some weird stuff.' She was grinning at me, but in a way that I didn't mind at all. She somehow seemed to express that it was all a cosmic joke, that the whole situation was absurd and not just me.

Before we could discuss the cosmos further, my phone rang again. This time it was Suraya. I apologized and took the call.

'If I kill my father, do you think I'll inherit when I get out of prison?' she asked.

'No, and I don't think it's a good idea to advertise a murder when you work in a call centre,' I told her. 'Your calls are all recorded, aren't they?'

'Yes, but I can steal the recordings.'

'OK, go ahead and kill him and then tell me why you called.'

In fact it was partly a courtesy call, to make sure I'd cleared things up with Tyler. But she also wanted to know what the French were up to. Not just the events – which Tyler knew about – but the ways Elodie might have tried to sabotage my campaign. The Brits were finally getting worried about the competition, it seemed.

'I'm seeing Elodie tomorrow. I'll do some detective work. I can let you know what she got up to in New Orleans and Miami, though. Pretty sneaky stuff.'

I promised to send an email and curtailed my call so that I could get back to talking about puffer fish and puffy jackets.

But when I turned back to the aquarium, the girl had disappeared.

11

I woke up next morning to find a text message from Juliana: 'crossed texas, nothing happened'. Poor old Texas, I thought. It must hate being so uneventful.

Juliana estimated that they'd arrive in Las Vegas in the early afternoon.

There was also a message from Alexa, saying she was getting here 'before the evening'.

It looked like being a crowded teatime.

I spent a relaxing morning at the hotel, getting a massage in the spa, floating around in the indoor swimming pool, and being photographed in my branded-entertainment outfit while eating another sushi meal. I looked out for the aquarium girl, but didn't see her.

After lunch, I headed back to the room and vegged out in a T-shirt and boxer shorts to wait for my guests. There was football on TV – two armies of gladiators trying to break each other's bones. I was amazed to see how the Americans had managed to take rugby, a violent but fast-flowing game, and turn it into trench warfare. I wondered why they didn't go all out and create an armed version. The team with possession of the ball could soften up the opposing defence with artillery, while the other team would be trying to take out the quarterback with a sniper rifle. At least if there were explosions, it'd be more exciting than this stop-start affair in which the players took a five-minute break every time one of them passed the ball. No wonder they had cheer-leaders to liven things up, I thought.

It was somehow inevitable that I should be ogling pom-pom girls when Juliana arrived. She whistled in appreciation at the sheer enormity of the room and sat at the end of my bed to see what I was watching on TV.

'Hmm,' she said disapprovingly. Not about my choice of viewing, though. 'They look jaded. Haven't been training hard enough. They need me.'

'Where's Jake?' I asked, half expecting that she'd got fed up with the poetry and abandoned him in the desert.

'He couldn't wait to go gambling. I left him at a poker table downstairs.'

'You can't put chips on a hotel bill, can you?' I asked.

'No. He's got the rest of the cash you gave us. Hundred dollars or so. Now I'm going to take a shower and have some sleep. Hey, three beds. Whose is which?'

'Well, I thought . . .' I had been giving this a lot of con-sideration, but hadn't come to a real conclusion. 'You two can share a bed, and then . . .'

'You're not sure if you're sharing with Alexa?'

I did a Parisian shrug. That was up to the great French architect of the universe.

12

An hour or so later, the footballers were still head-butting each other, the cheerleaders were looking even more jaded and Juliana was asleep in her queen bed.

I heard someone trying to open the door and swearing in French because they couldn't manage the electronic key. It had to be Jake.

To stop him hammering or yelling, I went to let him in.

'Paul!' I smelt booze on his breath. 'Man!' He fell across the threshold into my arms.

'You lose it all?' I asked.

'Lose? Huh, man. I footed them one in the girl.'

I guessed that this was a French phrase meaning he'd shafted the casino.

'You won?'

'Oh, oui, man. I am very good in poker. You forget, I am un homme de Las Vegas. Merde!' He suddenly looked more confused than before. 'Your room, there is no beds in it!'

'This is the hallway, Jake. The bedroom's through here.'

'Oof.' This was the French exclamation of relief. 'I must sit myself. I have made a rendezvous.'

'Who with?'

'Aha.' He tried to wink at me, but succeeded only in looking as though he was trying to stick his tongue up one nostril. 'You will see.'

Before he could say anything else, he passed out. I hauled him as far as the second bed, then returned to watch the football – or the advertising, anyway.

A few minutes later, there was a businesslike rap at the door.

I opened up to be greeted by a kind of Batman and Robin of the sex trade. Although they were more like James Bond and M, one of them obviously up for it physically, the other too old to do anything other than give advice from an armchair.

The older one was tall and White. She had large, suspiciously upstanding breasts, a wrinkled cleavage and no apparent waistline. She was in a short red dress with a zipper down the front and glossy black high-heeled boots. The younger partner was Black, short and almost totally spherical. Her breasts, stomach, backside and thighs all bulged out, chubby but firm – she only needed to touch a switch somewhere and her glittery Vegas T-shirt and black hot pants would ping off and hit the walls.

'I got a call from Jake,' the older woman said. 'He not here?'

I assumed the worst. The sex-mad lunatic had phoned out for in-room entertainment.

'Sorry, there's been some mistake,' I said. 'I'll go and get your money, but you really can't come in.'

'What?' She looked insulted, as if she'd actually prefer to earn the cash.

'I'll pay you right now, don't worry.' I did my best to look honest and friendly, realizing too late that I was now smiling at a third woman – Alexa.

She looked from me to the women, to me again. From the half-dressed hookers to the guy in his underwear.

'This isn't what it seems,' I said hopelessly. In my limited experience, women usually care more about what a situation seems than what it is.

'No?'

'No.'

'You collect these phrases, Paul,' she said. ' "I can explain", "It was an accident" and now this.'

'But it's *not* how it seems, I *can* explain, and it *was* an accident.'

I was intensely conscious that we were having a row while being watched by two prostitutes, and something very English inside of me wanted to go somewhere private and explain things in a civilized way. But Alexa had obviously been in America long enough not to care that she had an audience for her emotional outburst.

'You mean it is an accident that there are two hookers in your room? Because that is exactly how it seems to me.'

'Yes, but they haven't even been in the room. And anyway, talking of how things *seem*, in Miami you weren't exactly—'

'Oh yes, that's it. Attack me to defend yourself. You're the one with two hookers in your room.'

'No, this is my mom,' Jake groaned from somewhere behind me.

Alexa laughed.

'Jake, keep out of this, please,' I said, even more pissed off than Alexa about the lameness of the excuse.

'Pathetic,' she said, and stormed away down the corridor.

I dashed after her, begging her to stop, but quickly remembered that there were two prostitutes trying to get into the room. And it struck me now that their eagerness to go through with the deal might have something to do with them wanting to help themselves to my credit card, laptop, phone, passport and anything else they could lay their hands on. I had no choice but to let Alexa stomp away towards the elevators.

To my horror, I found that Jake had actually invited the hookers inside, and was sitting half-unconscious on the corner of a bed, with the two women standing over him, whispering to each other.

'This is my mom,' Jake repeated.

'Alexa's buggered off now, so you can stop bullshitting,' I said.

'It's my mom.'

'I'm his mother,' the tall White woman said, tugging on the hem of her dress as if covering an extra half-inch of thigh might make her look more maternal.

Juliana had been woken up by all the noise, and was blinking at us from her bed.

'His mom?' she said. 'Even that's legal in Vegas?'

12A

There was another knock at the door, which I'd left ajar.

Oh shit, I thought, the management. I couldn't believe that these two women had snuck up here unnoticed. I was going to get evicted.

But no, it was Alexa again. And she was looking worryingly calm under the circumstances.

'Sorry,' she said. 'Sorry to doubt you.'

I was confused as to how she'd stopped doubting me so quickly.

'I decided to give you a chance, so I returned and I heard. She really is his mother.'

She kissed me – on the cheek – and came in to say hello to everyone.

I got the coffee machine working, and we all sat down in the lounge area of the suite to talk about what on earth was going on.

Jake's mum – who introduced herself as Sam – was totally upfront about her job. Or part-time job. She was doing this to earn extra money. She'd just borrowed heavily to buy a nail bar.

'Great business, though,' she told us. 'Every woman in Vegas needs nails.' She held out her own hands, and her friend – Nayna – did the same. Both of them had what Americans call French nails – white varnish with an even whiter tip. Short, presumably to prevent painful accidents with their customers' delicate regions.

It sounded as though she'd always been on the fringes of

the sex industry. Dancing and waitressing in clubs, mainly, she said. This seemed to explain a lot about Jake's own casual attitude to sex.

'But a poot, mom?' Jake was now sober enough to feel pain and humiliation.

'Poot?' Of course, mother and son had lived apart so long they were now divided by language.

'Hooker,' I translated.

'So what? I did it for free with your goddam dad, and that taught me a lesson.' Now I understood why Jake had fled to Paris. Home life can't have been too homely. 'And you're only here so you can beg for more money,' she went on. 'Where you think I'm going to get that?'

'That's not why I came,' he said.

'It's not?' This was news to his mum.

'No.' He explained about the name change, and said he was planning to do the legal stuff in Nevada, where all you had to do was prove that you weren't just trying to shake off a criminal record by changing your name from Mugsy Slaughterhouse to Fred Niceguy. In France, he said, they only let you change if you could prove that your old name was uncool – a Frenchman's biggest hangup. So people called Aimée Moncul (which sounded like 'love my butt') or Jean Cultamaire ('I sodomize your mother') were the only ones in with a chance. Even the French didn't 'respect posy' enough to let Jake change his name to Rimbaud.

'Wo.' It looked as though his mum's day was getting much too complicated for her.

'Anyway, I won't need your frick any more,' Jake said.

'Frick?'

'Money,' I interpreted. 'Why not?' I was as keen as her to know how Jake was suddenly going to achieve financial independence.

'I got a job. A new job. In New Orleans.'

'Really?' We all seemed to say this at once – Sam, Alexa and me. Juliana's smile told us she was in on the scoop already.

'Yeah. I'm going to be a prof in a school.'

'Teacher,' I told those who needed help.

'The Cajuns need me,' Jake said. 'They need French. They need Baudelaire.'

Here, he lost his mum for a moment. She, like almost everyone else on the planet, didn't understand why anyone would need this 'Baudelaire', whatever that was.

'What you're saying, Jake . . .' I was still trying to come to terms with this, 'is that you're going back to New Orleans to work in a school?'

'Yeah. I was bavarding with the musicians, and they said no kids talk French these days, their culture is in disparition.'

I at least understood what he meant. Alexa did, too, apparently. For the first time ever, she looked at him with something other than distaste.

'*C'est super*,' she said, honouring him with some French. 'It's strange, how in America you can discover your real roots, whatever the roots are.'

The others nodded at this, but I didn't quite understand. It was too abstract for me. And besides, I hadn't discovered any roots at all.

'I have rediscovered my French roots,' she explained. 'I wanted to make a film about the American lifestyle, but it has transformed into a movie about why Americans should love France and French culture.'

'Like French nails?' Nayna asked.

Alexa didn't laugh this off as she might once have done.

'Yes,' she said, 'French everything.' She explained that she'd filmed the French influence on design in Miami, Americans' love for French clothes and food, the French train in Boston. (I couldn't remember her filming it with me – I wondered if she'd returned there with the hairy Irishman.) And now she wanted to interview Americans about the Paris Las Vegas resort. 'Even as far away as San Francisco, they love French culture,' she added.

'San Francisco?' I asked. 'You going there next?'

'Yes, and you must come with me, Paul.'

We went to sit by the pool. The sun was dipping down below the dark ridge of mountains, and the palm trees in the hotel gardens were beginning to stand out stark and prickly against the sky.

Alexa took the offensive.

'Did you sleep with Juliana?'

'No.'

'You looked like you wanted to.'

'Well, I did not have sexual relations with that woman, or even ask to.'

The Clinton reply seemed to satisfy Alexa, who started to explain what she wanted from life – love, she said, to know that she'd be loved.

'When a Frenchwoman knows she is loved, she'll do anything. And as well as love, we need trust,' Alexa went on. 'Do you trust me?'

Wow, I thought, a real trick question. Who can you really trust? Your bank manager? No way. The police? Forget it. Your folks? They start telling you lies the first time they take you to the dentist – 'No, this won't hurt, darling' – and they don't stop till you've left home.

So did I trust Alexa, who had sold the news photos that had dropped me in the merde in Boston, who had fixed up a sly rendezvous in Miami with Mike, and dumped me so that she could hang out with him and the arty lesbians Cherry and Gayle? Did I trust her?

There was only one possible answer.

'Yes, of course,' I said.

'Good.' She put a cold hand on my arm. 'So you will come to San Francisco with me?'

'Why San Francisco?'

'Ah.' She smiled as if she was about to unveil some sexy lingerie. 'I got an offer to have an exhibition there. You know, the same one I had in Paris.' This was the collection of arty photos of me that she'd taken when we'd first started going out. The ones that had been illicitly posted on the Visitor Resources website. 'A gallery saw some of them on the internet and they contacted me.'

'Great,' I said, before I started getting an uncomfortable jabbing sensation in my memory. 'But last time we spoke, you were giving me hell because someone had put those photos on the web. You were going to sue Visitor Resources, and have the website shut down.'

'Yes, well . . .' She blushed. 'Sorry. I was listening to the wrong people. I know that now. Will you come to San Francisco? After your voting ceremony, of course.'

'I don't know, Alexa. Will I have to wear my kilt? The kilt that you thought looked stupid. Do you want me to do a Scottish dance to publicize your show?'

'No, of course not. Let's just finish the American trip together, like we started it. You, me and Thelma.' She looked me in the eye and seemed to upload a photo album of memories into my head. All the fun things we'd done together, the closeness we'd shared. 'Please, Paul. We'll drive to Los Angeles, we'll finish your job. Then you must come to San Francisco with me.'

LEAVING LAS VEGAS

Uzi Does It

1

THE FLAMES WERE BUBBLING up through the water. I wondered how fire could survive in a pool of water. But this was Las Vegas, where anything is possible.

The firepool was in a circular pit below the main floor level. All around it were couches, arranged so that you had to sit staring into the mesmerizing flames. I couldn't tell what colour the couches were because everything was bathed in a pinkish-purple light coming from the tubes of neon set along the walls and reflected in the mirrored ceiling.

I was sitting by the fire admiring a tall woman with thick black hair and a cute Cindy Crawford mole. Like practically every woman working in the city, she had no qualms about showing most of the surface area of her chest to the general public. It wasn't her chest I was looking at, though. I was admiring the length of outer thigh revealed by the split in her floor-length dress.

She was perched beside me, bending over a menu and

listing her favourite cocktails. She'd already said she'd recognized me from the TV, and inquired about the well-being of my Mini. Even Thelma was getting her fifteen minutes of fame.

'The Scorpion's our signature cocktail,' she said. 'It has—'

'I see you have American *champagne*?'

The waitress smiled at Elodie's interruption. I'd decided to accept the forceful invitation she'd left on my answering machine, even though I knew she was less trustworthy than a horny female praying mantis. It was like Tony told me back in Miami – know your enemy. And I wanted to find out what she was up to, both here in Las Vegas and more generally.

What was more, Elodie had provided me with an excuse to get away from the hotel and think about the Alexa situation. This sudden suggestion that we get back together and go to San Francisco was a bit like flames in a pool of water. I needed to figure out how it worked.

'We have American champagne, French and Spanish,' the waitress said.

I could see Elodie preparing a speech about how only French bubbles can make champagne. Knowing her, she was probably on a retainer from the French wine industry to report any bars or restaurants misusing the trademark.

'We'll take two glasses of American sparkling wine, then, please,' I said, to defuse the diplomatic incident.

'Great.' The waitress stood up, smoothed down her dress and strolled away. The mood of the bar was zen-like cosiness, and no snooty French girl was going to spoil it.

'Look at those two, they're going to make love.' Elodie nodded towards a couple in a dimly lit corner booth. I could just make out two silhouettes almost horizontal on the couch.

'It's going to be a bit difficult on those curved sofas,' I said. 'They'll roll off.'

'Oh, you Englishmen have no imagination. I should know.' She gave me a lascivious smile.

She was the most glamorous thing in the bar apart from that endlessly dancing water flame, and she knew it. Her dress was the same colour as the waitress's costume, but you would never have mistaken her for one of the staff. On her right wrist was a gold bracelet that looked so heavy she probably had to do special weight training to lift her hand. Her necklace was a string of pearls as big as blueberries, and the dress itself had that classic simplicity which tells you it had cost thousands of euros in the designer's own Paris boutique.

There was no danger of her charms working on me, though.

'Are we going on to McDonald's after our aperitif?' I asked her.

'Honestly, Paul, you've become so American. No, we're going to France.' She meant the Paris Las Vegas resort, of course.

The waitress brought the drinks, told us she was there if we needed *anything* else, and left us to clink glasses.

'To survival,' Elodie said. 'I'm very impressed, Paul. Your absurd, underfunded campaign started out as a total disaster, you have been obliged to make yourself look a complete jerk, but somehow you have survived.'

I thanked her for her kind words.

'I'm very surprised you're even in Vegas. What was wrong with the car?' she asked.

I told her.

'Is that all?' she said. She seemed glad that the problem was so minor. 'You know, after the ceremony, to recuperate from your defeat, you must come to Clint's house at Venice Beach. It's on the canal.'

'Does it have gondolas?' I asked. 'And what makes you think I'm going to lose?'

'Oh, come on, Paul. You are on TV, OK, you have your website and stuff, but that is not what counts at this level. You Anglo-Saxons, you know nothing about the subtleties of negotiation. You have given them their TV coverage, you have been filmed with their logos. They have everything they want already. Why should they vote for you?'

It seemed to be a typical French rhetorical question, so I didn't answer.

I finished my drink, letting the bubbles fizz on my tongue. I looked over at the couple in the dark booth. They were sitting more or less upright now. They'd stopped short of making love.

Maybe Elodie was right, I thought. I'd done everything that people wanted, and now I was waiting passively for a favour in return. The French, on the other hand, were promising help with the Big Dig in Boston, hurricane protection in Miami and aid for New Orleans.

But no, Tyler had said that they'd vote for the famous guy. And Renee had seemed more pleased with the work I'd done, even without the Mini, than with Elodie's promise of a Revolutionary reconstruction. Elodie was just playing mind games. She'd probably learnt the tactic during her MBA course. She was, after all, the most manipulative, treacherous woman I'd ever met. Every time she kissed me on the cheek, I felt the prick of the blade in my kidneys.

'I hear Alexa is in town,' she said. 'Will you go to Los Angeles and San Francisco with her?'

'I don't know.' The more I thought about it, the less I liked the idea. After all, she'd never explained what had gone on with the Boston strangler. And the way she talked about it, she wanted me to go to San Francisco for her own reasons, to help promote her photo exhibition, not for the sake of our relationship.

'Perhaps she came back because she thinks you need France's help to conquer America?' Elodie said.

'Perhaps.' She was fishing for information, but the one person I wasn't going to discuss my private life with was Elodie.

'Come, let me show you how France can help Las Vegas,' she said.

2

I didn't see how Elodie was going to win any votes at all.

I was looking out from the side of the stage into a theatre half full of middle-aged people, almost all of them women, searching for their seats and admiring the fake baroque Frenchness of the décor.

These people were genuinely French. Elodie told me they'd all been shipped into Vegas from the Paris region. They were fans of Clint Highway, who was shut away in his dressing room with a 'pardee' pack of drugs. Just enough to keep him going, Elodie said. She didn't want him falling into the crowd again and turning into a matchstick, even if American fire restrictions meant that there wouldn't be any naked flames in the room.

'Why will this persuade Las Vegas to vote for France?' I asked. Wasn't Elodie giving the city what it wanted too quickly, just as she'd accused me of doing?

She answered my question as we sat in the box closest to the stage, only a matter of yards from the large white line on the boards that told Clint where to stand. He had been briefed that if he crossed the line, there was a danger of diving into the front row. Apparently, to make sure he didn't forget, Elodie had had the instruction implanted in his shrivelled brain by a hypnotist, the only inconvenience being that he was now incapable of crossing a road. Not that he often had to do so. He was flown, limo'd or cabbed everywhere.

'This concert is just a sample,' Elodie said. 'The rest is a secret, but you are an honest Englishman, so I can tell you.' She leant close and whispered, 'But not yet.'

As her self-satisfied laugh faded away, the house lights dimmed and the roar of conversation from the audience changed to a mixture of applause and very un-middle-aged squeals.

'Cleent, Cleent, Cleent,' a few women started to chant.

A drum roll boomed out from the speakers right next to our box.

'And now, for the very first time in Vegas,' an announcer brayed hysterically. An organ swelled a dramatic chord. 'All the way from Paris, France . . .' The organ added a second chord and took us to new heights of anticipation. 'Paris Las Vegas is honoured to give you . . .' The organ seemed about to explode with excitement. It stayed at the same frantic fever pitch for ten, fifteen, twenty seconds. What was happening behind the curtain, I wondered – were they having trouble rolling Clint on stage or was the announcer just trying to remember the name of this unknown Frenchman?

'Clint Highway!'

Simultaneously, the curtain disappeared, a white explosion covered the stage with smoke and a rock band appeared against a giant French Tricolor backdrop. The band was playing a chugging rock beat and someone was singing a melody that I vaguely recognized, but it wasn't clear where the voice was coming from. Then the mist dissipated enough to reveal a leather-suited Clint, who'd been swallowed up by the dry ice like an elf in a two-foot snowdrift. First-night rustiness, I guessed. The theatre's special-effects guys hadn't been told that their star was even smaller than Elton John.

The ex-girls in the audience were on their feet, singing along. And I had to admit Clint had a lot of stage presence. He was doing all the rock-star poses that a pair of skin-tight leather trousers encourage a man to do, and only occasionally did he wince as he pulled himself back to the vertical.

The musicians seemed to arrive at a chorus. Now I got it. He was opening with his hit, the re-hash (with the emphasis on the hash) of 'Strawberry Fields Forever' – 'Tarte Aux Fraises' – and I managed to pick out the words as the audience chanted them over and over.

'*Je suis une tarte aux fraises, croque-moi à ton aise. Couvre-moi de crème, fouettée c'est ce que j'aime.*' Which translates more or less as 'I am a strawberry tart, eat me at your own pace. Cover me in cream, whipped is what I like.' Typically French. While John Lennon was singing about psychedelic visions, Clint stuck to sex.

It was all building to the third or fourth chorus when my phone began to vibrate.

I'd received a text message saying simply, 'Call me NOW Larry'. I showed Elodie the screen and went out into the corridor to phone.

Larry, I quickly found out, wasn't happy. He wasn't exactly pleasant when he *was* happy, and now he was like a guard dog who's just been ordered not to bite the intruder's balls off. A mass of barely controlled rage.

'I warned you about fucking around,' he said.

'What?' Pretty well everything I'd done in Vegas could have been classified as fucking around, so I really needed specifics.

'In the casino. When you started balls-aching about the odds.'

'Ah.'

'Yeah, *ah*.'

'Is there an issue with that?' I asked, trying to tone things down American-style.

'Yes there's a fucken *issue*. One of the TV guys – and I'm gonna find out which one – let a fucken liberal national news fucken station see the pictures and they ran the fucken story. Brit guy lifts the kilt on Vegas, or some shit like that. The odds at blackjack, and you being a smartass about craps, and me placing the dice. Made the whole fucken operation look like a total fucken scam.'

I didn't think that a 'sorry' would help. It had always struck me that he wasn't the kind of guy you could apologize to other than by falling off a high building.

'What can I do?' I asked.

'Do? Undo, you mean. You can't undo a fucken TV story. Once people see something on TV, it fucken exists. You can't unexist it.'

'Ah.'

'Will you stop fucken saying "ah". You sound like a guy who's getting a blowjob from a rat.' Which was, in my opinion, a weird image to have in stock. 'There is one thing you can do. It won't undo the damage, but it will help me pay off a debt to a friend of mine.'

'Yes?'

'Where are you?'

I told him.

'I'll pick you up in twenty minutes. Be out front under the Ark D. Triumph.'

There is a time and a place for French pronunciation lessons, and it wasn't now.

3

The car that pulled up wasn't a limo. It was a long silver saloon of some kind, a car that would be impossible to park in Paris but was just another mid-range luxury vehicle over here in the land of the extreme.

I got into the passenger seat, and Larry dropped a heavy black weight on my groin. The violence was starting already. I began to feel glad that I'd told Elodie where I was going. If I disappeared, she'd be the last person to see me alive. She might even get arrested as an accomplice and ruin France's reputation once and for all.

'Open it,' Larry said.

It was a box. I unclipped the lock and swung a lid upwards.

'Shit,' I said, recoiling instantly.

'Take it out.'

I did as I was told, lifting the dead thing inside as if it might wake up and sink its fangs into my arm. Which it could have done if I'd mishandled it, at a rate of God knows how many fangs a second. It was an Uzi.

'Ever fired one? No, don't answer that. You look like the kind of guy who'd shit himself paintballing.'

'Well, no, actually I used to go paint—'

'It's not loaded. But it soon will be, and you're gonna fire it. OK?'

'At what?' I asked.

He didn't answer. He gunned the engine, and swung us around the Arc de Triomphe and out into the flow of traffic on the Strip.

The drive gave me fifteen long minutes of agonizing about what to do. At every traffic light or traffic jam, I thought about jumping out of the car. But like the law-abiding idiot I am, I'd put on my seatbelt. Undoing it would have made my next move too obvious.

I could have phoned for help. But who?

I could have hit Larry over the head with his gun, but it might not have knocked him out, and that would only have made him more furious. And besides, I was the one holding the gun. Unloaded or not, he'd given it to me, which presumably meant that no actual bullets were coming my way. Not yet, at least.

We passed floodlit malls, neon motels, gas stations. We headed five or ten miles away from the Strip, and the river of cars didn't ebb at all. Everyone in Vegas seemed to have to be somewhere else very quickly. Somewhere else in Vegas, that is. In the distance, the desert was pitch black.

Larry pulled into a parking area outside a row of low-rise retail outlets. There was a pawn shop and cheque-cashing office – 'Open 24/7', it boasted – a pizza-delivery service, and a building painted with stars and stripes and topped with a flashing sign saying 'Girls 'n' Guns'. Beside the lettering, a red neon cowgirl was rodeo-riding a pistol.

Larry parked in front of the pizza place, but I didn't think we'd come to demand a calzone at gunpoint.

'Let's go get some ammo,' Larry said. 'And put the goddam gun back in the case.'

I looked down at my lap. I'd been holding the Uzi all this time, a finger wrapped round the trigger.

Inside Girls 'n' Guns, the first thing I saw was the kind of wall display that you don't get in your average European shop.

I recognized the AK-47, the M-16 Vietnam rifle, an old English Sten and even one of those Nazi machine guns you see in the movies – a Scheisser or something like that. There were also heavier weapons on tripods, their barrels as thick as a dog's snout. All in all, there must have been twenty or thirty guns decorating the room.

Below this display was a rack of ammo, with magazines in little plastic drawers like sweets at a pick and mix. The sales counter was made of glass, and underneath it were shelves of handguns, dozens of them lined up waiting to be taken home.

A gigantic Black guy was examining one of the guns through the glass, squinting as if he was wondering whether the shade of steel would go with his watch.

A girl in a gold halter top and red mini-skirt came out from the back of the shop.

'Yes gents, how may I . . . ? Oh, hey.' An embarrassed smile froze on her face.

'Candy?' I said.

'Yeah, I . . .' She didn't need to explain. So many Americans have more than one job. Her two jobs were pretty similar, really. Both involved putting on a short skirt and pulling in the punters. A lot like my own work.

'Go get Dave, will you?' Larry told her.

Candy disappeared and I had time to look around. Behind us were stands of accessories – gun cases, telescopic sights, cans of oil. And to one side of the counter was a row of posters that seemed way out of place in here. Osama bin Laden, Saddam Hussein, a turbanned guerrilla. Surely these guys weren't poster heroes in Las Vegas, I thought.

Just then a war seemed to break out in the back of the shop. A clatter of machine-gun fire – akakakakakakak – answered by a slow volley from a rifle or pistol – dah dah dah dah. I was the only one who flinched.

Candy returned, the slap of her gold thigh boots against her legs almost as loud as the pistol.

'Dave's coming,' she told us. She made a gesture that said she'd like to stop and chat but she had to see to the Black guy. She bent low across the counter to help him find his weapon of choice. He looked more than grateful for her shapely offer of assistance.

A small stocky White man came out from the back room, a pair of blue earphones around his neck. He was much more in tune with the shop's décor theme than Candy. He had an army crew cut and hard stubbly beard, and wore a black uniform that was bristling with pouches and pockets.

'Hey, Larry,' he said.

The two men shook hands, unsmiling, comrades in arms.

'This is him,' Larry said.

Dave nodded and crushed my hand. I crushed back as hard as I could. No way was I going to let him know he'd just fractured my knuckles.

'I brought your Uzi back. We'll need fifty shells,' Larry said. 'No, make it a hundred.'

''Kay.' Dave swivelled and picked up a rectangular white box that he slammed down on the counter. 'Five seconds of pure pleasure,' he said, grinning at me.

'Five seconds?'

'Amazing, huh?' Dave seemed to think I was impressed.

'I prefer to make my pleasures last a bit longer,' I said, earning a chuckle from the Black guy and a weak smile from Candy.

Dave and Larry didn't like that.

'I see what your problem was,' Dave said. 'A joker.'

'Yeah.' Larry gave me the look I'd seen in the casino. Kind of, How shall I kill him – slowly or very slowly?

'What do we want a hundred bullets for?' I asked loudly, as another war started up behind the scenes. I wanted witnesses to the fact that I didn't know why I was holding a gun.

'You didn't tell him, Larry?' Dave laughed at this, making his pectorals shake through the black material of his combat shirt. 'Come out back,' he said, 'into the killing zone.'

4

A row of tall girls in mini-skirts and thigh-boots were hugging men of all sizes and types. A short guy in camouflage fatigues had a long bare female arm around his shoulders. A lanky kid in an ice-hockey shirt was being gripped around the waist.

Everyone – including Dave, Larry and myself – was wearing ear protection now. The shots being fired registered more in my stomach than in my ears. The smell, though, was strong. A sort of firework-display tang in the air.

I saw what the posters had been for. The clients were firing at a human-looking target rather than a bull's eye. Osama seemed to be the firing squad's favourite, and was getting ripped to shreds in at least four of the ten shooting lanes. Saddam had also lost his head a couple of times. Here, it seemed, the War on Terror was getting played out with real bullets and fake terrorists.

Dave beckoned us into a soundproof booth. Well, sound-proof-ish. It still sounded as though someone was hitting the windows with a baseball bat.

'Look at this,' he said, and pushed a leaflet at me.

It was an ad for the shop, promising customers 'the experience of a lifetime'. They could shoot a machine gun and then relieve the stress of battle with 'the best massage in town'. Shit, I thought, so Candy has to do that, too? No wonder she looked embarrassed. Though it was also no surprise she was building up a real-estate empire. All those tips were being put to good use.

The photo on Dave's ad showed a girl licking the barrel of a machine gun. Standing over her was a blobby tourist with a cigar in his mouth and a manly grin on his face, suggesting that he'd just wiped out world terror single-handed and still had enough energy to shag a whole women's army. And maybe win a million-dollar poker game as well.

'What do you want me to do?' I asked.

'Fire a few rounds,' Dave said. 'You're a famous guy, kinda. I'll film you, you give us an endorsement, you'll bring in a few customers. Some a them Europeans don't like the idea of shooting a machine gun.' He shook his cropped head and tutted.

'Is this part of the contract with Visitor Resources: Britain?' I asked Larry.

'Contract?' He guffawed. 'You tore that up in the casino.' His voice suddenly became more appeasing. 'You do this, though, and we might just reconsider.'

I personally hadn't signed any contract, so there was no way I could have breached one, but what the hell. It was just a schoolboy fantasy come true, really. You blast a couple of bullets (well, a hundred) at a piece of paper and that's that. It was just like mechanized darts.

Dave seemed to sense my assent. He put a clipboard on top of the leaflet.

'Sign this.' He pointed a gold-ringed finger at the weirdest contract I'd ever read.

I would have to acknowledge that 'guns can cause injury or death' – OK so far. It sounded no different to the warnings about hazelnuts in Boston and oysters in New Orleans. I also had to swear that I was over eighteen, and not mentally ill or under the influence of illegal drugs. Legal drugs and alcohol were presumably OK, though. I then had to agree that it wasn't a good idea to fire a machine gun while pregnant. Well, I thought, doctors do say that Mozart is better for the foetus than deafening explosions. And finally, I was meant to absolve the store's owner, employees and their goldfish from all responsibility for an accident, 'even if it is caused by the inadvertence or recklessness of an employee'. So if one of the girls tickled me as I pulled the trigger and I wiped out everyone in the shooting gallery, it'd be my fault. Great.

'Can't sign that, I'm afraid,' I said. 'My contract with Visitor Resources stipulates that I can't sign anything without getting it read by their lawyers. Who are in India,' I added.

This was pure bullshit, and Larry treated it as such.

'What the fuck, I'll sign for him,' he said. 'My responsibility. What can go wrong?'

As he scribbled on the bottom of the contract, I looked out of the booth and counted the number of things that could go very wrong indeed. Ten guns, times as many bullets as each one could hold, times all those people not wearing body armour.

And so here I was, a half-dressed Candy wrapped around me, my finger on the trigger of one of the world's most lethal weapons – a product that is as famous a brand as any perfume, sports shoe or phone in the world. Its barrel was pointed at a poster of Saddam Hussein that Dave had selected for me.

'Just squeeze,' Candy said, breathing on my cheek.

I looked along the row of other guys getting fondled by their personal instructresses. Dave had told them to hold their fire so he could film me without too much background noise. Most of the men wore the expression of a guy in a night club when he's got a girl dancing and knows he's going to score. They were looking at me as if I'd just got lucky, too.

'Come on, Paul.' Candy reached down and seemed about to give my trigger finger a decisive press.

'You gonna shoot the fucker or what?' Larry said.

Something clicked, and it wasn't the trigger.

'You know what?' I said. 'I'm not.' I put the gun down, backed out of Candy's grasp and made for the sound-proofed door.

Larry followed me out into the main part of the store.

'You fucking up again?' he growled at me.

The girl who'd taken over from Candy behind the counter looked ready to hit the floor. Raised voices in a gunshop cannot be good news.

'Me fucking up?' I turned to face Larry. '*Me?* In this country where oysters and hazelnuts are considered as dangerous as bullets? Where you can't sleep with a woman without going on three dates, but you can fire a Nazi machine gun? Where you can't compliment a female colleague without getting fired for sexual harassment, but where waitresses all have to show their boobs? Where everyone books a window seat and then refuses to look out the window? You call *me* fucked up?'

The desert night air was probably full of car fumes from the rushing traffic, but it smelt somehow pure, like the stuff they pump into the casinos. Allegedly.

I'd thrown my earphones on to the counter and walked out. Larry hadn't tried to stop me.

Now, though, I realized that I'd just created three major problems.

First, I was going to have to explain to Tyler that I'd blown the whole Las Vegas deal – money and votes – because I'd refused to do five seconds of overtime. And without Las Vegas's vote, I might have thrown away my chances of winning the competition.

Second, I'd probably dropped Candy in it. They'd be bawling her out for not seducing me into emptying my gun. But she looked like a survivor. And she was beautiful enough to get a job anywhere in this town.

347

Third, and most immediately, I didn't know how to get back to my hotel without Larry's help. This wasn't the kind of neighbourhood where there were bus stops. And I couldn't go back in the gun shop and ask for the number of a taxi service.

It was only when I was sitting next to the pizza guy, getting myself delivered to the hotel along with a couple of Quattro Stagiones, that I remembered the last thing Larry had said to me as I walked out of the shop. I couldn't recall the exact words, but they were something along the lines of it being wise for me to leave the hotel before he got there. If I wasn't mistaken, his last words had been, 'Ya got till midnight ya fucken fuck.'

I offered the delivery guy an extra ten dollars if we reached the hotel before the pizzas got cold.

5

I found Jake in the casino. He was smoking a thin cigar and was engrossed in a game of three-card poker.

'If he throws you or your baggages in the pool, just come here. We will play poker.'

'Very helpful, Jake, but I'm off to LA straight away,' I told him. 'You want to come with me?'

'No, I will gain some money, change my name, and then return to New Orleans.'

He groaned – he'd just lost a hand.

I told him that the small pile of chips on the table was probably enough to get him there by Greyhound, and that it might be better to cash them in rather than risk losing the lot.

'No, man,' he said. 'You know, everything in America is genetic, yeah? You are obese, it is genetic. You're a criminal, it is the fault of your ancestors. Well, I have the poker gene. I am writing a poem about my genes. You want to hear it?'

'I haven't got time right now.' Neither did I have the necessary genes to withstand Jake's poetry. 'How much do you need?' I asked him.

'Oh, enough to get to New Orleans. I must maybe buy an old car. Not much. I will gain it from this or I can borrow it from my mom.' He coughed smokily, and leant away from the table to tell me a secret. 'Her, uh, work, you know? It is just until she has the cash to pay her nail salon. And she never kooshes with the men.' He was using the French '*coucher*', meaning 'sleep'. 'She only does some SM things and, you know, la branlette.' Fortunately he didn't mime the handjob he was talking about.

'She told you all that?'

'Yeah.'

'I believe her,' I told him, and we said a manly goodbye with one of those American sex-free hugs.

Juliana was in the resort's business centre. It was open 24/7, just like the casino. She was looking at apartments for rent and checking out cheerleader-equipment sites. Now that she'd got where she wanted geographically, she was trying to do the same professionally. She was certainly no time-waster.

'You're planning on staying here, then? Not going to New Orleans with Jake?' I asked her.

She laughed. 'He's a nice guy, and I think he's only just realizing what potential he has. But he's got too many nationalities left on his list. And I got stuff to do with my life.' She nodded towards the computer screen.

I apologized for screwing up her free-suite deal and told her I'd left my credit-card number with reception so she could get another room.

She wished me luck with the voting ceremony, and gave me a chaste peck on the lips.

'I know Alexa thinks we did, but I'm glad we never – you know,' she said. And somehow it didn't sound at all like an insult.

The one person I couldn't track down was Alexa. Neither Juliana nor Jake knew where she was. Apparently she'd taken her bags and disappeared. And now her phone was on voicemail. She clearly hadn't thought much of my suggestion that we needed to carry on talking before we made any decisions about San Francisco.

I left her a message starting with 'It's me.'

I added 'Paul,' just so she'd be sure.

LOS ANGELES

Mini Ha-ha

1

THE LAPD SEEMED to take traffic offences very seriously.

'Speed limit enforced by aircraft,' the sign said. What happens if you go over 55mph? I thought. Do you get strafed?

As usual, though, no one was taking any notice of police threats. The speeders, swervers and inside-lane overtakers were just as carefree as they'd been in New Jersey, Florida and everywhere.

I was steering Thelma along her seventieth or eightieth mile of LA urban highway, and it was impossible to imagine that the planet contained anything other than roads, bridges, service stations and shopping malls, stretching to the horizon and beyond, covering the whole globe, with lone dusty palm trees like the umbrellas in a giant concrete cocktail. I was doing my best to use the lesson I'd learnt on the east coast – I was ignoring all attempts to sidetrack me, and was sticking doggedly to highway ten as it rolled westwards to the Pacific.

The drive had been pretty exhausting. The road atlas predicted that it would take exactly four and a half hours to cross the Mojave Desert and get to the coast, but they must have done their test drive at two in the morning. I'd been on the road for six hours and still there was no sign of sand, waves or migrating whales.

At last the highway petered out, and a sign told me I was in Santa Monica.

I called Suraya, and got through to her stand-in, Hemang.

'Hey, I got a cousin in Sanna Monica,' he said.

'Is he a Dennis?'

'No, an anaesthetist,' he replied, not picking up on my tired teasing.

'When will Suraya be in?' I asked. I preferred to explain my Las Vegas problems to her.

'She might not be back for a while. Her pop's threatening to throw her out of the house.' He explained that Suraya's dad had found out about her gallant neighbour. There had been a huge row, and when Suraya had summoned the scooter-borne knight in shining armour to rescue her, he had chickened out of a conflict with the older generation. Now Suraya was off work with 'nerves'.

'You have no idea how deeply I sympathize,' I said. He thought I was being sarcastic, but I meant it. I begged for the name of the chain hotel where all the lesser voting-ceremony guests like myself were being put up.

Hemang found it in a matter of seconds, and dictated it over the phone.

'Wo,' he added. 'It's, what, six in LA?'

'Yes, about that.'

'Check-in's not for another three or four hours. You've got time for some tourism.'

I felt more like going to see his cousin and getting a dose of morphine.

*

The hotel was one street back from the ocean. I was told that I was welcome to leave my luggage in the car, my car with the valet, and come back at around noon when my room would be ready.

All I wanted to do was crash out, but I took a beaker of coffee from the thermos in reception and strolled the last few yards to the Pacific.

If this was the climax of my trip, it was a bit disappointing. Wasn't the Pacific meant to be blue? It was almost coffee-brown, the small waves rippling like the topping on a caramel latte. The tropical palms were here – immense trees swaying in the breeze, their oildrum-thick bases tapering to pencil-thin beneath their parasol of leaves. But the trunks were smothered in graffiti. You couldn't see wood for at least the first five feet. And they were set in lawns that had been squatted by homeless men – scruffy, bearded figures who were emerging from improvised shelters or lying stretched out in sleeping bags, still unaware that another roofless day was just beginning.

I decided to avoid crossing the lawns, and followed a path that led along the seafront. This was even riskier than tiptoeing between sleeping tramps, though, because the dawn rollerbladers and cyclists made no concessions for a drowsy traveller at the end of his transcontinental odyssey.

'Pedestrians on the boardwalk!' a cyclist barked at me. With his floppy T-shirt, bare feet and premature sunglasses, he looked much too laid-back to get angry, but he was gesticulating furiously at the pictograms on the tarmac that seemed to indicate I was walking in a wheel-only zone.

Los Angeles, I decided, wasn't making me feel too welcome. I made a silent wish for things to improve very noticeably very soon, culminating of course in a victory at the voting ceremony in around thirty-six hours' time.

I had barely finished uncrossing my fingers when a dark blur materialized from behind a palm tree. It was a homeless man with a black bandana knotted on his head and an insane glint in his eye. He was holding a bike chain. The idea that he might just have stolen it from the guy who yelled at me was no consolation.

'That coffee?' he said. His teeth were definitely not those of a rich American.

'Yes. I hope you take sugar.' I put the beaker on the ground and got out of there.

2

I blagged my way into a room a few hours early, and shut the curtains on the rising sun. I squeezed between sheets that, as always, were too tightly tucked in, and instantly lost consciousness.

I was woken by my mobile phone. It seemed to be having a panic attack. It rang, stopped, rang again, stopped, and then had a third go at driving me mad. It was obviously an urgent call.

'Paul? It's Suraya.' I hoped for her sake that she hadn't phoned to give me the latest on her scooter saga.

'Hi. You're back at work?'

'Yes. You've got to get to Hollywood. They want you to do a dress rehearsal at the theatre. They're in a frightful tizzy.'

'A tizzy?' Another of her phrases from 1950s England.

'Yes, there is a problem with the voting system. Apparently lots of the delegates think that they will have to vote countries *out*, like on reality TV. The organizers are having to hold briefing sessions to explain that voters must choose the country they *want*, and not the one they want to eliminate. So they are in a panic and they want to rehearse the bits that they still have under control.'

'And they have me under control?'

'So they think, yes. They have not met you yet.'

Thelma drove as if she had never felt more at home since the Mini-fan-club rally in Miami, perhaps because there were lots of her brothers and sisters cruising the city. I doubted that any of the others had a kilted guy at the wheel, though. They were mainly driven by desperate-housewife types in wraparound sunglasses.

Familiar names came and went with every set of traffic lights – Wilshire Boulevard, Beverly Hills, Melrose Avenue, Sunset Boulevard, and finally Hollywood Boulevard.

Just like my first view of the Pacific, my initial impression was anti-climax. Was this really where everyone wanted to come and get made into a star, I wondered. This anonymous strip of malls and souvenir shops?

I finally saw evidence that the street was home to more than the everyday business of harvesting tourist dollars. A truck was unloading spotlights, tripods and other showtime gear on to the sidewalk. I pulled up in front of the lorry and was instantly chased off by a small guy with long hair and a headset.

'Not here,' he said. 'Just drive on.' He returned his attention to shooing pedestrians over to the other side of the street.

I didn't move, and took a look at the place where my trip would truly come to a climax the following day – Grauman's Chinese Theater. It was a tall, pagoda-style construction in a semi-circular courtyard. Marking the entrance to the theatre were two bright-orange columns. The doors to the temple were golden, and decorated with sabre-toothed-dragon masks. It wouldn't have been out of place in Las Vegas – except that there, the Chinese temple would have been several dozen storeys taller and the dragons on the facade would have been spitting real flames.

Technicians were mounting floodlights on tripods and heaving a roll of red carpet into the courtyard.

'Get outta here or we'll have you towed.' The human guardian of the temple rapped on my roof.

'I'm here for the dress rehearsal,' I told him through my open window.

'Oh.' Without apologizing, he asked my name and had a short discussion with his headset. 'OK, leave the car here and wait by the entrance. Someone'll come and meet you.'

I did as I was told, and wandered over to look at the handprints and autographs that the theatre is famous for. Tourists were milling around, taking photos of the legendary names who had left their mark in the courtyard's cement. Marilyn Monroe seemed to be the people's favourite. Her dainty handprints were black, presumably from all the people who'd pressed their palms into hers rather than because she'd forgotten to wash before coming to be immortalized. Groucho Marx, I saw, had left an imprint of something that looked suspiciously like his willy, but I guessed that it was probably his trademark cigar. Meryl Streep seemed to have sunk deeper into the concrete than anyone else. Was it a watery mix that day, I wondered, or an unflattering comment on her weight?

The workers were showing a distinct lack of respect for these famous names. A security guy was crouching down with his butt hanging over Jean Harlow. And the technicians were in the process of obscuring large expanses of the courtyard with their carpet. The guests at the voting ceremony were going to be treading on all those stars.

'It's OK, they don't need you after all.' It was the guy with the headset.

'They don't?'

'No, they just wanted to make double sure you were here with your car. Someone heard on the news that you'd broken down.'

'Wow, they reported that?' I hoped they hadn't spread the malicious rumour that the breakdown was caused by my running out of petrol.

'Yeah. So you just need to be here three fifty-five tomorrow—'

'Three fifty-five? That's got to be at least three hours before the ceremony.'

'No, it's an afternoon show. You didn't know that?'

'No,' I confessed.

'Yeah, the theatre's booked for an evening premiere. That's why timing's essential. So you pull up right in line with the doors –' he pointed towards them with outspread hands, as if he was guiding me in to land on an aircraft carrier '– you get out, go to be photographed on the red carpet, and your car will be valeted away. OK?'

'OK.'

'See you tomorrow, three fifty-five prompt. Have a good one. Hey, you people, the temple's closed, move outta here, please.' He began herding off the nobodies who were getting in Hollywood's way.

The sun was shining directly along the boulevard now, giving everyone the excuse to put on their sunglasses. I decided to pay an exorbitant parking fee and mooch around. Might as well have a look at Hollywood while I had the chance, even if it meant getting stared at for wearing a skirt.

I bought a coffee at a mall that was open at the back, so

that you could look up at the fabled white letters on the hillside. Tourists were taking photos to prove that they'd made it to Hollywood.

In the floor of the mall, forming a trail towards the viewing point for the white lettering, there were mosaics telling dream stories along the lines of 'I was cleaning sewers in Chicago when Steven Spielberg fell down my manhole and offered me a role as a sewer-cleaner in *Indiana Jones*.' It was the American Dream laid out for everyone to follow. Call me a cynic, but it felt like walking down Wall Street, hoping you might magically earn a million on the stock exchange.

People come to Hollywood thinking they're close to the action, but they couldn't be further from it. I mean, here was I, in my semi-famous costume of kilt and logo'd anorak, and no one was offering me movie work. They probably thought I was the sandwich-board guy for a Scottish pub, off on a quick coffee break.

I browsed through my texts, giving my phone a clean-out. My inbox was filling up about three times a day with messages from weirdos making lewd offers or sending me pictures and movies of their own undercarriages. I zapped them all, except one that looked vaguely professional – this I decided to refer to Tyler. It might fit in with his branded-entertainment plan.

There was a cinema in the mall, so I killed a couple of hours watching a slick thriller, a Hollywood product-placement deal for chic cars, watches, laptops and – yes – Uzis, in which the baddies got killed, the goodies made love with the sheets covering their private parts, and an un-corruptible cop proved that one solitary American is more powerful and resourceful than the whole of the world's secret services put together.

After this, buoyed up by the idea that the small guy can

achieve anything, I called Alexa, hoping to get our dialogue going again. It was our only chance of salvaging something before we hit the rocks once and for all. Predictably enough, I failed to get through. Life just isn't like Hollywood, even when you're in Hollywood.

3

Maybe I'd had too much coffee, or too much daytime sleep, but I just couldn't get any rest that night. What made things worse was the noise. American buildings are so damn loud. Even at night they won't shut up. Entire hotels shudder and whir twenty-four hours a day like ancient washing machines.

I turned off my air-conditioning, which was hissing out warmth from three or four grilles in the walls and ceiling. I jammed the bathroom door shut so that I wouldn't hear the constantly whistling air extractor. I reached inside my fridge and turned its motor to zero. And still there was a rattling mechanical sound coming from somewhere.

I finally tracked it down to an alcove out in the corridor, diagonally opposite the door to my room. Here, below a sign saying 'ICE', was a silver machine that sounded like a bus idling at traffic lights. It was shaking so much that if it hadn't been too heavy it would have waddled away and tumbled down the stairs. I kind of wished it would.

It was three in the morning, but I phoned reception and asked if someone could come and turn the machine down. Surely, I said, it didn't need to be on full blast all night?

'Sorry,' the night porter said, 'I don't think you can turn it down. And no one's ever complained before.'

Now you can't fob a customer off with that pathetic excuse. 'Excuse me, there's a king cobra in my bathtub.'

360

'So? No one's complained before.' The guy was just asking for trouble.

After all, it was the day before my big Hollywood début. I needed my sleep. So by my reasoning, I was perfectly entitled to take extreme individual action, like the cop in the thriller I'd seen. It was within my rights as a paying guest to go and unplug the ice machine.

The management didn't agree.

Two guys with white shirts, ties and logo'd name badges opened my door, poked me awake and told me I was being thrown out.

I felt like I'd just got off to sleep, but my bedside alarm said eight o'clock.

'Coffee and wheat toast with orange marmalade, please,' I said, but it didn't distract them.

They whined on about a flood, damaged carpets and a short circuit, all (they alleged) caused by a leaking ice machine. And wasn't I the one who'd called down to ask for the machine to be shut off?

Yes, I said, but how could they prove that I was also the one who'd unplugged the machine?

Well, they answered smugly, apart from the fact that they hadn't mentioned that the machine had been unplugged, no one else had ever complained before.

Half an hour later, I was sitting in the Mini wondering what to do. I had the company credit card, so I could just drive around and find another hotel. These days, Suraya seemed to have forgotten about the budget constraints that had caused so much hassle back in New York. But then I saw a road sign pointing to Venice Beach, and I remembered – Elodie had said I was welcome to stay at Clint's fabulous house, hadn't she?

Any port in a storm, and now that I knew my enemy, taking shelter in Elodie's port could even count as a useful bit of espionage.

'You are welcome, Paul,' she said when I called her. 'You haven't lost the competition yet, but come. I am very good at consolation.'

4

Elodie might have been a witch, but she certainly avoided living in a hovel. So far I'd seen her in her dad's apartment overlooking the chicest woodland in Paris, in her pied-à-terre at the heart of the Marais, and in Clint's department-store-sized Manhattan hideout.

This place beat the lot.

It was a newish brick-red villa, a simple cuboid construction that would have looked mundane in a town like Miami. But it wasn't the building itself that was so impressive. It was the whole context.

The villa stood on a wide canal lined with modestly sized houses, ranging from old cabins with leafy gardens to modern glass boxes that used up every inch of their building plot. The surviving old houses, often just wooden shacks with peeling paint and overgrown yards, seemed to be inviting architects to rip them down, and I guessed that it wouldn't be long before someone bought them and took up the challenge. The neighbourhood was a life-sized architecture catalogue showing off all the best ways to create roof terraces, tinted glass facades and sunken patios.

Not that the area looked overdeveloped. The houses were small and overshadowed by the canal itself, a peaceful ribbon of clear, fish-infested water. Boats were moored here and there along the towpath – not mega-yachts but pedaloes and canoes. A white ibis was perched on the prow of a small punt, peering down into its liquid breakfast buffet.

Clint's villa was one of the few new houses with a decent-sized garden. It had orange trees, a rose bed, and a lawn with a set of teak dining furniture. I even saw a hummingbird buzzing from flower to flower on one of his shrubs. It was peaceful enough to hear the tiny bird. The only sounds were the distant hammering of workmen on a building site, a propeller plane overhead and the tinkling of water in a small ornamental fountain.

I went in through the garden gate and knocked on a crimson door that glistened in the sun as if its paint was still wet. It struck me that I'd come a very long way since I was banging on a similarly shiny front door in the Bronx.

The door opened, and a young guy fell out into the garden.

'Oh, sorry. Hey. Bye. Later.' He mumbled a party mix of hello and goodbye noises, and jogged off down the canal path, stretching his arms and back.

Elodie stepped out to watch him go. She was in a kimono, unmade-up, straight out of bed.

'And don't forget the muffins!' she shouted.

The departing guy raised an arm in acknowledgement.

'That's Jerry,' she explained to me.

'He's not one of your French campaign team, then? He doesn't look like an engineer.'

Her face fought between blushing and laughing. 'No, I found him at the beach last Christmas. He's an actor but he wants to be a waiter.'

'Isn't that the wrong way round?' I asked.

'Yes, I guess he just wants to be different. That's the trouble with these Californians. They all want to be different, but they're all the same.'

Typical Elodie, I thought. Always has to be superior to everyone.

I had breakfast on a terrace that caught the morning sun but was hidden from potential snoopers by a row of gigantic plant pots. Which was lucky because despite the cool breeze, Elodie insisted on lounging around with her kimono strategically arranged to drive any watching men insane.

Moi, for example. I mean, I knew how manipulative she was, and that seduction was like a PlayStation game to her – totally without consequences. But seeing her do her *Basic Instinct* act was hard for a poor relationship refugee like myself to bear. I was here to uncover her secrets, but I'd have told her all mine in an instant. I'd even have made some up just to please her. The French government wouldn't have to build a Guantanamo to brutalize inform-ation out of their suspects – they could just send Elodie in to interview them, and the most hardened terrorists would start singing like a canary.

I did my best to focus my attention on the muffins and coffee that Jerry was laying out on the table. He fussed about, fed Elodie chunks of banana-and-pecan muffin and called her 'babe', while she pumped me for the lowdown on Las Vegas. I wasn't surprised when my moral stand over the Uzi made her laugh. Of course, to her, getting thrown out of a city for refusing to lower your ethical standards for five seconds was completely absurd.

'It was the straw that broke the camel's back,' I said.

'What?' She didn't know the idiom. Maybe, I thought, she didn't have limits. I tried to explain the concept of even the largest pack animal feeling overloaded.

'In French we say it's the drop that – how do you say it? – overspilled the vase,' Elodie said.

'But that's different,' I objected. 'One drop will just spill out of the vase, it won't break it.'

Elodie screamed with laughter and clapped her hands.

'This is wonderful, Paul. You have become French. You are more capable of arguing about the way of explaining something than discussing the real problem.' She flashed me another glimpse of her thighs as a reward, then spoilt everything by adding, 'I really think Alexa was wrong to ditch you.'

'Ditch me?' Now she was the one with some explaining to do.

'In Las Vegas. She called me asking where you had spent the night and I said I didn't know. You had left in the middle of Clint's concert, and disappeared.'

'But I went back to the hotel – she wasn't there.'

'No, she was angry because you went out for the evening without her, and she took a different room in the hotel. Don't you understand women at all? You were supposed to go and find her. Stupid Englishman.'

Talking about hotel rooms seemed to give her an idea.

'Chéri,' she said to Jerry, 'I think I'll have my next cup of coffee in bed. Will you bring it to me?'

She stood up and stretched erotically. I thought she might even throw off the kimono to save time in the bedroom.

'You can relax here before the ceremony,' she told me. 'Clint won't bother you.'

'Clint's here?'

'Oh yes, somewhere. I don't think he knows he has a garden, though. Or maybe he's forgotten how to get out here. He spends his time in the basement. It's where he has his *pardees*.'

She went in through the French windows, and then popped her head out again.

'Oh, by the way, Papa will be here for lunch. He will be happy to see you.'

5

There are people who could cause a riot in paradise. The angels would be up there on their clouds, strumming on their harps, and one troublemaker could goad them into ripping each other's wings off. The problem was that Elodie and her dad Jean-Marie were both that type of person. And Tyler was the kind of guy who'd make angels throw their harps at him in frustration. All in all, it was probably inevitable that our lunch in paradise would turn into a war.

Objectively, things couldn't have been more perfect. Here we all were, sitting in February sunlight that was strong enough to make us feel glad to be alive, but not so harsh that you needed to worry about sunblock. We were in one of the most peaceful gardens on the American Pacific coast – even the workmen had shut up now, and all we could hear was the artificial fountain, a distant whoosh of traffic no more intrusive than a bubbling river, and, yes, the hummingbird that had returned for lunch.

The food was excellent. The Mexican cook had laid on a Californian feast of salads and fresh fish, and Jerry was giving an Oscar-winning performance in his role as wannabe waiter. He was keeping the golden Napa Valley wine flowing, too, which might have been part of the problem.

The other lunchers were Elodie, myself, Clint, Jean-Marie and Jack Tyler.

Now call me slow, but it took me a few seconds to realize that there was something decidedly odd about the fact that those last two should show up together, in the same limo. It pushed back the boundaries of coincidence just a bit too far. Besides, there was no such thing as coincidence where Jean-Marie was concerned. If he walked out of his apartment one day with a suit that happened to be exactly the same grey as a cloud passing overhead, then either he or the cloud was up to something, or more likely they were in cahoots.

Today he was wearing slippery mercury grey, with his favourite salmon-pink shirt as crease-free as if it was being constantly ironed from the inside, and his silk tie apparently immune to any danger of getting splashed by salad dressing. His hair was slicked back off a perma-tanned forehead. Next to him, floppy-haired Tyler looked a total slob, his jacket baggy and his shirt rumpled round his midriff.

'Don't tell me you're involved in the French campaign, too?' I asked Jean-Marie.

'Yes,' he said, giving me his most charming – and least trustworthy – smile. 'When Elodie told me that she was going to be, how do you say, *implicated* in the World Tourism competition, naturally I decided that I must help. I am her father, after all.'

He was also a born liar, a sneaky French politician, and someone who had a lot to gain if I didn't manage to pay off my fine and was forced to sell my half of the café to him. But I didn't think it polite to question his motives and darken the sunny ambience.

'Yes, Papa will help me get a job after the competition, when we have won. Right, Papa?'

'Naturally, *chérie*,' he said, and planted a paternal kiss on her forehead. A touching scene, I thought, like the king and princess cobra deciding who was going to set a trap in my bathtub.

Tyler left it to Jean-Marie to explain that the two of them

had spent the morning at a meeting for all the heads of the different countries' campaigns. Jean-Marie had invited his British rival to lunch when he'd heard that I was staying at the house.

Clint – still dressed as a miniature leather Elvis – thought he was back in Las Vegas, and was keeping us amused by regularly asking Elodie when he was due on stage. Every time she told him he'd done the show, he'd say, 'OK, babe, less pardee!' and try to find his way into the house. And each time he'd fail to find a door – or one that he could remember how to open – and come back to the table until he got another urge to sing and/or party.

'It's a fantastic house,' Tyler congratulated Jean-Marie as if he and not Clint was the host. He slurred the word 'fantastic' slightly. The sun, wine and jetlag seemed to be getting to him. That and his medication. I figured that this combination had to be the reason why he hadn't immediately started whinging at me about Las Vegas. Unless he was trying to save British face in front of these foreigners and was waiting until we were alone to rant at me for screwing up the deal with Larry Corelli. He did seem nervy. He was licking his teeth even more restlessly than when I'd last seen him in London.

'The house is unique,' Elodie said. 'If you look carefully, you will see that there are no ninety-degree angles at all. You know it was designed by California's only blind architect?'

The scary thing was, I don't think she was joking.

'I hear that you are an exile here, Paul,' Jean-Marie said. 'You had to quit your hotel and were – what is the word – *expulsed* from Las Vegas?'

I examined him for signs that he was taking the piss about the gun shop. But no, he was looking at me with what I can only describe with a French word – *bonhomie*. It was impossible to believe that he wished me anything but good luck and happiness. I guessed that that was how the smiling cobra looked to its hypnotized prey.

'I think they were mad at me in Las Vegas because I wasn't losing enough,' I said. 'I managed to get away when I was only eighty dollars down. My own money,' I emphasized for Tyler's sake.

'I hope you did not ...' Jean-Marie mimed putting money on the table, and looked to Elodie for linguistic support.

'Gamble? Bet?' she guessed.

'Yes. I hope you did not *gamble* on Britain for the ceremony,' he said.

'You think I should have bet on France?'

We laughed, and the exchange would probably have been passed off as gentle jousting between opponents if Jack Tyler hadn't mumbled something into his glass of wine.

'Not much point in that, either,' he said.

I didn't pick up on it, but Elodie was on to him in a flash.

'What did he say?' she asked Jean-Marie in French.

Jean-Marie shrugged ignorance, which is usually a Frenchman's most reliable means of defence. If a Parisian shrugged hard enough, he could convince a nuclear missile that it wasn't worth landing on the city. Elodie, though, had progressed way beyond mere nuclear-war tactics, and kept up her offence.

'Why did he say that, Papa?'

'I don't know,' her dad said. 'You know these Anglais and their so-called sense of humour.' For once in his life he looked almost flustered. Tyler, meanwhile, was staring fixedly into his wine glass with those lazy eyes of his.

'Then why are you acting bizarre? You're bizarre.' Elodie sat back as if to get a better look at Jean-Marie.

'It's nothing, nothing.' Her dad was almost pleading her

to let the subject drop now, which was like rolling over and offering her your jugular.

'No, you must tell me,' she ordered him. 'If there's a problem, I have the right to know. I have been working hard on this campaign while you have been lazing around back in Paris, making sure you are on the committee so you get your free trip to sunny California.'

'Ah, so that's how you see things, is it?'

Elodie had successfully goaded Jean-Marie into losing his temper.

They proceeded to have a long row in French, which had Jean-Marie throwing his arms above his head to express that his daughter was being naïve, and Elodie alternately gaping in horror and spitting venom. They were speaking at Uzi speed, and I struggled to follow.

'Me, lazing about?' he seemed to be saying. 'Who do you think arranged for those engineers to extend their visit?'

'Huh, you're only doing this to get a foot on the political ladder,' Elodie countered. 'And what about my bonus if we win, will I get that?'

'Think yourself lucky you're getting a job. Do you know how many French kids are on the employment scrap heap at twenty-five?'

They started hammering out the issue of the bonus, and things got especially nasty. My French was sinking under the weight of so much concentration, but when they finally ran out of breath, I had understood enough to want to empty a bottle of wine over Elodie's head.

'You gave Alexa's photos to the website, didn't you?' I accused her.

'What?' Elodie hardly seemed to have heard. She was still charged up with the adrenaline of yelling at her dad.

'And you tried to persuade Alexa to sue Visitor Resources, didn't you?' Now I was getting charged up, too.

'I bet you even got that guy from Toulouse to mess up my tea party.'

'Yes, yes, yes,' Elodie hissed, letting off a surplus of pent-up steam. 'And yes, I got Jerry to sabotage your car in New Orleans.'

'Jerry?' I turned and saw the actor doing a very bad mime of guilty regret.

'You would have done the same to me if you'd known my plans,' Elodie said.

'What?' I did my best to look affronted, though I wondered if she was right. How far would I have gone to win my bonus? 'I wouldn't have sabotaged your car,' I said. 'You could have got me killed.'

'No, I told him to do it safely,' Elodie said. 'I didn't want you to have an accident. And it was a kind of om-ahj, really.'

'What?' Like turning a lion into a hearth rug was a hunter's idea of respect.

'Yes, it was because I really thought you could win the campaign. I wanted to win for myself. I didn't know . . .' She mimed strangling her dad and Tyler.

'Know what?' I asked.

'Oh, *franchement*, Paul, didn't Alexa teach you any French?' she snapped. 'Have you understood a word of what's going on?'

'I understand that you tried to screw up my events, yes. Even though you knew I had to win to save my share in the tea room. Bloody hell, compared to you, Lady Macbeth was a guardian angel.'

Elodie gave a stifled scream of despair and turned to Tyler.

'You must tell him,' she commanded. Everyone looked at the slouching Englishman – even Clint, who didn't seem to know or care what planet he was on.

'Tell me what?' I asked, but Tyler seemed incapable of

eye contact with anything other than the remains of a sliced pineapple.

'You British really are pathetic,' Jean-Marie said. 'Why can't you do things the French way? We know that the worst thing you can do to a person in politics or business is tell them that you have, how you say, *screwed* them. We French, we are the masters of silent diplomacy, and people respect us for this. We screw people, but we don't humiliate them. We do not tell the world they have been screwed.' He seemed to have fallen in love with the word. 'OK, French is not the language of international negotiation, but we are conquering the world in front of you Anglos. So yes, we have made the deals in Boston, in Miami, in New Orleans. Our engineers will help Las Vegas with its water supply and Los Angeles with forest-fire control. We have done all this, and have, er, will have . . .' His English broke down, but only temporarily. 'We *would* have accepted our defeat in the vote discreetly, with grace, and guarded the secret, not like you.' He gave Tyler a sneer that would have persuaded an eighteenth-century English gentleman to go out and commit honourable suicide. Tyler, though, was in silent communion with his wine glass.

'I don't get it,' I said. 'You're talking as if you already know you've lost.'

'My dear Paul, don't you see?' Jean-Marie looked at me with even more bonhomie. 'You were screwed, too. It was all, how do you say, *une arnaque*, a cheat. China is going to win. It was agreed from the start. They will win, and in return they will publicize our countries to their citizens. It is the logical result of globalization. China is the next big market. We cannot insult them by winning.'

'What?' I only just managed to squeeze the word out of my constricted throat.

But the full horror of the situation had already sunk in. My God, I thought, I must have the stupid-git gene. The blind, naïve-dickhead gene. This was why the campaign was outsourced to India and only half organized. This was why Tyler only got interested in my progress when the kilt thing took off and looked like making some money. And this was why the bastard had linked my bonus to victory at the ceremony. To avoid paying a bonus. It was also why the show was at the Chinese Theater, and in the afternoon because they 'couldn't book it for the evening'. Every single detail was a sham, a scam.

Now everyone was looking at me. Except Clint, that is. The sudden silence had convinced him that the meal was over and it was time for his show. He was looking for a door handle again.

'You mean it was all for nothing?' I asked Tyler. His only answer was a lick of the teeth. 'Starting a war in Boston, nearly getting shot in Miami, pushing the Mini halfway through a Louisiana swamp?' OK, that last one was an exaggeration, but I was owed a bit of pity.

'Not for nothing,' Tyler said. 'It made you famous. And it's not a defeat. Do you know how much money Chinese tourists are going to bring into London in the next twenty years?'

'But you might have told me, instead of letting me make a twat of myself.'

'A general never reveals his plans to the ground troops, you should know that,' Tyler said.

'No, he just sits on his fat backside while they do the fighting, and then turns up to sign the surrender.'

Tyler simply chuckled at this.

'There was no battle, really,' he said. 'So there was no surrender. That reminds me – I'm going to need your tank.'

'What?'

'The car. Suraya's posting it on a website. We'll be auctioning it straight after the ceremony. Now that it's been on TV, it'll be worth even more.'

I can't explain why, but that was the drop that overspilled my vase. I grabbed the jug of orange juice and emptied it over his head. He looked so beautifully shocked that I followed up with a pint of cranberry juice down his shirt-front and a pitcher of iced water into his gaping mouth. The ice cubes bounced off his cheeks, forcing Jean-Marie to leap out of his chair to avoid the ricochets. As usual, the fast-moving Frenchman escaped stain-free.

Until, that is, he was hit by a trayload of fresh-fruit salad, and then the tray itself, launched in a neat surprise attack by Elodie. My splash-therapy session seemed to have inspired her, and she was screaming French swearwords at her dad and looking for new weapons.

'*Calme-toi!*' Jean-Marie did his best to sound authoritative. His plain suit had now been brightened with a colourful pink-grapefruit-and-mango-chunk motif, and from the look of ecstatic fury on Elodie's face, he was going to have to run for it if he wanted to limit the damage to the expensive fabric.

'Pardee!' Clint cheered, and upended a bowl of crème brûlée over his wig.

Jerry the car crippler was standing clear of the action, grinning at the food-splattered guests, so I gave him an unpeeled banana to chew on and jammed the neck of an opened wine bottle down the back of his jeans.

'That'll fill your petrol tank,' I told him.

'Elodie!' Jean-Marie made one last attempt at crowd control and then bolted across the lawn, with his crazed daughter running after him, playing fresh-strawberry darts with his back.

The party seemed to have broken up, so I decided to take my leave.

'Car keys,' Tyler croaked damply as I vaulted the garden fence.

'Fuck that,' I told him. 'You're not getting Thelma. I'm keeping her.'

6

I parked the Mini by the pier and got through to Juliana. I wanted her to pass on a message to Jake, but she said that he was standing right beside her. She was visiting an apartment and had offered to put him up until he got the money together to go back to New Orleans.

She handed the phone over to him.

'Jake?'

'Hey, Paul. You on your planch?' He sounded pretty happy with life.

'My what?'

'Your surf. You know, surfboard?'

'No. Listen. Have you won enough money to take you to New Orleans?'

'No, not yet.' He sounded slightly sheepish.

'Well, I think I can help you out.'

'How?'

'Come to LA.'

'Uh?'

I didn't blame him for sounding confused.

'Come to LA and pick up the Mini.' I honestly didn't think Tyler would call the cops on me. It would create too much of a stink. In any case, I was willing to bet he didn't even know the registration number. 'Get the next bus here, and I'll meet you with the keys.'

'Wow.' He gabbled his gratitude in a mix of French, English and bad poetry, and I cut him off to tell him to go and buy his ticket to LA.

Besides, I had other calls to make.

'Suraya?'

'Yes. Oh, Paul, you'll never guess what.'

'What?'

'My daddy bought me a new scooter. Isn't that wonderful?'

'Yes it is, Suraya.' What a great life, I thought, when the gift of a car or a scooter can solve all your problems. 'Now I have some news for you.'

I told her all about the fixed vote, and was relieved to hear from her shocked disbelief that she was an innocent victim, too.

'So you won't post the ad to sell the car?' I asked her. 'And can you warn me if Tyler starts asking the police to track it down?'

She agreed to both.

'Get some cash,' she told me. 'Pay for a hotel in advance. He'll make me cancel the credit card, you know.'

'Thanks,' I said. 'I'm sorry if we got off on the wrong foot at the beginning. I probably yelled at you a bit. But I know it wasn't your fault, really. And I couldn't have been outsourced to a nicer person.'

'Oh, thank you.' I thought I heard a sob from the other side of the world.

'And I just hope your bonus wasn't at stake, too.'

'Bonus, here? Fat chance,' she said. 'But what about you? Why don't you sell the car and use the money to pay your fine?'

'No,' I said. 'I think I might have an idea how to earn the money I need.'

I explained my plan, and she giggled.

'You will show me the results if it works out, won't you?' she said. 'I've started up your Indian fan club.'

I thanked her for this, and we said a sentimental farewell.

'Safe scootering,' I told her. 'And don't forget to erase the tapes of you telling me to commit car theft.'

I crossed my fingers and opened my message inbox. And there, below a list of new weirdo spams, was what I was looking for – the professional text I'd saved. I dialled the phone number.

'Hi,' I said, introducing myself.

'Oh wow,' an excitable woman answered. 'Thank you *so* much for getting back. Are you interested?'

'Maybe,' I said. 'What exactly does it involve?'

'You, a kilt, your legs and a brand of sneakers. A poster campaign first, maybe a TV commercial. I'd have to meet with my clients again to hammer out the details.'

'And how much are we talking about, minimum?' I asked. She told me. '*How* much?' I said, just to make sure I wasn't hallucinating. She repeated the sum – I'd heard right the first time. 'I'm *very* interested,' I said. 'You just saved my British bacon.'

So I was in an unexpectedly bulldoggish mood when I made my final call. It might have been better to be a little more vulnerable, a bit less assertive. But sometimes a dose of self-confidence can help you see your problems more clearly.

'Alexa,' I began. 'Hi, it's—' No, I couldn't say it. It was the final proof that we'd failed the 'it's me' test. She was on voice-mail, anyway. What did that mean? She might be in a meeting about her photo exhibition, or on a plane. She might be having a siesta. Or maybe she just didn't want to talk to me.

Ultimately, though, it didn't matter, because I didn't know what to say to her any more. There was no point telling her that the whole coast-to-coast trip had been a sham. It would only confirm what she'd thought about me ever since the Boston tea party and the Cape May ferry.

No, before that – ever since the mix-up about which flag to paint on the car.

She'd said that I needed dreams. But she wanted my dreams to be planned. It was the French way. If you want a dream, you go to dream school and get your diploma in dreams. To her, a man in a kilt was just a guy with no trousers, and a Mini driving across a continent without knowing exactly where it was going was just a car getting lost.

OK, so it'd been anarchic. I'd set off on a simple PR consultant's job, and looked like ending up as a semi-naked footwear model. But that was how people had found gold in California. They'd been looking for a decent place to plant potatoes, and tripped over an ingot. They had probably started to panic that the desert would never end, and that the only place to plant anything would be on the piles of skunk droppings. And then they struck lucky. And so, in my own absurd, un-Parisian, unplanned way, had I.

Against all odds, I'd wrenched my share of the tea room out of Jean-Marie's clutches. And I'd done it without Alexa. Despite her, almost. Jake and Juliana were the ones who'd stuck by me, and they were the people she'd wanted me to leave stranded in Miami. Even Elodie, in her perverse style, had been there throughout. But Alexa had threatened to sabotage the website that was making me famous. Making *her* famous, too. If she got her exhibition in San Francisco, it would be a direct result of my cock-up with the kilt and my uncool dancing. The very stuff she had laughed at.

That was it. I couldn't say 'it's me' because that real 'me' just made Alexa laugh.

One for the Road

'YOU LOOK HAPPY,' I told the pelican.

Actually, I was flattering it slightly. Pelicans can look pretty morose with their down-turned beaks and their permanent frowns. But this one did seem content with its lot. It was perched on a post halfway along Venice pier, dripping after a successful fishing trip. Its friends and relatives were still out there, dive-bombing amongst the dozen or so surfers who were sitting on the swell in their black froggie suits, waiting for the perfect wave.

'You're lucky,' I told it. 'You just have to catch fish. You can go for a swim or a glide whenever you want. And if there ever is a giant earthquake, you'll just hover around till the shaking stops and the tsunami has passed. Sounds great, doesn't it?'

The pelican looked silently smug about its perfect lifestyle.

'But isn't it a bit monotonous?' I asked. 'I mean, I love sushi, but not for every meal. And if you get bored, all you can do is go and poop on a surfer. It must be fun once or twice, but surely the novelty wanes after a while?'

The pelican shook its heavy white head. It seemed to be telling me to get lost.

I took the hint and turned towards the beach. I was level with the tideline, where a frothy collar of foam was continually forming and disappearing as each wave broke on the custard-coloured sand. A tall blonde girl was walking barefoot, her shoes in her hand, her feet and ankles getting immersed every few seconds. She was the only person visible on that stretch of beach, and there was something spectacularly melancholic about seeing her walking there alone.

My phone began buzzing in my pocket.

It was Tyler, trying to sound diplomatic.

'Paul, you've got to come to the ceremony. Please.'

'Why, to earn you more money?'

'No, because people will expect it. Your country expects it.'

'Bollocks. My country expects me to lose, Tyler. You go and be the loser.'

'I've got some more events sorted out for you in LA. Don't you want to earn that bonus?'

'You do them. Get yourself a kilt.'

I heard him garrumph.

'If you're not at the theatre in one hour, you won't get a penny,' he said. 'Not a cent, not a euro.'

'Merde,' I told him.

'Pardon?'

'Merde. It's what the French say when they've had enough, when they're getting threatened but they don't care, when they want to say fuck you and fuck everything. Merde. OK, Tyler? Meeerde.'

I rang off, thinking that Jean-Marie was wrong. French was a damn good language of negotiation.

'Paul?'

Someone was talking to me, and it wasn't the pelican.

'Is that you, Paul?'

380

I looked down. The girl had stopped just below me on the sand. The last time I'd seen her, she'd been gazing into an aquarium in Las Vegas.

'Wow,' I said. Suddenly the beach didn't look so melancholic. 'What are you doing in LA?'

'Looking for you.'

'How did you know I was at the beach?'

'I didn't. I was planning to grab you at the ceremony.'

'Oh.' I didn't know what else to say.

She smiled up at me. 'Were you really talking to that pelican?'

FIN?

A YEAR IN THE MERDE
Stephen Clarke

'Edgier than Bryson,
hits harder than
Mayle' *THE TIMES*

Paul West, a young Englishman,
arrives in Paris to start a new job
– and finds out what the French
are really like.

They do eat a lot of cheese,
some of which smells like pigs'
droppings. They don't wash their
armpits with garlic soap. Going
on strike really is the second
national participation sport
after pétanque. And, yes, they
do use suppositories.

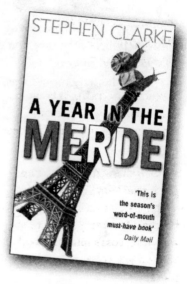

In his first novel, Stephen Clarke gives a laugh-out-loud account of
the pleasures and perils of being a Brit in France. Less quaint than *A
Year in Provence*, less chocolatey than *Chocolat*, *A Year in the Merde*
will tell you how to get served by the grumpiest Parisian waiter;
how to make amour – not war; and how not to buy a house in the
French countryside.

'The must-have book for Francophiles and Francophobes alike . . .
this comedy of errors has almost certainly done more for the
entente cordiale than any of our politicians' *DAILY MAIL*

9780552772969

BLACK SWAN

MERDE ACTUALLY

Stephen Clarke

'Edgier than Bryson, hits harder than Mayle' THE TIMES

A year after arriving in France, Englishman Paul West is still struggling with some fundamental questions:

What is the best way to scare a gendarme? Why are there no health warnings on French nudist beaches? Is it really polite to sleep with your boss's mistress? And how do you cope with a plague of courgettes?

Paul opens his English tea room; samples the pleasures of typically French hotel-room afternoons; and, on a return visit to the UK, sees the full horror of a British office party through Parisian eyes.

Meanwhile, he continues his search for the perfect French mademoiselle.

But will Paul find l'amour éternel, or will it all end in the merde?

9780552773089

BLACK SWAN

TALK TO THE SNAIL
Stephen Clarke

The only book you'll need to
understand what the French
really think, how to get on
with them and, most
importantly, how to get the
best out of them.

With useful sections on:

- Making sure you get
  served in a café
- Harassing French estate
  agents
- Living with bacteria
- Pronouncing French swear words
- Surviving the French driving experience
- Falling in amour, Paris-style

And beaucoup beaucoup more!

DON'T GO TO FRANCE WITHOUT READING THIS BOOK!

9780552773683

BLACK SWAN